PRAISE FOR

THE ANGEL OF THE CROWS

THE ANGEL OF THE CROWS

THE ANGEL

OF

THE CROWS

KATHERINE ADDISON

SOLARIS

First published in the United Kingdom 2020 by Solaris
an imprint of Rebellion Publishing Ltd,
Riverside House, Osney Mead,
Oxford, OX2 0ES, UK

This edition published 2021

www.solarisbooks.com

ISBN: 978-1-78108-910-1

10 9 8 7 6 5 4 3 2 1

A CIP catalogue record for this book is available from the British
Library.

Designed & typeset by Rebellion Publishing

Printed in Denmark

This book is
absolutely
for Beth Meacham

SHERLOCK: I may be on the side of the angels, but don't think for one second that I am one of them.

—Steve Thompson,
"The Reichenbach Fall," *Sherlock* 2.3

Nothing is more deceptive than an obvious fact.

—Sir Arthur Conan Doyle,
"The Boscombe Valley Mystery"

PART ONE

THE ANGEL OF LONDON

1

THE EXILE'S
RELUCTANT RETURN

WHEN I LEFT London in 1878, I intended never to return. I had my medical degree and a commission in Her Majesty's Imperial Armed Forces Medical Corps. If I died on the plains of Afghanistan in the service of my Queen, I would ask for nothing better. And if I did not die and somehow the war with Russia ended, one great truth of the world is that there is always need for doctors, whether you are in England, India, or Brazil. I could go wherever I pleased and be sure of earning a living.

The possibility that did not occur to me was that I would neither die nor see the end of the war. In May of 1888, a convoy of which I was part was ambushed in a narrow defile near Kandahar. Two Afghani Fallen led the charge, and in my attempt to defend my patients, I took a blow that broke my left femur in two places and missed severing my femoral artery by only a fraction of an inch.

I should have died—as I had always expected to—and been torn apart by the Fallen's monstrous claws, if it had not been for my faithful orderly Murray, who flung me across a pack mule and thus ensured that I was part of the retreat and not part of the carnage left behind. It was a long time before I was able to be grateful to him.

I was fortunate again: the nearest hospital happened to be under the direction of Dr. Ernest Sylvester, who has become famous in recent years for his theories about spectral injuries. Anyone else would have amputated my left leg and I would have died, as soldiers were dying throughout Persia. But Dr. Sylvester set the bone and cleaned my wounds with salt and silver, and I survived.

I was racked with fever after fever, the Fallen's poison festering and erupting in my body like malignant flowers. Dr. Sylvester's hospital was too small and too new—and withal too flimsy, being mostly flapping canvas and filthy straw—to have acquired an angel, and I was far too ill to survive transport to Scutari. I was healed with silver and salt and well-wishing from every doctor, nurse, and patient who knew how. Word spread, and when I finally woke clear-headed, my bed was surrounded by tokens from (it seemed) every soldier in Afghanistan.

"There are many people who have reason to be grateful to you, Dr. Doyle," Dr. Sylvester said, after a particularly trying and bitter interview with my superiors, and I endeavored to remember that; endeavored—with greater or lesser success—to remember that I had done good work, saved lives.

Was being shipped home a useless cripple.

Pack mule overland, rusty steamer to Istanbul. Another week in Scutari with a relapse—the young doctor there was very intrigued by the infected matter he drained from the raking wounds in my thigh, and I told him, wearily, to write to Dr. Sylvester with his questions. The Angel of Scutari I saw only from a distance. She walked among the dying men, who needed her comfort most. I was not dying, and there is nothing—not hell-hounds, not even demons—angels fear so much as the Fallen, their own murderous kin.

When finally I was deemed strong enough for the journey to England, I was almost glad of it, for it is agonizing to be on the edge of a war in which you are forbidden to fight. My paltry belongings and I were packed on the air-barque *Sophy Anderson,* and we began the three-day journey home—I had never developed the Raj habit of audibly capitalizing the *H*, and I certainly did not feel it now, surrounded by civilian businessmen with soft hands and fishy eyes. England was not my home, and I only wished I knew where home might be.

I was still so depleted that I slept something like sixteen or eighteen hours in the twenty-four, but not even a stone could have slept the last leg of the journey, from Paris to London; the unpleasant assortment of businessmen and invalids was increased by two North American Colonials. One, a giant, ugly bull of a man, was drunk when they boarded, but he bothered me less than his companion, who was cold-eyed and watchful in the manner of a man who dug voraciously for others' secrets because he was hiding so many of his own.

The drunken bull made a beeline for the only young woman among the passengers, the daughter of one of the businessmen; she had spent the past two years (I had learned from the inevitably overheard conversations) keeping house for her father in Athens. I had noticed her because she seemed another for whom England was not Home with a capital *H*. I had seen her in the Athens Elef-therion on Lykavittos, saying tearful and animated farewells in demotic Greek to a stout henna-haired lady whom I guessed to be the housekeeper. I had seen no such vivacity from her since; she sat silently by one of the tiny portholed windows, staring out at whatever there was to be seen and ignoring her father talking shop beside her.

The American took the unfortunately vacant seat across from her and announced, in a voice loud enough that they probably heard him at the base of M. Eiffel's ridiculous and majestic mooring tower, that he was Enoch J. Drebber of Salt Lake City, Deseret, and he was very pleased to make her acquaintance. The emphasis he put on "very" was obscene.

"And I to make yours," she said with the cold politeness that was only one step removed from *How dare you*.

I could have told her it was no use. Even if Enoch J. Drebber of

Salt Lake City, Deseret, would have heeded that cue sober—a matter which was frankly open to doubt—he was roaring drunk. He merely leaned in a little closer and began talking in a much softer voice, a voice too low to carry at all. The young lady's father had descended to the tower's café for—no doubt—a quick cognac, and the other American, who might have been hoped to provide a curb to his friend's objectionable behavior, merely offered a pale, chilly smile and wandered away to the other end of the cabin.

I did not want to care. I was exhausted and feverish, and my leg ached with a dull, endless throbbing that no position I tried seemed to ameliorate. I wanted to go back to sleep and be free of my body until we reached London. But from where I sat, I had a perfect view of the growing distress on the young lady's face, and when Enoch J. Drebber leaned forward and, with the suddenness of a snapping pike, caught her hand in his ham-hock-sized paws, I saw her gasp and her futile attempt to draw back, and I could abide it no longer.

I heaved myself to my feet and said, loudly enough to carry through the entire cabin, "Sir, I must ask you to unhand the young lady."

The abrupt quiet was exactly what I wanted. If nothing else, the other passengers would be made aware that there was a lady in need of protection, and one of them might—although I would not stake any large sum of money on it—have the fortitude to pick up the cudgels if I failed.

My immediate goal was achieved. Mr. Drebber released the young lady in order to stand up and snarl at me. "And what business is it of yours, sir, if the lady and I wish to have the pleasure of a few moments' conversation?"

"None," I said amiably, "if that is indeed what the lady wishes."

He was not so drunk that he did not know just how strongly the lady had been wishing him at perdition. He scowled, an expression all the uglier for how naturally it seemed to fit his face, and said, "I still don't see what call you've got to go nosey parkering around in my business, Mister—"

"Dr. J. H. Doyle," I said, "late of Her Majesty's Imperial Armed Forces Medical Corps. I wouldn't give a halfpenny for your business, Mr. Drebber, but I think you should find a seat somewhere else."

"Eavesdropping, were you?" he said, scowl metamorphosing to sneer. "Jealous, huh? Lady not interested in a cripple?"

"It can hardly be eavesdropping when you bellowed your name loudly enough for the entire cabin to hear."

Mr. Drebber took a step forward, and suddenly his friend, who had cared nothing for the lady's distress, was there, deftly insinuating himself into the aisle between Mr. Drebber and me, murmuring pale, cold phrases about "nothing regrettable" and "no rash gestures" with the polish and fluency of a man who had done the same thing many times before. But, for no reason that I could see, Mr. Drebber took the intercession in extremely poor part, shouting that he'd brook interference from no man living; he advanced into the aisle, shouldering his friend aside, and swung one massive fist in a ponderous haymaker.

I had to lean back only slightly to dodge, which also happily put my weight on my good leg. I swung the end of my cane in a neat sharp arc, striking solidly upon the inner condule of Mr. Drebber's forward ankle. His howl of agony was remarkably satisfying, as was the way he fell to the floor, clutching his wounded appendage and promising me the fiery torments of Hell. His friend, eyes suddenly awake, began to make threats about legal action and lawsuits, a higher-pitched contrapunto to Mr. Drebber's more sulfurous imaginings. I said, "It is no more than a bruise, sir. Please help your friend to someplace where he will not be blocking the aisle." I gave the young lady a meaningful glance and added, "I fear he is upsetting the lady."

I do not know whether she had ever had occasion to practice that sort of mendacity before, but she played up gamely, saying promptly—and perhaps not untruthfully, judging by her color— "Indeed, I am feeling a little faint."

The American's sharp-featured face for a moment indicated his profound hatred for all of us, including Mr. Drebber. But cabin stewards were starting to appear, drawn by Enoch J. Drebber's continuing howls, and he knew as well as I did how the story was going to look when all the participants and witnesses were interrogated. He and I awkwardly maneuvered past each other, he hampered by Drebber's uncooperative bulk and I by my cane and untrustworthy leg, and at the moment we were closest to each other, he caught my gaze and said, softly, "My name is Joseph Stangerson, Dr. Doyle. When you hear it again, I want you to remember who I am."

It was an oddly elegant threat. I said, "No fear of my forgetting, Mr. Stangerson," and then we had edged past each other and the moment was mercifully gone.

I sat down in Drebber's vacated seat and said to the young lady, "*Are* you all right?"

She had her color back, in the form of a blush dark enough to make my face hurt in sympathy. She said, "I am fine. But I must thank you for . . ."

"You needn't," I said. "I did not act in order to earn your gratitude."

She was pretty enough (and no doubt wealthy enough) that this puzzled her for a moment, but then her face relaxed into a more genuine smile. "I see," she said. "You are a preux chevalier."

"*Sans peur et sans reproche,*" I said, and although I intended the words lightly, they emerged with unexpected bitterness.

She drew back a little. I could not tell whether she was offended or frightened, and I did not care. The access of anger and the sharp addictive thrill of a fight, which had carried me this far, were draining out of me. I was aware again that my leg ached abominably, and the combination of fever and fatigue was beginning to make me light-headed.

Finally, well behind the fair, a steward reached us. "Are you all right, miss? Sir?"

"I am fine, thank you," said the young lady, "but I fear Dr. Doyle is not well. Is there somewhere he could rest until we reach London?"

I should have been angry at her for being interfering and high-handed, but I didn't have the strength for that, either. I barely had the strength to say, "Really, I'm all right. I've mastered the trick of sleeping in these seats."

"You'd be better off lying down," said the young lady, and the steward was clearly no more deceived than she was, for he said, "There's a bunk in the back, for the night watchman. You're more than welcome to the use of it, Dr. Doyle."

There seemed no point in continuing to deny that what I wanted most in the world was to lie down. I allowed the steward to escort me into the back of the cabin, behind the swinging port-holed door that protected passengers from crew and vice versa. I started to say, *Wake me if there's need,* before I remembered that I was no longer an Armed Forces surgeon. I fell asleep on the *Sophy Anderson*'s narrow bunk, and when I woke, we were in London, safely moored at the elaborate and ominous spires of Victoria's Needle, which had still been under construction when I had left the city ten years before.

2

A MEETING IN
ST. BARTHOLOMEW'S
HOSPITAL

LONDON IS NO place for an invalid, nor for anyone required by the exigencies of fate to be thrifty. And I did not love the city with either maudlin or clear-eyed passion. But one thing London possesses in greater quantity than any other location in England, Scotland, or the Alliance of Ireland, and that is privacy. One rebuffs the avid curiosity of the country at one's peril, but city dwellers have so many more opportunities to pry, among so many strangers whom they will never see again, that one missed chance is hardly worth the notice.

This alone made London the inevitable answer to the question of where I would choose to dwell, no matter how uneasy the Nameless Ones made me as they swept silently through the streets or congregated, like rooks, on the Underground platforms; no matter that regardless of how hard I pinched my pennies, they still seemed to slip through my fingers at a slightly faster rate each month. No matter that the obverse face of privacy is loneliness. I spoke to no one save the Armed Forces doctors to whom I reported once a week to have my leg assessed, and they, uncomfortable with my presence, unable either to treat me simply as a patient or to bring themselves to treat me as a colleague, were ill at ease and only became more so as the weeks passed and it became clear that, as so often with spectral injuries, my recovery was going to be less than complete. The leg would bear my weight, which was indeed more than I had hoped for when I first woke in Dr. Sylvester's tent, but it was sluggish, always dragging slightly no matter how I strove with it, and without my cane to lean on, I lurched rather than walked. Running was out of the question.

I knew that bitterness was mere self-indulgence: I had chosen to join the Medical Corps knowing full well that something such as this could happen, even if I had stupidly believed it would never happen to me, and there was no sense in laying blame or holding on to this pointless anger. Better to pick myself up, whether literally or metaphorically, and go on from where I stood.

And I had almost reconciled myself to doing so when my body finally recovered enough for the *secondary* effects to make themselves known.

The sense of shame I felt, when I woke that first morning, battered and aching and dizzy with dreams that were in truth memories, was literally nauseous. I lurched across my tiny room to the washstand and retched for what felt like hours, though I brought up nothing but ugly green bile. It was, in a way, a relief, for at least I knew I hadn't killed and eaten anything. Or anyone. But I was physically miserable all that day—as well as terrified, for I had no idea whether I might change that night.

I became more than ever determined to stay in London, and I said nothing to my doctors of this new development.

But, of course, the natural perversity of all things dictated that the more reasons I had to stay in London, the more beset with difficulties that prospect seemed to be. I could not afford London on my own, not with my health still so precarious that I could not hope to find regular employment, but finding someone to share lodgings seemed every bit as chimerical a goal. Although Armed Forces training made me at least *capable* of sharing my living space with another person, I harbored no illusions about the difficulties my temperament would make for anyone trying to share *their* living space with *me*. A natural tendency toward the autocratic had not been curbed by either my experiences as a surgeon or as a serving officer, and I had been accused more than once of being dour and pedantic and impossible to live with. Added to that were the new difficulties caused by and associated with my injury; pain made me short-tempered. And I now had a large and ugly secret to hide. I had a good deal of practice in keeping secrets, but this one . . .

At one point I began making a list of the traits I should look for in a potential flatmate. "Amiable" was the first, "dim-witted" the second. I considered for a moment, added "possibly deaf," and burst out laughing for the first time since Kandahar.

The conundrum remained unresolved, my savings dwindling at an alarming rate but not yet extinguished, on the day the doctors pronounced me healed—or as close as they thought me likely to come—and I decided on the strength of it to have a drink in the Criterion Bar, where once I had felt myself to be the ruler of all creation.

"Oh, how the mighty have fallen," I said, saluting the indifferent bartender with my glass, and a voice behind me said incredulously, "Doyle? That's never Johnny Doyle!"

I swung around and cried, "Young Stamford!" in disbelieving delight. Stamford of course was not young—he had been middle-aged when we struggled through Human Anatomy together, and he had to be nearly sixty now—any more than my name was "Johnny." But the sophomoric humor of medical students had bestowed fitting soubriquets: "Young" Stamford, who was old enough to be our father, and "Johnny" in retribution for my refusal to reveal more of my given names than my initials. And it could have been much worse.

Stamford and I shook hands, and he said, "Good gracious, Doyle, what have you been doing with yourself?"

"I am only recently returned from Afghanistan," I said, "and I have been devoting my attention to the question of whether there is a man in London mad enough to share lodgings with me."

I meant it mostly as a joke, for Stamford had known me well enough to appreciate it, but instead of laughing, he got a very odd expression on his face and said, "Do you know, you're the second person today to say that to me?"

"Who was the first?"

His expression became assessing. "I'm not at all sure . . . But then, you might just be cold-blooded enough to put up with him."

"But who is this paragon? One of those terrifying German lecturers?"

"Nothing like that," Stamford said cheerfully. He consulted his watch. "If you care to, you can come along and meet him, and it will spare me trying to explain."

"I have nothing better to do," I said truthfully and gripped my cane in preparation to follow wherever Stamford might choose to lead.

Outside the Criterion, he hailed a hansom and told the driver, "St. Bartholomew's."

"Bart's?" I said, when we were settled. "Are you teaching, then?"

He gave me a wry smile. "The fate of any man who cannot afford a London practice and yet cannot bring himself to leave London. But it's not so bad. I like to think that I'm doing my part to save lives by improving the pool of available doctors."

"I can almost guarantee you that you are," I said, and I told him stories of some of the so-called doctors I'd met in Afghanistan until we reached Bart's.

Stamford led me to one of the chemistry laboratories. It was deserted except for a man hunched over a lab bench in the back of the room. As we came in, he straightened up, and my first, puzzled thought was, *Why is he wearing an overcoat in here?* But then, as he turned toward us, the overcoat flexed around him, spreading slightly before pulling back in, and I realized that it wasn't an overcoat at all, but a pair of coal-black wings, crow's wings, and the man wasn't a man, but an angel.

I looked at Stamford in confusion. "Is that the Angel of St. Bartholomew's? I thought surely I remem—"

"*Him?* Oh good Lord, no." But before he could explain, the angel was striding toward us, his wings spreading and mantling around him. "Human blood!" he said. "I need a drop of human blood!"

"Oh, no, you don't," Stamford said, putting his hands protectively behind his back. "If you're turning vampire, I don't want any part of it."

"Don't be ridiculous," the angel said and turned his attention to me. He was tall but slight-built, with an angel's long, light bones. His complexion was marble-white, his hair white and as fine as a child's, and his eyes so pale that they seemed transparent and lit from within—although nothing could have been farther from the terrible light of the Fallen's eyes. He wore a subdued fog-gray suit.

"Human blood," he said again. He had a lovely voice, clear and measured, and perfect enunciation. "I only need a drop. I promise it isn't for occult purposes of any kind."

"Then why do you want it?" I said.

Stamford said, "Don't get him started."

The angel hunched both shoulder and wing—which quite effectively created a barrier between Stamford and the two of us—and said, "It's a question of stains, you see."

"Stains?" said I.

"Yes! After a few days, the police have no means of determining whether a particular stain, say on a shirt cuff, is blood or rust or perhaps paint. And they can't distinguish between human blood and animal blood at all. I'm working to find a reagent that will change color in the presence of hemoglobin, but not in the presence of other similarly colored substances. I think I've got it, but I can't test it without a drop of human blood." He looked at me beseechingly. I saw that despite the looming darkness of his wings, which made him look taller, we were very much of a height.

It was a bizarre request, but not an unreasonable one, even if it did seem oddly personal, and no matter what the *metaphysicum morbi* had done to me, I was still human. "All right," I said. "But I want to watch this test of yours."

His smile made his rather beaky face quite beautiful. "Of course! Here, I have a clean bodkin just over here—" He did not actually grab my hand to drag me across the laboratory, but it was obviously a very near-run thing. "Here, a beaker and a liter of distilled water. Here, your finger and the bodkin. Just a drop, really, I was being accurate. And I've got a bit of sticking plaster ready." His enthusiasm was weirdly touching—and more than a little contagious. I pricked my finger and pressed a drop of blood into his beaker, then applied the sticking plaster and watched as he stirred the water vigorously until the blood was invisible.

"There!" he said. "Undetectable! But now if we just . . ." He picked up a small phial from the bench; its contents were equally colorless, and when he tipped a drop into the beaker, it looked at first as if he had simply added water to water. "Come on," he muttered, stirring vigorously once again.

Then the liquid clouded up, and as we watched, a bluish-green sediment began to precipitate at the bottom of the beaker.

"Blood!" the angel shrieked in delight, and behind us, where I had forgotten about him, Stamford laughed.

The angel turned to scowl at Stamford; then he blinked, his wings rustling like those of a startled bird, and turned back to stare at me. "I beg your pardon," he said. "I don't know you at all, do I?"

"Crow," said Stamford, "this is Dr. J. H. Doyle. It's no good asking what the J or the H stand for—he won't tell you. Doyle, this is the angel Crow, who is looking for someone to go halves on a flat in Baker Street."

"But . . . how?" I said weakly.

The angel—Crow? Truly?—made that shoulder/wing hunching gesture again and said, "It's unimportant. I'm very pleased to meet you. Have you been back from Afghanistan long?"

"Only a few months," I said on reflex, but then realized with a jolt—"Wait. How did you know I'd been in Afghanistan?"

The angel giggled, and I could feel myself trying to decide if it was worth the effort of taking offense. It was a very peculiar feeling, and one I did not care for, showing as it did how weak and exhausted I still was. Thus, I was doubly grateful when Stamford said, "No, no, it's his parlor trick. Crow can guess everything about you just by looking at you."

"I never guess," Crow said stiffly. "If I were to *guess,* I would say that Dr. Doyle returned to London four months ago. But it might be as many as six, depending upon frugality."

My jaw dropped open. "That's astonishing!" I said.

"It's nothing," the angel said, although he looked pleased. "A parlor trick, as Dr. Stamford says."

"But truly. How did you know I had been in Afghanistan at all?"

He gave me an odd, sidelong look, halfway between coquetry and apprehension, then said, "It was really not very difficult. You came in with Dr. Stamford. You were clearly comfortable in a laboratory and familiar with St. Bartholomew's, indicating that you were a doctor yourself. Your manner toward him and his toward you indicated that you were his colleague rather than either patron or patient. But I had never met you before—and you had clearly never heard of me. Given my notoriety in St. Bartholomew's and other hospitals, that means you cannot have lived in London, or even come to London regularly, for several years at least. You have been in the tropics, as the contrasting color of your face and wrists shows. You have been recently and grievously wounded, as the stiffness and hesitancy with which you move demonstrates. All of that indicates an Armed Forces doctor serving in the endless conflict in Afghanistan. You were wounded by a blow from one of the Fallen, for the miasma lingers about you—I could have known where you had been from that alone, of course. I include the other details so that you can see I wasn't cheating. But really, as Dr. Stamford says, it's just a parlor trick."

"Then I have been spending my time in entirely the wrong parlors," I said, "for I have never encountered anything so remarkable in my life."

Angels lack the wherewithal to blush, but he was clearly both pleased and flustered. "The rest is easily deduced from the fact that Dr. Stamford brought you to meet me. It was only this morning that I was asking him if I had any hope of finding someone with whom to share lodgings. Therefore, you are trying to live in London on an inadequate pension and have come to the conclusion that you cannot do so alone. Four months probably, but certainly not more than six. Really, it's quite obvious."

"Four and a half," I said.

"There," said Crow, and his wings shook into place as if smoothing literally ruffled feathers. "And you're interested in the flat?"

"Definitely," I said and could not even bring myself to frown at Stamford when he gave me an irritating and supercilious smirk, as one who would be congratulating himself loudly on this success every time I ran into him for the rest of our natural lives.

There were reasons I had never been particularly close to him.

3

THE FLAT IN
BAKER STREET

I worried, of course, about what else Crow might have observed about me. I was encouraged by the fact that, whatever he had seen, he had held his tongue—except for that ambiguous hint about miasma—and felt no hesitation in keeping my appointment with him the following evening.

The house was narrow but high-ceilinged, and the flat was actually the top two floors: sitting room, bedroom, lavatory, and even a tiny W.C. on the first floor, and a finished bedroom on the second floor with a half-sized door leading to the attic. It was a splendid amount of space for its location, and the rent, when split between two persons, was within my financial grasp.

The landlady's name was Climpson, and she was one of those women born to give meaning to the word "respectable." I wasn't at all sure why she was willing to rent to an angel, but the look in her pale blue, exophthalmic eyes told me not to ask. Crow himself provided no hints, although he was clearly anxious for this venture to succeed, saying things like, "You should definitely have the first-floor bedroom. The second flight of stairs is practically a ladder. And you'll be nearer what I believe are called the 'usual offices,' which I of course don't need."

Angels did not eat, nor did they excrete. I had never come across a clear answer on whether they slept or not; I might now find out.

"They're lovely rooms," I said, "but before I make any decisions, there is a question I must ask."

Crow did not roll his eyes, but his wings hunched and flared, and his voice was full of disdain when he said, "No, I am not Fallen."

"Yes, I can see that you are not," I said, but this was far too important to allow myself to be deflected, and I continued obstinately, "but I need to know that that isn't liable to change. How can you be an angel, and have a name, and yet not be bound to a dominion?"

"London is my dominion," he said with grand melodrama.

"That doesn't exactly answer my question," I said dryly.

Crow gave me a sharp, unmelodramatic look. "You don't believe me." He didn't sound angry or hurt; he sounded intrigued.

"I don't know enough about angels to say, but I've never heard of one having a dominion as large as London—and do you mean *all* of London, or just the City? In which we are currently not standing, I might add. And how do you decide which suburbs are in and which are out? Woolwich? Streatham? What about Balham?"

Now he was trying to look hurt, but his laugh bubbled over. "All right! All right! It is not a well-thought-out answer, although I maintain it to be a true one. I *do* consider London—and all its suburbs, thank you, Dr. Doyle—my dominion, but not in the sense you mean." He hesitated, looking at me with visible uncertainty. "I can provide a . . . a character reference. The Angel of Whitehall can assure you that I have existed as I am for many years—and that my position is in no way precarious." And he looked so delighted at his own pun that I could feel my caution melting.

I was starting to say, "All right," when he interrupted me with a great rustle of feathers.

"But listen—we should know the worst of each other if we're going to share these rooms. I don't sleep, which I've been told is very annoying. I sometimes don't speak to anyone for a day or two. It won't be anything you've done, and I'll come 'round before long.

I dislike music."

"Music?" I said weakly. "I thought angels sang to each other through the aether."

"Exactly," he said, showing his teeth in something that might not have been a smile. "Is that a problem?"

"Not at all," I said, for I was not musical in the slightest. "I, ah, I'm still in a good deal of pain with my leg, and it makes me abominably short-tempered. At present, I have no stamina and spend most of my time asleep—and you needn't worry, I sleep like the dead. Except for the nightmares."

"The Fallen bring bad dreams," Crow said, with a mixture of sympathy and puzzlement, for, of course, dreams were a phenomenon he could not experience.

"In any event, just ignore any noises you hear coming from my room at night." And as long as I could remember to keep my mouth shut, that should keep my secret safe.

"Indeed," said Crow, and again I felt a moment of unease about what he had guessed—or inferred—about me from his observations. I might have challenged him, but Mrs. Climpson came click-clacking back up the stairs, and after all, whatever Crow knew or didn't know, he showed no hesitation about sharing lodgings with me.

We made arrangements that I should move in that very evening, and Crow followed over the next several days, accompanied sometimes by medical students lugging crates, sometimes by men who looked like dockyard brawlers carrying tea chests and steamer trunks. Crow had apparently bargained with Mrs. Climpson for the attic space as well. He demonstrated boundless energy, racing in and out at all hours, taking the stairs two or three at a time. I became resigned to the fact that he made no noise, no matter how vigorously he plunged in and out; only the brush of his wings against the walls or the furniture—or once, catastrophically, the tea tray—betrayed his movements.

For my part, I moved stiffly and haltingly from bed to armchair and back again, trying to stay out of the way, and sleeping more, and more heavily, than I had since I left Dr. Sylvester's care. Mrs. Climpson and her cook and her shy little Scottish maid-of-all-work focused on feeding me as if they had somehow to make up for not feeding Crow, and although I still did not eat much, my appetite did begin to improve. It helped that the cook, who seemed never to emerge from her basement den, like the ogre in a fairy tale, was uncommonly good at her job.

On the morning of August seventh, I emerged from my room, so late as to very nearly not be able to call it "morning" at all, to find Crow kneeling on the hearth rug in a drifted mound of newspapers.

He was a fanatical reader and collector of London newspapers, subscribing to both dailies and weeklies in a bewildering array and clipping articles from them with patient fervor; anything connected to crime caught his eye, but it was murder he was after, and the gorier the better.

He did not look up at my approach, but said, "Doyle, this is fantastic!"

"What's fantastic?" I said cautiously.

"They've found a murdered woman in Whitechapel. She was stabbed at least twenty-four times!"

"*Not* fantastic," I said. "Try fascinating, since you are clearly fascinated."

"Fantastic as in outré?" he offered.

"I'll give you that," I said, amused despite myself. "Twenty-four times?"

"At least. The newspaper reports are not very clear. And nobody knows who she is."

"That's not terribly unusual for murdered women in Whitechapel." I rang the bell for Jennie and sat down at the table.

Crow hunched his wings at me irritably. "And it's Elliston's case. Well, *he* won't let me in."

"Let you in?"

"To George Yard Buildings. It's idiotic—he wasn't the detective in Emma Smith's case. He won't have the least idea of what to look for."

"I must be very stupid this morning," I said. "What on Earth are you talking about?"

"The murder!"

"Yes, I did grasp that." Jennie came in, soft-footed and apologetic, and I asked her for toast and a fresh pot of tea. "Chandler could do you a poached egg, Dr. Doyle. If you wanted."

"Not this morning," I said.

She nodded humbly and slipped out. I knew she'd only asked because Mrs. Chandler or Mrs. Climpson had told her to. (Being respectable women of a certain age, both cook and landlady rated the "Mrs.," even though I had seen no evidence that either Mr. Chandler or Mr. Climpson existed—or ever had.)

"Emma Smith," Crow said in precise, thin irritation, "was murdered on the third of April, also in Whitechapel, also with an excessive degree of violence. They have not caught her murderers. It is not unreasonable to ask if the two cases may have some connection—which one might also ask about the Millwood and Turner assaults. And that's not even counting the dismembered woman they found in the Thames last year. But no one will, because the police of London are idiots."

"You are very harsh."

"I have reason to be." He shook himself, wings half spreading and settling back. "Have you ever heard of the Ratcliffe Highway murders?"

"Er," I said, dredging up a vague memory. "De Quincey, right?"

"Yes, although abysmally inaccurate," Crow said. Jennie brought in my breakfast, and we were silent for a long time. I was dealing with the last toast crust when I looked up and found him watching me speculatively. He said, "Are you up for a walk?"

"It depends how far we're going." I could not deny my desire to get out of the house.

"We'll walk as far as you're able and take a hansom the rest of the way," Crow said.

I had watched the amazing spectacle of Crow folding himself

into a hansom cab once, and I felt a private, ridiculous thrill at the thought of getting a second chance to observe. "Lay on, MacDuff," I said and levered myself slowly out of my chair.

4

THE SKULL OF
JOHN WILLIAMS

NO ONE GAVE us a second look as we came into the public taproom, from which I deduced that Crow came here fairly often. I did wonder why, since he neither consumed alcohol nor could even taste it, but I had learned that Crow did things for utterly unfathomable reasons—even when he could be coaxed to explain himself, which was not often.

The landlord said, "Mornin', Mr. Crow. The gentleman with you?"

"Yes," Crow said. "I've brought my friend Dr. Doyle to see Williams's skull."

The landlord made a pursed-lips, eyebrows-raised face, and said, "Ah, well then." He turned and reached up for what I had taken to be an odd porcelain decanter; as he brought it down and set it on the bar, I could see that, yes, it truly was a human skull, mandible-less, toothless, and brown with age. I picked it up. There was a strange feeling to the skull, a feeling of incompleteness that had been associated with no skull I had ever handled before.

I looked at Crow. He said, "John Williams was a seaman. Granted, he does not seem to have been of particularly sterling character, if the men who were his companions are anything to go by. But it still doesn't seem reasonable to assert that because that is so, he was able to split himself into two persons."

"That does seem most unlikely," I said cautiously.

He gave me a sidelong flicker of a smile. "And yet, at the scene of the Williams murders, two men were seen running away. Two sets of footprints were found. He cannot have been both men. It does lead one to wonder if he was either of them. In the aftermath, there were certainly persons who seemed overeager to see that the crimes were fastened irrevocably on the late John Williams."

"But what *were* the crimes? You say de Quincey is inaccurate, and to be truthful, I hardly remember him."

"So," Crow said, cocking his head to the side like his namesake bird. "On the seventh of December, 1811, Timothy Marr, his apprentice, his wife, and his infant son were found viciously hacked and beaten to death inside his home. It was later determined that the assailants—and again, there were plainly more than one—had escaped across the barren land behind Marr's house. No one knew of any person with a compelling reason to wish Mr. Marr dead— still less his wife and apprentice—and least of all his son, a child too young to speak and entirely incapable of bearing witness against his parents' murderers. Someone must have hated Timothy Marr with a most passionate hatred."

"Are they certain it was a person?"

"Footprints," Crow reminded me. "And at the second murder site, they were seen fleeing, a tall stout man and a shorter lame man, having murdered a public house owner, his wife, and his servant just as viciously as they murdered the Marrs."

"Are they *quite* sure they were the same men?" I said and saw the delight on Crow's face.

"An excellent question, Dr. Doyle. On the evidence of the sheer brutality of both attacks, it does seem likely—more likely than that two such beasts—I beg your pardon, four—*four* such beasts were roaming the Ratcliffe Highway at the same time."

I hoped devoutly that he had not noticed my twitch at the word "beast." "Then are they sure it was a man?" I pursued.

"A demon would not have stopped," Crow said. "The Williamses—no relation to John Williams—had both a granddaughter and a lodger above-stairs who escaped unscathed. A demon would have gone after the girl *first*. They are drawn to innocence."

"There are other . . . creatures," I said, for somehow I could not bring myself to say the word "beast."

"True again," Crow said. "But there was no stink of the unnatural about the scenes, and I think you know as well as I do, Dr. Doyle, that such creatures—even demons—leave a distinct odor behind them when they kill."

"Yes," I said, thinking of the terrible stenches I had encountered in Afghanistan. And I noticed that Crow spoke as if he had examined the scene of the crime himself. "Is it the killing itself that does it?"

"Generally," Crow said. "It's why angels have no such scent. Now, a very ancient and powerful Fallen—who has killed many hundreds, if not thousands of people—will carry that stench wherever they may go. But no such creature has ever alighted in London, I assure you."

"Thank you," I said, not specifying what I was thankful for. "Thus, you believe that the murders were the work of human hands, which doesn't surprise me. Humans are more than capable of evil. But from what you said, these seem to be quite *in*-human murders."

". . . Yes," Crow said, having considered my choice of words. "Whether committed by a human being or not, they were definitely inhuman murders. Eight people, including an infant, brutally murdered, and for what seemed to be no reason. Naturally everyone was terrified. Naturally the magistrates jumped at the first halfway plausible suspect they encountered. Naturally when he committed suicide before he could be brought to trial, everyone was only too glad to take it as proof-positive of his guilt."

"Suicide."

"Maybe," Crow said. "He was found hanged in his cell."

"Ah," I said. "He must have been rather ingenious to contrive that."

"Quite. A determined man can be shockingly ingenious. But there is also the fact that at his arraignment, Williams said very clearly and loudly that he was innocent."

"Bravado."

"Oh, very likely. But if he meant it—or if he thought he could brazen it out—then it was much too soon for that kind of despair. But if he *knew* something—and he very well might have—then it was not at all too soon for someone else to silence him."

"Permanently."

"Oh yes. No clairvoyant would have touched him regardless." Crow regarded me thoughtfully. "A gentleman named William Ablass keeps showing up around the edges of the case. He was a tall, stout man, very much like one of the men seen running from the scene of the Williams murder. He seems to have been an unpleasant sort of fellow. And it's possible he knew Timothy Marr."

"But even if he had a grudge against Marr," I said, "why did he murder the Williamses? Or I suppose, conversely, if he had a reason to murder the Williamses, why did he murder the Marrs?"

"Would that the magistrates had asked that," Crow said. "I don't have an answer. It's one of the reasons the case has never satisfactorily been resolved—even if John Williams *were* the sole perpetrator, which I don't believe. So far as anyone knows, the Marrs and the Williamses did not know each other and had nothing in common— except that they were both within the orbit of a man with a great lust for murder."

"But it only happened the twice?" I said. "If he did it for the love of killing—and he *wasn't* John Williams—then why did he stop?"

Crow made one of his shoulder/wing shrugs and said, "If the true—or second—perpetrator was William Ablass, then presumably he was too canny to strike a third time, especially after John Williams's 'suicide.' Also, he was a sailor. We don't know that he stopped."

I shuddered. And then I thought of something else. "Did the public house have an angel?" Some public houses did and some didn't, on a basis that I had never fully understood, but that seemed both arbitrary and self-contradictory.

"No," Crow said. "The murderer or murderers were seemingly very careful, for they did not allow their path to intersect an angel's dominion on either night. The Pear Tree, where Williams lived and where a variety of peculiar evidence was found both before and after his death, *did* have an angel. But I regret to say that the Angel of the Pear Tree was a sodden drunk."

"I didn't know angels *could* get drunk."

"We can't via literal alcohol," Crow said. "But there is a metaphysical equivalent, a kind of corruption. It often leads to the Fall."

"Could the angel have . . ."

But Crow was shaking his head hard enough to disarrange his hair. "It isn't the sort of thing one can conceal, Dr. Doyle. If the Angel of the Pear Tree had Fallen, everyone in London would have known. No, that angel embraced the Consensus in 1835." His wings mantled defensively and he twitched them back before they started to spread to their full span, which would be a debacle of no small proportion—or expense—in this public house, which was not overlarge and which was becoming steadily more crowded around us.

I knew, of course—every schoolchild knows—that an angel can only be left in an abandoned building for so long before they will inevitably return to the ranks of the Nameless; some angels can maintain their integrity for centuries, but those are the angels of great castles and churches, not the angels of seedy rooming houses. A very few angels choose to Fall and a very few angels choose dissolution—to be destroyed without hope of any kind of resurrection.

"The Angel of the Pear Tree provided no useful evidence," Crow said briskly, and I deduced that we were not going to mention that he felt about the word "Consensus" the way I felt about the word "beast," nor that he had clearly known the Angel of the Pear Tree personally. "If anyone knew the truth, they never confessed it. John Williams's corpse was paraded through the streets in a barbaric spectacle. They buried him"—he jerked his head toward the door—"out there. The body was accidentally dug up again during some road repairs. And," raising his voice, "the skull *somehow* ended up here."

The landlord smirked and said nothing.

"So," Crow said, picking up the skull and turning it pensively in his hands, "this is the skull of a murderer and/or a murder victim and/or a suicide. He might have been a completely innocent man."

"Makes a better story if he wasn't," said the landlord.

"That depends on what kind of stories you like," said Crow.

"What happened to the rest of the skeleton?" I said.

The landlord shrugged. "Potter's field, probably."

"Or the nearest storm drain," Crow said.

"You're a braver man than I am," I said to the landlord. "What if John Williams wants his skull back?"

The landlord shrugged, with another of his grins, as Crow handed him the skull. "Hasn't happened yet."

PART TWO

THE DISSOLUTION FEATHER

5

AN APPEAL
FOR HELP

JUST BEFORE MIDNIGHT on the eighth of August, my new problem reasserted itself.

This time, instead of merely waking in the morning with a head full of nightmares and a body full of cramps, I woke to cloudy consciousness in the middle of the night. It is hard to describe, for I was not human and my thoughts were not a human being's thoughts, but I was still myself. I still knew that I would be human in the morning.

And I knew I had to be quiet. I didn't understand my human fear of discovery, so that I had a confused belief that there were predators in the sitting room. In the morning, I would recognize the predators as Fallen, but in the night, all I knew were shadows and red eyes that glowed like hot coals and a sharp musty smell that meant only terror. I wanted to be outside, running, *hunting*, using the great muscles of my jaws to bite and rend and break. The door I had carefully locked was irrelevant; in the morning, I would understand that I could simply have pushed through it like a lion at the circus through a paper hoop. But there were predators in the sitting room, predators thronging the stairs.

I whined, but softly, and pulled the blankets off the bed to make a nest in the closet.

And that was where I woke in the morning, aching and unbelievably cramped and almost sick with gratitude for the locked door that had meant so little in the night. It took me twice as long as usual to complete my morning routine, and when I finally hobbled out to the sitting room and the breakfast table, Crow said, "You look horrible. Are you ill?"

"No," I said, pouring a cup of tea—blessed, miraculous tea that helped the whole thing seem like a nightmare instead of bitter reality. "I spent a bad night. And it isn't, by the way, considered polite to tell someone how bad they look."

"I don't know very much about diseases," Crow said, and I had lived with him long enough by then to recognize it as an explanation, if not exactly an apology.

It had never occurred to me before beginning this living arrangement what a skewed and partial view angels—whose dominions are public buildings, not private residences—must gain of human nature and behavior. Crow, who had the curiosity of nine particularly persistent cats, was fascinated by sleeping, by eating, by a thousand details of daily life about which I, for the most part, never even thought, and he was dreadfully offended that I would not let him follow me into my bedroom or the bathroom or, God forbid, the W.C.

Also, although his public, formal manners were perfect, as angels' manners always were, I had discovered that he had no real understanding of how to treat someone with whom he did not have a strictly defined, formal relationship. I often caught him staring at me as if he had simply no idea what to do with the fact of my existence. It was not that he disliked me or that he did not wish us to be friends. He simply had no idea *how* and in some ways only the vaguest conception that the thing was possible at all. Everyone knew that angels could speak to each other mind to mind, but Crow's behavior made me wonder just what kind of communication that was.

Thus, I did not take offense and said merely, "Trust me, if I'm ill, you will know about it."

"All right," said Crow, rather in the manner of one accepting a promise, and left me alone with my tea and toast and boiled egg. But I had barely reached for *The Times,* bracing myself as always for the complaints about the I.A.F.'s ineffectualness, when there was a sharp staccato knocking on the front door.

Crow's head came up sharply and eagerly. I watched him tracking the activity downstairs as Jennie emerged from the back of the house and answered the door. I could only distinguish the heavy thump of the bolt being drawn, but I had already learned that Crow's hearing was exceptionally acute and that the concept of "eavesdropping" meant about as much to him as it did to a fish. By the time I could hear someone's feet mounting the stairs, Crow was already regarding the door with pleased anticipation. He barely gave the visitor a chance to knock before he called, "Come in!"

The man who opened the door was short and stocky. In face as much as in body he resembled a bulldog, having a heavy jaw, a rather square forehead, and a prizefighter's much broken nose. His dark hair was slicked straight back and flat to his skull. He wore a blue serge suit that was only just beginning to be shabby and square-toed black leather shoes without the slightest pretense of fashion about them. His hat, already in his hand, was the bowler it had surely been destined from birth to be.

"Oh, it's you," said Crow. "Do you have something for me?"

"I think I might," said the visitor.

"Do you want me to leave?" I said, reaching for my cane with a certain amount of dread. Crow certainly had every right to use our sitting room for a private conversation, but short of shutting myself in my bedroom like a naughty child, there was nowhere I could go, and I was in no condition for a long, bracing walk.

"No," said Crow. He had turned his unnerving, searching stare on me, a thing I had by no means gotten used to. "You were an Armed Forces doctor. You must know a great deal about unnatural death."

"Well, yes, but—"

"Splendid!" His smile was like a crack of lightning, and he turned back to the little man with the bowler. "What can I do for you?"

"We've got a tough one," the little man said. He had a painstakingly corrected Cockney accent—a man who would never misplace an *H*, but who would never sound like he belonged anywhere but the East End. "And Gregson and all them are in Whitechapel."

"Of course," Crow muttered. "What can you tell me, then, Inspector?"

"Inspector?" I asked.

"This is Inspector Lestrade," Crow said. "Inspector, this is Dr. Doyle."

"Wait," I said. "Wait. Am I correct in understanding that there is an officer of the *Metropolitan Police* standing in our sitting room and apparently asking for your help?"

"Of course," Crow said. "It's what I do."

"It's *what*?"

His wings flared and mantled. "I'm a consulting detective, the only one in the world. I *told* you London is my dominion."

"You work for the police?"

"No!" he said, clearly insulted by the mere idea. "I work for anyone who has an interesting problem. My clients merely happen to include police officers."

It was not the most complimentary way to phrase the matter; I could not help glancing at the police officer still standing in our doorway, and he understood, for he said, "Not to worry, Dr. Doyle. I know what he's like."

"When you say you've got a tough one . . ." I said.

"Murder," Lestrade said. "Don't know who the fellow is or how he died, but me and my sergeant—my sergeant and I—we can't believe that anyone would commit suicide that way. So we agreed it was best to ask Mr. Crow."

Crow snorted and resettled his wings.

"Then you really don't want me along," I said regretfully, for I could use a puzzle to get other things out of my head. "I'm sure the last thing you need is more members of the public gawking."

"I'd be greatly obliged if you *would* come, Dr. Doyle," said Lestrade. "Our divisional surgeon's tied up in Whitechapel, too, and we could use a doctor to look at this fellow."

"Then of course I'll come," I said.

"Oh, *splendid*!" said Crow. He was clearly sincere, his wings half spreading before he caught himself, and although I knew his enthusiasm was more likely for my expertise than my companionship, I could not help being warmed.

After a night spent sleeping in a closet, any scrap of comfort would do.

Lestrade gave us the address, and I once again had the tremendous pleasure of watching Crow fold himself—like a conjuring trick—into a hansom cab.

I climbed in after Crow—I was learning rapidly not to be squeamish about feathers, and Crow was actually a good deal less fragile than a bird. His wing-feathers *behaved* like feathers, but they were made of the same stuff as he was himself. When he molted, what he actually shed was not his own material, but the accretion of the world: not the dust and dirt and plaster that he groomed assiduously out of his feathers, but the residue of this plane of existence. He had not been satisfied with that explanation when he gave it, and periodically would interrupt whatever I was doing to try to improve it, but thus far had not succeeded.

On the way to No. 3, Lauriston Gardens, he chattered so brightly about the investigation in Whitechapel that I finally said, "You don't seem very exercised about this dead man."

"There's no point in discussing him until we've actually seen him," Crow said. "If I let myself, I'll come up with all sorts of theories. And they'll all be wrong. It wastes a shocking amount of time. I will bet you a buttered scone Lestrade has been theorizing away like a mad thing."

"He seems sincerely perplexed."

"Oh, he is," Crow said. "He always is, when he comes to me. And it's because he made up a theory instead of looking at the facts in front of him. I cannot seem to get it through his skull that he's going about it backward."

"Do you work often with Scotland Yard?"

"Not often enough. They'd save themselves a good deal of time and embarrassment if they'd just let me investigate for them."

I did not laugh, although it was a struggle. Crow's vanity was sometimes endearing and sometimes exasperating, but it seemed deeply ingrained in him. I'd found myself speculating—theory in front of facts, Crow would chide me if I were to tell him—about whether all angels were hiding this o'erweening self-esteem behind their demure faces or if it was perhaps part of the reason he could survive without a habitation where no other angel could.

It certainly made me more *aware* of angels, this new curiosity: the silent throngs of the Nameless, the Angel of Victoria's Needle (a very young angel, as these things went, a delicate female with shining golden hair, like an angel doll for the top of a Christmas tree; but she had the astonishing wings of an albatross), the Angels of St. Pancras and Waterloo, starling-winged both of them, dark and iridescent and grimy. I hadn't realized how few people looked at angels' faces until I started doing so myself, how few people bothered to speak to them.

I always said "thank you" to the Angel of the Baker Street Station when he extended his wings (sparrow wings, brown and barred) to clear me a path; the shock on his face was worth the irritation of his help.

6

No. 3,
Lauriston Gardens

No. 3, Lauriston Gardens, off the Brixton Road, was one of a series of small, drab, yellow-gray brick houses—it would have been drearily respectable when new and now, clearly abandoned, was merely wretched.

A crowd of gawkers had inevitably gathered, errand boys and unemployed men and a few women of questionable virtue. They were thronging the constable who stood in front of the house, pelting him with their curiosity, but they all turned at the sound of the hansom, and I could see the brightness in their faces. Not malice, although it could become that in an eyeblink, but eagerness—eagerness for anything that might disrupt the endless anxious sameness of their lives.

I exited the cab first and paid the cabbie. Money baffled Crow, although he listened earnestly to my explanations time and again, and I had learned that, since he would either forget to pay or hand over all the money in his pockets, it was better if I took care of payment. Crow had begun simply giving me all the money he made, currency and checks alike, with a sort of indifferent trust that made my blood run cold. I had not asked him how he earned the money; I wondered now if he had wanted me to.

I heard the crowd gasp and knew Crow had just stepped down from the hansom.

In general, people assumed he was Nameless, and in general, he let them; it was so much simpler than embarking on any kind of explanation. It wasn't unheard of for a prosperous medical man to hire the services of a Nameless, and I had my cane, which suggested a simple reason for Crow to be dogging my footsteps—and he was, in fact, carrying my medical bag. Probably none of the gawkers had ever heard of a Nameless using a hansom cab—indeed, neither had I—but the truth was so much more improbable that I felt sure it would never occur to them.

Not that we necessarily had anything to fear if it did, but I knew how quickly a crowd's mood could change. Moreover, the first thing anyone thought when they realized Crow was *not* Nameless was that he was Fallen, and that was something I most certainly did not want to deal with in this shabby-genteel street with only a young, florid-faced constable to help.

"Go slow," Crow hissed at me.

"Do I have a choice?" I muttered back, but I kept my pace slower even than was necessary. I had not the first idea why Crow wanted to linger in front of the house, but it was almost always easier to give in than to argue with him, and this was not one of the places, such as the W.C., where I had drawn the line.

"There was a cab here," he said, just barely audible. "Not Lestrade's—that's still there, half a block down. Four-wheeler. Horse had one new shoe, on the off-fore. Nothing else to be made out of the general puddle."

The path from the sidewalk to the front door was a mix of gravel and mud and water standing in deep footprints. Crow made an agonized little noise which I recognized as a cri de coeur. I'd heard him discoursing on the astonishing number of things one could learn from footprints; I knew what he'd say the instant he'd closed the front door behind us, and I was not wrong.

"Why didn't you just call for a herd of buffalo?" he said to Lestrade, who was waiting in the tiny front hall.

"Not my doing," Lestrade said. "They'd had five constables in and out of here before anyone thought to send for the C.I.D. Every constable on the beat wants to prove himself by solving a murder— they all think they're in the penny bloods."

"Well, it's a simple matter in the bloods," Crow said more cheerfully. He was as passionate a devotee of the penny dreadfuls as he was of the penny press; I had yet to be brave enough—or foolhardy enough—to ask him how on Earth an angel benefited from that kind of reading material. "You look at the body, you see a clue no one else has seen, it points you straight at the murderer."

"And Bob's your uncle," Lestrade agreed. "None of them had that kind of luck with this fellow, and frankly we haven't had any luck, either." He waved us ahead of him into the room. "About all we've found out is his name, which is—"

It was a dreadful little room, even without the corpse, bare of all furnishings and the wallpaper—a petit bourgeois and utterly hideous pattern of cherries and ribbons—peeling in long, ragged strips. It felt desolate, like a place where no one had ever been happy.

And then there was the corpse, whom I recognized at once. "Enoch J. Drebber," I said. "Oh dear God."

"You *know* him?" Crow and Lestrade said in unintentional chorus.

"I encountered him," I said, "on the airship from Paris to London."

"Well, that's a real piece of luck," said Lestrade. "Are you sure it's him?"

"Vividly," I said.

"What do you know about him?" Lestrade said.

"American," I said. "A drunken boor. He was traveling with another man, a fellow named Stangerson, who seemed to be the brains of whatever their operation was."

"Do you know where they went when you reached London?"

"Not a clue," I said. "To be perfectly honest with you, Inspector, I was simply glad to see their backs."

"Which ship?"

"The *Sophy Anderson*. Barnhart line from Istanbul to London.

They only joined the ship in Paris."

"And the date?"

"The eleventh of March."

"Huh," said Lestrade. "Well, I admit, Dr. Doyle, I wasn't expecting you to be able to tell me anything about this fellow's *life*. But do you think you can tell me anything about his death?"

I looked at the body and wondered how I would make it off the floor again. But there was no help for it. I knelt down, slowly and awkwardly, hiding my wince as best I could.

His limbs were violently contorted, as was his face. "My guess," I said, "would be some sort of convulsant poison—strychnine is the most common. But if he didn't take it by his own choice, and I can't imagine that he did, the murderer either tricked him or forced him. There are no bruises on his face and"—I looked at his clawed, straining hands—"no bruises or other defensive wounds on his hands, so he must have been tricked."

"It must have been someone he knew and trusted," Lestrade said. "Can you imagine swallowing a pill because a stranger told you to?"

"People do strange things," I said. "But I agree, it seems more likely it was a friend or at least a colleague of some sort, whatever Mr. Drebber's business might have been."

"I guess this Stangerson is the one we want to talk to," said Lestrade.

Crow had been drifting about the room, apparently paying no attention to us, although I knew that wasn't true. He'd inspected the fireplace and the stump of red wax on the mantelpiece that had been a candle; he'd inspected the bloodstains on the floor (odd, since there was no sign that Drebber had been wounded), the baseboards, the hideous gas lamps. And he'd been peering at the walls, the peeling wallpaper and the plaster behind it. Out of the corner of my eye, I saw him startle—the twitch of his wings gave him away every time—and bring his head closer. "Hello," he said. "What's this?"

Lestrade joined him. I stayed where I was, to conserve my limited energy and the number of times I'd have to ask for help in getting up.

"RACHE," Lestrade said, "and is that . . . did the lunatic write it in blood?"

"I believe so," said Crow. "And if you look closely, that smudge might be the start of a sixth letter. Or he might just have been startled."

"Constable Rance found the body still almost living temperature," Lestrade said. "Probably he scared the murderer away."

"Quite possible," said Crow. "The question is, what word did the murderer mean to write? RACHE is German for 'revenge,' but it looks like a downstroke . . ."

"Rachel," I said.

They both turned sharply to look at me. "Rachel?" said Crow.

"A common woman's name," I said and shrugged. "Plus, my encounter with Drebber makes it all too plausible to me that he would have been killed for his treatment of someone's wife or sister or daughter."

"It's certainly a possibility," Crow said.

"But what if it's *not* another letter," said Lestrade. "The East End is full of German Jews and Socialists, and heaven knows what kinds of secret societies and cabals those people have."

"Oh *really*, Lestrade," Crow said crossly. "Don't talk nonsense. This man came here with one other person, not a cabal."

"How . . . how do you make that out, Mr. Crow?" Lestrade said, doing a poor job of appearing nonchalant.

"Well, aside from the mud wallow left by your constables, I make out the tracks of two men. One is our friend there with his fashionable patent-leather boots. The other was a man something over six feet in height who wore rough square-toed boots. His tracks are distinctive, for he has quite small feet for a man his size."

"Go on," said Lestrade, a sharp look gleaming in his pouched eyes, and I understood why he had asked Crow to come.

"They arrived together," Crow said, "sometime after that largest puddle formed on the walk. Mr. Drebber's patent-leather boots went carefully around—so that he cannot at that point have been in fear of his life—while square-toes stepped across. They came straight to this room, where patent-leather stood still for some time while square-toes paced up and down. He got steadily more excited, as his stride got longer and harder. The blood must have been his, if the corpse has no wounds?"

"None," I said. "And no bloodstains."

"And square-toes used his own blood to write RACHE—or most of RACHEL—on the wall at a height which again suggests he is a very tall man. And the fact that he wrote in his *own* blood, not his victim's, again suggests the lack of a secret society in this case. At present, I have no idea how he compelled Mr. Drebber to swallow a strong convulsant poison without laying a finger on him, but he clearly *did*. We will assume for the moment that his powers of persuasion are remarkable. Let us find out about Mr. Drebber's belongings."

He came and knelt across from me and began a catalogue that had Lestrade scribbling frantically to keep up. "A gold watch, fifteen-carat, Barraud's of London, Number 97163. Not new, but in good condition. Gold Albert chain, probably twenty-carat, very heavy and solid. Gold ring with Masonic device—there's your secret society, Lestrade."

"Very funny, Mr. Crow," the detective said sourly.

"Gold pin, fifteen-carat, bulldog's head with ruby eyes. I can't say I care for it. Russian leather card case, with cards of Enoch J. Drebber of Cleveland, Ohio, matching Dr. Doyle's identification, so that's convenient. No purse, but loose money"—he counted rapidly, long fingers dipping in and out of Drebber's clothes as easily as a pickpocket—"seven pounds thirteen. Pocket edition of—oh dear—Boccaccio's *Decameron*, with the name Jos. Stangerson printed very legibly on the flyleaf. Two letters, one to E. J. Drebber, at the American Exchange, to be left 'til called for, the other to Joseph Stangerson, the same. Both letters are from the Guion Steamship Company about the sailing of the *Lone Star* from Liverpool. Clearly Mr. Drebber was making his way back to the Colonies. I imagine, Lestrade, that Mr. Stangerson will be endeavoring—possibly with a new sense of urgency—to do the same."

"We'll cable Guion," Lestrade said. "The *Lone Star* can watch for him."

"Could square-toes have been Mr. Stangerson, Dr. Doyle?" asked Crow.

"Not if he was a noticeably tall man," I said. "Stangerson was shorter than Drebber, and I can't somehow see him wearing square-toed boots."

"Pity," said Crow. "It would make this a tidy murder instead of the messy sprawling thing I fear it is." He was straightening the dead man's clothes—as best he could given the corpse's contorted position—and all three of us heard the distinct metallic clunk of something hitting the floor.

Crow pounced on it, as swift as a cat, and then sat back on his heels with an expression of blank astonishment. "What in the holy . . ." He extended his open hand to me—and to Lestrade, who was by now breathing down the back of my neck. The thing on his palm made no sense for a moment and then I was able to resolve it: a feather. It looked like one of Crow's pin-feathers, or like the husks of them he molted, except that it was made of gold.

Lestrade and I both flinched back from it. Lestrade said, "Is that . . . ?"

"Yes," Crow said. "It's a dissolution feather. A real one."

"But how . . ." Lestrade said helplessly. I knew a little about dissolution feathers: when an angel's habitation was destroyed and the angel itself was dissolved, rather than Fallen or made Nameless, there might be left behind one or perhaps two feathers, transmuted by the forces of dissolution into gold. There was a fashion among the wealthy for young women to carry replicas as tokens of virginity. On her marriage, a girl gave her feather to her younger sister or her best friend. I found the tradition unspeakably macabre—but finding a true feather of dissolution on Enoch Drebber's body was far, far worse.

Crow was still completely *bouleversé*. Lestrade looked as baffled as a bulldog trying to understand a doorknob. He said tentatively, "That seems an unlikely thing for this gentleman to have."

"I don't think he did," Crow said. "I mean, I don't think it was his. It wasn't in one of his pockets, just caught in the lining of his coat. I think his murderer dropped it."

After another long silence, Lestrade said, "I'm not sure that's any better."

"He leaned over his victim. To gloat? To be sure he was dead? And it must have fallen out of his pocket." Crow considered a moment and said thoughtfully, "He'll be horrified."

"But what kind of murderer carries a dissolution feather?" protested Lestrade.

"This one," said Crow. "Who was it who found the body again?"

"Constable John Rance 299P," said Lestrade. "Why?"

"There's something I want to ask him."

"He's off duty right now." Lestrade consulted his notebook. "He'll be in the Camberwell Division dormitory, but have a heart, Mr. Crow, and let the poor man get some sleep first."

"Ah," said Crow, who obviously hadn't thought of that. "Yes, of course. I suppose it doesn't matter now. Anyone he encountered would be long gone."

"What on Earth are you talking about?" I said. I was fairly sure he wanted to be asked.

"A dissolution feather isn't the sort of thing a man carries around as a casual trinket. It must be important to the murderer somehow. Vitally important. When he realized that he'd lost it, I don't think he'd be able to keep himself from coming back to look for it. But we know Constable Rance found the body while it was still warm. And the feather is still *here*. Therefore, we know the murderer must have discovered the law already in possession of No. 3. And it seems certainly worth inquiring whether the worthy constables might have discovered *him*."

Lestrade made a noise that was probably intended to convey that he himself had been about to say the exact same thing.

"In the meantime, however," Crow said, "it might be a very good idea to find Mr. Joseph Stangerson. For whether he knows it or not, I fear he is in a great deal of trouble."

7

THE CONSTABLE'S STORY

ON OUR WAY back to Baker Street, Crow bought every newspaper he could find, and he spent the afternoon collating accounts of the murder in George Yard, ferreting out every fact possible and making a neat tabulation of the number of newspapers in which any particular item of information appeared. The process was instructive to witness: the range of facts presented by the newspapers was quite astonishing, as was the degree to which they cribbed from each other.

"There's only so much news to go around," Crow said. "They all circulate and recirculate it endlessly. You have to read quite carefully to glean any new facts."

I looked at the stacks of newspapers once again flooding our sitting room and could only agree.

"I find it abominable," he added after a moment, "that they can't discover this poor woman's name."

Names, of course, are of the most desperate importance to angels; they don't properly exist without them. For a moment, I imagined the dead woman in Whitechapel as one of the Nameless, and then shuddered at how accurate an image that was for the wretched people of that district. Certainly, most of them had no one who cared whether they had a name or not.

At four, Crow stood up in a great rustling of feathers and paper and said, "Time to roust Constable Rance. Do you come with me?"

It was asked diffidently, and I noticed the way his verb choice spared him from actually *asking me to come* and spared me from having to refuse such a request—if I had been capable of doing so, which was doubtful. "Of course I'm coming," I said.

❖

THE CAMBERWELL CONSTABLES' barracks were new, redbrick, and rather pathetically dreary. Constable Rance was still in his shirt sleeves, a stout young man with brown hair, already thinning but neatly combed. He was earnestly eager to help in our inquiries.

He was able to tell us a great deal about his beat, including Lauriston Gardens. It was a dismal part of east London, prone to typhoid; the last resident of No. 3 had in fact died of typhoid and the house was empty because the landlord had yet to do anything about the drains.

"When I saw the light in the windows," Constable Rance said, "to tell you gentlemen the truth, I thought that maybe it was him that died o' the typhoid inspecting the drains what killed him."

That wasn't an unreasonable fear, and I said so.

The constable reddened. "Thank you, sir. Sergeant says I was being a nervous Nellie. But I *did* go in, and I found him."

"Inspector Lestrade said the corpse was still warm?"

"Yessir. But he was stiff all over, like you woulda had to break his bones to lay him out straight."

"Yes," Crow said, "I thought you'd tried. It's a kind impulse, but really you shouldn't."

"I never—"

"You walked around the room several times," Crow said. "And you knelt down by the body. Then you walked through and tried the kitchen door. Then—"

Constable Rance staggered up and back from the table. "Where was you hid to see all that? You ain't the Angel of Lauriston Gardens, because there *ain't* one and never has been, and how can you—"

"Peace!" Crow said, laughing. "I am one of the hounds, not the wolf. I am not the murderer, and I am not Fallen. Inspector Lestrade will vouch for that."

"Beg your pardon, sir," the constable said, now brick-red. "I didn't mean nothing by it."

"Of course not," Crow said and flashed his dazzling smile. "As Dr. Doyle said, it's not an unreasonable fear. Come sit down and tell me about the man."

"The man?" the constable said, obediently resuming his chair.

"When you went back out in the street. There *must* have been one."

"You mean that drunk fellow?" He grinned. "I've seen some drunk men in my time, but never anyone so cryin' drunk as that cove. He was a big man, too, so I was just glad he was too drunk to fight."

"What sort of a man was he?"

Rance was puzzled but willing. "A big bloke in a big shabby coat and a muffler. Me and Murcher had to prop him up an' he was singing the whole time. Oh! He was a Colonial, he was singing one of those Rebellion songs like they do."

"That's very interesting," Crow said. "What became of him?"

"We would've taken him in for causing a public nuisance, but we didn't have a man to spare. So me and Murcher, we walked him down to the Brixton Road so he'd be out of our way, and I imagine he got himself home all right."

"I imagine he did," Crow said dryly.

Rance, as a truly sterling example of the London bobby, missed the inflection, and while he was clearly ready to offer any help he could, it was equally clear that he had nothing more to provide. In the hansom, Crow was bitter. "He could have solved the case!" he said. "Right there! All he had to do was his job!"

"He had no reason to expect the murderer to come back," I said, more out of a vague sense of obligation than any belief that Constable

Rance was not an idiot.

"If he'd arrested him!" Crow said. "We'd have him right now!"

"Yes, I suppose this will teach us all not to prioritize murder before drunkenness," said I.

It startled him—I felt his wings twitch—and then he burst out in his slightly hysterical but infectious laugh. "Well," he said, "and he did give us some useful information. The murderer seems to be an American—which makes some sense, since Mr. Drebber is an American."

"One thing puzzles me," I said. "On the *Sophy Anderson,* I distinctly remember Drebber saying he was from Salt Lake City, but his cards say Cleveland. I admit that my knowledge of the Colonies is not perfect, but I didn't think those two cities had anything to do with each other."

"No," Crow said. "Cleveland is in the Western Reserve, while Salt Lake City is the capital of the Mormon Territory of Deseret. Those are very different points of origin." He pondered a moment, then added, "When we do find Mr. Joseph Stangerson, there are a number of very interesting questions I wish to ask him."

8

THE
MOUSETRAP

"Will you keep a secret, Doyle?" said Crow as I turned from hanging my hat on our hat stand. He was giving me a look compounded of hope and mischief, and I noted his wording again: not "*can* you" but "*will* you."

"As long as it harms no one," I said, for I had drawn that line for myself a long time ago.

"Oh, well, that's simple then," Crow said. "No harm to anyone, I promise."

"Then, yes, I will keep your secret."

"Splendid! They should be arriving—yes, there's the bell."

I tried to be open-minded and prepared for anything, but I was still surprised when eight of the Nameless filed into our sitting room.

"Behold!" said Crow, who was honorably trying not to laugh at my expression. "The Baker Street Irregulars!"

"I beg your pardon?" I said, and he did laugh, though more with delight than anything else.

"They go everywhere, Doyle! They see everything! And no one thinks twice about them. They are of far more use in an investigation than a police constable."

"But I thought . . ."

"That they are mindless as well as Nameless?"

"No, of course not. How could they be? But I had always thought that the Nameless had no self-volition?"

"Well, they haven't," Crow agreed. "But if I ask them to find something out for me, that's perfectly within bounds and there's no reason they can't."

"Is it that they *have* no volition or that they are forbidden to use it?"

"Um," said Crow, and there was a susurrus of feathers from the line of Nameless. "A bit of both, I suppose? They have no individual identity or will. But they're quite capable of making decisions in pursuit of a goal once they've been given one—which can come out rather close to the same thing on occasion." He added, "Just because they don't *act* on what they hear doesn't mean they don't hear it."

"What are you going to have them listen for?"

"We need to find the cabdriver who brought Mr. Drebber to No. 3 Lauriston Gardens," he said to both me and the Nameless. He described Drebber and the horse with one new shoe and said, "I think the setting was chosen as a matter of opportunity, so that I don't think the cab ride can have been very long. Start around the Brixton Road, and only widen your search as you have to."

The Nameless nodded their understanding and Crow dismissed them.

"They like having missions," he said. "It gives them a sense of identity, which of course is what they all long for."

"Do you remember being Nameless?" I asked and then realized what a dreadfully tactless question it was.

But Crow didn't seem to mind. "Yes, of course, but it's quite hard to describe. There's no sense of self to anchor what I remember. Thus the memories are very hard to"—he gestured widely with both hands—"hold on to. I have heard people discussing their dreams, and I think that's the best analogy. I remember the *sensation* of being Nameless more than anything else—the rest is disjointed and quite nonlinear. And I can't make narratives out of any of it."

"That sounds unpleasant," I said.

Crow shrugged, shoulders and wings flexing together. "There was no self to find it so. Just the longing to have a name." And then he shook himself, like a dog coming out of the water, or a person emerging from a dream, and said briskly, "It seems to me that our point of leverage is the dissolution feather. It is clearly something the murderer values, since he made the reckless move of attempting to return to the scene of the murder. Ergo, it should be possible to induce him to do something reckless again."

"Your hypothesis seems sound as far as it goes," I said. "But how do you intend to set this trap? You can't just place an advertisement in the papers: 'FOUND, one dissolution feather.'"

"I can't?" He sounded disappointed.

"Dissolution feathers are too rare and too valuable. Your mousetrap will attract far too many mice."

"Oh dear," he said. "Do you have an alternative in mind?"

I almost laughed at him, but then I had a thought. "You *could* put an advertisement in the paper. 'FOUND, an item believed to be of great value to its owner. Inquiries to 221 Baker Street.' That way, anyone who comes has to tell us what the thing *is*."

"That's rather clever, Doyle," he said. "Do you think it will work?"

"I think it might. As you say, he clearly wants to retrieve it very badly. And desperate men do stupid things." I'd seen that often enough in Afghanistan.

"It's worth a try," he said. "We won't tell Lestrade. He'd have a thousand fits."

"How did you persuade him to let you keep the feather anyway?" I said.

The corners of Crow's mouth curved up. "I implied strongly that it was sacred and had already been profaned by being found on a murdered body. I think he thinks I'm going to pray over it all night."

"*Is* it sacred?"

"Eh." He pulled it out of his pocket and considered it, tilting it to watch the firelight gleam off the delicate lines. "It's a bit like a cremation urn. This *was* an angel, once. I certainly don't like the idea of it being mucked about by a bunch of ham-handed constables. But it's mostly, I don't know, symbolic."

"And you know it's real," I said, because his identification of it had been immediate and certain.

"I can feel . . ." He paused for a long moment, clearly trying to think of the right word. "Harmonies? Does that sound at all right?"

"Don't ask me," I said. "The precious little I know about angels mostly involves how to avoid the Fallen on the battlefield."

"Well, let's call it harmony, anyway. It's the last trace of the angel, of their song, held in this lump of transmuted gold."

"Their song?"

"We sing to each other," Crow said simply. "Always."

"As birds do?" I said doubtfully, trying to imagine the dignified angels of St. Bartholomew's and St. Paul's squawking at each other like parrots.

"Birds aren't actually an awfully good analogy. You'd do better to think of us as bees."

"Bees?" said I, taken aback.

"Well, we've too many limbs to be mammals," he said reasonably. "And our social structure is much better represented by a hive than by a warren—or even by a rookery. And bees do sing, in a way."

"I suppose so," I said feebly and spent the rest of the evening trying very hard not to think of Crow as a bee.

❖

I WENT TO sleep that night fully expecting to wake up in my closet again, but although I had terrible dreams about the Fallen, I woke up still human and still in my bed, which I supposed amounted to a victory. Of sorts.

I'd overexerted myself the day before, running around after Crow like a fool, and I paid for it with aches and chills and bleak ennui. I got out of bed only because I knew either Crow or Mrs. Climpson or poor overworked Jennie would come tapping at my door to find out if I was all right.

I wasn't all right, but I was alive, and that would have to do.

Crow was in the sitting room, surrounded by the inevitable drift of newspapers. He was bent over one intently, his hair already rumpled—for he had an inveterate habit of raking his fingers through it when perplexed—and falling into his eyes. "I say, Doyle," he said, not looking up as I folded myself gingerly into my chair at the table, "they still don't know the name of this poor woman murdered in George Yard."

"She has no one to notice that she's gone," I said bleakly.

He raised his head sharply, and I got the full force of his stare. "You're not all right."

I shook my head. "It's nothing to worry about."

He looked profoundly unconvinced. "What you mean is that there's nothing to be done."

I winced, rattling my teacup against the saucer. "I suppose that's true. I warned you that my health was bad."

"I wasn't complaining," he said. "If there *is* something that can be done, will you tell me?"

Concern or curiosity? It was hard to say; I knew he liked me, but I had no sense of how deep that liking might run, or indeed how deep it *could* run. I had learned that angels, while they mimicked human manners and emotions perfectly, did not always feel them, and Crow had suggested, just last night, that it was an error to imagine that they felt as humans did.

Bees, he had said, and it occurred to me to wonder, if the angels of London were the bees of a hive, who was their queen?

"Doyle?" said Crow.

"I'm sorry," I said. "My mind was wandering. Yes, if there's anything you can do, I will tell you."

"Good," he said, still watching me. "But there isn't?"

"No," I said and decided my hands were steady enough to pour tea. Mrs. Climpson had learned just to leave the teapot (in its garish knitted cosy) on our dining table; I habitually went through an entire pot in a morning, needing both its warmth and its invigoration.

I was not at all sure tea was going to be enough today.

Crow returned to his newspapers after a moment and regaled me with tidbits while I drank my first cup of tea—necessary before I rang the bell. Crow was in an odd way an infinitely undemanding, and thus restful, companion. If I wanted to say *My leg hurts like a bonfire,* Crow would not judge me as a whiner or a malingerer; he had no expectations about maintaining a decent reticence, nor any experience of the stoicism I had been raised to expect of myself.

I wasn't, of course, going to say any such thing, but there was some comfort in knowing that I could, and Crow would not think less of me.

When I rang the bell, Jennie appeared like a magic trick.

"She was waiting on the landing," Crow said mildly, and Jennie blushed a hard scarlet that clashed with her hair.

"I'm late," I said. "I know, Jennie, it's all right."

"Please, sir," she said. "Cook's got a lovely pair of kippers, if you'd be wanting—"

"No," I said and added, "thank you," because I'd been much more fervent than I'd intended. "Just toast, please. But bring the good marmalade." I smiled at her and got the faintest responsive dimple.

"Yessir," she said and scurried away.

Crow said, "I've put an advertisement in the East End papers. He's more likely to read them, I think, than *The Times.*"

"You're sure he reads?" I said.

"He found Drebber somehow."

"Then you think—"

"I don't think it's like this woman in George Yard, no. Something that needed to kill found someone who wouldn't be missed. But Drebber had a traveling companion. He had visiting cards—even if we think they weren't accurate, due to that telltale difference between Cleveland and Salt Lake City. No one searching for a victim of convenience would choose him. *Ergo,* he was killed because someone *knew* him and wanted him dead very badly. And since Drebber is merely a visitor to London, that means his killer stalked him. Like a lion stalking a gazelle."

"I have a little trouble thinking of Drebber as a gazelle," said I.

Crow laughed. "No, I suppose not. But you see my point. I don't know if this person followed Drebber from Paris or was waiting here in London. But either way, their encounter wasn't by chance. And I think that does imply strongly that the murderer can read."

"Fair enough," I said. "And even if *he* can't, he probably has friends who can and who will read the papers for him."

"That's true," said Crow, much struck. "I hadn't considered that he might have confederates. Oh dear." He muttered to himself for a moment—of which I only caught the words "bait and switch"—and then burst to his feet. "I'll be right back!" he said and flung himself out the door.

Jennie, bringing in my toast, stared after him in amazement, but said only, "Please, sir, Cook said if you'd be liking a poached egg or such like, she'd be glad to—"

"No, thank you," I said. "Toast and marmalade is truly all I want." The exchange with Crow had lightened my mood, and I refrained from snapping at the child. That in turn meant that Mrs. Climpson, who ran her household with an iron fist, wouldn't be up later to scold me for making Jennie cry.

I appropriated Crow's newspapers and found myself drawn to the articles about the death in George Yard. The woman, unknown, was middle-aged, plump, shabbily dressed. There could be no doubt she was what polite London termed an "unfortunate"—a fallen woman instead of a fallen angel, and I lost myself for a moment in considering the hopeless plight of the woman and the equally hopeless plight of the angel, and yet how differently that hopelessness played out. In the case of the woman in George Yard, since none of the residents recognized her, it seemed obvious enough that she had chosen that landing to conduct a transaction, equally obvious that her client had had other ideas.

Thirty-nine stab wounds, up from the earlier estimate of twenty-four. It was hard even to imagine an attack that frenzied. She couldn't have put up much of a fight in the face of so much rage; she would have bled to death in a matter of minutes at the outside.

There was speculation, naturally, about paranormal activity—what polite London (those who called the woman an "unfortunate") termed the "unusual." But the wounds had distinctly been made with a bladed weapon, which ruled out hell-hounds, rogue werewolves, and any other creature incapable of holding a knife, and none of the body was missing, which ruled out necrophages and ghouls, while neither vampires nor any desperate hemophage would have been so *wasteful.* All the signs pointed toward human agency, and although it was only a matter of time before the howls of "witchcraft!" started up, none of the witches I had met was any more likely to do this sort of thing than their respectable neighbors.

All of which led to the inevitable question: what sort of person *was* likely to do this sort of thing, and would you recognize him if you saw him on the street?

I had seen men in Afghanistan who had been driven mad by the Fallen, or by the experience of being buried alive in a mass grave, or by having their best friend's brains painted across their face. All of them had indeed *looked* like madmen, wild-eyed shivering wretches who wept uncontrollably or held conversations with people who were not there. But they were mostly not violent, and those that were would not have been able to act normally long enough to persuade a Whitechapel prostitute to go anywhere with them. On the other hand, I had known a number of exceedingly sane men who had reveled in the butchery of war, and my most uncomfortable image was of one of them, returned to London but still on the battlefield in his heart, realizing that there was an infinite supply of targets in the East End, women who would be so little missed that no one could even identify their ravaged corpses. It was a terrible image, and I strove to rid myself of it. But a man like that, a soldier, *would* be able to persuade a canny woman—and the women who made their livings on the streets of the East End were as canny and cunning as wild creatures—to find a dark and quiet spot to be alone with him. And she wouldn't realize her mistake until it was too late to scream.

Enough, I said to myself and deliberately turned to contemplation of Enoch J. Drebber—of either Salt Lake City or Cleveland, depending on which source you believed—and the peculiar circumstances of his death.

I agreed with Crow that the dissolution feather had not belonged to the murdered man, not because I believed him incapable of carrying such a macabre relic, but because if he had had it, I felt certain he would have tried to impress the young lady on the *Sophy Anderson* with it. That led me only to the question of why his murderer would have been carrying such a thing *on his person* when he set out to commit a murder—and I could not but assume he had set forth with that goal in mind, for otherwise he would not have *also* been carrying the poison necessary to do the job.

But how on Earth could anyone have premeditated the murder of a transient? Drebber had arrived in London five months ago, and he had been planning to leave soon, on the *Lone Star.* Was it mere happenstance that he had crossed paths with his murderer? Or had his murderer stalked him from Paris to London, like Crow's simile with the lion and the gazelle? Why *was* Drebber in London? Why had a man like that been in Paris, for that matter? Drebber had seemed to me, in our admittedly brief encounter, to be the worst kind of Colonial, the sort of man who asserted that because America was new, everything old was bad. What would bring such a man to Europe?

I lurched up out of my chair and over to my desk, where I found a sheet of foolscap and my pen and began making fierce scribbled notes.

1. STANGERSON

Clearly the first order of business had to be to find Stangerson, both for the information he had and to warn him. Anyone who hated Drebber that much must surely also loathe Stangerson.

2. dissolution feather

I had a terrific number of questions about the feather and how it came to be on Drebber's body, starting with the angel to whom it had once belonged and ending with, if the murderer treasured it so greatly that he carried it with him on his errand of murder, how could he possibly have been so careless as to leave it on Drebber's body?

3. Drebber

What had Drebber been doing in France? What was he doing in London? Where was he lodging? What had he done the last day of his life? I was sure Lestrade was pursuing all of these questions, but it hurt nothing and no one if I wrote them down as well.

4. How had the murderer found Drebber?

Possibly unanswerable.

5. How had the murderer persuaded Drebber to enter No. 3, Lauriston Gardens with him?

Also possibly unanswerable.

6. How had the murderer persuaded Drebber to take poison without putting a mark on him?

What alternative was so dreadful? What threat could the murderer possibly be holding over Drebber? Or, alternatively, did Drebber not know it was poison? Was the murderer someone he *trusted*?

7. RACHE

Why write that on the wall? Was the murderer a German socialist? Was the word really *RACHEL*? If so, who was Rachel and how was she tied to that damned dissolution feather? No one could have *two* such fearsome causes, even against a thug like Drebber. Could an angel be named Rachel?

I stopped and thought about that. There was, so far as I knew, no reason an angel *couldn't* be named Rachel. They generally got their names from their habitations, but Crow was proof that they could have names even without one.

Had Crow picked his own name? Could an angel *choose* to be named Rachel?

I wrote those questions down and continued:

8. The murderer

Speculating about his motive was an alluring but ultimately pointless exercise. I simply didn't have enough information. But there *were* things worth writing down: *The murderer was (a) someone Drebber knew and trusted or (b) someone Drebber DID NOT KNOW.* A chance-met acquaintance was much more likely to arouse suspicion than a complete stranger—which perhaps said something odd about the human psyche. *The murderer knew London well enough to know that No. 3, Lauriston Gardens was abandoned— possibly even that people were worried about ghosts.* If a constable admitted to unease, the anxiety had to be pretty widespread. But the murderer—apparently not afraid of ghosts, but I supposed a man who carried a dissolution feather with him probably wouldn't be—knew that No. 3 was a safe place to go to conduct a quiet bit of murder.

PERSUASIVE, I wrote and then went back and underlined it. The murderer had either persuaded Drebber to kill himself, which seemed ridiculously improbable, or had persuaded him to swallow something under the pretense that it would . . . And there I was stumped. In an abandoned house in the middle of the night, what in God's name would you agree to swallow? What could you possibly have that needed to be cured that badly?

Another avenue of useless speculation.

Before I could regroup and try again, Crow burst back into the room as precipitously as he had left. "I found one!" he said triumphantly.

"One what?"

"A wedding band with an inscription," he said and held out a gold band, chased with a delicate pattern of ivy leaves and with a line of engraving running around the inside.

"What on Earth . . . ?" I couldn't even articulate the question.

But Crow understood. "If someone comes, and it's not the right person. We can't just say, 'Oh yes, we found a dissolution feather.' Now we've got something to show them."

"You went . . ."

"To Oliphant's pawnshop. They know me there; they'll send a bill."

"And bought someone's wedding ring?"

"Well, they'd *pawned* it."

"Some poor woman had to pawn her wedding ring, and you're going to use it as a ploy?"

". . . As a ploy to catch a murderer," Crow said, frowning.

"What does the inscription say?"

"Just a date and some initials. Doyle, the whole case was covered in dust. She's not going to come back for it."

"I don't know that that makes it any better," I said. I would have liked to slam out of the room, the way I had done in my parents' house, but I could neither spring to my feet nor stride to the door. My dramatic exit would be a farce.

"I don't understand your objection," Crow said stiffly.

"No, I'm well aware that you don't," said I.

"Do you have a better suggestion?"

"No, of course not." I felt myself deflate, my anger vanishing like a soap bubble. "And who knows, perhaps she pawned her wedding ring for money to escape her husband. Perhaps she never intended to come back for it."

Crow's head was tilted in his most birdlike fashion. "Your objection is based on the feelings of the woman who once owned the ring?"

"No . . . yes . . . maybe, I don't know."

"Well, that was comprehensive," he said dryly.

"I'm trying to prevent the words 'common decency' from coming out of my mouth," I said.

Crow looked, if anything, more baffled. "Is there something indecent about the operation of pawnshops? I thought they were perfectly legal."

I started laughing, which only worsened his perplexity. Finally, I said, "No, there is nothing illegal about pawnshops. I meant only that it seems callous to purchase a wedding ring, which has a great deal of symbolism and emotional freight, for use in a distinctly Machiavellian ploy."

"Oh," Crow said. He had read *The Prince;* I knew because we had discussed it before, particularly the infamous passage about ends and means. He pondered for a long moment and said, "I think I understand your objection, but I don't agree with you."

"You believe that your means are justified by your end?"

"I think my means do not need any particular justification. It's not as if I walked up to the woman on the street and demanded her wedding ring. *She* pawned it, Doyle, not I."

"No, I know," I said. "You are correct. You have done nothing wrong."

He frowned at me—Crow was unfamiliar with human beings' more private emotions, but not insensitive to them.

"Never mind," I said. "Do you truly think we are likely to get false claimants?"

Crow said, "I have every faith in the average Londoner's curiosity and acquisitiveness. I only hope we may not be mobbed."

In the event, we had four callers that evening, three of whom were bowled out by their own lack of imagination, one of whom correctly/incorrectly guessed a wedding ring—and had a particularly affecting story to go with the guess—but could not supply the inscription. After she had left, I said to Crow, "I've been thinking about some things," and read him the notes I had made earlier.

"That's quite good, Doyle," Crow said, with such enthusiasm that it was not at all patronizing. "I didn't think you'd take such an interest."

My face heated. "I've little enough to do," I said, "and I have never been able to resist a puzzle."

"Well, it's good news for me. I was afraid you'd leave once you realized I was entertaining police officers."

I snorted. "I was a battlefield surgeon. My sensibilities aren't so delicate."

"People can be surprisingly finicky," Crow said, but before I could decide whether there was perhaps a hint of sadness in his voice, he said briskly, "Well. What next?"

"I trust that question is rhetorical," I said.

"No, I'm quite serious. You're an intelligent person, and I value your opinion. What do you think should be our next step?"

"We still don't have any idea why Drebber stood still to be murdered."

"No, you're right," said Crow. "And that honestly makes no sense at all. Unless he didn't know it was poison."

"But why would he take it? What could the murderer *possibly* have claimed it was and been believed in the middle of the night in an abandoned house? You're quite sure the murderer couldn't have been Stangerson?"

"From your description, yes, I am perfectly sure. But that reminds me, I must send word to Lestrade that the mouse has eluded our mousetrap tonight. I shall be back directly."

"I won't have gone anywhere," I said.

But before Crow reached the door, we heard the bell.

He stopped as abruptly as a child playing Statues, neck craned just slightly, listening. He said, "I think that's Lestrade now. Yes, I'm sure of it." He finished his rush across the room and flung the door open before Lestrade could have been halfway up the stairs. "Good evening, Inspector!" Crow said cheerfully. "Won't you come in?"

"Good evening, Mr. Crow," Lestrade said, pausing on the threshold as he had before, as if checking for lurking assailants. "Dr. Doyle."

"Good evening, Inspector," I said, my mother's voice in my memory snapping at me to be civil to guests.

"You look like a man with much to impart," said Crow.

The Inspector did indeed look as if he was about to explode with the force of the words pent inside him. "It's one in the eye for Gregson!" he cried.

"Whatever do you mean?" said Crow.

"We've got him!"

"The murderer?"

"Yes, indeed. Lieutenant Arthur Charpentier of Her Majesty's Navy."

"Charpentier," Crow said sharply. "That's a lupine name, isn't it?"

"Yes," said Lestrade.

"You think a *werewolf* murdered Mr. Drebber?"

I was as taken aback as Crow. Werewolves, tending as they did to live in their enclaves apart from human society, rarely had any reason to murder human beings. And when they did, it was almost always a matter of lupine justice, and the murderer torn to bits by the rending teeth of the pack.

"I think a werewolf with a beautiful sister murdered Mr. Drebber," Lestrade corrected.

". . . Oh dear," said Crow.

"Mrs. Charpentier is a widow, and to support herself and her children, she runs a boardinghouse. Most of her clientele are cabmen and factory workers, but she accepts transients from time to time, and she told me that Drebber and Stangerson were paying a pound a day each. That was why she put up with Drebber accosting the servants and being over-familiar with her daughter Alice. But finally Drebber got stinking drunk and actually grabbed Alice and kissed her."

"He was lucky he wasn't dead then and there," I said.

"Alice was apparently too stunned to react," Lestrade said. "She seems to have been quite sheltered despite her mother's rough customers."

"You don't have to be bourgeois to know better than to insult a werewolf like that," I said. "Arthur must not have been home at the time."

"No," Lestrade agreed. "His ship is in dry dock, so although he's sleeping at home, he is exceedingly busy."

"And Mrs. Charpentier herself?" said Crow.

"Mrs. Charpentier did not come upon the scene until after Stangerson and one of the other boarders had got Drebber off Miss Charpentier, and she is a woman who has lived among humans for a long time. She told me she almost never shifts anymore except with the moon."

"A hard way to live," Crow said somberly.

"The Charpentiers are a poor family, even by werewolf standards," Lestrade said. "She had two small children, and her son has apparently been Navy-mad since he was quite young."

"Some werewolves feel a call to the sea," I said. "No one understands why, but it is apparently unassuageable."

"She's just paid for Arthur's commission," said Lestrade, "so that fourteen pounds a week got her to overlook a great deal—but she couldn't overlook this. Even Stangerson was disgusted. She asked them to leave, and they did. But Drebber came back." Lestrade seemed to enjoy our horrified silence. "Drebber came back, even more drunk, and proposed to Alice."

"Proposed?" I said.

"Proposed. He said"—Lestrade consulted his notebook—"'You

are of age, and there is no law to stop you. I have money enough
and to spare. Never mind the old girl here, but come along with
me now straightaway. You shall live like a princess.' That was when
Lieutenant Charpentier entered the room."

Crow and I exchanged an eyebrows-raised glance.

"Well, young Charpentier shifted, all right," said Lestrade. "He
chased Drebber out of the house, and the last his mother saw of him,
he was trailing Drebber down the street."

"If he were going to kill Mr. Drebber, he would have done it then,"
Crow pointed out.

"If he'd meant to kill him," Lestrade said. "Which I don't think
he did. Not then, at any rate. He'd come back inside long enough to
shift and dress, and his mother and sister both swear he wasn't in a
killing rage."

"Was Drebber too drunk to have the wits to run?" I said.

"Charpentier's a tracker," said Lestrade. "And Drebber was afraid
of the wolf, not of the man. He saw the wolf go inside and must have
thought that was all he needed to worry about. Now, don't make that
face at me, Mr. Crow. This isn't one of your hypotheses. This is what
all three of the Charpentiers agree happened."

"Drebber may not have known enough about werewolves to
realize," I said. "In the Colonies, werewolves have their own
settlements, or they go over to the native tribes."

"And any found in Deseret are driven out," Crow said reluctantly,
as if it pained him to have to give support of any kind to Lestrade's
story.

"And anyway," said Lestrade, "Charpentier *admits* it. He says
that he followed Drebber until Drebber noticed him and hailed
a cab to get away from him. Then he says he encountered an old
shipmate and took a long walk with him, but couldn't tell me where
the shipmate lived or what ship he's serving on now, and the name
he gave me is almost certainly false. That's *his* story. I say that he
encountered the shipmate *before* Drebber noticed him, and the two
of them persuaded Drebber into that empty house with them."

"Where they persuaded him to take poison?" Crow said. "Don't be absurd, Lestrade."

"Ah, now, we don't *know* it's poison he died of," Lestrade said. "A hard enough blow to the stomach can kill a man without leaving a mark. I don't think young Charpentier and his friend meant to kill Drebber. But when they did, they did their best to throw us off the track by writing on the wall in blood and so on."

"And one of them just happened to have a dissolution feather on him?" demanded Crow.

"Sailors pick up all sorts of strange trinkets," Lestrade said.

"Yes, but don't you see," Crow started and then clearly realized the effort was pointless.

"You do this every time, Mr. Crow," Lestrade said, more in sorrow than in anger. "You get so caught up in the little details that you can't see the big picture."

Crow's wings mantled at that, and he snapped, "And how many times have I been wrong?"

"Well, you've made some lucky guesses," Lestrade allowed, "but—"

"Guesses nothing! I've made deductions and extrapolations from those 'little details.' And I have been *right*."

"Well," said Lestrade in a tone I recognized from years of my brother arguing with my father, and I realized I had to intervene. They could easily be here all night.

I said hastily, "It won't wash, Inspector. You can kill a man with a hard enough blow to the solar plexus, but you can't send him into convulsions. And Crow only found footprints for one murderer."

"Charpentier and his friend could have been wearing the same sort of shoes," Lestrade said stubbornly.

"And carefully walked only in each other's footprints even before they killed him?" Crow said scornfully. "I assure you, even if they had, it would have shown in the marks they left. Dr. Doyle is right, Inspector. It won't wash."

Lestrade looked both annoyed and rather hurt. "Well, we'll see," he said. "We're still looking for Charpentier's friend and I've a number of other things to do, what with Gregson and them wasting their time in Whitechapel. I just came by to give you the news. Good evening, Mr. Crow, good evening, Dr. Doyle." And he stalked out.

"Poor Lestrade," said Crow. "He tries so hard and there's no one more dogged, but he's just dreadfully bad at putting the story of a crime together."

"Do you think Lieutenant Charpentier is in any danger?" I said.

"Of having a very uncomfortable couple of days? Yes. Of being convicted? No. Gregson will laugh this theory of Lestrade's to scorn as soon as he hears it. They hate each other."

"Which is such a splendid method for Her Majesty's justice to be served by," I said.

"At least they have the wits to come to me," said Crow.

❖

I SPENT A restless night, but no worse than that.

I had not yet finished dressing when there was a tap on my door. It was Jennie, looking scared. "Please, sir, there's a policeman asking to see either you or Mr. Crow, and Mr. Crow's gone out."

"All right, Jennie. Show him up."

I came out in my dressing gown, expecting Lestrade, but it was someone else.

Detective Inspector Gregson was taller than Lestrade, fair-haired, with gray eyes in a square, bullying face. I disliked him instantly.

And it seemed the feeling was mutual, for he said, "So, Dr. Doyle, I've heard a great deal about you from Inspector Lestrade," in a way that indicated a profound disbelief in everything he'd been told. I half expected him to demand to see my medical diploma.

I said pleasantly, "Lestrade has also said a great deal about you, Inspector."

Gregson took my meaning easily and flushed brick-red. He said, "I understand you knew the murdered man?"

"I encountered him once," I said, "on the airship between Paris and London."

"Not an amiable encounter," he said.

"No, decidedly not."

"Have you encountered either Drebber or Stangerson since you arrived in London?"

"No."

"Do you know the Charpentiers?"

"No." I fell prey to a horrid suspicion. "You don't think that I . . ."

His face was stony. "It seems like a remarkable coincidence."

"That Drebber should be murdered, or that I should happen, by virtue of being Crow's flatmate, to encounter his corpse? Because I can assure you there's nothing remarkable about the former at all, and the latter seems even *more* implausible if you assume it was somehow planned. Why should I do such a thing?"

"To divert suspicion from yourself," Gregson nearly snarled.

"But that's ludicrous. I wasn't under suspicion to begin with, for the very good reason that I've had nothing to do with Drebber since disembarking from the *Sophy Anderson*. And I didn't kill him."

"You're a doctor," Gregson countered. "It'd be no great difficulty for you to get your hands on poison."

"But I didn't," I said through my teeth. "I had reason to detest Drebber, but not reason to kill him. And Crow will tell you I neither go out nor have visitors. In fact, since he never sleeps and can hear everything that happens in this house, he can tell you I was here all night the night that Drebber died." I wondered, with a chill, what else Crow might be able to tell someone who asked the right questions.

Gregson was scowling, and he said, "Lestrade warned me you were clever," as if "clever" was the worst thing he could say about anyone. "But just because you have an answer for everything . . ." He shook his head like a man trying to rid himself of a gnat. "You see, it's ridiculous to think a strong young man like Charpentier would resort to poison—"

"Lestrade doesn't think Drebber *was* poisoned," I said, mostly to goad him.

"Lestrade's an idiot," he said. "Drebber was obviously poisoned, and the man who uses poison is the man who doubts his ability to defeat his opponent any other way." And he looked meaningfully at my cane.

"Tell me how I compelled him to swallow poison," I said.

Gregson's smile was not pleasant. "You're a doctor—as Drebber knew—and Drebber was very drunk. If you'd told him it was a hangover cure, I think he would have believed you."

"That's really rather good, Gregson," Crow said from the doorway, and Gregson and I both jumped a foot. "Much better than your usual efforts—but I'm afraid it just won't do. Dr. Doyle did *not* make the footprints I found at the scene, and did not leave the flat on the night of Drebber's murder. I will swear any oath you like."

Gregson's scowl swung from me to Crow. It was deliberately nonsensical for Crow to talk about swearing an oath; Gregson knew as well as I did that angels do not lie. "He could have suborned someone into acting as a proxy."

"*Who?*" Crow said. "Me? Mrs. Climpson? Jennie MacArthur? Dr. Doyle doesn't see anyone else—certainly not on the sort of terms you'd have to be on to ask someone to commit murder on your behalf."

While I was grateful for Crow's support, I wished he could have found a more tactful way to say I had no friends.

Gregson looked unconvinced—half (I thought) his unwillingness to give up a beautiful theory and half the mutual antipathy that had sprung up like a thicket of swords between us. But he got no chance to argue, because there was a commotion at the front door we all could hear, and Crow swung nimbly out of the way as Lestrade came up the stairs.

Crow said, "Inspector! What can we do for you?"

Lestrade looked from Crow to me with troubled eyes—and winced at the sight of Gregson. "We've found Stangerson."

"And yet somehow this seems not to be splendid news," Crow said cautiously.

"He's dead," said Lestrade. "Stabbed to death in his hotel room."

"*Stabbed* to death?" Crow said.

"Viciously," said Lestrade.

"Well, *that*'s not surprising," Crow said. "This murderer hates his victims as much as anyone has ever hated their fellow creatures. But . . . stabbed. Tell me about the scene."

"So I had my constables canvass around Euston Station, and one of them struck gold at Halliday's Private Hotel in Little George Street. He came and fetched me first thing this morning, and I got the boots to take me up—which he wouldn't do for a constable. He'd got orders to wake Stangerson at six o'clock. I told him I'd take care of it, but as it turned out Mr. Stangerson was beyond waking. The first thing I saw when we turned the corner was a trickle of blood, red as anything, running from under Stangerson's door to puddle against the opposite baseboard. It was already clotting."

Crow's wings rustled, but he said nothing.

Lestrade continued, "The boots turned green, and I thought he was going to faint, but he pulled himself together and ran to get the passkey from the head housekeeper, which spared me a sore shoulder. I unlocked the door, since the boots had used up his courage, and went in."

Lestrade sighed. "The room was a shambles. Stangerson hadn't sold his life cheaply: the chair was overturned and everything had been swept off the writing desk, the bedclothes were all in a wad on the floor, and there were bloody handprints everywhere. I asked the boots—him wringing his hands in the doorway like an old maid—and he said the rooms to either side were unoccupied. The gentleman had specifically asked for a quiet room. The body was huddled on the floor under the open window. He'd been stabbed in the side and had slashes on his hands and forearms like he'd been fending off a knife. The word 'RACHE' had been written in blood on the wall right beside the window and—oh yes—there were two pills in a chip ointment box on the windowsill."

"Pills?" Crow said, almost quivering, like a hunting dog who has found a scent. "What sort of pills?"

"They were rather odd," Lestrade said, although he looked puzzled—as was I—at Crow's intensity. "I think I've still got them." He dug in his pockets, while Crow watched, looking as if he would rather just turn Lestrade upside down and shake him. "Here we go."

Crow was immediately there, inspecting the pills minutely. "May I show these to Dr. Doyle?" he asked and did not wait for Lestrade's nod to snatch the box and bring it across the room to where I was sitting. "What do you make of them, Doyle?"

"They're very odd," I said, and they were, translucent gray and almost perfectly spherical. "And I must tell you that I will not volunteer to swallow them."

"Good heavens, no," Crow said. "I can't lose the best flatmate I've ever found. And in any event, we don't need to test them to know they contain poison. Mr. Drebber did that for us."

"But how on Earth did the murderer persuade him?" I asked. "It's not like you can just walk up to people on the street, hand them pills, and expect them to swallow them."

"And why are there two of them?" Crow said, scowling. "Is there some third man in danger of his life?"

"We won't know until he turns up dead," said I.

Gregson was frowning. "You think those pills are poison?"

"Strychnine, to be exact," said Crow. "If Mr. Lestrade will remember, Dr. Doyle said as much over Drebber's body."

"Why would the murderer leave them behind?" Lestrade said, also frowning.

"He must not have needed them anymore," Crow said, although dubiously. "And why are there *two* of them?"

"And how did the murderer escape?" I said.

Lestrade snorted. "Bold as brass down a ladder. We found a man who saw him and thought nothing of it. Said he was a big man with a long, dull-colored coat, but that's as much description as I could get."

"He has the Devil's own luck," I said.

"He does, at that," Lestrade agreed.

Crow was still scowling at those two innocent-looking pills. "I would understand the whole sequence of events if I could just figure out why there are *two*," he said. He started pacing the length of the sitting room, an alarming practice, both because the sitting room was not truly large enough to accommodate it and because it was a sign of agitation, and if sufficiently agitated, Crow *would* forget—no matter how heartfelt his apologies were afterward for the overturned furniture and broken china. I had taken a wing full in the face once and could only count myself lucky it hadn't broken my nose.

Gregson and Lestrade looked alarmed enough that I surmised they had witnessed the phenomenon—and its consequences— before. Lestrade said, in an obvious attempt at distraction, "We've released Lieutenant Charpentier, of course, and I wrote him a letter for his captain. He was quite decent about it, said he was only sorry that Drebber had been so drunk there'd been no chance of a fair fight."

"A fair fight," Crow said absently. Then more slowly, "A fair fight." Then exultantly, "A fair fight! That's it!" Gregson and I ducked as his wings swept wide, just barely missing the breakfast table. The sensation of being brushed by Crow's feathers never stopped being unearthly and a little unpleasant.

"*What's* it?" I said crossly.

"Oh, sorry. But that's why there's two. For a fair fight."

"That doesn't make any sense," I said. "How can two poison pills be more fair than one?"

"That's just it!" said Crow. "One of them isn't poison!"

"One of them *isn't* poison?" Lestrade said.

"Yes! He offered them a wager. Two pills, one harmless, one lethal. Each man swallows one. One man dies. Drebber must have taken the wager, while Stangerson preferred to make a wager of his own. Both of them lost. And because this murderer is in some ways a very careless man, he left the pills meant for Stangerson behind. He didn't need them anymore."

"But why would anyone proceed in such a lunatic fashion?" I said.

"Why would you deliberately give yourself a fifty-fifty chance of death by strychnine?"

"The answer to that question must lie in the history between the murderer and Drebber and Stangerson. I haven't even a guess. It does seem a terribly inefficient way to go about the matter."

"Inefficient is one word," I said dryly.

"This is all well and good," Lestrade said, in a tone indicating it was neither, "but it gets me no closer to *finding* the man."

Crow's attention had been attracted by something outside. "If you'll give me just a minute, I believe I can help you with that, as well. I say, Lestrade, have you ever seen handcuffs like these? They've got a spring mechanism and they lock on themselves. It's quite beautiful."

Lestrade gave me an eloquently baffled look. I could only shrug in return.

"They do seem rather clever," he said—a bachelor admiring his neighbor's infant—"but what do they have to say to anything?"

"You'll see in a minute," Crow said, eyes gleaming mischievously as he tucked the handcuffs in his inner coat pocket.

There was a tap at the door.

"Come in!" Crow shouted.

It was a Nameless, who said, in the soft, genderless, idiosyncrasy-free voice that all the Nameless shared, "The cab's downstairs, sir."

"Excellent," said Crow. "Have the cabdriver step up here a moment, and come back yourself. I've got something bulky to transport."

The Nameless slipped silently out, and Crow smiled apologetically. "Sorry about the interruption, but this shouldn't take long."

We could hear the cabman thumping up the stairs. He was a big man, very red in the face, wearing a long overcoat the same color as his mouse-brown hair. I realized who he was and how the pieces fit together at the same time I realized that Crow, drat him, was all too capable of lying by omission.

"Thank you for coming up," Crow said to the cabman. "I'm afraid this may be a little difficult, but I had to get your help. Because, you see, I know what you've done."

The cabman wheeled to bolt, but the Nameless was in the way, whether on purpose or not I could not tell. I saw the snarl on the cabman's face, more like an animal's than anything human. Crow caught his wrist and fastened the handcuff on it in one motion, and the cabman went berserk. I use the word precisely, for I had seen the phenomenon before, although never in a Marylebone sitting room.

He dragged Crow almost to the window before the Nameless jumped on his back. Both angels' wings were flaring and flapping as the cabman roared with fury and tried to shake them off. Lestrade, showing a bulldog's courage as well as its lack of common sense, leapt into the struggle. Gregson stood and tried to look superior. I did the only thing I could and rescued the teapot from certain destruction.

The cabman's strength was as extreme and convulsive as an epileptic's, and he seemed not to feel pain, although his nose began to drip blood almost immediately. It wasn't until Lestrade actually hooked his fingers in the man's neckcloth and began cutting off his air that the two angels and the police officer gained the upper hand. Finally, though, the cabman dropped to his knees and a spark of sanity returned to his eyes. He and Lestrade were both panting, and the cabman's face had turned an alarming shade of fuchsia. Neither Crow nor the Nameless was winded, of course, but their wings were ruffled, the feathers plainly askew, and Crow's hair was standing mostly on end. But he was also beaming triumphantly. "Are you all right, Dr. Doyle?"

"Yes," I said, carefully restoring the teapot to the tempest-tossed table.

"Then, gentlemen, allow me to introduce you to the man who murdered Enoch Drebber and Joseph Stangerson."

The cabman sighed and used his sleeve to wipe sweat and blood off his face. "Dead to rights," he said in a flat, strongly American voice. "My name is Jefferson Hope, and I'd better tell you to start with that I'm not sorry and you are welcome to hang me tomorrow."

Even Crow was a little taken aback, while Lestrade and Gregson

looked like they'd swallowed a live goldfish each. The cabman—
Jefferson Hope—said, "I don't have any reason to deny it now. There
isn't a lot of time remaining to me, and I'd've rather not spent it in
a jail cell, but I'm not going to complain. Providence saw fit to give
me my vengeance."

"What do you mean?" Crow said at the same time Gregson said,
"I must warn you that you are under arrest. If you choose to speak,
your words will be taken down and used against you." Lestrade
already had his notebook out.

Hope laughed. "What does that matter? I'm not about to deny
what I've done."

"Then tell us?" Crow said.

"I'd like someone to know," Hope said, sounding faintly surprised.
"Here, are you a doctor?"

"Yes," I said.

"Then come have a listen," he said. "You'll understand."

There isn't a medical doctor alive who can restrain his curiosity,
which I think is the true lesson of both *Frankenstein* and *Dr. Jekyll
and Mr. Hyde*. I went and fetched my medical bag. When I came
back, Jefferson Hope was in one of our armchairs, a handkerchief
pressed to his nose, with the Nameless standing behind the chair
as a guard.

I got out my stethoscope and put the bell to Hope's chest. The
commotion inside his chest was exactly the sound of a death
sentence. "That's an aortic aneurysm," I said and only then realized
how close I was to a man I knew for a cruel and violent murderer.
Curiosity.

His eyes were dark and fierce, the eyes of a hawk in a man's
ordinary, florid face.

"Underfeeding and overexposure in the Salt Lake Mountains," he
said, and the fierce eyes begged me to agree.

"Overexposure would certainly do it," I said. It was unnecessary
to specify overexposure to *what*—unnecessary to embarrass Hope
by announcing that he had gotten himself infected with syphilis.

"I went to see a doctor about it last week," Hope said, "and he told me it is bound to burst here soon. So you may consider that you are looking at a dead man. I won't lie to you, gentlemen, and you may take what I say as the Gospel truth."

Lestrade flipped to a fresh page in his notebook. Gregson said, "Is this true, Dr. Doyle?"

"Absolutely," I said. "He might as well be carrying a lit fuse and a charge of gunpowder in his chest."

"Thank you," Gregson said, although it sounded like it pained him.

"The seed of this matter," said Jefferson Hope, "was planted in Deseret some thirty years ago. I suppose the ins and outs aren't important. There was a man named John Ferrier, one of the wealthiest Gentiles—as Mormons call all non-Mormons—in Deseret. He ran a trading post, started it in the crazy Gold Rush of 1848 and then traded with the Indians and all the settlers taking the South Branch of the Oregon Trail. Supposedly, he'd traded with the Donner Party, but I was never sure of the truth of that. His trading post was called Fort Ferrier as a joke, but it was busy enough and successful enough that it attracted the only Gentile angel in all Deseret. Ferrier called her Lucy after his dead wife, and she never seemed to mind."

"A name is a name," Crow murmured.

"I suppose," said Hope. "Lucy was the kindest creature I've ever met, and she was lovely, tall and blond and with a snowy owl's silent white wings. She was good to me whenever I stopped at Fort Ferrier—and it was rare to find a friendly face in Deseret if you weren't a Saint yourself. I can't tell you the degrees by which we fell in love with each other."

He stopped and stared at us defiantly.

"Oh *dear*," said Crow.

Gregson looked shocked; Lestrade merely looked worried. I had known many young soldiers in love with the Angel of Scutari, but this was the first suggestion I had ever heard that an angel could love back.

"Ferrier was a good man, and I guess he liked me. He said he wouldn't interfere as long as Lucy wasn't hurt, and I swore a Bible oath I'd never harm her. So the next time I brought my gold ore and trade goods to Fort Ferrier, I was going to stop and settle down and let Ferrier teach me how to be a trader instead of a miner. But when I got there, it was burned to the ground. I found Ferrier's body in the ruins, murdered by a shotgun blast to the chest, and in Lucy's chapel I found her dissolution feather, and I am not ashamed to tell you gentlemen that I wept like an orphan child." He wiped his face on his sleeve again.

"I went to the nearest farmstead and asked what had happened. They told me it was the Danites—Brigham's Avenging Angels, they called themselves, which is the cruelest joke I've ever heard, for they were nothing but a roving gang of murderers. The Danites put the word around that Ferrier was living sinfully with Lucy, which I didn't dare say otherwise. But I knew who was behind it, because I knew who wanted Fort Ferrier to burn."

"Drebber," Crow said softly.

"And Stangerson. I remember Lucy thought Stangerson knew about us. She said he'd ask her questions, when he and Drebber came to trade, and I said, 'What kind of questions?' but she wouldn't tell me. Drebber and Stangerson both made their fortunes on the destruction of Fort Ferrier, and I swore salt and iron vengeance on them both."

Hope sighed. "I kept Lucy's feather, although there were times when I could surely have used the money from selling it, because it was a little like having her near me. And I watched and I waited. I couldn't get at them in Deseret, not both at once, and I couldn't afford to move against one if by doing so I guaranteed the other's escape. I knew it was Drebber who'd killed John Ferrier, as surely as if I'd been standing there to watch him do it. When Stangerson was unfellowshipped—it's like excommunication, but not as bad—not long after, I knew he was the one who had destroyed Lucy. Not even Brigham Young could stomach destroying an angel."

"He may have realized how close Mr. Stangerson came to destroying all of Deseret," Crow said. "If Lucy had Fallen . . ."

"She wouldn't," Hope said positively.

"No, clearly not," Crow said.

"I missed them when they left Deseret—I was back at the mines in Arizona, trying to scrape together a grub stake—and it has taken me all these years to catch them again. I read somewhere that RACHE was the German for revenge and I wrote it over Drebber's body in my own blood." And he held up the bloodstained handkerchief in explanation.

"Why two pills?" Crow said.

"A fair chance," Jefferson Hope said and smiled an ugly smile. "The fair chance they didn't give Lucy. Drebber was sure he'd detected a difference between the two pills. He hadn't, for I couldn't tell them apart myself. Stangerson believed it was a trick because it was just the sort of trick he would have pulled, and he jumped me. I was glad to spill his blood. Really, there's nothing more to say."

Lestrade and Gregson looked as if they wanted to disagree. Crow said, "You need tell us nothing more if you do not wish to."

"You are nothing like her," Jefferson Hope said, "but I perceive that you are kind. Thank you. I bear you no grudge."

"Thank you," Crow said in turn.

Lestrade said, "I can drive a four-wheeler, if we may bespeak your Nameless to help us with the prisoner, Mr. Crow?"

"Of course," said Crow, and between them, the two police officers and the pigeon-winged angel removed Jefferson Hope from our sitting room.

❖

JEFFERSON HOPE DIED that night. Lestrade told us that they found him in the morning, stretched out on the floor as peaceful as a statue.

"Probably yesterday's exertion was the last straw," I said.

"I suspect he wanted it to be," said Crow. "He had quite literally nothing to live for. I wish I could have given him Lucy's feather back. But Gregson and Lestrade wouldn't have stood for it."

"They would have taken it as evidence," I said, "and it would be lost."

"At least we can keep that from happening," Crow said and put the dissolution feather of the Angel of Fort Ferrier, Deseret Territory, carefully on the mantelpiece.

PART THREE

AN UNEXPECTED TREASURE HUNT

9

A Visit to New Scotland Yard

ON THE NIGHT of August thirtieth, I dreamed that I was Mr. Hyde, trying to find my way out of Dr. Jekyll's house. It was the sort of dream in which as ardently as I, as Mr. Hyde, wished to escape from the house so that I might go marauding through London, just so ardently did I, as J. H. Doyle, wish that I should be thwarted. I was at once mad with frustration and sick with dread, and I suppose really I shouldn't have been surprised when I woke myself falling out of bed and discovered I had changed. The allegory was all too embarrassingly clear.

Unlike Mr. Hyde, however, I had no desire to leave my bedroom. I ended up in the closet again, trying desperately to be silent so that the angel wouldn't hear me. There was something wrong about that, something askew, but I couldn't remember what, and it was too complicated an idea to hold on to for long. I curled up in the closet and lay watchful and awake 'til dawn.

When I changed back, I at once remembered what had concerned me dimly in the night: what did Crow hear when I changed and what did he think was going on? He had to know *something* was happening; even if the change itself was silent, the noise of me dragging the bedclothes into the closet had to be discernable to him, even if not identifiable. But he hadn't said anything, which meant either he knew *exactly* what was happening and chose to treat it as a secret or . . . I could not imagine Crow not asking, if he was at all puzzled by what he had heard. That was his nature.

Ergo, he knew.

That conclusion was mortifying. I wanted to stay wedged awkwardly in the closet; it seemed far preferable to saying anything to Crow, starting with "Good morning" and going on from there. But if he knew . . . I couldn't leave it a strained semi-secret between us; it would drive me mad and that in no great length of time.

I dressed with particular care and went out, only to discover that a newspaper bomb had exploded in our sitting room.

"I say, Doyle," said Crow from the floor, "there's been another one."

I didn't have to ask "Another what?" The headlines were all too visible.

"They found her in Buck's Row," Crow said, "with her throat cut from ear to ear. She was still warm—I think the carman who found her probably scared off her murderer."

"Do they know who she is?" I asked, instead of any of the things I'd planned to say. Crow's attention was ferocious when focused, and it was pointless, as I knew from any number of experiments, to try to talk to him about anything else.

"No, but she was clearly a prostitute," said Crow, who bothered with euphemism only irregularly. It was, to be perfectly truthful, a relief to me, for it meant I did not have to mind my tongue. I had had a—not complimentary—reputation at Bart's for plain speaking, and Afghanistan had, if anything, made the habit worse. A flatmate with conventional sensibilities would have been as offended by me as I would have been exasperated by him.

"And of course they haven't caught the murderer."

Crow laughed. "No, there's no trace of him. And there's a slaughterhouse a stone's throw away. No one would think anything of a man covered in blood at three in the morning. Aside from the inconvenient carmen walking to work, he couldn't have picked a better spot."

"Do you think it's the same man?"

"Whitechapel is dreadful," Crow said, "but *two* men with a knife and a taste for unfortunates? That seems a bit much."

"What kind of man do you think he is?" I said, thinking of my dream. By this time I had unearthed my chair and sat down, although I was putting off ringing for Jennie.

"Comfortable with a knife," said Crow, "but I don't think a slaughterman or a butcher would have gone after Martha Tabram so wildly. And despite everyone going on about blood-boltered maniacs, he obviously *isn't*. Or someone would have noticed him by now."

"Dr. Jekyll and Mr. Hyde," I said bleakly.

"Yes, or something *like* that. If they ever catch him, he'll be quite ordinary."

"A sort of spiritual werewolf."

"That's quite the slander on honest werewolves, but I see what you mean. Perfectly ordinary until he turns into a beast. He *has* to be, or he'd never persuade an East End prostitute to go anywhere with him."

"No."

"They know they're easy prey," Crow said. Then his attention was caught by something in the newsprint around him. I rang the bell and tried to compose my thoughts around breakfast rather than around savage murder.

I was only marginally successful.

❖

UNLIKE THE CASE of the unfortunate woman in George Yard Buildings, this time the police invited Crow in almost from the start. He said it was a sign of how desperate they were. I did not go with him, for I did not want to step on any medical toes, but Crow reported everything, as much for the chance to say it aloud as for any desire for my opinion.

We had followed the George Yard investigation in the papers—Crow by obsession, me by proximity to Crow—so we knew that her name was Martha Tabram, age thirty-nine and identified by a husband who hadn't actually seen her in years. The sordid tale of her past unspooled in the sad and unfortunately predictable pattern. We also knew that that was essentially all the evidence that had been discovered. Another prostitute had come forward, admitting that she had been with Tabram on the last night of her life and telling a story about two soldiers; a story that, since she could not identify them, led exactly nowhere.

And that was all there was. No other clues, no other leads, and the inquest jury brought in the only possible verdict: willful murder by person or persons unknown.

This new victim was identified as Mary Ann Nichols. She'd gone by Polly. She was also a prostitute and of the same sort as Martha Tabram: a homeless alcoholic who sold herself daily for the pennies to rent a bed in one of Whitechapel's notorious and vile doss-houses. Everyone seemed to have liked her well enough—even her erstwhile husband—and there was absolutely nothing to suggest she'd been murdered by someone she knew. Which, unfortunately, left the investigation exactly where it had started.

Polly Nichols's throat had been cut, and she had been savagely disemboweled.

"It wasn't an autopsy cut," Crow said. "This fellow knows how to use a knife, but I don't think he has any medical training. Probably knows how to dress a cow."

"Do you still think it's the same man, then? Because Martha Tabram's killer didn't exactly show any skill."

"No," Crow agreed. "But it still seems like too much of a coincidence. Two savage knife murders in one month? And the rest of the modus operandi is depressingly similar: murder a prostitute and disappear without a trace."

Lestrade, too, had been drawn into the Whitechapel investigation, and he started appearing at all hours to argue about it with Crow. One night, I came out of my bedroom, drawn by the raised voices, and found Lestrade trying to argue that Tabram and Nichols had been murdered by a Fallen.

Crow rolled his eyes at me. "No matter how much you want that to be the answer, Lestrade, it can't be done."

"You—"

"I did not commit these murders," said Crow. "There. Settled."

"The Fallen don't commit murder, Inspector," I said. "All the stories to the contrary."

"But what if one *could*?" Lestrade said doggedly.

"Then it wouldn't look like that," I snapped, startling myself nearly as much as Lestrade. "The Fallen don't kill one at a time, and they don't bother waiting until the middle of the night."

"Besides," said Crow, "every angel in London would know if there were a Fallen among us. They can't hide themselves."

"This man must have been a hide-and-seek champion as a child," I said.

"Reid keeps sending his constables around," Lestrade said gloomily. "And I really think if anyone had seen *anything*, they would have come forward by now. Everyone in the East End is scared out of their wits."

Crow was pacing, his wings pulled tight against his back. "Your constables have probably talked to him," he said. "Some ordinary little man."

"Some ordinary little man," I said, "with a very sharp knife."

❖

AND THEN HE struck again. The eighth of September in the backyard of a perfectly respectable house on Hanbury Street. This time, the murderer hadn't stopped at disembowelment. He'd pulled his victim's intestines out of her body, and he'd taken her uterus with him when he left.

"He took . . . what?" I said when Crow told me.

"Her uterus," Crow said. "It's nowhere to be found. He got part of her bladder, too. But I think that was accidental."

"But . . . but why would he want her uterus?"

"I have not the foggiest idea. Why would he want to cut her throat and disembowel her?"

"Yes, I suppose motive *is* a useless avenue of exploration. What did he do with it? Put it in his pocket?"

"He must have," Crow said. "Even in Whitechapel, I think someone would have noticed a man carrying a blood-dripping internal organ in his hand."

"One can only hope," said I.

This victim, the third, was named Annie Chapman. Her story was much the same as Polly Nichols's and Martha Tabram's: alcohol, desperation, and a chance encounter with the wrongest of men, a man far worse than a werewolf. Werewolves were honest folk, and honest wolves. This man did not change his form—for no werewolf would need a knife to kill, or would think of using one—but the beast he was on the inside was far worse than any wolf.

The *Star* was beside itself, proclaiming, "London lies today under the spell of a great terror."

"Which I suppose is true," Crow said, "but it seems rude to point it out. And, oh dear, they go on to announce 'There is another Williams in our midst.'"

"Could it *be* Williams?"

"What? No! You've seen his skull. No revenant can go running around without its head."

"I've seen *a* skull. Unless you can attest its provenance?"

"Oh. I see what you mean." He considered for a moment, head tilted birdlike to one side. "Well, even if the skull isn't Williams's—and even if Williams *was* the killer, which I'm by no means persuaded of—revenants follow the script, as it were, of their former lives. The Ratcliffe Highway man beat people to death with a ripping chisel. And he preyed on people he could rob. *This* fellow isn't out for money."

"And he's very fond of his knife, yes. Point taken."

"Also, honestly, if it were a revenant, I think they could track him. Revenants . . . aren't very tidy."

"Do you think he's a demoniac?"

"Despite all the newspaper theorizing, no. There's no disturbance in the aether, not around Nichols, not around Chapman. Even a deep-buried demon betrays itself with its *metaphysicum morbi*."

"The papers would be very disappointed if they asked someone who knew that."

"That's why they won't ask anyone who does," said Crow.

"At least it would be a clue," I said.

The most awful thing about this succession of murders was that the investigations ended in the same place every time: nowhere. Even when they finally found a witness who thought she had seen Chapman with a man, less than an hour before the body was discovered, she had only seen the man from the back and her description was useless.

"She thought he 'looked foreign,'" Crow said, still exasperated hours later. "By which we all know she meant she thought he was a Jew. But she's basing that assumption essentially on the back of his neck, which is a deeply uninformative part of the body."

"True," said I.

"I suppose if she'd said he looked *African* that would be different. But her description is utterly meaningless, even if she's right. Do you know how many thousands of Jews there are in London?"

"I can't even hazard a guess," I said.

"Neither can I. Gregson is all puffed up and pleased with himself. But it's over *nothing*."

And that was as close as the investigators got. The doctors disagreed over whether the man was skilled with a knife, and if so, *how* skilled. The newspapers got hold of the ambiguity and howled that the murderer had surgical training, which was manifestly nonsense. The prostitutes of the East End, when asked, agreed that they were scared of a man they called Leather Apron. He bullied them, extorting money and roughing them up if they refused to pay. Several said he'd threatened them with a knife. And, of course, he was Jewish.

But when they found him—sensibly enough in hiding, since being identified as the Whitechapel murderer on the streets of the East End was becoming perilously close to an immediate death sentence—he had an alibi.

"It was almost worth it," Crow told me, "for the look on Gregson's face. Exactly like the frog that burst in the fable."

But the utter nothing of the investigation frustrated Crow horribly. The crime scenes were useless by the time he was called; the bodily mutilations were horrible, but if they meant anything, it was only to the murderer, and Elizabeth Long—she of the "foreign-looking" man talking to Annie Chapman outside 29 Hanbury Street—was the best witness they had.

"It's like he can turn himself invisible," Crow snarled, then stopped short in his eternal pacing. "Do you suppose he can?"

"You mean like a warlock?" I said dubiously. Witchcraft practitioners claimed—in their anonymously printed pamphlets—to be able to do all sorts of things. Invisibility was a popular one.

"Well, I wasn't thinking warlocks *specifically*. Mystics in several religions are supposed to have the power of invisibility."

"Are any of them religions that would condone what this chap is doing? Because my understanding has always been that mystics have to be quite observant."

"Um," said Crow, clearly going down a mental list. "Drat. Even the Mithrates wouldn't butcher women."

"I've seen theories that it's someone Christian who believes he has a mission from God to rid London of prostitution."

"He's chosen a shockingly inefficient method," Crow said.

"There is that. And it doesn't explain the uterus."

"*Nothing* explains the uterus," Crow said. "The best lunatic theory thus far is that it's a doctor trying to obtain specimens."

I boggled at him.

"I know!" Crow said. "No doctor would just rip a woman open on the street to take her uterus."

"No doctor would *need* to," I said. "There are far safer and easier ways of acquiring specimens. Some of them are even legal."

"Aside from which, this fellow took two-thirds of her bladder, too, which I think says he was guessing."

"Blundering about in the poor woman's pelvis. No, you're quite right. Any doctor would take either all or none of the bladder, and that goes double for surgeons."

"Is there some other reason he could possibly need a human uterus?" Crow said.

"You mean like a Hand of Glory? We're back to warlocks."

"At least, if there *is* such a spell, it would be a *reason*."

"No, I quite see the attraction. Are there any secret societies or mysteries bloodthirsty enough to demand something like this as an initiation rite?"

"Not that I know of," said Crow. "But none of the angels of the mysteries will talk to me anymore. They say I've Fallen."

"But you haven't," I said blankly.

"You can't argue with the angel of a mystery," said Crow. "But if it *was* an initiation rite, we'd have a lot more than three butchered corpses. Where are all the other initiates? Who are *they* killing?"

This turned out to be an uncomfortably prescient question, for it was the next day that we received a desperately scribbled note, of which the only thing we could decipher at first was the signature: *G. Lestrade.*

It took much squinting and trial and error, but we finally decided the note said: *Please come at once. Arm found near Ebury Bridge Road.*

"Oh my word," said Crow. "It's *him*."

"It's who?"

"No one knows." He raised his hands mock defensively. "It's true! People have been finding neatly butchered body parts in the Thames for years, and there has never been the slightest clue as to the identity of the butcher."

"You don't think it's . . ."

"Oh, no. *Miles* apart. This fellow never does anything in a frenzy. Couldn't be more different from the chap in Whitechapel. But I do see why Lestrade is so agitated. Will you come?"

"Of course," I said.

❖

WE FOUND LESTRADE standing on the side of Ebury Bridge Road, looking as miserable as a molting sparrow. He greeted us gloomily and said, "I hate this cove."

He jerked his thumb at a burlap-covered object on the embankment behind him. "It's over there if you want to take a look."

I followed Crow, although I did not kneel down with him as he twitched the burlap aside.

I didn't need to. The scent of the arm was immediate and horribly compelling, a mix of the foul water of the Thames, the stifling reek of old blood, and the sweet nauseous miasma of decay.

I staggered a little, and Crow twisted to look at me. "Are you all right, Doyle?"

"Yes, I'm fine," I said, although I did not sound either certain or as dismissive as I wanted to. The scent was so vivid that it was distracting, and I found myself bifurcated, part of me wanting to retreat to where Lestrade was standing, another part wanting to move closer.

Get hold of yourself, I said to myself sternly and was at least partially successful. I did not change on the spot.

"Are you *sure* you're all right?" Crow said, eyes as sharp as diamonds, and at that moment I knew for certain that he knew. He knew, and he was offering to help.

I shook my head. "I just lost my balance for a moment," I said, willing it to be true.

"If you're sure," Crow said doubtfully, but he turned back to his grisly prize.

Lestrade, who could never stand to be left out of anything for long, came down the embankment to where I was standing and said, "A workman found it. Not a single solitary clue except what you've got right there. As per bloody usual, begging your pardon."

"You sound like this happens frequently, Inspector," I said to distract myself from the dreadfully alluring (alluringly dreadful) scent of the arm.

"Frequently enough," Lestrade said disgustedly.

"The first body—or I suppose I should say, the first *part* of a body— was found in 1873," Crow said without looking up. "In Battersea."

"*1873?*" I said, horrified. "You mean this has been going on for fifteen years?"

"Intermittently," said Crow. "One in 1873, one in 1874. Then nothing until 1884."

"We thought we'd gotten lucky and he'd died," Lestrade said.

"Then one at Rainham in 1887 and now this. I can tell you nothing you don't already know, Lestrade. It's a woman's right arm. It's neatly butchered and has a string knotted around the shoulder cap, presumably for ease in carrying. It was removed from the body using seven separate cuts. Judging by the lack of calluses and the neatly kept nails, this was a bourgeoise. Either someone else earned her keep or—far more likely—she worked in an office."

Lestrade said, "But—"

"No," said Crow firmly. "A prostitute of this class would be missed—by her madam if by nobody else. Especially right now, with everybody jumping at shadows. Decomposition has already started. This poor woman has nobody to miss her."

Lestrade made a grumbling noise but didn't argue.

"The person who did this is definitely skilled," Crow said. "Not like the man in Whitechapel. I don't think you'd ever catch this man stabbing anyone thirty-nine times."

"So we're looking for two men, not one," Lestrade said. "That's just grand."

"Don't be sarcastic, Lestrade. It's not becoming to a Scotland Yard detective. This man must be a butcher or a surgeon. Someone who cuts up dead—or anesthetized—creatures for a living."

"Do you know how many men in London fit that description?"

"Probably not as many as the number of women who fit what we know about the victim. Nor as many men as look foreign from the backs of their necks."

Lestrade winced.

We knew more than that.

She had been a young woman, not more than thirty. She had never borne a child. Her last meal had included fish. There was no fear scent. She hadn't known, in the last minutes of her life, what was going to happen to her, which meant at least that he killed them first, *then* carved them up, rather than the other way around.

I could not tell where she had come from, but there was something else, something that was not exactly scent, although I had no better word for it. Let us call it scent, and let us therefore say that I could smell where the rest of her body was. I realized that I had felt—smelled?—the same thing when I was holding Williams's skull, but the rest of his body was apparently truly lost. Not like this woman.

Before I could think things through, or think at all, I heard myself say, "We need to find the rest of the body."

"Easier said than done, Dr. Doyle," said Lestrade. "He never dumps all the pieces at the same place, and some he doesn't dump at all. We think he keeps the heads."

"No," I said. "We need to find the rest of her body *right now*."

Crow moved in a swirl of feathers and was suddenly between me and Lestrade, although whether he was protecting me from the inspector or the inspector from me is a question I have never had the brass-faced nerve to ask. "Doyle," he said in a low, urgent voice, "do you mean you *can* find the rest of her?"

"I think so," I said. "I can find *something.*"

"Something is always better than nothing," Crow said. "Let's go."

IT WAS ALL very well to *say* "Let's go," but I could not move at any pace swifter than a brisk crawl and—as we rapidly discovered—whatever it was I was following, I could not find it from a carriage. The driver of that growler surely thought we were lunatics, as we made him stop every two hundred yards or so in order for me to cast around like a blighted beagle to make sure we were still going in the correct direction. My leg objected quite strenuously to all the climbing in and out of the growler, but it soon became clear that we were going a distance considerably further than I could have walked.

Lestrade *did* think we were lunatics, but he came with us uncomplainingly, using his authority to smooth things over when the cabdriver began to complain about our glacial progress. I was fairly certain that Lestrade thought Crow was a lunatic ninety percent of the time anyway (and a miracle-working genius the other ten percent); I was only sorry to be losing whatever credibility I'd had as a sane and rational person—and that only in the narrow back corner of my mind that was always assessing how other people saw me. The overwhelming majority of my consciousness was fixated on this not-exactly-a-scent and finding its origin.

Also, not changing in the middle of Grosvenor Road.

This was the first time I had ever been aware of that shift as something I had any control over. Previously, I had always and only changed in my sleep. But now I could feel the change wanting to happen, and I could resist it. It was not *easy;* it felt a little like holding back a sneeze, or, at least, I can come up with no better analogy. But it was *possible,* and I fought the urge fiercely.

At some point in our endless procession along the Embankment, the fiftieth, or sixtieth, or one hundred sixtieth time I climbed back into the growler, Lestrade said inconsequently, "I had a brother, you know."

"Did you?" Crow said with obvious surprise.

"He was a soldier, and he came home from Afghanistan with a terrible secret." I could feel Lestrade's gaze on me and carefully did not look at him. "We kept it for him as long as we could, but he got caught. Them bastards at the Registry trapped him. He committed suicide before they could send him to Colney Hatch."

"Oh!" Crow said, as shocked as a child. "Oh, Lestrade, I am so sorry."

"Eh. It happened near ten years ago, now, and we were never close. But he was my brother, and they hounded him to death." A long, long pause. "Pardon the pun, Dr. Doyle."

He knew. I went cold, then hot, and broke out in a sick sweat. I managed to croak, "Your dreadful puns are no concern of mine, Inspector," acknowledging what he had said without making a confession. And there, if we were both very lucky, the matter would rest.

On and on, along the Embankment, until Lestrade said with some surprise, "Here! That's the new Yard building." But that was nothing compared to all our surprise when I said, "How can we get in?"

Lestrade looked fairly well dumbfounded. Crow said, "In?"

"She's in there," I said.

"There's only one way to find out," Crow said to Lestrade.

"You can't stop here, guv," the cabman added.

Lestrade scowled frightfully but said, "All right. Wait here." He strode across to the Westminster Pier, where I lost sight of him. It was a long, awkward, and increasingly difficult quarter of an hour before he returned.

Crow had succeeded in enticing the cabman into telling stories about the strange things he'd seen driving a growler in London. I paced—slowly and haltingly—and tried not to imagine what the cabman would tell future passengers about *us*. And tried not to change.

In that, at least, I succeeded. I was still human when Lestrade came back.

"All right," he said. "They want us to go around to the gate on Cannon Row."

The cabman drove us around the massive construction site to the side opposite the river. At the gate, Lestrade paid him off, and he said cheerfully, "Thanks then, guv. Good luck!" and rattled away.

As we proceeded into what would one day be the basements and cellars of New Scotland Yard, the urge to shift grew stronger and stronger. I knew I would be able to follow the almost-scent much more easily. I was in more and more pain and walking more and more slowly and railing in furious inward invective that I had to bite my tongue to keep from spilling into speech.

We were forced to stop while Lestrade commandeered a couple of lanterns: the darkness was simply too thick, and there were building materials scattered everywhere, like the toys of a giant child who needed to be told to pick up the nursery before bed. Crow asked, with unusual caution in his voice, "Doyle, are you all right?"

"Oh, I'm just fine," I said bitterly and then caught myself. "That is to say, I'm as well as I can be. You needn't worry."

"I'm not certain I agree with you," Crow said, but then blessed Lestrade returned with two lanterns, and Crow was obliged to drop the subject we both knew we were talking about.

I had one lantern and Lestrade the other, and we were able to proceed much more safely, if not necessarily more rapidly. Even following the quasi-scent as directly as I could, our path still wound and twisted like Theseus's path through the Labyrinth. We had to backtrack more than once.

"This place was originally going to be an opera house," Lestrade said after a while. "Dunno how it's going to feel, coming to work in an opera house."

"Well, you'll have all the oubliettes you could ever need," I said. "The architect was clearly a megalomaniac."

"I've never been in a police station yet that wasn't bursting at the seams with files," Lestrade said. "This will all get used, never fear."

"I hope it will also get better lit," I said. Even with a lantern, the darkness was a thick, heavy, utterly unignorable presence, pressing in from all sides, almost seeming to wind around our feet. It was the sort of darkness in which you imagine you see things out of the corners of your eyes.

And all the while, even as our progress remained excruciatingly slow, the scent that wasn't a scent grew stronger and stronger until finally I said, "Here. She's here."

It took only minimal investigation of the corners and cubbyholes before Lestrade said, "Augh. God in heaven, I think I've found her."

From a corner so swallowed in darkness that even a lantern didn't help, Lestrade pulled out the most incongruous possible object, a paper parcel, tied up with string.

But the paper was black with foul, seeping ooze, and the reek of it was discernable to Lestrade and Crow as well as to me. "I don't want to open it down here," Lestrade said.

"No, don't," I said.

Lestrade said, "You two wait here. I'm going to fetch a constable." He strode off with one lantern, leaving Crow and me to eye the parcel uneasily by the light of the other.

"That can't be all of her," Crow said.

I had been doing the same geometry of solids in my head. "It can't hurt if we look around a little more," I said; no sooner had I turned my back on the parcel than I knew, with terrible urgency—"Here." I thumped painfully down on my knees in the same recess out of which Lestrade had dragged the paper parcel, though not in quite the same place. I managed to restrain myself from clawing at the earth with my fingers, but it was a near thing.

"Doyle?" said Crow.

"It's been buried," I said.

"Buried?"

"There must be something to dig with around here somewhere."

I gave Crow the lantern and he obligingly started poking around, even as he continued to voice objections: "But why would he bury part of her and leave the rest done up in paper?"

"God only knows," I said and meant it. "I don't think it's buried very deeply."

"I can't imagine somehow that it would be," said Crow. "Here." He handed me something, a tool, a ripping chisel. Not ideal for the task, but better than bare hands. I dug carefully and within minutes found something that was not dirt.

Crow by this time had wedged himself in with me; I did not object, even though it meant I had one wing draped over me like an opera cloak. Crow's presence was not the same as a human being's—he did not smell human, and his temperature was about five degrees lower—but he was a living creature all the same, and a great comfort against the reek of death in my nostrils and the cold clay under my fingernails.

We unearthed the length of a human leg, and I knew by no defensible method that it belonged to the arm at Ebury Bridge and to whatever was in that horridly seeping parcel.

"What on Earth has happened to Lestrade?" Crow grumbled.

"Can't you hear him?"

"There are too many echoes down here," he said, "and too much noise above us. I won't hear anyone *actually* here until they're right on top of us—which is why I would like Lestrade to come back so that we can *leave*."

"You didn't have to come," I started, but he said, "Doyle, surely you aren't seriously suggesting you would have left me *behind*?"

He made me laugh, which was the last thing I was expecting. "No, of course not," I said.

"Good," said Crow, "for you wouldn't have succeeded."

He stood up, and despite the fact that I disliked the touch of his feathers, I found myself missing the slight weight and static prickle of his wing. "Where on *Earth* is Lestrade?" he said. "Maybe I should just—"

"Don't leave me here alone." I didn't recognize my own voice.

"Doyle?" Crow sounded both alarmed and uncertain. "I won't take the lantern."

"It's not that," I said, although "that" was certainly part of it. "But if you leave me here by myself . . ." I couldn't force the words "I'll change" out of my throat, although that was certainly what would happen, and I did not know how else to explain how close I was to the edge, how little it would take for me to fall over.

Mercifully, Crow was an intelligent creature. "Oh," he said, and then, "*Oh*. All right, Doyle, I won't go anywhere." He hesitated, and his voice was wary when he said, "Do you want me to help you up? Would it be . . . easier if you were a little farther away from the body parts?"

It *would* be easier, of course, since the actual reek of the leg was combining with the vile and overwhelming stench of the Thames and the not-exactly-scent I'd been following all morning in a fashion that was both sickening and relentless, so that although it was a sore wound to my pride, I said, "Yes, I could use a hand."

Crow was my height, and his wings made him appear bulkier, but angels being built more like birds than mammals (for all that Crow said birds were a bad analogy), it took all of his strength and considerable care on my part to ensure that his help did not end with both of us sprawled across the grave of this nameless woman's right leg. Still, I could not have made it to my feet by myself, and although he had never said so, I knew that Crow did not like touching, or being touched by, human beings.

Therefore, I said, "Thank you," although I could not make the words come out as anything other than a growl.

"You're welcome," Crow said, laughing at me, and handed me my cane.

I steadied myself, then limped a few cautious steps out into the darkness. Crow had the lantern and was leaning close over the leg, obviously determined to collect all the observational data he could before Lestrade found his way back.

The darkness coiled around me and caught in my throat. It

was impossible to breathe deeply, given the stench, but I breathed steadily and regularly, and by the time Lestrade finally reappeared, with reluctant constables in tow, I had better control over myself than I had had since Crow had moved the burlap covering this poor woman's arm.

The constables had brought an ambulance, onto which they carefully—cringingly—loaded first the parcel and then the leg. Lestrade demanded to be told whether the leg belonged to the arm from Ebury Bridge Road. I choked off the words that wanted to spill out, and Crow said, "Your guess is as good as mine. *Really,* Lestrade."

"It depends on what's in the parcel," I said, my voice as hoarse as if I'd spent the morning yelling to be heard through the racket of heavy machinery. "I suppose there's no necessary reason they all have to be part of the same person"—even though I knew they were.

"Bite your tongue, Doctor," said Lestrade, and I thought he was not joking.

The constables started away with their macabre load, and I was about to tell Crow to bring the lantern, so that we could follow them—I'd found my way here by means that would not serve to lead me back to daylight—when I took an incautious step toward that damned alcove, and the scent—or not-scent and I could no longer tell the difference—hit me like a cramp.

For a white-out panic moment I thought I had shifted. The scent was so strong it seemed impossible I could be smelling it with mere human senses. Then Crow said, "Doyle?" which grounded me enough that I could open my eyes and see that nothing, including me, had changed.

"Doyle? Don't you dare tell me you're fine."

I exhaled a shaky half-laughing breath and said, "There's another piece."

"There's *what*?" said Crow, his voice ringing in the vault, and I heard Lestrade yell at the constables to stop.

"It's in the same place," I said disbelievingly. "He must have buried one on top of the other."

Crow muttered something I did not wish to catch and then said loudly, "Lestrade, did you bring a shovel?"

"What?" said Lestrade. He came back into the room where Crow and I were still standing and said, "I beg your pardon," as though he were pleading with us to tell him he'd misheard.

I think we both would have liked to tell him we were joking, but I had never felt less facetious in my life. Crow said, "Dr. Doyle believes we've missed a piece."

Lestrade did not swear, which I thought showed admirable restraint on his part. He called his ever-more-reluctant constables back in, and they, under Crow's nitpicking supervision, exhumed a left arm that looked, on hasty inspection, to be a match for the right arm found by the Ebury Bridge.

"I *really* hate this cove," Lestrade said while the constables unhappily added the arm to their awkward pile of body parts. I realized with a breath-stealing sense of relief that, wherever the rest of this woman's body was—and in how many pieces—I could not sense it.

Magnanimously, Lestrade said, "You've done us quite the favor this morning, Dr. Doyle. God only knows how long it would have been before someone noticed the poor wretch."

"Years, maybe," Crow said.

"Or never," said Lestrade, and we followed the constables and their sad burden back toward the light.

10

SECRETS SHARED

WE BARELY MADE it into the flat (past that watchful dragon Martha Climpson) before I could endure it no longer. I fled in lurching strides to my bedroom, slamming the door behind me, and stripped out of my clothes with none of my usual care. I was only just in time, for I was still shaking my bad leg free of my undergarments when the change rolled over me like a wave, quite literally knocking me off my feet.

I was still human when I started to fall, but I was not still human when I hit the floor.

I grumbled at the light, pulled the bedclothes off the bed, and was dragging them toward the closet when there was a knock on the door.

I froze.

"Doyle?" The angel's voice. I whined soundlessly and tried to crawl under the bed.

"Doyle? You know I can hear you. I'd ask if you're all right, except I'm fairly certain you're not." And the door, which I had stupidly forgotten to lock, opened.

From my awkward position wedged half under the bed, I turned and bared my teeth at the angel in the doorway.

There was a long silence, during which neither of us moved. Then the angel said, "Well. There's definitely a difference between knowing your flatmate is a hell-hound and actually seeing it. I, um . . . Doyle, can you understand me?"

I managed to get half an inch further under the bed.

"Well, let's try this," said the angel. "I'll assume you understand what I'm saying—I know werewolves understand human speech when they've shifted, so that it's at least logical to assume that hell-hounds do, too—and when you're . . . when you're yourself again, you can tell me if I'm right."

The angel closed the door and knelt down, buttocks resting against heels. It was a familiar posture and somehow comforting. "So," said the angel, "I'm hoping you'll shift back soon. You usually stay a hell-hound for about six hours—did you know that?—but this seems a rather exceptional case. Thank you, by the way, for *not* shifting in front of Lestrade. I'm afraid he would feel he had to arrest you. Which I cannot imagine being anything but a complete disaster for all concerned."

The angel's voice, soft, rapid, and clear as water, was soothing, and I could only fit the front half of my body under the bed, no matter what I did. Cautiously, I rearranged myself so that my hindquarters were under the bed and protected, then laid my head on my paws and watched the angel's lively gestures as the words rolled over me.

The angel said, "Yes, that's better. Although to be perfectly honest with you, Doyle, you're a little unnerving at present. It's the eyes, the phosphorescence, and d'you know, Doyle, I can't see if you have pupils. I suppose you must still have them, since you're not blind, but it's definitely much more eerie than I'm really looking for in a flatmate. By which I mean, please change back quickly, as this is all very disquieting. Also, I have a thousand questions I want to ask you. I doubt you'll answer them—since you don't like talking about yourself—but my word, Doyle! I've never seen a hell-hound this close before."

The angel moved as if thinking about coming closer, and I showed my teeth again.

"All right, message received. I shan't move. I should have brought a newspaper in, then I could read to you about the Chapman woman. But I suppose I'm more than capable of filling the silence regardless. You're welcome to change back any time and tell me to shut up."

The angel paused, then said, "Really, the other thing—and at least I know you're curious about this—is the fellow who butchers his victims so neatly. At least, I'm operating on the assumption that it's one person. It might not be. Once you've murdered someone, there's only so many ways you can get rid of the body. And I can see that the Thames would be a tempting solution."

I sighed and uncramped my body a little.

"So. The first one—yes, *do* get more comfortable, Doyle, you look ridiculous crammed under the bed like that—the first one was found in Battersea. The left quarter of her torso, then her right thigh, and her right shoulder with part of the arm. They kept finding pieces of the poor woman, all just floating merrily downstream in the Thames. The most gruesome part is, they found her face. Not her skull, mind you, just her face. And they still couldn't identify her. Eventually, they found all of her except her right foot—and, of course, her skull. As I think Lestrade mentioned, it looks like he keeps their heads. Or he disposes of them in some other fashion. And even with almost all of her body, no one could identify her. And it's not as if people didn't try! Half London must have gone and gawked at her. They really thought for a while that she was a woman named Mary Ann Cailey—her landlady and two of her brothers identified the body, except then, most inconveniently, Mary Ann Cailey came back alive and well from a trip to Scotland. And that was as close as they've ever come. I know losing your name isn't as disastrous for you as it would be for one of us. But it still seems terrible to me that all of these women, either nobody *noticed* they were gone, or nobody cared enough to go to the police and tell them the dead woman's name. Which I suppose comes to the same thing in the end, although— Just a moment, that's Mrs. Climpson on the stairs."

The angel twisted around and got up in one motion, and slipped out of the room. I growled, although I remembered not to do so loudly enough to be heard.

And then, whether it was the new threat of discovery or whether some necessary amount of time had elapsed, I was abruptly and uncomfortably human again.

I managed, by dint of a mad scramble, to be at least partially clothed and properly under the bed covers (*in* the bed) when Crow came back in.

"I don't know, Doyle," he was saying as he came in. "I think Mrs. Climpson could teach Lestrade a thing— Oh! You're you!"

I started forthrightly enough, "Thank you for . . ." but then I didn't quite know what I was trying to express gratitude for.

He waved it aside. "I've nothing against hell-hounds."

"The eternal enemy of your people?" I said dryly.

"Oh, Doyle, that's a mad exaggeration. You didn't fall on me and rend me limb from limb, did you?"

I shrugged uncomfortably. "I was too afraid of you to try."

"Afraid of *me*?" He sounded appalled and intrigued in equal measure.

"Afraid of angels," I said. "I think the Fallen in Afghanistan still . . . smelled like an angel?"

I was afraid he might be insulted, but his eyebrows went up, and he said, "I don't believe I've ever considered the olfactory aspect before. Now, are you sure that it's the Fallen that smelled like an angel, or do I smell Fallen?"

"You don't smell like the Fallen at all," I said. "I couldn't share a flat with you if you did." The Fallen in Afghanistan had smelled of salt and gunpowder and blood. Crow smelled, insofar as my human nose could determine, of tea and newsprint and the flesh of a newly cut apple. Whatever common scent the hell-hound recognized between the two was something much too subtle for me to detect.

"Well, that's some comfort," he said.

"Crow, you aren't Fallen," I said. "I don't know how it is that you aren't, but—"

"Let's trade secrets," he said abruptly. "I know yours. Let me tell you mine."

"You don't have to," I said, taken aback.

"No, but I want to," he said. "I want *someone* to know. And I know I can trust you. Here. Here's how I do it." Out of his inner waistcoat pocket, he pulled a chunk of marble about the size of a hazelnut. It looked like it had chipped off something larger, like a balustrade. "This is all that remains of my original habitation."

"And you carry it with you. Crow, that's genius."

"Desperation, my dear Doyle." He regarded the chunk of marble thoughtfully for a moment, then tucked it back in his pocket. "It doesn't work if your habitation remains intact. And the timing is exceedingly dicey."

"But how was your habitation razed when it still had an angel?"

"Bribery." He saw my incomprehension, for he said, "The builders paid off the inspectors."

"But, my God, they took a terrible risk. By all rights, you should have Fallen."

He shook his head. "No British angel has Fallen since the Angel of the Great Fire in 1666. We're all imbued with self-sacrifice. But even those of my . . . shall we call them colleagues? Even those of my colleagues who *don't* think I'm Fallen think I should have gone back to the Nameless, which is what most London angels do when dishabited. You have to have a fairly large pool of Nameless for that to be possible, and it's just as much death as dissolution, for the nature of the Nameless is such that it's impossible for them to retain any memories. They're not individuals in any meaningful sense— you truly never meet the same Nameless twice."

"But then how can they possibly run errands or, for example, look for one particular cabdriver in all of London?"

"Oh dear," he said. "This is rather complicated."

"You don't have to tell me."

"No, I quite want to. And it's not secret at all, just difficult to explain. When you give a Nameless a task, you are providing a brief taste of having a habitation. The task is something like my piece of marble. The Nameless carries it until the task is finished, and then it dissolves—I use the word advisedly—back into the hive. They have no more real individuality than worker bees."

"It sounds a horrid existence," I said.

He shrugged shoulders and wings together. "That's a value judgment the Nameless can't make. They all long for a name, but they don't know why." He gave me one of his sudden, blinding smiles. "It *is* a horrid existence. But the great blessing of it is that you don't know that until you've received your habitation."

"Meaning that angels and Nameless are . . ."

"Think of them as caterpillars," Crow suggested. "They don't spin cocoons, but they do undergo a metamorphosis. The butterfly—or moth—isn't the same creature as the caterpillar, except that it is *exactly* the same creature, which you can prove with a very little exertion in natural history."

"Yes," I said. "I do follow you, but I'm not sure caterpillars are any better than bees."

"You have a great prejudice against the order *Insecta*," he said. "What's wrong with being a moth? Some of them are surpassingly lovely."

I noticed that he did not claim to be a butterfly.

"Whoops!" he said before I could answer. "There's Mrs. Climpson again. I told her you were under the weather—such a blessing, idioms are—and she's insisting on making you tea."

"Oh God," I said. "If I make it true, will you tell her I'm asleep?"

"Too late," said Crow.

I wanted to growl at Mrs. Climpson's knock, but I could not afford to alienate her any more than Crow could. I could not risk the gamble on finding another living situation so cheap or—despite some of Crow's eccentricities—so congenial. Thus, I suffered Mrs.

Climpson's tray and tea and gimlet eyes. I could at least take comfort in the fact that I was decidedly "under the weather," my leg howling like the Furies and the rest of my body aching with exhaustion, so that Crow's little pas de deux with truth-telling was accurate after all. To tell the truth myself, the tea was welcome, and I managed to say "Thank you" and have it sound sincere.

"You don't take care of yourself, Dr. Doyle," she said. "You need a wife." She swept out in a great rustle of bombazine without waiting for an answer. Which was just as well, for my answer would have been unprintable.

Crow looked puzzled. "What did she mean?"

"In an ordinary household"—a thing he had never experienced—"the wife would do things like making sure her husband had something for tea that he liked or reminding him to wear galoshes." Or endlessly nagging him, as my mother had nagged my father. "It's why they talk about a wife being the angel of the house, just as your . . . colleagues are angels of public buildings."

"That never has made sense to me. But—should I be doing those things for you? Is that—"

"Good God, no!" I said. "Number one, I don't need anyone to look after me. I'm an adult and can look after myself. Number two, you are in no sense *my* angel and I would be wrong to ask that of you, even if I wanted to. Number three, you are an angel of the res publica and shouldn't be anything else. And number four, *I do not want a wife*."

"I like that," Crow said. "An angel of the res publica. That practically sounds respectable. I shan't worry about your galoshes, then."

"Thank you," I said, and I meant it from the bottom of my heart.

PART FOUR

THE MYSTERY

OF

CAPTAIN MORSTAN

11

A Second
Appeal for Help

My brother died on the fifteenth of September. I did not attend the funeral. I would not have been welcome; his wife had never approved of me, and the angel of their church would have recognized the miasma of the Fallen that still lingered about me, even if she did not denounce me as a hell-hound forthwith. I expected the telegram notifying me of his death to be the end of it. I certainly wasn't expecting to receive a small, flattish parcel through the post from Edinburgh. I opened it, more than a little unnerved, and found my brother's watch, which had been our father's and was the only truly valuable piece of jewelry my brother had owned. There was a note, in my sister-in-law's handwriting, that said only, *He wanted you to have this.*

Crow had watched with avid curiosity, and I said, "Here. What do you make of this?" and handed him my brother's watch. I was curious to see just how much the power of deduction could do.

Crow examined the watch closely, the case, the dial, the works, both with his unaided eyes, which were still far sharper than human eyes, and even with a magnifying lens. He snapped the case shut and returned it to me.

"There are hardly any data," he said plaintively. "The watch has been cleaned recently, which robs me of all sorts of useful facts. But I could make some deductions. First, that you had an elder brother, who has recently died."

"Correct," I said.

"He inherited the watch from your father, who—I further deduce—was either a towering egotist or . . ."

"Yes," I said. "But how . . ."

"I'm cheating a little," said he, with a flash of a smile, "for I know a bit about your father from your conversation. But! The initials H.D.D. on the watch. They're as old as the watch itself, which I judge to be some fifty years old, much too old for any sibling of yours. Therefore they are your father's. And I note from the wrapping"—he nodded toward the brown paper in a wad beside my chair—"that your brother's widow is *Mrs. H. D. Doyle*. Therefore, your brother's initials were the same as your father's. And it is not an unreasonable step to assume that he was the eldest son and named for your father. That's not unusual. However, I further note that your middle initial is H, and thus I speculate—perhaps unwisely—that you also bear his name, or some variation on it."

"His name was Henry," I said. "Anything else?"

"Well, your brother seems to have been a rather untidy man, careless in his habits. The case is dented and marked—he kept this fifty-guinea watch in the same pocket as his keys."

I hesitated.

"What?" said Crow. "Am I wrong?"

His almost childlike anxiety made me smile. "No, it's quite true. Henry was chronically untidy. He was a Latin master at a crammer's school in Edinburgh, and if the watch hadn't been cleaned—no doubt my sister-in-law's doing—I daresay you would have found a good deal of chalk dust as well. But I have always wondered about the way he'd jumble his keys in with his watch."

"What did you wonder?"

"We both hated our father," I said. "When he died, he could have done Henry a great deal of good by leaving him some of his rental properties. But all he left him was the watch, with a remark in the will about the eldest son's share."

"That seems . . ."

"Insulting? Yes. Father felt Henry had squandered his potential. He meant Henry to be a barrister, but Henry couldn't stick law school at any price. Thus, Father left Henry the watch and my younger brother got all the property."

"And you?"

"Oh, I was disinherited years ago," I said lightly. "But I have always wondered if that was why he was so careless with the watch."

"Then was leaving it to you also an insult?"

"To Father," I said. "Flouting his dictates one last time."

"Oh," Crow said, his face clearing. "Yes. I understand."

"And he would have thrown it off the Dean Bridge before he let our brother have it. James *is* a barrister and is very much like a second edition of our father. But what else does the watch tell you?"

"Your brother was chronically short of money, but with periods of prosperity." He raised his eyebrows at me.

"He only got paid when school was in session, and he had his wife and two little girls to support. He got private tutoring jobs when he could, but my understanding is that those weren't a dependable source of income. How did you know?"

"Easy," said Crow. "The pawnbroker's ticket numbers scratched on the inside of the case. Better than a label, since the number can't be lost. I count four such numbers on the inside of this case. Therefore his finances were frequently in a desperate state. But he had bursts of prosperity—doubtless at the beginning of term—which enabled him to redeem the pledge. He must also have been a proud man, to redeem a watch he hated."

"Yes."

"Finally, the keyhole is surrounded by scratches where the key has slipped repeatedly. I infer that your brother was a drunkard. He wound the watch at night, thus scratching the plate. These marks are hardly the tracks left by a sober man."

I cleared my throat. "The disease which killed my brother palsied his hands." I watched Crow's face fall.

"Oh dear," he said. "*That* is embarrassing."

"You misstepped," I said, without any feeling of triumph at having caught him out. My childhood nurse would have said Crow lived too much on the outside of his skin. He was too easy to wound.

"In any event, I apologize for calling your brother a drunkard." Angels cannot blush, but his wings had crept up and around, as if to shield him.

"Apology accepted," said I. "Tell me the latest from Scotland Yard."

"Nothing!" Crow said. "Nothing, nothing, and more nothing! They've no more leads on the man in Whitechapel and no leads at all on the fellow with the sense of humor."

"I suppose if you disjoint dead bodies as a pastime, that *is* the sort of thing your sense of humor would run to."

"There's no other reason for him to *bury* her body—well, parts of her body—under Scotland Yard. Not when he had all of London to choose from. And almost anywhere would have been easier. No, that was a joke on Scotland Yard. I should like to think that he will be caught by his own cleverness. But I do not believe it's going to happen. And the poor woman is still as nameless as a cobblestone. It all adds up to a giant nought. Really, we might as well be playing noughts and crosses for all the good we're doing." He sighed dejectedly. "Which brings us back to our theme at, nothing."

I was opening my mouth to reply to this tirade, when heralded by a crisp knock, our landlady came in, bearing a visiting card on a salver.

"A young lady for you, Mr. Crow," she said.

Crow picked up the card. "Miss Mary Morstan. Not a name I recognize." By which he meant that no one of that name had been convicted of murder in London for the last fifteen years, perhaps longer. "Well, show her in. Don't go, Doyle," he added as I prepared to haul myself out of my chair. "I should much prefer you to stay."

"Of course," I said, but rose to my feet anyway, so as not to be either uncivil or unbearably slow when the young lady entered the room.

Miss Morstan was a delicate blonde, no more than five feet and two inches in height. Her features were undistinguished, her clothing in exquisite taste, but with the simplicity of cut and materials that generally betokens a lack of funds. Her eyes, her one remarkable feature, were luminously blue and held an expression of great kindness.

She looked from me to Crow and blinked hard, but she had clearly been warned, for she came forward and extended her hand gamely. "Mr. Crow? I am Mary Morstan. Thank you for seeing me."

"Not at all," Crow said, shaking hands with her. "This is my colleague, Dr. Doyle."

"How d'you do?" she murmured, and we shook hands. Her hand was very small, but her grip was firm. Her gloves were kidskin, and I felt a mended place on one finger. Not a young lady of means.

We sat down, and Crow said, "Tell me what brings you here."

Miss Morstan folded her hands together carefully in her lap. "You once solved a problem for my employer, Mrs. Cecil Forrester."

"Did I?" said Crow. "Oh, yes. But it was quite simple, barely a problem at all."

"She had not found it so. She was most impressed by your kindness and skill, and she suggested that you might be able to help me, for certainly nobody else can." Her folded hands were now gripping each other tightly.

"I shall certainly endeavor to do so," Crow said. "Please, tell me your problem."

She nodded and said, "Briefly, the facts are these. I was born in India, where my father was an officer in an Indian regiment. My mother died when I was very young, and my father sent me home to Scotland, where I was educated at a very respectable boarding establishment until I was seventeen. In 1878, my father obtained twelve months' leave and came home. He telegraphed me from London that he had arrived safely and that I should come down and meet him at the Langham Hotel. I reached the hotel, which is werewolf-run, clean, and respectable, only to be told that Captain

Morstan had gone out the evening before and had not come back. All of his belongings were at the hotel." She swallowed hard. "I contacted the police; I advertised in the papers. The Langhams, who naturally did not like having a guest vanish, had their pack do a block hunt around the hotel, but they found nothing. And nothing it has been ever since. My unfortunate father has disappeared as if the earth simply opened beneath his feet and swallowed him."

"The date?" said Crow.

"The third of December, 1878—almost ten years ago."

"You said his luggage remained at the hotel. What did it contain?"

"Nothing to suggest a clue. Some clothes, some books. He had been one of the officers in charge of the convict guard at Port Blair in the Andaman Islands, and lived a very Spartan life."

"Had he any friends in town?"

"Only one that I know of—Major Sholto, of his own regiment, the Thirty-fourth Bombay Infantry. Major Sholto had retired some years previously and lived in Upper Norwood. But when I wrote to him, he wrote back, expressing considerable dismay. He said he hadn't even known my father was in England."

"Most singular," murmured Crow.

"Now," she said, with a quick—almost furtive—but lovely smile, "we come to the truly singular part. Six years ago, on the fourth of May, 1882, an advertisement appeared in *The Times,* asking for the address of Miss Mary Morstan, daughter of Captain Morstan, late of the Thirty-fourth Bombay, and stating that it would be to her advantage to come forward. There was no name or address appended. I had just entered Mrs. Cecil Forrester's household as governess, and I have no family. I consulted with her, and we agreed that it might be word of my father's whereabouts, and I could not afford not to answer, for the mystery was eating at me, as it does still." Another furtive, nervous smile. "With her kind permission, I placed a reply in *The Times,* giving her address. The same day there arrived through the post a small cardboard box addressed to me, which contained a very large, very lustrous pearl. There was no note, no address, not a scrap of information. Only the pearl. Every year since then, upon that same date, I have received another pearl in precisely the same fashion. I have consulted an expert, who said they are of a rare variety and quite valuable. You can see for yourselves that they are very handsome."

She produced a flat box from her reticule as she spoke and opened it, showing us six unusually beautiful and perfectly matched pearls.

"Gracious," said Crow. "Has anything else happened to you?"

"Yes, today. And that is why I have come to you. This morning I received this letter." She gave it to Crow, who read it quickly and gave it to me. The letter was written in a small, tight, looping cursive. I read: *Be at the third pillar from the left outside the Lyceum Theatre tonight at seven o'clock. If you are distrustful, bring two friends. You are a wronged woman and shall have justice. Do not bring police. If you do, all will be in vain. Your unknown friend.*

"Do you still have the envelope?" Crow asked Miss Morstan. She gave it to him, and he assessed it quickly: "Postmark, London S.W. Date, September 20. Same handwriting as the letter. Good print of a thumb on the corner. Probably the postman. Best-quality paper, envelopes at sixpence a packet, no letterhead or address. A very particular man in his stationery. This is a very pretty little mystery you have brought us, Miss Morstan. What do you intend to do?"

"That is what I have come to ask you about," she said.

"But surely you know what my answer will be," said Crow. "Of course you must make this rendezvous, and Dr. Doyle and I will go with you."

"Will you?" said Miss Morstan, her face lighting up in a way that made my mouth go dry.

"Of course," I said.

"You are both most kind," she said. "I lead a very retired life, and my few friends are not people I could ask this favor of. Will it be acceptable if I return at six o'clock?"

"Certainly not later," said Crow. "But one other point. Is this handwriting the same as that upon the pearl boxes?"

"I have the wrappings here," she said, producing a half-dozen pieces of paper.

"You are now my favorite client!" Crow said delightedly. "Let us see here." He spread the papers out on the table and glanced between them. "This is a disguised hand. But the writer knows very little about disguising handwriting—and he isn't very good at it. See how the irrepressible Greek ε will break out, and that twirl to the final *s*. They are undoubtedly by the same person. I don't want to raise false hopes, Miss Morstan, but is this hand at all like your father's?"

"Nothing could be more different," she said promptly and firmly.

"Yes, I expected as much. *That* answer was much too simple. But the question had to be asked. We shall see you at six, then. May I keep the papers between now and then?"

"Yes, of course," she said.

"Thank you," said Crow and ushered her to the door. *"Au revoir."*

"Au revoir," she said, including me in her smile, and was gone.

"An attractive young lady, don't you think?" said Crow, crossing to the window to watch her out of sight, as he often did with clients. He said he learned more from the way they walked than from anything they said.

"I did not notice," I said and winced at the sound of my own grating voice.

"No?" Crow said disbelievingly. "Come now, Doyle, you aren't such an automaton as all that. And even I could see that you found her charming."

I realized that my denial had boxed me in where simple and truthful agreement would have left me free. "Crow," I said and sighed. "Yes, she is a lovely young lady."

I had puzzled him, which was the thing above all others I had learned to dread doing. "But why would you not just say so? What did I miss?"

"Nothing." But he wouldn't let go of it now. A dog with a bone was nothing compared to Crow with an unanswered question, and I had a lively appreciation for the feelings of the bone. I shoved myself to my feet, said, "I'm going out," and suited the action to the word.

12

THE
UNKNOWN FRIEND

I GOT NO farther than the corner of Baker Street and Upper George Street before I turned and came back, feeling embarrassed and ashamed of myself, only to find a note in Crow's beautifully illegible handwriting that read, *GONE OUT. BACK BEFORE SIX.*

I was relieved, and then felt like a heel of the worst sort.

Crow had left Miss Morstan's papers spread out over the table, and I amused myself by picking out the "irrepressible Greek ε" and the twirling *s*. Then I found I had gotten interested, and for my own edification I made a list on a piece of foolscap of the characteristics I could observe. It was better than thinking about Mary Morstan, whom I could not have, or my foolish behavior with Crow.

The writer—and I thought him a bit impudent to call himself Miss Morstan's friend—tended, in both the addresses and in the letter, to large and quite ornate capitals which reeked of egoism and self-esteem, but the rest of his letters, no matter how he formed them, stayed all much the same size, *d*s and *l*s no higher than *e*s or *a*s. Once I saw that, it was unmistakable. The same went for his *g*s and *y*s, their loops barely managing to descend far enough to be seen. Although it was not a cramped hand in the usual sense, it nevertheless gave an intense sense of oppression, of being squashed between two unyielding forces. I began to see weakness in the letter writer—quite aside from his handwriting, what on Earth was this cloak-and-dagger business about the third pillar from the left? And why be so insistent about not going to the police when thus far, there was no evidence of illegality, save the disappearance of Miss Morstan's father ten years ago? Either this was some sort of criminal operation—but then, why suggest she bring two friends? And why choose an obviously impoverished governess?—or the writer was more than a little paranoid. But it was all of a piece with sending her a single pearl in the post every year for six years and with his refusal to give his name. It all seemed almost childish, but the value of the pearls and the disappearance of Captain Morstan (and I wondered just how thorough the police investigation had been) put the lie to that.

And why did he talk of justice when he specifically forbade her to go to the police? *You are a wronged woman,* he wrote in his squashed and fussy cursive on his very expensive paper. The only "wrong" I could see was that she had been deprived of her father—and yet having one's father vanish wasn't really a *wrong* per se. And why was he sending her those blasted pearls?

At this point, I realized I was going in circles—and possibly thinking more of Miss Morstan's kind blue eyes than of the mystery she had brought. "Fool," I said savagely to myself and tried to turn my attention to an article in *The Lancet* about the comparative pathology of werewolf bites and vampire bites, but with only middling success.

Crow reappeared at half past five and began talking almost before he was in the door. "Success, Doyle! The back files of *The Times* produced an obituary for Major John Sholto, of Upper Norwood, late of the Thirty-fourth Bombay Infantry. He died on the twenty-eighth of April, 1882."

"1882 was when Miss Morstan began receiving pearls," said I.

"Exactly!" said Crow. "Six days later, Miss Morstan observed the advertisement in *The Times*. Major Sholto was clearly blocking what *someone,* as yet unknown, felt to be the right course of action."

"Sending her single pearls for six years?"

"I didn't say it *was* the right course of action—merely that someone felt it to be so."

"Fair enough. But why is he changing the game now?"

"Either he is exceptionally timorous or something else has occurred very recently that changes his situation. I have no idea what, so don't ask." I laughed, as he had intended, and a ripple of satisfaction went through his feathers.

If he wanted to pretend I hadn't inexplicably stormed out on him, I was hardly going to argue. "Major Sholto begins to present rather a sinister figure."

"He certainly does," said Crow. "The Captain's only friend in London, and he somehow *hasn't* heard from him? It's not likely. And combined with the very suspicious timing . . . I want to know a good deal more about Major Sholto and his heirs. And I suspect strongly I am going to get the chance. *The Times* also told me that the Major was survived by his sons Bartholomew and Thaddeus. I would be very surprised if Miss Morstan's unknown friend were not one of them."

"That does seem likely," I agreed, "insofar as anything seems 'likely' about Miss Morstan's experience."

"It's a very Gothic situation," Crow said. "But I expect the mystery will be cleared up by our expedition this evening. Speaking of which, will you bring your service revolver?"

"Of course," I said. "You think tonight's work is likely to be serious?"

"I fear the disappearance of Captain Morstan can have had no happy outcome," said he. "And I would greatly prefer we not join him."

"I cannot fault your reasoning," I said and went into my bedroom to get my revolver.

When I came out, Crow said, "I commend your observations on Miss Morstan's mysterious correspondence," and I realized that I had left my jottings on the table.

I felt the blood rush to my face. "Those are nothing," I said. "Just meanderings."

"But you raise some excellent points," said Crow. "Calling her a wronged woman *is* an odd choice of words. It certainly suggests that Captain Morstan's disappearance is not a mystery to this person. Also that that disappearance was neither accidental nor fortuitous."

"You mean that he was murdered," I said.

"Yes," said Crow. "I think the pearls are preemptive blood money. He's trying to pay her back before she realizes what she is due."

"Or he *was*," I said. "Why is he writing to her *now*?"

"Something has changed," Crow said thoughtfully. "Hopefully, he can be induced to tell us what. But here is Miss Morstan in a four-wheeler, well upon her hour. Let us join her."

I chose my heaviest stick, and I admit the weight of the revolver in my pocket was a comfort.

We squashed into the four-wheeler, Crow's wings as ever another passenger and a half. Miss Morstan, muffled up in a dark cloak, looked somewhat nervous, but she was composed and perfectly ready to answer Crow's questions.

"Major Sholto was a particular friend of my father's," she said. "The letters Father wrote me were full of allusions to the major and the things he said. He and Father were in command of the troops at Port Blair in the Andaman Islands, so that they were thrown a great deal together. By the way, a curious paper was found in Father's room. No one I have shown it to has been able to make any sense of it. I don't suppose it is of the slightest importance, but I thought you might wish to see it."

"You were quite right," Crow said, surprising a smile onto her pale face. He unfolded the paper carefully. "It looks like the plan of a large building. Or part of the plan. A very elaborate building. Is it anywhere you have ever been?"

"Not unless it was when I was too young to remember," said Miss Morstan. "I have always assumed the building was somewhere in India."

"I agree, that seems likely," Crow said. "So. At one point there is a small cross in red ink and above it is '3.37 from left' in faded pencil. Which rather makes it look as though the cross and the instructions were written by different persons. In the lower left-hand corner is an odd little hieroglyphic like four crosses in a line with their arms touching. Beneath it is written in very coarse characters, 'The sign of the four—Jonathan Small, Mahomet Singh, Abdullah Khan, Dost Akbar.' You are right, Miss Morstan, it is most curious. I confess I do not see what bearing it can have upon the matter. Yet it is evidently a document of importance. It has been kept carefully folded in a pocketbook, for the one side is as clean as the other."

"It was in Father's pocketbook that I found it," said Miss Morstan.

"I have not the faintest idea of what it means. But by all means preserve it carefully." He handed it back to her, and she folded it carefully away again.

Crow proceeded with lively curiosity to ask her about being a governess, and she found, as I had, that he was extremely easy to talk to, not in the slightest judgmental, and eager for details by which most people were bored. And one could tell that he had no ulterior purpose—he wasn't asking to make small talk or to distract Miss Morstan from the grimmer aspects of our errand. He asked because he truly wanted to know, and she responded to that with the pleasure people always feel when asked sincerely about their lives.

I listened silently. The joke at Bart's had been that I would never make it in general practice—I'd scare all my patients into coronaries the first week. I have neither patience nor skill for conversation; I could only admire Crow's natural, unthinking ability to make a reserved woman like Miss Morstan open up and chatter to him like a girl. It transpired that she was a most accomplished governess, being able to teach French, music, and clairvoyance along with the standard subjects, and Mrs. Cecil Forrester's ever-increasing brood of children meant that her employment prospects looked good for at least a decade.

The day had been a dreary one, and although it was not yet seven, a dense, drizzly fog turned London into a city of ghosts. Every face that emerged from the fog was as waxy white as a vampire's, and even the omnibuses seemed insubstantial, as if we could drive straight through them.

The Lyceum was already thronged with playgoers. Miss Morstan's "unknown friend" might be a paranoiac, but he was shrewd. No one watching—assuming such a person to exist—would have noticed the addition of three more people (a couple and a Nameless hired for the evening—hardly the only one) or seen anything suspicious in our movements.

We had barely reached the third pillar from the left when a small, dark, brisk man in a coachman's uniform approached us. He had a werewolf's light and penetrating eyes, and I felt confident in wagering that he had fur on his palms.

"Beg pardon," he said, "but are you the Morstan party?"

"I am Mary Morstan," Miss Morstan said, "and these are my friends."

He looked us over with sharp curiosity, his gaze lingering on Crow. "You will excuse me, miss," he said, "but my instructions were very clear. Will you swear that neither of these persons is a police officer?"

"I give you my word that neither of my companions is a police officer," Miss Morstan said readily, and we all felt the momentary static shock of the oath.

The werewolf nodded. "Thank you, miss." He gave a shrill whistle, and a Nameless led over a four-wheeler and opened the door. The werewolf took his place on the box while the three of us climbed inside. The door was barely closed before the coachman clucked to his horse and we plunged into the fog at a remarkable clip.

Crow and Miss Morstan continued talking like old friends. I thought about what Crow had said, that you never met the same Nameless twice. The idea was both eerie and sad. I wondered if the memories were truly lost or if there was some sort of collective memory where everything was stored. I had never heard anyone complain about having to teach a Nameless the right way to do anything—and how else could they understand English? This Nameless had certainly known how to lead a horse, which it couldn't know if it were a true tabula rasa. I would have to ask Crow at some more opportune moment.

At first, I had some idea of the direction we were going, but our pace, the fog, and my own patchy and limited knowledge of London soon had me in hopeless confusion. Crow was never at fault, though. He punctuated his conversation with Miss Morstan with the names of streets and squares. "Vauxhall Bridge Road. We are making for the Surrey side, apparently. Yes, here's the bridge. You can see the Thames."

I did indeed catch a glimpse of the river, lamps shining through the fog on her broad back, but we rattled on, and I was quickly lost again.

"Wandsworth Road," said Crow, abandoning conversation. "Priory Road. Lark Hall Lane. Stockwell Place. Robert Street. Cold Harbour Lane. Our quest is not taking us among fashionable London."

It was getting darker and foggier, and the neighborhood was one of dull brick row houses with the tawdry yellow glare of public house lights like punctuation at the corners. Every so often there was a red light in a first-floor window, indicating a vampiric hunt. Then came the villas, stodgy and respectable, with their tiny identical gardens, and then yet more row houses, new staring brick soldiers in the war London waged against the countryside around it. Our destination lay among them, on a terrace so new that only one of the houses was inhabited—and that, it seemed, only barely, for there was no more than a glimmer of light from the kitchen window to show there was anyone within. But when I knocked, the door was opened immediately, as if the person on the other side had been waiting impatiently for us.

He was a wildly incongruous figure in the banal English kitchen, an Indian in soft white clothes with a yellow sash and yellow turban.

He stood aside to let us in. His eyes widened when he saw Crow, and he bowed deeply, murmuring something in his own language to which Crow replied briefly.

The Indian stepped outside to speak to the coachman, and I whispered to Crow, "What did he say?"

"Welcome to this household, messenger. And I said thank you."

The Indian returned, shutting the door, and said in excellent, almost accentless English, "Mr. Sholto awaits you."

Even as he spoke, a high, piping voice called from some inner room, "Show them in to me, *khitmutgar*. Show them straight in to me."

"If you will follow me," said the Indian and led us down a corridor in keeping with the kitchen: sordid and shoddy and badly lit. He stopped and opened a door on the right; a blaze of yellow light streamed out, and in the center of the light stood a small man with a massive bald head, decorated only by a bristle of red hair around the edges. His eyes were protuberant, and his face not unlike a frog's. He was much younger than his dramatic baldness would suggest. I judged him to be about Miss Morstan's age.

"Your servant, Miss Morstan, your servant, sir. Please—" And then he got a good enough look at Crow to realize he was not Nameless, and his words stopped with a squeak.

"My name is Crow, and I am the Angel of London," said Crow, who quite relished moments such as this. "I am a friend of Miss Morstan's."

"Come in," the redheaded man said faintly.

The room was astounding, as opulent as the house was shabby and as out of place as the Indian servant. Rich tapestries hung on the walls; the carpets were beautiful and as soft and welcoming to the foot as a bed of moss. There were tiger skins, a hookah in the corner, a lamp in the shape of a dove that filled the air with a soft and not unpleasing scent of spices.

"I am Mr. Thaddeus Sholto," said our host, wringing his hands together. "That is my name. You are Miss Morstan, of course, and you have brought a . . . an angel and . . . ?"

"This is Dr. Doyle," said Miss Morstan.

"A doctor?" said Sholto, his face lighting up as if he'd been told I was Father Christmas. "Have you your stethoscope? Could you possibly be so kind? It's my mitral valve, you see. I have every confidence in the aortic, but the mitral . . . if you *would* be so kind. I have such grave doubts."

I had indeed brought my bag, on the theory that we had no idea of what might happen, and I obligingly listened, but found nothing amiss save that his heart was beating much too fast and he was trembling head to foot in an ecstasy of fear.

"It sounds normal and healthy," I said. "You have no reason for concern."

"Oh the relief! Thank you, Doctor. Forgive me, Miss Morstan, but one cannot be too careful when it comes to matters of the heart. Indeed, your father might be alive today if he had exercised a little more care."

I acquitted him of any malice—indeed of any awareness of the effect of his words—but it was still a stunning display of tactlessness. Miss Morstan paled but said resolutely, "I knew he had to be dead. How did he die? Were you there?"

"No!" Sholto cried in something near panic. "No no no! I do have information, which I am happy to share"—that part, I believed— "but my knowledge is all secondhand."

"It is better than no knowledge at all," Miss Morstan said. "Tell me everything you can."

Sholto was flustered now, tugging fretfully on the fringe of red hair around the bald dome of his head. "It is a complicated story," he said, "and I must explain my part in it. I have done the best I could!"

"I did not mean to accuse you of anything," said Miss Morstan. "Please, tell me your story."

"Well," said Sholto—then, "You must indulge me. My hookah calms me and helps me think." He got the contraption going while we stood in a semicircle watching, like three cats with a timorous and exceptionally bald mouse. But finally he was settled and puffing, like Alice's Caterpillar, and began his story: "As I'm sure you have guessed, I am one of the sons of Major John Sholto, your father's close friend."

"Yes," Miss Morstan said encouragingly, but Sholto had thought of something else: "You must promise me that what I say will go no further. No police or officials or"—he shuddered—"newspapers. We can settle it all quietly among ourselves."

"I promise," said Miss Morstan, and Crow and I murmured assent.

"Very good," said Sholto. "Very good." He puffed on his hookah, clearly steeling himself for his task. Then he said, "My father retired some eleven years ago and came to live at Pondicherry Lodge in Upper Norwood. He had prospered in India and brought back with him a considerable sum of money, a large collection of valuable curiosities—my father had quite the connoisseur's eye, which I flatter myself I have inherited—and a staff of native servants. With these advantages, he bought a house and lived in great luxury. He had only myself and my twin brother, Bartholomew, as heirs, my mother having died long ago, and there being no other children."

I thought "prospered" was a nice choice of word, vague and agencyless and so much better than words like "despoiled" or "plundered."

"I remember vividly the sensation caused by the disappearance of Captain Morstan. We read the details in the papers, and, since we knew Father to have been his close friend, we discussed the case with him, and he joined in our speculations quite freely."

Another pause while he resorted to the hookah. I hoped it really did calm him, for he was a man in sore need of calming. He continued, "We never had the slightest idea that he alone of everyone on Earth knew the true fate of Captain Morstan."

Miss Morstan said, "Pray continue," and sounded more than sincere.

"We did know that Father had brought more back from India than just treasure. He was very nervous about going out alone—eventually ceasing to do so altogether—and he employed two werewolves as bodyguards. He hired a witch to hex the estate to drive away trespassers. He would never tell us what it was he feared—nor, indeed, discuss the matter at all—but he had a most marked aversion to men with wooden legs. He once actually fired his revolver at a wooden-legged man who turned out to be a harmless and respectable tradesman. By the greatest good fortune he missed, and we were able to hush the matter up, although it cost us a great deal of money. My brother and I used to think this was merely an eccentricity of my father's, but events since have led us to change our opinion."

Another pause: the smoke from the hookah was starting to wreathe his head like fog.

"Early in 1882, my father received a letter from India which was a great shock to him. He nearly fainted at the breakfast table when he opened it. What was in the letter, we could never discover—I believe he burned it that same day—but I was close enough to see that it was short and written in a scrawling hand. It was my father's death sentence. Toward the end of April we were informed that he was beyond all hope and that he wished to speak to us."

Sholto sighed, exhaling smoke. "He had been moved into a room on the ground floor. When we entered, he besought us to lock the door and come close. I cannot give you his exact words, but he told us that when in India, he and Captain Morstan had come into possession of a remarkable treasure. My father brought it to England, and when Captain Morstan arrived, he came straight to Pondicherry Lodge to claim his share. There was what my father called a difference of opinion over the division of the treasure, and Captain Morstan's anger so exacerbated a weakness of his heart that he had a thunderclap coronary and died on the spot."

"I don't believe you," said Mary Morstan.

The words were like a thunderclap themselves. Crow and I both startled, Crow's wings flaring and resettling, and Sholto nearly jumped out of his skin.

"Oh, I beg your pardon, Mr. Sholto!" Miss Morstan said, reddening.

"I didn't mean that I think you are lying. But none of that sounds in the slightest like my father. He was the most even-tempered of men, and he had very strong opinions about the pillaging of India's treasures. He wouldn't have wanted a share in your father's loot. And his heart was perfectly healthy."

Sholto looked intensely uncomfortable. "My father claimed that Captain Morstan's heart trouble was a secret between the two of them, but I confess I have always had my doubts. My father was a man in whom the sin of avarice was particularly strong, and there was very little he would balk at in order to keep what he coveted. As an example, he had taken a pearl chaplet from the treasure to send to you, but he could never bring himself to do so. So that I suppose I would not be *horrifically* shocked to discover he had committed murder. But it must be true that your father came to see him, for by then my father, as I have said, never went out."

"They were friends," Miss Morstan said sadly. "Or, at least, my father thought they were."

"My father sincerely regretted his death," Sholto said anxiously. "And we cannot know the truth, as both of them are dead."

"We *could* know," Miss Morstan contradicted him. "I am certified in clairvoyance."

"Clairvoyance?" said Sholto, looking more than ever like a frog.

"They both died in your father's house, didn't they?" she said. "There's nothing simpler."

"Wait!" shrieked Sholto. "I haven't *explained*!"

"What is there to explain?" Miss Morstan said. "And can you not explain on the way there?"

"You've got me all muddled," Sholto complained. "My father, you see, had hidden the treasure, and as he was about to tell us where it was, he let out a most dreadful yell: 'Keep him out! For Christ's sake keep him out!' We both twisted round to stare at the window behind us, and we both, Bartholomew and I, saw a face looking in on us out of the darkness. We saw the whitening of the nose where it pressed against the glass. It was a bearded face with wild, cruel eyes and an expression of concentrated malevolence. I should know it again in an instant. We rushed toward the window, but the man vanished, and when we returned to my father's bed, we found him lifeless. I suppose it is not really too much to say he was scared to death. We had the grounds searched immediately, but found no trace of him save only a single footprint in the flower bed beneath that particular window, and a cheap all-hex ward on the gravel just beyond the gate. It was melted all around the edges."

"No hex can actually stop someone who is determined enough," Crow said.

"It was certainly proof that my father had a determined enemy," said Sholto. "And although he never said so, we both felt that this enemy was part of the secret of the treasure, or why in the world should he have hidden it?"

"It's not as if he had done anything prosecutable," murmured Miss Morstan, who apparently shared her late father's feelings on the despoliation of India.

"Quite," said Sholto with a nervous giggle. "My brother and I spent weeks—months, years!—digging up the grounds and sounding the walls, all with no success."

"Why did you not hire a clairvoyant?" Miss Morstan said in perplexity.

"No outsiders!" Sholto said so vehemently that he choked, and it was a moment before he could continue. "Finally Brother Bartholomew, who is a clever fellow, took measurements and did a horrific series of calculations and found that, when you had taken the width of the roof and the floors and all that into account, the house was four feet shorter on the inside than the outside, and that led us to a garret above the attic that neither of us had had any clue existed. Brother Bartholomew climbed up and found the treasure chest resting on two rafters. He and I lowered it down and there it sits. He says he cannot compute the value of the jewels."

"But what has this to do with me?" said Miss Morstan. "And why have you been sending me pearls?"

"I *knew* I should get muddled," Sholto muttered. "That was why Father wanted to talk to us. He felt that you were owed recompense."

"Blood money," said Miss Morstan.

"No no no no no!" Sholto cried. "He said he did not murder your father! But he said half of the treasure was rightfully your share, and he was most sincerely ashamed of the greed that had kept him from notifying you."

Miss Morstan looked unconvinced, but said nothing.

"He asked us to put that right for him, and I am afraid it is here that Brother Bartholomew and I began to disagree. He is too much like our father and resents any suggestion that the treasure should be divided. But I say we have plenty of money ourselves. I desire no more. We are your trustees—or, at least, that is my view—and I grew very angry at Brother Bartholomew. Our disagreement became so fundamental that I thought it best to remove myself from Pondicherry Lodge. But yesterday Brother Bartholomew summoned me to help him extract the treasure from its hiding place, and I notified you immediately. We need only drive out to Upper Norwood and demand our share."

Our share, I noted, not *your share*. He was not as indifferent to the treasure as he was trying to appear.

"But why the pearls?" said Miss Morstan.

"The chaplet that my father brought out and did not send. Brother Bartholomew did not want to send it, either, for much the same reasons. He said that sending you the chaplet might give rise to gossip, and that might lead to trouble. It was all I could do to persuade him to let me send you a single pearl once a year so that at least you might never feel destitute."

"It is exceedingly kind of you," said Miss Morstan.

Sholto waved her thanks away, but looked pleased. "I must confess that I share my brother's paranoia," he said, "and for this reason. The morning after my father's death, the window of his room—that same window—was found open. His room had been ransacked and upon his chest had been affixed a scrap of paper with the words

'THE SIGN OF THE FOUR' scrawled across it. As far as we could judge, nothing had actually been stolen, though everything had been dragged out into the light. My brother and I assume that it was the work of the same man who scared my father to death and that it was connected to the fear that had haunted him, but it is still a complete mystery to us."

"Do the words 'the sign of the four' mean anything to you?" Crow asked. I tried not to look like every nerve was thrumming in anticipation.

But Sholto said, "No. Brother Bartholomew and I racked our brains, but we could think of nothing."

"Did you ask the servants?" said Miss Morstan. Sholto looked baffled.

"The servants?"

"If they were with your father in India, they might have seen or heard something," Miss Morstan said.

Sholto rang the bell and the Indian servant appeared, brows raised inquiringly. Sholto released a flood of Punjabi, to which the servant—the *khitmutgar,* the house steward—listened with bafflement growing clearer and clearer on his face.

At last he said, "No, sahib. Those words mean nothing to me. We all knew of your father's fear of one-legged men, but none of us knew the reason for it, except perhaps Lal Chowdar, who is dead."

"It was a good idea," Crow said to Miss Morstan.

"Really, I just want to find out what happened to my father," she said.

"I think," I said, "that we ought to start for Upper Norwood. It is only going to grow later."

"You are very practical," Miss Morstan said, smiling at me. And I returned her smile even as I cursed myself as seventeen different kinds of fool.

Sholto still seemed inclined to delay, for all that the entire undertaking was his idea, but the *khitmutgar* allied himself with us and got his master bundled into a heavy astrakhan-trimmed topcoat and a rabbitskin cap with hanging lappets that covered the ears. "My health is somewhat fragile," Sholto said. "I am compelled to be exceedingly careful."

The werewolf coachman was waiting to assist Sholto into the carriage, and as soon as we were all inside, he set off, again at a tremendous clip.

Thaddeus Sholto talked incessantly, his voice rising above the clatter of the wheels, and I realized he was still nervous nearly to the point of terror, although whether his fear was of his brother or of the mysterious—and, admittedly, alarming—one-legged man, I could not say. He was a hypochondriac of the first water, taking great and obvious pleasure in reciting his symptoms. He would periodically ask for my opinion; since I was not listening to him, my answers were rather hit or miss, but since he was not listening to me, being too enthralled with the saga of his own health, it hardly mattered. Sholto just kept talking. It was an inexpressible relief when the carriage pulled up and the coachman leapt down to open the door.

"This, Miss Morstan," said Sholto as he handed her out, "is Pondicherry Lodge."

All we could actually see of it was the high exterior wall, topped with shards of glass that gleamed ominously in the moonlight. There was a single narrow door in this wall; iron-clamped and notably Gothic in appearance, and on this Sholto knocked with a peculiar sharp rhythm, a rhythm which was explained when the door opened and a cerberus bounded out, the moonlight showing its rivets but leaving its eyes as hollows of darkness with only the faintest, dullest gleam of red in their depths.

Some cerberus automata were actually built in the shape of dogs. This one was in human form, save for the three mastiff heads, which its body was built broad and squat to accommodate. It was two-thirds my height and probably that much broader.

"It knows me," Sholto said, "but it will want to examine the three of you. Brother Bartholomew is becoming more and more paranoid."

The cerberus inspected first me, then Miss Morstan, with polite thoroughness, but it was sorely baffled by Crow. It circled him twice, examining him first with one head, then with another. But finally it stopped solidly in front of him. The whir was very clear in the silence, and a ticker tape emerged from a slot in its chest. The cerberus tore it off and handed it to Crow.

"Oh dear," said Crow as he read it, then handed it to me. I read:

NAMELESS? FALLEN? WHAT?

Crow said to the cerberus, "I am not Nameless and I am not Fallen."

The cerberus cocked its heads, and although the whine it made came from the ball joints in its three-in-one neck, it sounded exactly like a puzzled dog.

"There isn't a word for it," Crow said.

"I vouch for all three of these persons," said Sholto; he sounded pleased with himself, as if he was relishing the opportunity to be someone who could vouch for others.

The cerberus spat out another ticker tape and handed it to Sholto. He said, "*Really,* McMurdo," and to us, "He won't let us in until he's sure Mr. Crow isn't Fallen."

"If Crow were Fallen," I said, "we would already be inside and the house would be on fire."

The ticker tape this time read:

I MUST DO MY DUTY

"No one's saying you *shouldn't* do your duty," Sholto said impatiently.

"I don't know a way to prove I'm not Fallen," Crow said, "aside from continuing not to wreak destruction on Upper Norwood."

"That's certainly a good start," I said, and Crow giggled.

"McMurdo, this is ridiculous," said Sholto. "You're asking us to prove a negative."

The cerberus made its baffled whine again.

"I need to see Mr. Bartholomew," said Sholto, "and I need these three people to come with me."

"You can recognize Crow is not Fallen," I said slowly. "There is no scent of burning and nothing is catching fire. The Fallen carry fire with them wherever they go. And you can recognize that he is not Fallen by his eyes. The Fallen's eyes glow red. You can see them from a hundred yards away."

"You sound as if you've seen the Fallen in person, Dr. Doyle," said Miss Morstan.

"I have," I said. "That's what happened to my leg. If this cerberus were one of the occult models, it would be able to detect the Fallen's miasma. Which would solve our problem nicely, since Crow wouldn't have it, and not being an angel, I can't Fall."

"It's being ridiculous and insubordinate," said Sholto. "McMurdo, *I vouch for them.* He isn't Fallen."

The cerberus seemed to consider for a moment; then it turned to Miss Morstan, heads cocked inquiringly.

She looked alarmed. "What does it want from me?"

"A third confirmation," said Crow. "That will allow it to accept the hypothesis—that I am not Fallen—as true. It's a built-in failsafe for situations like this where it's gotten hung up on something that can't be proved directly. I didn't think it'd work for this, but plainly McMurdo thinks it will. Just tell it I'm not Fallen—assuming you believe I'm not."

"Mr. Crow is not Fallen," Miss Morstan said firmly to the cerberus.

The whine of the dubious ball joints again, and then the cerberus nodded its middle head and stepped aside.

Inside, there was a gravel path that led us through the grounds, bleak in the moonlight, to a great ugly house, square and unyielding, that could never have been a lodge in anything more than name. "I cannot understand it," said Sholto, somewhere between grumbling and whining. "Brother Bartholomew never goes to bed before four o'clock—and I *specifically* told him I should be coming this evening—but there is no light in his room."

Indeed, the entire house was dark, save for a chink of light escaping from a window beside the front door. Crow pointed this out, and Sholto said, "That is the housekeeper's room. Mrs. Bernstone will know what's going on. But if you wouldn't mind . . . ? I don't want to overwhelm her, and my brother has as few visitors as I do."

We agreed, and in a surprisingly considerate gesture, Sholto handed Miss Morstan the lantern before he approached the house. She held it high to give him as much light as possible. The door opened in a sudden flood of lamplight, and we all heard a woman's voice cry, "Oh, Mr. Thaddeus, thank God you've come," before it closed again.

"An unlikely savior," I said, and Miss Morstan laughed.

"He seems to be a good-hearted man," she said. "But how strange that those same words, 'the Sign of the Four,' should be found both among my father's things and on Major Sholto's body. You did not mention the map, thus I did not, either, but I could not help thinking of it. Do you think it could be a map to the treasure's original hiding place?"

"I hardly think it could be anything else," said Crow. "Miss Morstan, I don't want to impugn your father's memory, but is there *any* possibility he was involved with Major Sholto in this . . ." He hesitated.

Miss Morstan did not. "Robbery," said she. "It is nothing else and it is unconscionable. I cannot imagine my father taking part in such an unethical scheme. But at the same time, I cannot deny the existence of the map."

"Is it possible," Crow said, "that your father found out about the treasure after Major Sholto left India and decided that he had to confront him face-to-face before he took any kind of action?"

"*That* sounds like my father. He would hate the thought of going against a friend."

"And of course he would seek out Major Sholto the instant he arrived in London," I said, half to Miss Morstan and half to Crow. "To get it over with."

"Of course," said Miss Morstan. "Poor Father. He would have hated it. I only hope he did not *know* in his final moments that Major Sholto was about to kill him."

"You reject the story of the heart ailment?" said Crow.

"Utterly," said Miss Morstan. "My father was not a stupid man. He would never have kept such a thing secret from me. How could he, when I might inherit it?"

"And it's awfully convenient," I said, "that the only person present when he died was the only person who knew of this alleged heart ailment."

"That is also true," said Crow. He asked Miss Morstan, "Do you still intend to take a reading?"

"More than ever. I want to know the truth, and I want to know where his body is." She looked around and added, "He clearly wasn't buried on the grounds."

"No," I agreed. The grounds of Pondicherry Lodge looked as though a thousand moles had tunneled for a thousand days and then, unsatisfied, had tunneled for a thousand more.

"He *said* they dug up the grounds," Crow murmured. "And I deduce from this evidence that at least one of the Sholto brothers is an extremely methodical man."

"Brother Bartholomew, at a guess," said I and caught the answering gleam of Crow's smile.

That was when we heard the shriek. It came from inside the house, and it was a terrible noise even at that distance, ripping the air apart like knives.

I discovered Miss Morstan clutching my wrist, and I did something stupid. Instead of gently extracting myself, I turned my hand over and returned her grip. She had remarkable hand strength for a woman her size; I glanced at her face and saw she still looked perfectly calm.

She caught my glance and said wryly, "Governesses must have nerves of steel."

"Should we go in, do you think?" said Crow, who was bouncing anxiously on the balls of his feet.

"We don't know the house," I said, "and no one except Mr. Sholto will know that we aren't intruders."

"Point taken," said Crow, and Thaddeus Sholto burst from the house, his eyes all but starting from their sockets, and his voice hoarse and cracking when he told us, "Brother Bartholomew is dead."

13

THE TRUTH ABOUT
CAPTAIN MORSTAN

FOR THE NEXT three-quarters of an hour, I was simply Dr. Doyle, reviving Mrs. Bernstone from the dead faint in which she lay across the threshold of the attic room where Bartholomew Sholto had died; making her and Thaddeus Sholto each take a slug of brandy for the shock; getting Miss Morstan to make tea, sweet and milky, and settling the two of them at the kitchen table to drink it, Miss Morstan there to remind Mrs. Bernstone at intervals that the tea was in front of her.

Thaddeus Sholto talked the entire time in a thin, bewildered thread of a voice, explaining disjointedly and repeatedly how Mrs. Bernstone had told him Bartholomew had locked himself in the attic all day and refused to answer her; how he, Thaddeus, had told her to bring the master key; how they had gone up to the attic and he had knocked and called, but Bartholomew had not answered; how he had unlocked the door and found Bartholomew dead, his face in a hideous rictus, and no sign anywhere of what had killed him or of the treasure. He kept saying, "What do I do? What do I *do*?" like a man told he must thread a needle without the use of his hands.

Finally, when there was some color in his face again and his hands had stopped chattering the teacup against the saucer, I said, "You must notify the police."

He was aghast. I said, "Your brother is dead by some means we do not know, at the hands of a person as yet unknown. At this point, if you don't notify the police, you will only create more questions that will be even more difficult to answer."

I herded him outside, toward the side gate where his coachman was waiting, but as we reached it I was struck with an idea. I asked Sholto, "Did your brother own McMurdo or was he leasing it?"

"Oh, he owned it," said Sholto. "Brother Bartholomew was very particular."

"Therefore, you own it now?"

"Yes, I suppose I do."

"Will you lend it to me?"

"*Lend* it to you?"

"If it has the tracking algorithm, it might be able to track your brother's murderer."

"Yes, of course," Sholto said. "That is, yes, I will be happy to lend the cerberus to you."

We had reached the gate. Sholto knocked to summon the cerberus, which appeared at once from its niche in the wall, heads up alertly and the tiny red sparks of its eyes bright.

Sholto said, "Oh dear, oh dear. McMurdo, my brother is dead."

The cerberus's eyes seemed to get brighter. It spat out:

WHO

"We don't know," I said. "Are you equipped with the tracking algorithm?"

YES

"Since my brother is dead," Sholto said in a rush, "you belong to me now. I wish to lend you to Dr. Doyle to track the murderer."

There was a long pause. Finally, it spat out another length of ticker tape:

MUST CONFIRM DEATH OF BARTHOLOMEW SHOLTO

"Oh dear," said Sholto, wringing his hands.

"That's not impossible," I said, "but you need to go for the police. McMurdo, can you come with me?"

Another long pause before the cerberus said:

IF/THEN SEQUENCE VALID. I WILL COME.

"All right," I said. "Just a moment."

I got Sholto out the gate to where his coachman was waiting, reading a newspaper by moonlight, as werewolves do. I bundled Sholto into the carriage and gave the coachman the bare facts: Bartholomew Sholto was dead and it looked like murder. He nodded, his eyes wide, and I knew I could count on him to ensure that Sholto made it to a police station and did not simply run off into the night.

The carriage rattled away. I swung the gate door closed, feeling the jar of it in my bones. By now, the house was wide awake, and the police would come in through the main gates. It occurred to me to wonder, as McMurdo bolted the door with a bar of wood about the size and weight of a railroad tie, why Bartholomew Sholto had a guard on this side gate at all, if it was true he had no guests. Why not just leave it bolted?

McMurdo kept pace with me to the house and followed me up flight after damnable flight of stairs, each step creaking under its weight, to the attic, where Crow was contemplating Bartholomew Sholto's body.

"I found what killed him. Hello, McMurdo."

McMurdo nodded courteously.

"McMurdo needs to confirm that Mr. Sholto is dead."

"Well, he's not getting any less dead, so come look. Doyle, come see this—but whatever you do, don't touch it. Unless you've a hankering for a quick and ugly death?"

"Not at the moment," said I.

Bartholomew Sholto's body was huddled in a wooden armchair, the limbs twisted and the head dropped to the right shoulder with a dreadful teeth-bared grin on its face. The resemblance to Thaddeus Sholto was exact, so much so that I had to remind myself that Thaddeus had gone for the police and could not be sitting here dead and cold.

McMurdo began a solemn examination of the corpse, much as it had examined us when we had arrived. I came to Crow's side and locked my hands together behind my back.

"Here," said Crow. He pointed, careful himself not to touch, although I wasn't sure that poison would have any effect on him.

"It looks like a thorn," I said.

"It is," said Crow. "Whoever killed him used a blowpipe."

McMurdo straightened. It looked from me to Crow and said:

DEATH OF BARTHOLOMEW SHOLTO CONFIRMED.

GIVE ME A HALFPENNY

"I haven't any," said Crow. "Doyle? McMurdo needs a token before it can do anything."

"And a halfpenny will do?" I said, digging through my pockets for loose change.

"It's symbolic. Any coin, really."

"Well, I have a penny, and McMurdo's services this evening are certainly worth that much." I gave the penny to McMurdo, who inspected it gravely, nodded in confirmation, and ate it.

READY

it said.

WHAT ARE YOUR ORDERS

"Crow can give you instructions, too," I said.

Crow said promptly, "Examine the room for signs of an intruder. We already know he took something. But I don't know how he got in and out. It wasn't by the door."

What he had taken, of course, was the treasure, and I remembered Thaddeus Sholto's reiterated dismay. His claim to be disinterested had gone up like flash paper; he seemed almost more grieved by the loss of the treasure than by his brother's death.

Grief could take strange forms—and I was aware of my brother's watch ticking in my waistcoat pocket—but I wondered about the avarice Sholto had described as riding both his father and his brother.

Crow was concerned with more practical matters. He said, "It's clear so far as it goes. But then it isn't clear at all. Bartholomew Sholto was killed by a poison dart. And he was killed either *by* a one-legged man or by someone *with* a one-legged man."

"How do you make that out?"

"By the footprints. Look. Here's a boot, a heavy one, nothing like Bartholomew Sholto's slippers. And here, about a pace away, is an ever-so-slightly irregular circle. Clearly the underpinnings of the same man—and proof also of Thaddeus Sholto's story, in case we were wondering."

"We might have been," I said.

Crow laughed. "No, the one-legged man was definitely here. What puzzles me is how he got in. The door was locked from the inside. The window is closed and locked. And there's a sixty-foot climb up a blank wall on the other side. Where did he come from?"

McMurdo whirred, like clearing its throat, and said:

THERE WERE TWO

"You're sure?" said Crow. "No, never mind, you wouldn't have said it if you weren't. That explains the rope, in any event."

"The rope?" I said.

He nodded toward the corner by the window, where a coil of rope lay in untidy loops. "The one-legged man could climb a rope let down by a companion—and he could lower the treasure the same way, before climbing back down himself. But, while excellent in and of itself, that merely backs the question up a step. How did the *companion* get in and out?"

"There's only one other point of egress," I said and quoted back to him something he was fond of saying: "When you have eliminated the impossible, whatever remains . . ."

Crow frowned up at the ragged hole in the plaster. "Yes, but that leads to a sort of oubliette, which by definition is a dead end—a hiding place isn't much good if your enemies can get to it from the outside."

"You should at least look," I said. "I would, but I can't get up there, and neither can McMurdo."

"You'll have to give me a leg up," Crow said. "I confess, I wouldn't have waited for you if I could have reached the hole unaided."

"I can do that much," I said and set my cane down so that I could lace my fingers into a stirrup.

Crow was absurdly light and really only needed a foot or so of boost. "Could've used your wings," I said, mostly joking.

"Doesn't work like that," he said, as he pushed and I lifted. "Besides—" And then his hands caught the rafters and he scrambled up, disappearing entirely for a moment and then reappearing as a face, disembodied in the blackness.

"Besides what?" I said.

"What? Hand me the lantern, please." He reached down, and I stretched up as best I could. He caught the lantern handle and disappeared again.

After no more than a few seconds, his voice drifted down to McMurdo and me. "Well, that answers one question. It isn't an oubliette at all. This stretches the entire length of the house. Hold on a minute."

We waited. In the silence, I could hear McMurdo ticking. Then Crow came back and said, "Yes, a little further along there's a trapdoor to the roof and a plastered-over space where I think there must have been a trapdoor to the rest of the house. I guess Major Sholto didn't think he had to worry about his enemies coming from above. Which only goes to show that really you can never be too careful."

"He probably wasn't expecting his sons to go hacking great holes in the ceiling," I said. "And certainly not on the same night his one-legged friend came calling . . . Isn't that timing a little suspicious?"

"Someone must have talked," Crow said. "The interesting question is who they talked *to*."

"Does someone in this house possibly know who the one-legged man is, do you mean?"

"Someone might," said Crow. "I'm coming down."

McMurdo and I stepped back and Crow descended, not gracefully, in a flurry of feathers. "I certainly think it's worth asking."

⋄

I FOUND MISS Morstan, Mrs. Bernstone, and a planchette in the dining room. Miss Morstan seemed embarrassed by the planchette. "It is not my usual method, but Mrs. Bernstone was so kind as to volunteer her help, and the planchette is the tool she is most comfortable with."

"Have you had any luck?"

"Depends on what you mean by luck," Miss Morstan said and made a face. "I cannot catch even a hint of my father."

"Don't be discouraged, dear," said Mrs. Bernstone. "It takes time for the planchette to warm up to a new sitter."

Mrs. Bernstone was seated at an angle that meant she could not see my face, so that I allowed my expression to reflect my incredulity.

Miss Morstan smiled. "Do you need me for something?"

"Yes, if you have a minute."

She looked inquiringly at Mrs. Bernstone, who said, "I think a break is a good idea. Let things settle."

"Then pray excuse me for a moment," said Miss Morstan and followed me out of the room.

When we were out of earshot, she said, "I would never teach my pupils such nonsense, but she so kindly offered to help, and it *can* provide a focus. But what about your investigations?"

"We've discovered some things," I said. "Crow and McMurdo are out in the grounds, trying to find the murderer's trail. I came to ask if you could scry for him."

"Yes, of course. All I need is a bowl of water and a focus. Something belonging to the murderer, or something you know he's touched."

I had anticipated this request. "As long as you don't open the phial," I said. "We aren't sure if the poison is only on the tip." I had had a small stoppered phial and a pair of forceps in my bag, and had very gingerly removed the thorn from Bartholomew Sholto's neck.

"Is that . . . ?"

"Yes. But I'm quite sure the murderer touched it."

"Yes," she said faintly, and it occurred to me that the scrying she was accustomed to was probably on the order of finding lost gloves. But she rallied gamely and said, "Just let me ask Mrs. Bernstone for a bowl."

We ended up back at the kitchen table, the planchette and its papers pushed to one side. Mrs. Bernstone watched as Miss Morstan set the bowl on the table, the phial right beside it.

"This may take a minute," she said. "I'm not as tranquil as I should be."

"I cannot imagine why," I said and got another smile.

Mrs. Bernstone came across to me and murmured, "She's very talented."

"Yes," I said.

"You must be very proud of her," she said, and I realized in horror that she thought Miss Morstan was my intended. In the split second before I refuted this idea, I realized with even more horror that without this belief, Mrs. Bernstone might take a very different view of Miss Morstan being out so late with a party of men. An angel was generally considered an impeccable chaperone, but Crow was different, and Mrs. Bernstone had been alarmed by him—which was why Crow had gone with McMurdo and I had come to find Miss Morstan.

"Yes," I said, truthfully enough—although clairvoyance was not a science and its results were not admissible as evidence, I had every respect for those who achieved their certification—and changed the subject. "Mrs. Bernstone, how many of the servants knew what Bartholomew Sholto was doing in the attic?"

She looked at me as if I'd asked her to eat her planchette. "All of us." She sighed at my expression. "Even the stupidest person would notice the two of them digging up all the gardens like a pair of rabbits, and then Mr. Bartholomew going up and down the house *measuring* everything and muttering to himself, and then he shuts himself in the attic, and you could hear the noise of him tearing a hole in the ceiling in every corner of the house. And *then* he sends for Mr. Thaddeus and they're up there yelling at each other and Mr. Thaddeus comes down all dusty—which is not like Mr. Thaddeus at all—and muttering about fairness and equal shares . . . how could we *not* know?"

"I see your point," I said. "Is there anyone, do you think, who might have mentioned the treasure to someone else?"

"What do you mean?"

"Well, it's the timing," I said. "How did the . . . the people who stole the treasure know it was here?"

Mrs. Bernstone's eyes widened, then narrowed. "You really think—"

"Not on purpose," I said hastily. "But if the thief had cultivated a relationship with someone, they might not think anything of passing along the latest gossip."

I thought for a moment I had mortally offended this gentle elderly lady, but she considered my proposition, then said, "No. The menservants are all Indians, and they would never discuss Mr. Bartholomew's business with an outsider. And the maids sleep out.

They weren't here when Mr. Thaddeus came and they weren't here when he left. Isn't it more likely that this person did exactly what you're trying to do to find him?" And she nodded at Miss Morstan, who was leaning intently over the bowl of water.

"It's too dark," she said. "Wherever he is, it's too dark to see anything."

"Do you receive anything at all?"

"Only the reek of the Thames, and that hardly narrows it down." She stepped back from the table. "I'm sorry, Dr. Doyle. That's all I have."

"Thank you for trying," I said and smiled at her more warmly than I should have. "I'll let you and Mrs. Bernstone get back to your planchette work."

She gave me a dryly unamused, very governess-ish look, but said only, "Good luck."

First we had to clear the hurdle of the police. They arrived in the person of a Detective Inspector Athelney Jones, who seemed inclined to treat Crow as a sort of dancing bear, and a dour Sergeant Forbes, who seemed to feel that Bartholomew Sholto had died with the intent of affronting him. They brought Thaddeus Sholto with them; he was, if possible, even more affronted than Sergeant Forbes, radiating wounded dignity like a wet cat. Mrs. Bernstone sprang into action when she saw him, making a hot toddy and fussing over him until he drank it—and did he look pleased by the attention!— and then bundling him willy-nilly off to bed.

I spent an interminable length of time talking to Sergeant Forbes, who was determined to make everything I said a lie—or at best simply wrong. If I thought he did it on purpose, I would call it a very clever technique, since there is nothing more infuriating than being called a liar when you're telling the truth and nothing more likely to make you say more than you meant to.

When finally I escaped from him, I found Crow and Miss Morstan waiting for me in the hall. She said, without preamble, "Dr. Doyle, I have to find my father."

"Of course," I said. "Do you need my help with something?"

She was blushing. "I tried to explain it to Mr. Crow, but I don't think he understands."

"And you think I will?"

"You have a family," she said, and I didn't wince. "I'm sure you know what it's like to lose a loved one, although"—and she managed a wan smile—"not quite as literally as I have."

"What can we do to help?"

I got a much better smile, and she said, "I think if I am to reach Father or get any information about his death, I need to use Major Sholto's study, but I've no idea where it is."

"Well, that, at least, is simple. We ask."

There were four of Major Sholto's Indian servants remaining, one having died and one having gone with Thaddeus Sholto to that awful row house. I was not sure what all of them did, but the butler was a man named Narhari Rao. We found him easily enough, in the kitchen, drinking a strong cup of tea, which I was sure he needed after being interviewed by Athelney Jones.

"Of course, sir," he said, his English as beautiful as the *khitmutgar*'s, when I asked about Major Sholto's study. He led us easily through a warren of dark-paneled hallways, all luxuriously decorated with Indian treasures and carpeted with Indian carpets. And what must it be like for him, spending his life in a foreign country, surrounded by stolen reminders of his home?

"I'm surprised Major Sholto returned to England at all," I said to Miss Morstan.

"He does seem to have been obsessed," she agreed and then was visibly struck by an idea. "Mr. Rao, did you know my father? Captain Arthur Morstan?"

Rao glanced back at her, sympathy in his eyes. "Of course, miss. He visited Major Sholto many times in Port Blair. He was a good man."

"Thank you," said Miss Morstan. "But you never saw him in England?"

"No, miss. Here is the Major's study. Mr. Sholto does—did not use it, preferring a room upstairs for his chemical experiments." He opened the door and gravely ushered us in, as if we were invited guests instead of nosy intruders.

"Thank you, Rao," I said.

He bowed to us both, and slightly more deeply to Crow, and departed, hopefully back to the kitchen and the cup of tea we had interrupted.

The study, like the rest of the main floor, was dark-paneled and littered with Indian art and artifacts at the value of which I could not even guess. It was like a much larger version of Thaddeus Sholto's room—or rather, I supposed, his room was a much smaller version of this.

"Oh dear," said Miss Morstan. "My father would have been very angry about this. He was a man of principle, and he believed very strongly that looting was criminally wrong."

Crow was frowning. "How could he have been friends with Major Sholto, who clearly believed the opposite?"

"I don't know," Miss Morstan said helplessly. "Unless the Major did not display his treasures openly in Port Blair."

"But felt perfectly safe doing so in England," I said. "And he could hardly clear the house of them before your father's visit."

"Not if Father arrived unannounced," she agreed.

"But it isn't as if your father could have done anything. Major Sholto is hardly the only—or the worst—offender."

"That's what angered Father the most, that almost no one even considered it a crime—certainly not a serious one. He used to say, 'Imagine if they were looting Buckingham Palace.' Oh, it *infuriated* him."

"This reunion of two old friends must have been anything but cordial," I said.

"If Father *did* have a weak heart, I would be inclined to believe that part of Major Sholto's story. But I know he would have told me." She looked around the room with mingled awe and distaste. "This collection must be worth thousands of pounds."

"What do you need for what you want to do? Not, I hope, a planchette."

"No," she said and turned a laugh into a cough. "Oh dear, it is just the most dreadful nonsense, but of course I couldn't say so. For this, I just need something . . ." She looked around the room. "Ideally, something they both touched, but something Major Sholto handled frequently will do."

"Here," I said. "I imagine this knife is on his desk because he used it as a letter opener." It was a lovely little thing, a paring knife with a jeweled handle.

"Perfect," she said and took it from me, our fingers brushing for an instant.

"And you don't need water?"

"That's for distance," she said. "Did your sisters not learn clairvoyancy?"

"I have no sisters," I said.

"Oh, I'm sorry," she said, divining from my voice that the topic was a sensitive one. Instead of prying, as most people would, she said, "Water doesn't help when you're trying to see spirits, and I've never had much luck with it in scrying the past. Mirrors are best for all kinds of clairvoyancy, but one can hardly carry around a scrying mirror all the time. They need to be at least a foot in diameter. But, although I don't like to brag, I *am* certified, and I think I can manage with just a focus."

She sat down in one of the wing chairs, the knife cupped carefully in her hands. I sat in the other chair and Crow paced thoughtfully back and forth in front of the desk. I was worried for a few moments that Miss Morstan would find him distracting; then I saw that she had her eyes closed, and he, of course, made no sound.

After a span of time that was more than five minutes but less than fifteen, Miss Morstan said softly, not opening her eyes, "I can feel Major Sholto's greed. It's all through this room like a suffocating fog. And I can see him at his desk, looking at his treasures and thinking about the hidden treasure, the Agra treasure. He almost panics when he thinks of it, because he stole it and he's afraid of the people he stole it from."

Crow had stopped pacing and was watching Miss Morstan with an intensity that suggested he was trying to dissect her with his gaze alone.

"And there's guilt," she said. "Guilt about my father. There! I've found it. I can see my father coming in. He *is* angry. They talk. He reproaches Major Sholto. He says they had an agreement. They argue. Major Sholto is defensive, desperate. He offers to share the Agra treasure, half and half, and my father leaps to his feet. He's going to go to the I.A.F. Major Sholto comes around the desk to plead with him, but my father is adamant, and he's deeply offended that Major Sholto would think he would accept a bribe. He says, 'This conversation is over,' and turns to leave, and Major Sholto picks up the paperweight from the desk and hits him over the head with it."

Crow and I stared at the paperweight, an elaborately etched brass globe that certainly looked heavy enough to kill a man.

"My father falls to the floor and Major Sholto looks down at him for a moment and then gets down on his knees and . . . oh *God,* no! No!" Her eyes snapped open; she flung the knife across the room, narrowly missing Crow, and burst into bitter tears.

Crow came and knelt down beside my chair and whispered, "What should we do?"

"Nothing," I said. "She's just learned that her father was brutally murdered by his best friend. Let her cry. I have no knack for comforting, and I beg you not to attempt it."

"All right," Crow said, although he looked worried.

As I expected, Miss Morstan did not cry for long. She regained her composure within a few minutes and said, "He deliberately beat my father's skull in until he was sure he was dead. Oh, that monster!" She shuddered. "I do not wish to stay in this dreadful house another minute."

Crow said, "But your father's body—"

"No," said Miss Morstan. "He is not in the house, and I cannot bear to imagine what that fiend might have done with his body."

"I do not blame you," said I. "Come. Let us find Williams the coachman and get you home."

"I will call on you and Mr. Crow this afternoon at six to find out what you learn."

"Of course," I said.

Williams, too, we found, had gravitated to the kitchen, where he was playing cards with Lal Singh, one of the Indian servants whose duties I did not know. Williams was astute enough to see that Miss Morstan had been crying, and he agreed at once to take her to Mrs. Cecil Forrester's house. "And you gentlemen?" he said.

"Thank you, no," Crow said. "We have a prior engagement."

14

TRACKING BY CERBERUS

WE FOUND MCMURDO in the garden, waiting by the wall where the two murderers had gotten into the grounds. The wall, with its glass shards, was as forbidding as ever, but there was, almost like an optical illusion, a pattern of missing half bricks, which, if you looked at them the right way, made an obvious ladder leading up to the exact corner, where there was no glass.

We walked down to the main gate, open for the police officers coming and going, and then back along the other side of the wall to the same corner, where, as Crow had confidently predicted, we found a hex-ward lying in the gravel. "It must have gotten too hot to be bearable," said Crow, kneeling to take a closer look. "It's a good one, though. Custom built."

"He learns from experience," I said. "A better hex-ward and a better escape method. That must be why Bartholomew Sholto bought McMurdo to watch that gate."

"Yes," said Crow. "And yes."

"Can we find out who made the hex-ward? That might be an easier way of finding the murderer's identity."

"Possibly," said Crow. He pulled out a handkerchief and gingerly picked the ward up. "It's still warm."

"Wait!" I said, assailed by a qualm. "Should we not show this to the police?"

Crow snorted. "Jones thinks Thaddeus Sholto killed his brother. I'm not going to give him more ammunition."

"But . . ."

"Later, Doyle! When we've gotten as much information from it as we can. For now, let us follow McMurdo, who has caught the murderers' trail."

Cerberus automata do not track by scent. They track the psychic residue that human beings leave on everything they touch. This makes them particularly formidable, for while you may disguise your scent or cross your trail, you cannot disguise your psyche. It is possible to "shake" a cerberus, but it is not easy, and we were wagering that the persons we were after, not expecting to be tracked by a prohibitively expensive cerberus, would not even try.

McMurdo proceeded steadily, but not fast—its short legs and broad body were not built with speed in mind—and Crow and I followed, away from Pondicherry Lodge and into a maze of alleys and side streets. We were headed toward the Thames, and after a while we left behind the residential neighborhoods, finding ourselves walking among warehouses and odd, secretive shops, and the air grew heavier and heavier with the indescribable stench of the river.

As we walked, Crow described his encounter with Athelney Jones. "It's not that he's a stupid man—he's brighter than Gregson, for one—but he comes up with a theory and then moves the facts around to match it. The *problem* is that he's so frequently correct, he's gotten out of the habit of imagining that he could be wrong." He sighed, then brightened. "At least I annoy him nearly as much as he annoys me, so that's something. Due north. He's heading for Whitechapel."

"Cheap doss-houses and no questions asked," I said.

"And right in the shadow of Victoria's Needle," said Crow. "Endless throngs of strangers to lose yourself in."

The damaged muscles in my leg were beginning to burn with

fatigue. To distract myself, I said, "If Inspector Jones has a theory, then you must have one as well."

"I do!" he said, laughing.

"Tell me your theory," said I.

"It is not very complicated," he said, but I could tell he was pleased to be asked. "An officer of a convict guard comes into possession of a treasure map. The most likely way for this to happen is that a convict draws it for him. Draws it and signs it in English with the rather dramatic 'the Sign of the Four,' which may suggest something about his reading habits. Now, of those four names, only one of them is obviously that of a native English speaker."

"Jonathan Small," I said.

"Exactly. Therefore, I think it's safe to proceed on the theory that Jonathan Small drew the map. And furthermore that Jonathan Small is the wooden-legged man of whom Major Sholto was so terrified."

"Economy of persons," I said approvingly.

"Just so. And we see that the Major was right to be worried, since Small caused the death of the Major's heir. Why this unrelenting anger? Either Sholto stole the map or he received the map in exchange for a promise that he did not keep."

"Release," I said. "The one thing every convict wants."

"I would guess that Major Sholto recklessly promised something he knew he couldn't—or wouldn't—deliver, secure in the knowledge that by far the most likely outcome was that all four men would die in prison."

"But Small did not."

"No. And in the meantime, somehow Captain Morstan learned what was going on—learned and was infuriated. I would guess that he was angry at Sholto for taking the treasure—but also for the entire transaction with Small, as Sholto effectively took a bribe and then reneged. *That*'s why Sholto had to silence Morstan. The Armed Forces might turn a blind eye to despoliation, but they feel very strongly about bribery. And most officers are gallant men, who pride themselves on upholding their oaths. But you know that better than I do."

I waved his apologetic grimace away. "Then Sholto, what? Gave Morstan the map to keep him quiet?"

"As token of an agreement of some sort. Remember what Miss Morstan said."

"But Sholto reneged again. He murdered Morstan and was scared to death by Small."

"Yes, for a treasure he hoarded up in that unspeakably grim attic, unseen and unknown. It hardly seems worth it, especially when one factors in Jonathan Small. I think the letter Sholto received in 1882 was either from a friend still in India, warning him that Small had escaped, or from Small himself, since clearly he knew where Sholto lived."

"Sholto must have thought he had nothing to worry about, with Morstan dead."

"The Major doesn't seem to have been much gifted with foresight," said Crow.

"Small escapes, makes it back to England, scares Major Sholto to death, and waits for the Sholto sons to find his treasure for him." I told him Mrs. Bernstone's theory about Small hiring a scryer.

"How very practical!" he said delightedly. "Certainly much easier than climbing that wall every month. And we don't have to explain how someone could have been chatting regularly with a wooden-legged man and not known it—which was a bit of a stumbling block."

We had come through Streatham, Brixton, and Camberwell, and now the trail McMurdo followed, while still sedulously avoiding main roads, began to bear away to the east.

"Not Whitechapel after all," murmured Crow. "I suppose it was a bit much to ask of Jonathan Small that he also be the Whitechapel murderer."

"A bit much, yes," I said. "His crimes are quite horrible and outré enough already."

Here, where Miles Street turned into Knight's Place, McMurdo stopped dead in its tracks. I heard the whine as all three of its heads turned in different directions—a notably eloquent expression of bafflement.

"Oh dear," said Crow. "McMurdo, what happened?"

THEY HAVE VANISHED

Even the whir of the ticker tape sounded disgusted.

Crow and I looked around futilely. "They *couldn't* have known we would be following them some eight-and-twenty hours later," Crow said, "but how do you disappear from a cerberus's view by *accident*?"

My eye had been caught by the brightly colored crescent moon painted on the sign of one of the shuttered shops that surrounded us:

MADAME SILVANOVA
scrying, divination, wards, hexes

"Crow?" I said and pointed.

"Do you think there's a ward?"

"If I were a fortune-teller in this part of town, I'd certainly ward my premises. And my clientele might have any number of reasons to wish not to be followed or observed."

"Besides," he said, "she advertises confidentiality." And he nodded at the door of the shop, where the words CONFIDENTIAL *and* DISCREET had been freehanded by someone with a fair amount of skill. Crow peered closer, reading the hours. "Well, Madame keeps fashionably late hours. We will have to try back this evening."

15

THE
MURDERER'S STORY

AFTER SOME LOOKING, we found a four-wheeler that could take McMurdo's weight and returned it to Pondicherry Lodge before going home ourselves, I to sleep and Crow to consume today's ream of newsprint about the Whitechapel murders. My dreams were murky, and I woke around noon feeling no better rested than I had when I lay down.

I came out into the sitting room to find Crow deeply ensconced with scissors and paste in compiling his eccentric collection of press cuttings. He did not save *every* word printed about the Whitechapel murderer—which was just as well, or there would have been no room in the flat for us—but he chose and rejected articles based on no list of criteria that I could decipher. He said he kept only the "essentials," whatever exactly that meant.

"Doyle!" he said, and it was pleasant to have one creature in the world who was glad to see me, even if it was only because he wanted someone to listen to his theories about the Whitechapel murderer, of which he had several. It maddened him that no one at Scotland Yard would listen to him—"Even though," he said ruefully, "I should be used to it by now. They never listen to me until I'm proved right."

That seemed foolish, and I said so. "Why do they ask for your help if they don't listen to you?"

"Lestrade's better," said Crow. "He *does* listen, even if he frequently doesn't understand. So does Gregson, although most of the time you can't tell. It's detectives like Athelney Jones that I find insufferable. They act like I'm a dilettante, even though I've solved more cases than any of them."

I asked the question that had been plaguing me. "How long have you been doing this?"

Crow looked embarrassed, and his wings shivered and almost mantled. "I'm not entirely sure. I don't keep track of time very well, and the first part of my existence without a habitation—honestly, the memories are pretty patchy. Up until the police officers—in Whitechapel of all places—gave me a name. They said I hung around their crime scenes like a carrion crow. Once they started calling me Crow, things got a lot clearer."

"You kept that bit of your habitation," I said. "Why did you not keep your name?"

"You ask complicated questions," Crow said, not complaining. "I suppose the best answer is that having a name isn't tied to one's habitation. Or, at least, not in a strictly material sense. Keeping a piece of my habitation didn't actually keep me from becoming Nameless—my wings weren't always crow wings, you know—it just let me keep a sense of my self until I got a new name. And of course it meant I didn't have to become tied to a new habitation."

"Crow, are you saying you *cheated*?"

He looked even more embarrassed. "That's what most of the others say. But it isn't as if there are any actual rules, and I say as long as I don't Fall, it isn't anyone else's business what I do."

"That opinion must make you wildly popular," I said dryly and startled him into laughing.

"It definitely makes me abnormal," he said. "Even angels with names and habitations and dominions tend to stay half or more in what, for a lack of a better word, I call the hive-mind. Bees, you know. *They* call it the Consensus."

"The Consensus?"

"We can't travel, but we can communicate with each other. All the angels in London form a consensus. And where one angel's range is barely enough to reach the public house on the nearest corner, the Consensus can communicate with the Consensi of York and Birmingham and Edinburgh and Dublin and can even hop the Channel to the Consensus of Paris. And the Consensus of Paris can talk to the Consensi of Rome and Berlin and so on. That's why the angels of embassies and consulates are so greatly valued."

"Good God," I said. "But you're cut off from that?"

"They were angry at me for surviving something angels don't survive," he said. "I should have just embraced the Consensus—that's what they call it, when you become Nameless, that you embrace the Consensus. I call it dying, and that makes me *very* unpopular. Thus, I can go talk to any angel in London in person—although some of them refuse to talk to me at all—but I can't join the Consensus. They're afraid that I'm going to Fall suddenly and take the whole Consensus with me."

"Is that even possible?"

"I have no idea."

"Do you miss it?"

"Oh, yes," he said cheerfully. "But not enough to die for."

<>

AT FOUR WE returned to Madame Silvanova's. The neighborhood was transformed, shops opening and the pubs already doing raucous business. In the window of the flat above a tobacconist's, a red lamp told the sensation seekers and the addicts where to find the vampires.

Madame Silvanova's establishment was better lit than I would have expected, and the woman who came to meet us, brushing aside the strings of anti-possession wards hanging from the ceiling, was small, with a sharply angular face and gray-brown hair that suggested she was older than she looked. She wore a blue silk dress trimmed with lace. Not, then, an ordinary shopkeeper.

"I am Madame Silvanova," she said, her accent distinctly Russian. "How may I help you?"

Crow and I had discussed possible gambits, based on whether or not Madame Silvanova was a knowing accomplice to murder, but we did not get the chance to try any of them. As she looked us over and realized Crow was neither a man in an overcoat nor Nameless, her eyes got wider and wider, and she blurted out, "It is you!"

"I beg your pardon?" said Crow.

"The mirror showed me," said Madame Silvanova. "You come and then the police come and all is ruin. You must leave. At once."

Crow's wings spread wide, wall to wall in the tiny shop. "If you throw me out," he said, "I *will* bring the police. But if you help me, that might not be necessary."

She had gone back a step when he spread his wings (in fairness, so had I), and her face was filled with fear, even though she had to know as well as I did that no angel could harm a human being—unless she actually thought he was Fallen, in which case she was a fool, and a fool twice over for still standing here. But then she glanced over her shoulder toward the back room of the shop, and I realized it might not be Crow she feared.

Crow saw the glance, too, and said, "What did he tell you? Did he tell you about the murder, or only about the treasure?"

"*Murder?*" We had given the poor woman too many shocks in a row. She staggered, catching herself on the store counter, and I hastened to support her before her knees buckled. There was a chair behind the counter, and I guided her to sit in it.

She stared up at me. "Murder?" she repeated. "Who is dead? Whom did he kill?"

"A man named Bartholomew Sholto," said Crow.

Madame Silvanova frowned. "But I read about that in the papers. It couldn't have been Jonathan. It wasn't—"

"It was I," said a thin and heavily accented voice; we all stared at the person standing in the doorway to the back room.

For a moment, as my mind struggled to interpret what I saw, I thought I was looking at a child. He was no more than four and a half feet tall, but the face, dark-skinned, was an adult's, with bags under the eyes and lines of anxiety and unhappiness graven into the forehead. "I did not want to do it," he said, "but it was too late. There was no other way to stop Mr. Small."

"To stop him from what?" said Crow.

"From feeding," said Madame Silvanova. "Jonathan Small is a hemophage."

Crow and I stared at each other. "Well," Crow said at last, "I suppose that explains how a wooden-legged man could be so agile. But why did you not kill *him*?"

"I am bound by oath to Mr. Small," said the little man. "And if he were dead, what would become of me? They would throw me in prison as a murderer or exhibit me in a circus like the Wild Men of Borneo. Mr. Small is my only hope of going home."

"Where is home?" I said, although I thought I knew.

"The Andaman Islands. Mr. Small saved my life and thus I serve him, but he promised he will see that I get safely home again."

"Jonathan Small seems to be a dab hand at keeping a promise," I said to Crow. "He's been in England at least six years."

"Six years and eight months," said the little man, and offered a shy, lopsided smile. "I keep count."

"We're going about this all backward," Crow said. "My name is Crow, and I am the Angel of London. This is Dr. Doyle. Madame Silvanova we have met"—with a little bow to the lady—"and your name is?"

"Mr. Small says it is unpronounceable. He calls me Tonga."

"I think I should like to know your *real* name," Crow said, frowning.

The little man rattled off a string of syllables, of which the only part I could catch did sound something like "tonga." He smiled at our expressions and said, "I have had many names. Perhaps you will call me Anuvadaka? It means 'translator,' which was my job."

"You were a translator at Port Blair?" I said.

"At Kala Pani, yes. That was why Mr. Small spared my life."

"*Spared* your life?" said Crow. "Not saved it?"

"With a hemophage," Anuvadaka said dryly, "they are much the same thing."

"But how did you come to be a translator?" I asked.

"The British soldiers found me wandering in the jungle, feverish and dying. They brought me back to the prison, where the doctor— his name was Somerton and he was a good man—cured me. But I was dead to my people, who would never accept me back once I had been among the outsiders, therefore I stayed as Dr. Somerton's servant and learned English. When the doctor died of one of the pestilential fevers that sweep through the Andamans, I stayed as a translator, for by then I had learned Punjabi as well, and there was always need for someone who could speak both the language of the overseers and the language of the prisoners. I knew who Mr. Small was, for there were very few English prisoners, and especially not Englishmen imprisoned for killing an Indian man—but then, he and Dost Akbar had killed the man by feeding on him, which I have noticed the British find particularly loathsome."

"Were all four of them—Jonathan Small, Dost Akbar, Mahomet Singh, and Abdullah Khan—hemophages?" asked Crow.

"No, though all four had encountered the Fallen of Agra, who raged in the surrounding countryside and howled for the angels of Agra to come out and fight. I am told that this Fallen was insane."

"Some of them are," I said.

"They go mad with grief," said Crow. "I think perhaps all the Fallen are insane—it's just that some of them stay rational, such as the Fallen of Afghanistan who fight with the partisans. They can make treaties. But they are still irrationally bent on destruction and revenge. Doyle, do you know if any Fallen ever offered a treaty to the British?"

"Not to my knowledge," I said. "It would have been refused."

"Yes, of course," Crow said. "Making treaties with the Fallen is something only the enemy does."

"The I.A.F. does have at least a principle or two," I said. "But no one could have made a treaty with the Fallen of Agra. From everything I have heard, she was truly insane."

"At their trial," said Anuvadaka, "the defense lawyer argued that the *metaphysicum morbi* had driven all four of them insane and that that was why they murdered the man Achmet. But it was really the treasure."

"Do you know the story of the treasure?" Crow asked eagerly.

"I know what Mr. Small has told me," said Anuvadaka. "I do not know how much of it is true. He says that he was guarding one of the gates of the fort when Singh and Khan ambushed him and told him he had the choice of joining them in betrayal, robbery, and murder, or being killed on the spot. He says he made them swear that they meant no harm to the fort and the people inside it before he would agree, but then he joined them, swearing an oath that bound the four of them together. So far as I can tell, that part is true. He is doing his best to keep faith with Dost Akbar, Abdullah Khan, and Mahomet Singh."

"Are they in England?" I asked.

"No. Only Mr. Small escaped Kala Pani, taking me with him. He plans to take the treasure back to India and find a guard he can bribe to let them escape. He says that part will not be hard, and perhaps he is right."

There was a commotion in the street. Crow turned to look and said, "Oh no, it's Jones! And at least three officers. How on Earth did . . . where is Small?"

"He went out," said Anuvadaka, whose dark face was going a terrible gray color as the blood drained from it. "To secure the use of a steam launch to take us to where the boat for India waits. But—"

Crow backed up to the door, his wings spreading and becoming jammed in the doorway just as a voice outside said, "Police!"

"Quick!" Crow mouthed at me. "Get him out the window!"

We were obstructing justice, then. But I did not want to see Anuvadaka arrested and Small left to go free. Madame Silvanova had already opened one of the small side windows, and she and I boosted Anuvadaka up to it. He was very light, and I saw his toes were splayed and strong.

"221 Baker Street," I hissed as he wriggled out the window, reaching for a hold on the bricks. "Tell them Crow said to let you in." Then he was gone, and I turned back to where Crow had somehow gotten one wing half out the door and seemed to be genuinely stuck. There was a fair amount of cursing from the officers on the other side.

I counted to ten. Madame Silvanova closed the window, and I said, "All right," softly, knowing that Crow could hear me and the officers couldn't.

Crow floundered and flailed. He really *was* stuck. It ended up taking me and Madame Silvanova on one side, and Jones on the other, to work him safely back into the shop.

"You startled me," he said fussily to Jones as he tried to smooth his feathers back into order. "There was no need for that."

Jones looked bemused, aggravated, and suspicious all at once. "What are you doing here?"

"We tracked the murderers to this corner, where they seemed to disappear," Crow said truthfully, and I picked up quickly: "We were canvassing the shopkeepers to see if they had noticed anything unusual."

Madame Silvanova recognized her cue and came forward. "I am Madame Silvanova," she said, and if not exactly gracious, she managed to sound not hostile. "I was telling these . . . gentlemen that I saw nothing that could help them."

Jones looked even more deeply suspicious. "D'you mind if we look around, miss? We have reliable information that Bartholomew Sholto's murderer is in your shop."

"*Bozhe moi,*" said Madame Silvanova. "Yes, by all means! I wish to have no murderers here."

"I thought you were reliably informed the murderer was Thaddeus Sholto," Crow said.

"He proved an alibi," Jones said disgustedly, gesturing to his officers to search the building. "I admit we were at a bit of a dead end when that wooden-legged fellow came in and said he knew where the murderer was hiding."

"Wooden-legged, eh?" said Crow. "Did he say *how* he knew?"

"I don't..." Jones looked perplexed. "Forbes! Where's that wooden-legged fellow?"

"He was right..." Forbes went to the door and leaned out, looking left and right down the street. "He's gone!"

"Shocking," I said to Crow, and he gave me a quick flash of a smile in return. We both pretended not to hear what Athelney Jones was muttering under his breath.

Another constable came down the stairs—I could hear his regulation boots clearly—and back out into the shop. "There's no one here, sir."

"If you'd let me last night," Crow said to Jones, "I could have told you you were looking for a wooden-legged man."

Jones's already red face became uniformly brick-colored. He said, "Yes, and I see that somehow you got here before us. Tread carefully, Mr. Crow, for you may not be able to commit murder but you have a friend who can. Mr. Gregson told me all about the Jefferson Hope case."

Crow's wings mantled, and his scowl was thunderous. "Are you insinuating—"

"Oh for God's sake go home!" Jones interrupted. "Go home and be glad I'm not *insinuating* anything."

"Thank you very much for your help," I said hastily to Madame Silvanova, caught Crow by the elbow, and would have dragged him out of the shop, except that we had to be careful negotiating the door.

We were a block and a half away before Crow started giggling. "Thank goodness!" he said. "I was afraid Jones wouldn't take the bait."

"You were *trying* to get him to throw us out?"

"Well, if he'd actually questioned me, we'd have been in an ugly fix. But I knew he didn't want us there more than he wanted to find out what we knew, therefore I provoked him and gambled. Also, I *did* try to tell him last night. And he said I needed to stop constructing castle-in-the-air theories and let real policemen do real police work. So . . ." He gave me a half-conspiratorial, half-guilty smile. "I do hold grudges, even though I know I shouldn't."

"I'll bear that in mind," I said, and he laughed.

—◆—

WHEN WE GOT back to the flat, we found Anuvadaka huddled miserably in front of the fire with my mouse-colored dressing gown—which I'd carelessly left draped over one of the armchairs— wrapped around himself like a blanket.

He stood up as we came in, and said, "I beg your pardon. I did not dare attempt the front door. I came in from the roof."

"Understandable," said Crow. "For the future, we'd best buy a lock for the trapdoor."

"Did you have any trouble evading the police?" I said.

"No," said Anuvadaka. "Like almost all your people, police officers don't often look up. And I have learned to navigate London in the five years we have stayed here. It is not so different from the jungle in its own way."

Crow said gently, "Small betrayed you."

Anuvadaka sighed and said, "I admit that I am not entirely surprised. He made no secret of the fact that his three friends—and the Agra treasure—came first with him. And he was very angry with me for killing Bartholomew Sholto."

"I still don't quite understand the sequence of events," said Crow. "I had thought Sholto must have been dead before Small made it into the room."

Anuvadaka shook his head. "He was not . . . killing him was no part of the plan. Mr. Small thought he wouldn't even be in the room.

I came down into the room through the hole in the plaster. He was frightened enough of me that he did not fight, which is ridiculous, really. He was a foot taller and could easily have overpowered me. But I yelled nonsense at him in my own language, and he didn't even protest. Then I threw down the rope to Mr. Small." He stopped and shivered, this time not from cold.

"What triggered him?" I asked.

"The treasure," said Anuvadaka. "He was so excited to recover it at last, and so angry at Major Sholto for stealing it . . . I saw his fangs come down and I did the only thing I could." From a pocket inside the waistband of his trousers, he produced a blowpipe and what was obviously a handmade pouch to keep the thorn-darts accessible but not able to prick anyone, including their wielder. "I was almost too late as it was. If he had bitten Mr. Sholto, he would have savaged everyone in the house. Perhaps I did the wrong thing, but I had sworn an oath to him, and at that point, he had not broken his promise to me. Thus I spared his life as he had spared mine. He showed his gratitude by beating me for it."

"Is your oath still binding?" Crow asked cautiously.

"He betrayed me," Anuvadaka said. "You cannot keep faith with the faithless."

"Then will you help us find him?"

"I must, mustn't I?" said Anuvadaka with another of his lopsided, half-sad smiles. "Since it is my fault that he is still out there to be found."

◆

ANUVADAKA EXPLAINED TO us the rest of Jonathan Small's scheme. He had hidden the treasure somewhere Anuvadaka did not know, and when he had left Madame Silvanova's he had said he was going to hire a steam launch, which was the next part of the plan: a steam launch to take them down the river to where a boat was supposed to be waiting for them. But now that he had diverged so spectacularly from that plan, it was a matter of guessing what he might do next.

"He will be doing everything in his power to get the treasure back to India," Anuvadaka said. "It is the goal for which he lives. He hated to leave India without his friends; he railed and raged all the way to England. Thus his first thought will be to return and effect their escape."

"If not by boat, he can leave England only to go to Scotland," said Crow, "therefore his plan must still rely on a boat, and he cannot expect to pass unnoticed—a wooden-legged man with a heavy box."

"It is a remarkable box, of Benares work," said Anuvadaka. "Anyone who got a good look at it would remember it."

"Does he have other friends in London?" I asked Anuvadaka. "How did he find Madame Silvanova in the first place?"

"Her brother is an unregistered necrophage," said Anuvadaka. "The unregistered in London stick together and help each other as best they can. She and Grigori are the only people we know in Southwark. Madame Silvanova was not happy to see us, but she agreed to let us hide above her shop—and you were right. He didn't tell her about Bartholomew Sholto's death."

"Perhaps what we need," I said, "is to talk to Madame Silvanova again."

"That's not a bad idea, Doyle," said Crow. "And let's see if she will come to us—a Nameless can run that errand, and I will ask her for tomorrow morning, not now when her business is best. She might be more talkative off her home turf. I will return directly."

I tidied away the map Crow had been staring at—he had a prodigious number of them, though none of London—and told myself not to think about Miss Morstan's blue eyes. If she received even a portion of the treasure, she would be a wealthy woman, and even if not, she was still well above my touch. But I admit my heart beat faster for more reasons than one when I heard Crow's voice in the stairwell: "Yes, of course, Miss Morstan. Just let me go see if Dr. Doyle is inclined for visitors."

Anuvadaka stared at me in mingled inquiry and panic; I pointed him into my bedroom and closed the door just as Crow came in. He glanced around, nodded approvingly at the absence of Andaman Islanders, and said, "So how *do* you feel about visitors?"

"Resigned," I said.

Miss Morstan was once again wearing a dress that combined elegance of design with simplicity of manufacture and material. She had most likely sewn it herself; certainly the embroidery of morning glories at the cuffs was her work and showed a resolute pride that I admired. And whether she or another had chosen the cloth, they had chosen well. The blue matched and accentuated the blue of her eyes, elevating her from "unremarkable" to "striking." She smiled when she saw me, and I smiled back even as I was thinking, *That is her best dress. She wore her best dress because she knew she would see you. You have to end this.*

But I could not do so now, not with Crow in the room and Anuvadaka in the bedroom and a treasure at stake. I held my tongue and some reprehensible part of me basked in the knowledge that she had worn her best dress on my behalf.

Crow described our adventures and conclusions to her; I listened carefully, but he managed to skirt the fact that there was a murderer in my bedroom all on his own.

And Miss Morstan did not catch him. She said, "I don't want you to be in trouble with the police!"

"We aren't," Crow said. "I've had go-rounds like this before with Jones. He won't stay angry—it is one of his few redeeming features."

Miss Morstan laughed. "What about the wooden-legged man? I don't care about the treasure, but he seems like a most undesirable person."

"He does, doesn't he?" said Crow. "We are working on that problem, and I hope to have news of him very soon."

"Really," Miss Morstan said, looking uncomfortable, "you shouldn't be looking for him on *my* account. I don't entirely know how I shall pay you as it is. I should have inquired about your fees before I engaged your services, but I am shockingly bad at business."

"You may pay us out of your share of the treasure," I suggested.

"And I can hardly charge you for something I would be doing anyway," said Crow, who was also shockingly bad at business.

"You are very kind," Miss Morstan said, although she still looked uncomfortable.

"Nothing of the sort," Crow said. "I am *intrigued*. But truly, Miss Morstan. The job you hired us for is complete. You have safely met your unknown friend, and as a bonus you have discovered the truth about your father's death. You are naturally interested in the sequelae, but it is certainly no fault of yours that we have been chasing a wooden-legged man all over London."

"But the treasure," said Miss Morstan. A lesser woman might have been wringing her hands.

"A happy coincidence," Crow said airily.

"You are *very* kind," she said. "I must go. Mrs. Cecil Forrester was generous enough to let me borrow her carriage, but I promised to do a number of errands. But perhaps, Dr. Doyle, you will come and tell me how the adventure turns out?"

It would be an opportunity to speak to her alone, which I now saw I must do. "Of course," I said. Her smile was shy and hopeful; I felt ill.

When she was gone, Anuvadaka came out of my bedroom and said, "What is to become of me now?"

"What do you mean?" said Crow.

"I am a murderer," said Anuvadaka. "Surely you cannot mean to allow me to go free."

"I think a good defense lawyer could win an acquittal," Crow said. "The laws surrounding oaths are complicated."

"Yes," I said, "but *we* don't have the right to make that decision."

Crow frowned at me. "Are you saying you want to hand him over to the police?"

"I don't *want* to do any such thing. But—forgive me, Anuvadaka—we are obstructing justice by hiding him."

"I would say we are *enabling* justice," said Crow. "You know Jones would forget all about Jonathan Small the instant he arrested Anuvadaka."

"Small did not murder Sholto," I said.

"He stole the treasure," Crow said. "And he would have done worse than murder if Anuvadaka had not stopped him. You must have seen what's left after a hemophage has gone berserk."

"Yes," I said, because I had, and the memory was not a pleasant one. "But that is still not the point. What Small would have done is a hypothetical. The *fact* is that Anuvadaka killed Bartholomew Sholto, and we do not have the right to decide he should go free."

"Where in London are you going to find a jury of his peers?" Crow said scornfully.

"Still not the point," I said through my teeth.

"Then what?" Crow demanded, his wings flaring. "You want to send a telegram to Athelney Jones and tell him to come arrest him?"

"Do you propose to send him back out among the rooftops of London? Or do you plan to keep him as a pet?"

"Well, I'm not going to hand him over to Athelney Jones," Crow snarled.

"And what will you do when they arrest Small and he tells them— truthfully—that they've got the wrong man? What will you tell Jones then?"

"How can you be so heartless?" Crow said, angry and—what was much worse—hurt. "Or does no one other than Miss Morstan matter to you?"

Although it took a Herculean effort, I did not say any of the things I wanted to. Instead, I said, "My feelings for Miss Morstan have nothing to do with the matter. It is a matter of ethics."

"Yes, it most certainly is!" Crow said. "But you've confused ethics with legality."

"And you've confused your liking for the suspect with an ethical principle." I was still hovering on the brink of saying something unforgivable. I grabbed my cane, stood up, and said, "I'm going out."

"You can't just leave in the middle of an argument!" Crow protested.

"We aren't arguing," I said. "We're fighting. And I am going out." I slammed the door behind me and hoped it rattled the china.

16

The Social Club of the Hemophages

I RETURNED MUCH later and, truthfully, in no better mood, to find Anuvadaka asleep on the sofa and Crow amidst his press cuttings. He started up when he saw me. "Doyle—"

"Not now, Crow," I said. "I'm going to bed." I went into my room, locked the door, and had no sooner finished undressing than I turned into a hell-hound.

Being awake for the transition, I discovered for the second time, did not make it better, and even if I had been prepared to fight it, I don't think I would have been successful. Werewolves are taught from an early age not to lose their temper unless they do so with intent.

I wormed out of my unbuttoned pajama jacket and groaned in dissatisfaction. There was an angel outside the door, and the room was too small to pace properly. Sullenly, I dragged all the covers off the bed and made a nest in the closet. It was going to be a long night.

I did sleep eventually, although "sleep" for a hell-hound is a strange state. I myself did not dream, but I was intensely aware of Anuvadaka in the next room, dreaming of the jungle and home. I was aware of Crow, too, like a bright and steady lamp in the night, and stayed away from him.

Downstairs, I found Jennie dreaming about burned scones and the cook dreaming about searching for her dead mother's umbrella. Mrs. Climpson was dreaming about standing at the top of Victoria's Needle, watching for the Spanish Armada, while the Queen, who was Elizabeth or Victoria or both, called up to her like the girl in the fairy tale, "What do you see?"

At dawn, I became human again and dragged the bed covers back to the bed for a couple of hours of real sleep.

When I came out of my room at eight o'clock, feeling only marginally refreshed, Crow was alone in the sitting room. "Anuvadaka went up to the attic," he said, pulling the bell to let Jennie know it was time to make tea. "So that we could have Jennie and Mrs. Climpson stomping in and out."

I muttered something that might have been "Good morning," and settled in at the table with the armor of *The Times*.

Crow waited until I had tea and toast and had fended off offers of kippers and oatmeal and eggs, until he could be sure Jennie wasn't going to come in again, before he said, "Doyle, are you still mad at me?"

"Yes," I said, because all the folktales say you should not lie to an angel. And because I was still mad.

"If . . ." He broke off. I was halfway down the casualty lists when he blurted, "If you have sexual congress with me, will you stop being mad?"

Tea went everywhere. If I'd had a mouthful of toast, I probably would have choked to death. As it was, I wheezed and gasped and finally said, "*WHAT?*"

"I don't want you to be mad at me," Crow explained unhappily. "I thought maybe—"

"That is not what sexual congress is for!"

"It isn't?"

"No! Who gave you that horrible idea?"

"It doesn't matter," he said, his wings curving around him protectively.

I had never been so keenly aware of how little I knew about his past. "Well, whoever it was, they were wrong. Good God."

"Oh," he said. "Oh dear."

"Did you . . . did someone . . ." I couldn't even formulate the question.

"It was a long time ago," he said defensively. "And it wasn't— Oh thank goodness, there's someone at the door."

He strode out to the landing to shout, "Come up!" probably before Jennie even had the chance to ask the caller's business. He came back ushering Madame Silvanova. In daylight, she was older than she had looked in her shop, with crow's-feet starting and lines of worry and aggravation marking her face. But her grace was undiminished, and she did not seem at all annoyed to be answering our summons.

Crow asked, tactless as ever: "Is your name really Silvanova?"

She laughed and said, "No. Silvanova I made up for the punters. My name is Oksana Timofeyevna, and forgive me, but I will not burden you with my real surname. Silvanova will do. One cannot be too careful, you understand."

"Anuvadaka said your brother is unregistered," Crow said.

She scowled. "Anuvadaka should hold his tongue. But, yes, since you already know, my brother Grigori is an unregistered necrophage. We left Russia one step ahead of the Tsar's hounds, and it is well known that the British Registry is shared with other governments. Besides, if Grigori registered, they would never let him continue to work as a sexton."

"Are the Tsar's agents still pursuing you?" I asked. "It seems a great deal of bother."

"For one common necrophage?" Madame Silvanova smiled bitterly. "But my brother is not a common necrophage. He was the youngest colonel in the Russian Army."

". . . Oh dear," said Crow.

"Since he is considered to have disgraced the Tsar by becoming a necrophage," Madame Silvanova continued, "they will never *stop* hunting him. At this point it would be quite a feather in the cap of the person who found him. We have lived in London for seven years."

"Were you always a diviner?" I said.

"I was trained at the Imperial Academy of Augury," she said, with old but still strong pride. "It is not suitable, of course, for a woman to hold an Imperial appointment, but I was allowed to act as my father's augur."

Meaning her father was a landowner. "It must have been quite a wrench to leave," I said.

She shrugged elegantly. "Grigori is my brother."

"Madame Silvanova," Crow said, "we need your help."

She immediately grew wary. "What kind of help?"

"We need to find Jonathan Small."

"He has not returned to my shop," she said.

"We didn't imagine he would," I said. "But you might have information that could help us."

Crow was watching her intently. "The treasure that Major Sholto stole from him, Small stole from another man, whom he murdered. He is not an honorable man. He betrayed you as surely as he did Anuvadaka when he went to the police."

"Worse than that," said Madame Silvanova, "he must have used one of my charms on them."

"How so?" Crow asked.

"All those police officers, and they didn't ask his name? Or how he came by his knowledge?" She shook her head. "I make a charm I was taught by a hedge witch in Danzig—not of invisibility, but a sort of . . . inconspicuousness. People forget you're in the room. They don't ask you questions when they should. I give them freely to the unregistered, but I didn't give one to Jonathan Small. He must have stolen it. If the policemen realize what happened, I will be fined for practicing unlicensed witchcraft, and that is attention I do not need. But I do not know that having Jonathan Small caught will help me. Or Grigori. There will be nothing to prevent him telling the police all he knows about the unregistered in London. And they will be *very* interested."

That was unanswerable, because she was entirely correct. And we could hardly make the argument from morality or ethics when we were currently harboring Bartholomew Sholto's murderer in our attic.

"He is a murderer and a hemophage," Crow said. "He was prevented from going on a rampage two nights ago. But you know that means he's more likely to go on a rampage now."

She did know; her frown deepened and she bit her lip.

"Do you want those deaths on your conscience?" Crow continued, playing the morality card regardless. "We can't stop him if we can't find him. And right now we can't find him. Not without your help."

"But I know nothing useful," Madame Silvanova protested.

"Then you harm no one by telling us," Crow said. "I promise we will not share any information you give us about the unregistered with the police."

She looked at me, immediately spotting the loophole. "I promise," I said and felt the spark of the oath binding.

"I am a fool," said Madame Silvanova, "but very well. I will tell you what I know and you may make of it what you will."

Her story matched Anuvadaka's, with the addition of a considerable exchange of gossip. She said, perhaps a shade defensively, "I don't know why women have the reputation for gossip when in my experience men are just as bad. Small certainly was. He was particularly interested in other unregistered hemophages."

"Did he say why?" I said uneasily.

"I did not ask him," she said. "I tried to engage him in conversation as little as possible. He was . . ." Her shoulders lifted, past a shrug, not quite into a hunch. ". . . encroaching."

"Did he proposition you?"

"Not in so many words," she said. "But he made it very clear what he wanted, and he seemed completely unable to grasp the idea that I was not interested. He was *vulgar*." It was clearly the worst insult she could think of, for she said it with utmost loathing.

Crow said slowly, carefully, "Is there a nest of hemophages in Southwark?"

He was right to be careful; it might not be illegal to be a hemophage, but it was definitely illegal to be a member of a nest. Hemophages in groups were far more likely to rampage. . . . And Small was already primed. Combining him and a nest was going to result in something very ugly.

She knew it, too. She said, "They would not," but then stopped. She knew—as I knew—that they *would*. She made a gesture expressive of defeat and said, "There is a nest near Waterloo Station. They call it a social club—I believe they even collect dues—but it is a nest. I know he knows of it, for he asked me about it: what was the address, how many members were there, and so on. He asked me just as many questions about the rumors of a hell-hound pack in Shoreditch—which are *not* true—so that I thought nothing of it."

"At the time it may only have been idle curiosity," Crow said. "I doubt he intended to go anywhere near them before he hit on his new plan. But if I were a hemophage in need of a bolt-hole, a nest is where I'd go."

"More than that," I said. "Hemophages are drawn to each other's company just as . . . as hell-hounds are." I almost managed the word without stumbling and could only pray Madame Silvanova did not notice. "Especially once he'd been triggered without being able to feed, he would be desperate to find others of his kind."

"I will take you," said Madame Silvanova. "And may God forgive us all if it is the wrong decision."

◆

THE SOCIAL CLUB of the hemophages was in a run-down warehouse, apparently derelict except for their comings and goings. "They are mostly here at night," said Madame Silvanova. "Few of the unregistered are as lucky as Grigori, to have a job that suits their needs and their hours so well."

"And their hungers," I said dryly.

She shot me a knowing look. "No unregistered has a job that suits their hungers, Doctor, a fact you know as well as I do."

She had noticed something. I could only hope that she assumed I was like her, the sibling—or parent or spouse—of an unregistered, not that I was unregistered myself. I said, "True enough, madame."

Crow had stayed at Baker Street; people as habitually, necessarily suspicious as unregistered hemophages would not wait for explanations about his not being Fallen—they would flee as soon as they saw him. I went with Madame Silvanova to the warehouse door, where she knocked briskly and called, "Ludwig, I know you are here!"

There was a long silence. She knocked again, harder, and finally the door opened a crack. "Who is your companion, Miss Silvanova?"

It was an obvious watchman, an elderly man who peered around the door at me like a suspicious rabbit.

"This is Dr. Doyle," said Madame Silvanova. "He is a friend."

The old man looked dubious, but did not demand that I present my bona fides on the spot. He said, "What brings you here, then?"

"We are looking for someone," Madame Silvanova said. "A man named Jonathan Small. Has he been here?"

The old man was no poker player. We both knew the answer before he opened his mouth to lie. "I do not know the name."

"You'd know him by sight," I said. "A man with a wooden leg."

"No, sir," said the old man, who might as well have been wearing a sign: *LIAR*. "I do not remember anyone of that sort."

"He is a bad man, Ludwig," said Madame Silvanova. "He will bring the police down on you."

The old man spat at the mention of the police, a petty warding that didn't do a damned thing, and said, "But I told you, Miss Silvanova. I do not know this man."

"Ludwig," Madame Silvanova said. "I know that is a lie, just as you do."

The old man hesitated a moment, then said, "I suppose you must come in." He swung the door wide; I gestured for Madame Silvanova to precede me.

As I was following her inside, I realized first how very dark it was, and then that I had no idea where the old man was, and then, like the solution to a theorem, what was about to happen.

I turned just in time to catch my stick in the closing door. The impact jarred up into my hand; I heard Ludwig hiss, and, grabbing the door to swing it open again, I said to Madame Silvanova, *"Run."*

She had fast reflexes, eluding the hands of two hemophages who emerged suddenly from the darkness, and she hauled up her fashionable skirts and ran like a deer, graceful and fast. They weren't fools enough to pursue her.

"You may regret that, Dr. Doyle," said the old man, and a third hemophage, all staring white face and gruesome teeth, caught me across the side of the head with something that felt like the Tower of London but was probably only a length of board.

I was not knocked fully unconscious, although I fell hard to the floor and lost my grip on my cane. I heard them arguing in half-grumbling whispers about what to do next, and then two of them picked me up—carrying me between them like a drunk—and followed the old man down what seemed interminable flights of stairs, into basements and subbasements, and finally through an awkward iron hatch, where the brutes dropped me, which made them laugh, and into a long, brick-lined tunnel.

"We'll take him to the hole," the old man said. "He'll keep there until we decide what to do with him."

That sounded bad, but I did not have enough control of my limbs to struggle effectively, and even if I had somehow succeeded in getting free from them, I did not have my cane and would be as easy to recapture as a newborn kitten. They hauled me briskly along, not caring when my bad leg hit something and I yelped, until they came to a sort of side tunnel, where the old man unlocked an iron grille and they half threw, half shoved me in. The grille clanged shut behind me.

There was a trickle of light coming from somewhere, and for a long time that was all I was aware of, as my head swam and pounded and I struggled neither to lose consciousness entirely nor to vomit. But gradually, as things inside my head began to calm, I saw that across from me, that strange trickle of light was picking out the line of a nose, a cheekbone . . . a man with a long nose and a sharp widow's peak, watching me intently with eyes that proved he was no hemophage, for they were the lambent, narrow-pupiled gold that the addict-poets have been singing about for centuries.

I had been imprisoned with a vampire.

17

THE
VAMPIRE

THE REALIZATION ACTED as a face-full of cold water. I was abruptly alert and if not terrified, definitely alarmed. I sat up much too quickly and had to shut my eyes against the consequent surge of nausea.

The vampire said, in a rich Irish voice, "You need not be frightened. I have neither the intention nor the ability to harm you."

The nausea abated somewhat, and I was able to open my eyes again. The vampire had moved farther into the light and extended his hands so that I could see the silver manacles on his wrists.

"They're keeping you captive?" I croaked.

The vampire said, both embarrassed and annoyed, "They caught me with my guard down."

"But why would anyone do such a suicidal thing?" I said.

It made the vampire smile, a careful, Mona Lisa–esque smile that did not show the teeth. "They wish to negotiate with my hunt."

"They've picked a phenomenally stupid way to go about it."

"They seem to feel the risk is worth it in order to get our attention." He paused a moment and added, "They have not harmed me, other than the insult of silver. And those cold iron bars."

"Well, I suppose that's something," I said.

"They assure me they will release me unharmed when they have completed their negotiations." This smile had an ironic curl.

"But what are they negotiating *for*?"

"That part seemed a bit confused, but in essence they want their nest to be recognized as a vampiric hunt."

"It's no such thing."

"No, it isn't. But they seem to think we can make them that which they are not, and then they will be protected from your laws."

And the peace the government had with the vampiric hunts was delicate enough that that part would probably work. But the premise was hopelessly flawed. The vampires could no more make a nest of hemophages into a vampiric hunt than a flock of peacocks could make a mouse into a bird. And they were unlikely to endorse the legal fiction, for they needed the delicate peace as much as did the government.

"How long have they had you here?"

"A couple of days. Nothing to signify, really."

Vampires can go for weeks without feeding, but they do not like to. Hence their red lamps and courteous ways. A true, deeply enthralled addict will let his or her vampiric Master feed daily if asked to—although vampires, wise and old and cold-blooded, and with a large population of addicts to choose from, generally do not do so.

"Introductions!" the vampire said briskly. "My name is Moriarty."

"Doyle," I said and, having observed the vampire's long, curved nails, did not offer to shake hands.

The nausea was almost gone; I asked, "Who has the keys to the grille?"

"There are two keys," Moriarty said, "and I think not more. Meier—the old man—has one, and the other is held by the hemophages' leader, a man named Overton."

"Bother." I touched the side of my head gingerly, finding the mess of bruising and sticky blood I had expected.

"And how did *you* come here, Dr. Doyle?" said Moriarty, adding, "I heard them call you 'Doctor' as they brought you down the stairs. But you are no hemophage. You have not their smell."

"I must smell like a hell-hound, then," I said sourly.

"Yes," said Moriarty. "But not, as I would have expected, in league with my—*our*—captors."

"I came here looking for a hemophage named Jonathan Small—a man with a wooden leg. Have you seen him?"

"Oh, yes," said Moriarty. "He and Overton came and threatened me last night."

"*Threatened* you?"

"Apparently, Mr. Small has fed on vampires before and has a taste for us. They want me to write a letter to my hunt telling them to negotiate. I told them that even if I did, it would not help them in the slightest, but they did not believe me. They promised me they would return; therefore, you will get to see Mr. Small yourself. Why are you hunting him?"

It could do no harm that I could see to tell him, and I rather badly needed his goodwill, since even chained with silver he was probably strong enough to overpower me. I told him the story, starting with Miss Morstan and ending with Ludwig Meier. Moriarty listened intently, golden eyes—the eyes of a beast in a man's ascetic face—fixed on me. He said when I had finished, "Mr. Small is a man of many surprises. I don't believe he has told his new friends about his treasure. I do not know that that can be used to our advantage, but it *might*."

"If Overton is greedy enough," I said.

"Greed seems to follow this treasure," said Moriarty. "And Overton is a venal man. I cannot believe that he would not want his share."

"It seems to be the only weapon we have," I agreed. "How do those manacles fasten?"

"They're rather ingenious," said Moriarty, as one reluctantly giving credit where credit was due. "They screw together, you see, but without a screwdriver with the correctly shaped head, they cannot be unfastened."

"They must have been very expensive to make," I said, examining the bulky lock that held the manacles stacked together like a hinge. The screw had an odd, irregular star-shaped head—not the sort of thing one could improvise.

"I would imagine so," said Moriarty, "although you will understand that I did not inquire. They held me down with an iron bar across my throat to fasten them, and I was not in the mood for conversation."

"I wouldn't have been, either. But it's all the more reason Overton might be interested in the Agra treasure."

"True," said Moriarty. He sighed as he tried to ease his arms into a new position. "Monstrously expensive they may be, but I must admit I find them tedious."

"Do they hurt?" I said.

"Not exactly. Not like iron, which burns. But silver makes my bones ache and it drains my strength. Like the influenza, if my friends have described it to me accurately."

"It does sound similar," I said.

It is not really possible to make small talk with a vampire, but we discussed the Whitechapel murders, about which he was nearly as well informed as I was, for he had been following the case avidly in the newspapers. He denied vehemently that it could be the work of a vampire. "The waste of all that blood? Even a starving vampire would never cut someone's throat back to the bone and sever all the major vessels in one go. And even if you imagine a vampire that insane, it would end up *covered* in blood—mouth, face, hands, everything—because it would never be able to resist feeding, and I think someone drenched literally head to foot in blood would have been memorable even to the people of Whitechapel."

"What about a hemophage?"

"Well, it's *more* like something a hemophage would do—all that needless carnage—but they don't usually leave their prey where they kill them. Some hemophages have traveled considerable distances to hide their kills. This doesn't really fit a hemophage's pattern, either.

I think it's an ordinary human being." And he smiled, this time showing his teeth.

I did not shrink back, but it was a near thing. Vampires' teeth are not as horrible as hemophages'—few things are as horrible as a hemophage's teeth—but they are no pretty sight.

"It's only the *Star* that's really pushing the 'insane vampire' idea," I said, "and they only like it because of the headlines."

At this point in our conversation, which had taken place intermittently over several hours and had meandered a good deal as the throbbing in my head waxed and waned, Moriarty said, "Someone's coming," and we both fell silent.

After a few minutes, I could hear them, too, thanks to the acoustical properties of the staircases. Among the dull thumping, the sharp *tock* of a wooden leg end was plainly audible.

I glanced at Moriarty, who nodded, a quick jerk of the head. "Small," said he.

Listening to Small's slow approach was far worse than if he had simply appeared in front of the grille like the Devil in a pantomime. Moriarty and I did not attempt to resume our conversation; we were both listening too intently to the irregular *tock* of Jonathan Small's wooden leg.

Voices became audible, too, although I could not distinguish words until they started down the tunnel toward us.

". . . be trouble, no doubt, but she'll have no luck getting the police to believe her. Not in this district." A round of laughter which meant either that the police in Lambeth were very stupid or that they'd been bought.

"Still," said a deep, scratchy voice that I knew immediately was Small, "hadn't we better take some precautions?"

"What do you mean?" said the first voice.

"More guards on the door," said Small. "Meier got lucky that there were people here to help him."

"Meier panicked," said the first voice. "There's nothing here to connect us to you. He could have led the doctor and the girl all over the damned place and they would have found nothing. As it is, now we have another prisoner to deal with."

"There's one easy way to deal with prisoners," Small said, and they all laughed again. I disliked the sound of their laughter; they sounded intoxicated, although not with alcohol. They had something—or they *thought* they had something—that would let them negotiate with a vampiric hunt. They were drunk on a feeling of invincibility. And that did not bode well for their prisoners.

There were four of them: a tall man who had the fussy look of a schoolmaster; two shorter men, one stocky, one slim, who looked indistinguishable from the thousands of clerks who flooded the City every day; and Jonathan Small, a broad-shouldered, bulky man with a grizzled beard and a fanatic's eyes.

"You must be Dr. Doyle," he said. "I hear you've been asking questions about me."

"Yes, Mr. Small," I said. "Where *is* the Agra treasure?"

It was a gamble and a foolish one, for if Small had already told the other hemophages of the treasure, I would achieve nothing but making all of them angry, but it paid off immediately, for the stocky man said, "Treasure?"

"He must have told you he's evading the police," I said. "The treasure is why."

"Shut up!" said Jonathan Small, realizing the apple of discord I had thrown at him, but it was already working, as it had done throughout its existence.

"You didn't mention a treasure," the schoolmaster said.

"You said you could never repay us for our help," said the stocky one. "It sounds as if perhaps you can."

"The treasure is nothing to do with you!" said Small. "It belongs to me and my friends and us alone. We murdered for it and served years in Kala Pani for it and no one else has any right to it. No one!" As he spoke and his fury grew, I saw his fangs drop and his eyes burn redder and redder; his face became a twisted caricature of a human face, the terrible fangs gnashing with every word.

The other hemophages drew back from him as he became more and more a beast and less and less a man. He needed to feed before he lost control of himself entirely, at which point he might very well turn on his fellow hemophages, and their glances at me said they knew it.

Moriarty saw those glances, too, for he said abruptly, "You cannot have him. He is mine."

It caught even Small's attention, and his face gradually returned to normal.

"You haven't fed from him," said the skinny hemophage.

"You only think you know that," said Moriarty. "You don't have the nose to tell."

"I think we'd bloody well know," said the skinny hemophage and giggled at his own pun.

"You hemophages are so unsubtle," Moriarty complained. "Doyle, give me your wrist."

My choice was between the vampire and the hemophage. Small's eyes were still glaring red and he looked more than ready to tear my throat out. Moriarty was a bad risk, but he was better than that.

I extended my arm.

Moriarty carefully rolled back my cuff, bending over my wrist so that the hemophages couldn't see. He nicked the vein in my wrist so delicately I barely felt it, and when he raised his head, he was ostentatiously licking my blood off his lips.

My nausea returned in a rush. I slumped over in a fashion I hoped might look like an addict's ecstasy and concentrated on not vomiting.

"Satisfied?" Moriarty asked the hemophages. "He is mine and you cannot have him."

"You're awfully presumptuous for a prisoner," said the schoolmaster.

"*You* threw him in here with me," Moriarty countered. "What did you expect to happen?"

"You could feed without bloody claiming him," said the skinny hemophage.

"I don't share," Moriarty said flatly, and I shuddered, remembering his beast's eyes.

"That's not why we came down here," said Jonathan Small, who had himself back under control. "We have a favor to ask of Mr. Moriarty." His faux-ingratiating tone made me feel even more ill.

"Even if I do what you want," Moriarty said, "it will not help you and will mean nothing."

"The legal position—" the schoolmaster began pompously, but Moriarty interrupted:

"Is based on facts that cannot be bent to your whims. Vampires and hemophages are different. A courtesy extended to a predator that does not kill its prey is not applicable to a predator that does. You commit murder every time you feed, and no contortion you go through will make that legal."

"You're overthinking your position," said the schoolmaster. "Either you do what we want or Small feeds on you while the rest of us feed on Dr. Doyle."

Moriarty stood up, a slow uncoiling of muscle like a panther in a man's respectable suit. "You're welcome to try," he said. "Go ahead. Unlock the grille."

The London hemophages suddenly seemed uncertain that four on one were favorable enough odds.

Small sneered at them. "You're all a bunch of pantywaists. Open the grille, and I'll fight your vampire for you."

"Please do," Moriarty said, smiling the smile that was all teeth.

Sick as I still felt, I knew what the next line was, and there was no one else to say it. I sat up and said to Small, "I don't think you can."

It infuriated him as only a sneer from someone you've already marked as *dinner* can. *"Open the bloody grille!"* he roared, and the schoolmaster—a sheep in wolf's clothing if ever there was one— fumbled his key out and complied.

Moriarty surged out, shouldering the door aside before it was even fully open.

As hemophages, Small and his friends were generally able to

overpower anything they encountered, but a hemophage, no matter how twisted, was still a human being. Moriarty was not. Even cuffed with silver he was stronger than a hemophage, and he had made the same assessment I had, that the schoolmaster and the two clerks would run at the first sign of serious danger. Which they did, so incontinently that the schoolmaster left his key in the lock of the grille and the stocky one dropped their lantern.

Small was a brawler with no science; his size and his condition guaranteed that he would almost never need anything more. Moriarty, on the other hand, closed and wrestled savagely, throwing Small across his hip to the ground and then kneeling on his chest. "You may have developed a taste for my kind," he said, "but I have not developed a taste for yours. I could kill you all the same, but it is part of our treaty with the city of London that we will kill no one unnecessarily, and we have abided by this treaty for four hundred years. I will not be the one to break it. I will let you up, and you will run, or I will reassess whether or not your death is necessary. Do you understand?" He wasn't even breathing hard.

"Yes," said Small, who was panting.

"Very well," said Moriarty and managed, in one smooth movement my eye could not follow, to get them both on their feet, Small staggering one direction while Moriarty leapt the other.

Small stood a moment, glowering, and Moriarty said, "I will begin reassessing your death in ten seconds," and while his voice was perfectly pleasant, it sent a chill down my spine—perhaps *because* it was so serenely pleasant and unbothered, as if it were no great matter to the vampire whether Jonathan Small lived or died.

It wasn't a bluff, unlike Small's glower. Small turned and ran, the lurch of his wooden leg offset by a hemophage's strength and agility. Moriarty watched him go until we heard the clang of him scrambling through the iron hatch; then the vampire turned to me and said, in much the same pleasant voice, "Can you stand?"

"If I can't, will you eat me?"

"No, I thank you," Moriarty said and made a face. "Hell-hound isn't a great deal more appealing than hemophage, and if you'll forgive the familiarity, I favor the *other* sex. No, if you can't stand, I will carry you, but I thought you might prefer I didn't."

"Yes," I said. "I would."

I crawled to my feet, using the wall for handholds and leverage. Once there, I wobbled precariously for a moment, but caught myself and did not fall.

I limped out of our prison and Moriarty said, "Are you hurt?"

"What? Oh. No, this is old. Got too close to a Fallen."

"And that's how you became a hell-hound," he said, as if the puzzle had been bothering him.

"Yes," I said.

"Are you all right to walk? I don't know how long it will take to find a way out that isn't swarming with hemophages."

"I can manage," I said grimly. I wasn't about to let him carry me. "But before we proceed, there is a question I require an answer to."

His eyebrows went up. "Then by all means ask."

"You claimed me," I said, though the words were nearly choking. "So far as I know, that isn't something you can simply lie about."

"You are blunt," he said.

"I have reason to be. Pray explain."

"It's really no reason for concern."

"That, I believe, you *can* lie about."

His eyes flashed bright yellow in the lantern light. "Are you calling me a liar, Dr. Doyle?"

"*Are* you a liar, Mr. Moriarty?"

We stared at each other. The gaze of a vampire was notoriously mesmerizing; I kept expecting my will to cave before his—and I thought perhaps he was expecting that, too—but I did not lower my eyes.

He looked away first. "My mark is on you," he said sullenly, "and no other vampire can touch you."

I turned back my cuff. On my wrist, where he had nicked me, there was a black mark like a tattoo, a sigil that looked a little like the tracery for a stained-glass window. "That's your mark," I said, not so much a question as a need to say the horrifying truth out loud. I was marked by a vampire.

"Yes," he said.

"How does it come off?"

"It doesn't. Would you prefer to have been eaten by a hemophage, because that was your other option."

"No," I said and forced the words past my gritted teeth: "I mean, thank you."

"Look at it this way. I *won't* feed from you and no other vampire *can* feed from you. And since you are obviously not the sort of person who wants a vampire's kiss, you are now completely protected from vampires. Think of it as an advantage."

I couldn't quite do that, but I fastened my cuff again and said, "All right. I still feel as if there's a catch you aren't telling me about, but I suppose I'll find out about it the hard way. Shall we go?"

"Very well," said he, not denying that there might be a hidden catch. "I shall give you the lantern which Simpson so carelessly dropped, and we shall proceed"—he hesitated, testing the air—"this way, away from the reek of hemophage."

"So that we can become lost in the ancient catacombs beneath London and die. Excellent."

"This isn't a catacomb," Moriarty said. "Nor is it ancient. This was probably a service tunnel two or three hundred years ago. It might even once have been an alley before it was built over. Come on."

I followed him into the dark, away from the hemophages' warehouse.

⸻◆⸻

WE WALKED IN silence for some time, but Moriarty did not find silence congenial, and he began to talk, aimlessly at first—*nervously*, I should have said in a creature other than a vampire—but then he began to talk about London. Vampires live a prodigiously long time, of course—some people claim they are immortal, which is nonsense—and at about three hundred, Moriarty was still comparatively young. He had come to London in 1732, a new husband for the seraglio of his vampiric Master's hunt, which was still rebuilding itself after the Great Fire. "It's how we ended up in Lambeth. Kate fled across the Thames when the City burned and afterward she could not bear to go back. She lost her oldest husband to the Fire—she was in mourning for him for nearly a hundred years, which the other Masters considered excessive—and of course vampires invest in property."

"Of course," I said. Jokes about vampire landlords were probably as old as London.

"She still keeps more sisters than most Masters," said Moriarty, "but I think that makes our hunt healthier, rather than the reverse. Vampires who try to become Masters too soon generally make a poor go of it."

"Has your Master managed to recoup her holdings?"

"She says the fortunes of our hunt are not what they were in King Charles's day, but we are one of the three or four wealthiest hunts in London—certainly the wealthiest on the Surreyside. She was *livid* when they started building the Needle—all the slum land they cleared in St. George's in the East just became worse and more crowded slums in Whitechapel and Bermondsey and Lambeth."

"The Queen gets her Needle, St. George's in the East becomes a model parish, and the rest of the East End can go hang."

"One foot taller than the Eiffel Tower because God forbid we don't outdo the Frogs," Moriarty said. He sighed and shook himself and said, "Let's try here." I followed him down a side tunnel so narrow and set at such an oblique angle that it was invisible practically until I was inside it.

I braced one hand against the wall to relieve some of the strain on my bad leg, and we had not been walking long before I heard a noise like thunder in the far distance and felt the vibrations in the wall.

"What on Earth is that?"

"*Under* earth, Doctor," Moriarty said. "Or, more precisely, the Underground. We're heading toward Waterloo Station."

"Was that your plan?"

"Would that I could take the credit," he said, "but no. It was just luck that I picked the correct direction."

"The luck of the Irish," I said, impressed, and he laughed.

"Hopefully, it doesn't bring us out directly in the path of an oncoming train."

The noise of the trains got louder as we went, a hollow rushing sound that I kept hearing as demonic laughter, as the voice of a Fallen. Soon I could feel the vibrations of the passing trains even when I wasn't touching the wall.

But before we came to an actual Underground tunnel, we found a wooden door, quite literally black with age. It was locked, but it might as well have not been, for Moriarty simply shoved it open as if there were no lock at all. On the other side there was a staircase, a tight, steep spiral that looked to me like pure unmitigated murder.

Even Moriarty looked a little daunted. He gave me an assessing glance. "Can you manage?"

"Yes," I said, because my other two options—being left behind or being carried—were equally unacceptable.

"God save me from stubborn Scots," he said. "All right, but if you cannot keep up, I shall leave you behind."

"Fair enough," I said, and we started up the stairs.

The climb was hellish from the beginning. The steps were unevenly worn, making for treacherous footing, and my muscles were already burning with fatigue. Periodically, the entire staircase would vibrate and hum with the roar of a train. I started slowly, which became slower and slower. True to his word, Moriarty did not wait for me, and I was glad: it was bad enough without an audience. I deliberately chose not to count the steps, so I do not know how high I climbed before Moriarty's voice came ringing down to me: "I've found another door!"

The news gave me a fresh surge of sorely needed energy, but I was still surprised to find Moriarty sitting on the landing when I finally reached the point where the half-size door was set awkwardly into the wall above the steps. He saw the question on my face and shrugged, saying, "I don't know what's on the other side. It seemed foolish to proceed alone."

He got up and turned his attention to the door. It proved not to be locked, although the hinges were so rusty it might as well have been. Moriarty forced it open and then had to bend double to fit himself through. I gave up on one more shred of my dignity and simply crawled.

On the other side, we were in the back of a storeroom—Moriarty had had to shove a box out of line to give us room even to get through the door. I got to my feet, using the boxes beside me for support, and immediately found myself festooned with cobwebs.

"Forgive me, Arachne," I said reflexively, even though the spider who spun this web was surely long dead; it had been drilled into me as a child to be courteous to spiders.

Moriarty said, "Do you want to rest a minute? I believe we're going to have to climb over this box to get out, for I can't push it any farther. The aisle isn't wide enough."

"I would appreciate a moment, yes," I said. Inwardly, I was railing against fate and the Fallen; a year ago I could have raced Moriarty up the steps and still had the stamina to climb over a box. But now I leaned against a box to take my weight off my bad leg, and I was, God help me, grateful for a chance to rest without being abandoned.

Moriarty observed, "The *metaphysicum morbi* is still very thick around your leg."

"I didn't know vampires could see that," I said, instead of snapping at him to tend to his own business and leave mine to me.

"Our eyes don't actually work the same way yours do. We see heat instead of light, and the *metaphysicum* shows itself to us as cold. Hell-hounds and hemophages and necrophages always look colder—and thus, I confess, less appealing even if I could not smell what you are—but you have a very distinct clot of coldness around your thigh. It hasn't healed properly, has it?"

"No," I said. "The Armed Forces doctors have done all they can."

"That's because they should have sent you to an aetheric practitioner," he said with considerable exasperation. "You're a doctor. You should have thought of that yourself."

He was entirely correct. My face heated—and burned all the hotter for the new knowledge that he could tell even in the dark—but I felt a rush of hope that I hadn't even realized I'd abandoned.

I said, "Doctors are always particularly dreadful at treating themselves, and the Armed Forces would prefer to think of wounds as purely material. Mostly, people don't survive an encounter with a Fallen as close as mine was."

"Did it touch you?"

"Glancingly."

"Then you are a very stubborn Scot to be alive at all."

"My orderly saved me," I said and realized I no longer resented him for it. Which was an odd epiphany to have in a cobwebby storeroom somewhere underneath Lambeth. "Which makes him, I suppose, an even stubborner Scot."

"Either very brave or very foolish," said Moriarty. "I'm afraid I would have left you to die."

"Oh, so would I," I said. "I was yelling at Murray to drop me right up to the point I passed out." I sighed, assessing the state of my aching body. "I'm prepared to go on, I think."

"Then let us waste no time in doing so. It's nearly daylight, and I prefer not to be abroad in the sun." Said loftily, as if it were mere eccentricity, although I knew better. Folklore said that vampires were blind in direct sunlight; I decided to take advantage of my forced and unwanted intimacy with a representative sample, and as I crawled laboriously over the box, I asked him if it was true.

"Not *blind,*" he said. "But bright sunlight hurts our eyes, and we sunburn fast and badly. We blister almost immediately, and it takes weeks to heal. I have scars on my forearms from a sunburn I took when I was a kit in Dublin."

Despite his manacles, Moriarty followed me easily over the box, and we began searching for the way out. Escaping the storeroom was easy enough, for while it was long it was very narrow, and there was really only one way we could go, but once outside the storeroom, we found ourselves in a spiderweb of tunnels, and the clamor of the trains, seeming now to surround us on all sides, had gone from being a beacon to being a bewilderment, throwing off Moriarty's innate sense of direction. The best we could do was look for staircases going up, though we could not seem to find one that ascended more than a flight—leaving us still somewhere short of attaining the platform.

"What I would not give for a simple egress sign," Moriarty said. "Or a map. Or some passing and benevolent Virgil to take pity on us poor benighted wanderers."

I was about to say something about Dante and only wanting to go to London, not Paradise, when a voice behind us said, "Are you gentlemen lost?"

I think I knew who that high, husky tenor belonged to before I turned around: only an angel could move so silently that a vampire could not hear them coming.

We had been found by the Angel of Waterloo.

He was a tall, gaunt angel with unkempt dark hair and eyes like a hawk's—pale amber ringed with dark brown. He had a hawk's wings, too. They were mantled up around him defensively; he was expecting trouble.

"Sir," said Moriarty, "you come well upon your cue. Yes, we are lost, and we would be deeply obliged for some guidance."

The Angel of Waterloo stared at him unblinkingly for several seconds. Then he tilted his head, even more birdlike than Crow, and looked at me. "A vampire," he said, "and a hell-hound."

"We are not banned from the precincts of Waterloo Station," Moriarty said and got another stare, while I bit back the urge to protest that I was not a hell-hound. The angel had spoken no more than truth; a hell-hound was exactly what I was.

"How did you come here?" said the angel.

"The story is a very long one," said Moriarty.

"From below," I said.

"Yes," said the angel, and I saw that he was looking at Moriarty's manacles. Then he looked directly at me. "Where do you wish to go?"

"The surface," I said instead of staggering back under the impact of the angel's gaze.

"Very well," said the angel. "Follow me."

18

THE MASTER
OF THE HUNT

WHEN I RETURNED to Baker Street, some twenty hours after I had left, I had scarcely closed the street door behind me when Crow came barreling down the stairs and enveloped me in a hug that seemed like a combination of entanglement in a deck chair and assault by a pack of feather-dusters. I managed, after several intensely uncomfortable, nerve-jarring seconds, to free myself, and he demanded, "Are you all right? Oksana Timofeyevna and I were certain you'd be killed."

"Can I sit down first?"—and while I meant to be peremptory, it came out decidedly plaintive.

"Oh, good grief, what's wrong with me? Yes, yes, yes, come upstairs! Do you need help?"

"I can manage," I said, reckoning to myself that the odds of that being true were about fifty-fifty. I leaned heavily on the wall all the way up, and I was aware of Crow just behind me, waiting to catch me if I fell, which was infuriating and ridiculous—my mass being greater than his, he would succeed only in pitching us *both* to the bottom of the stairs—and yet for all that, it was also somehow comforting.

I achieved our flat and my armchair and finally felt as if it was possible—although perhaps not entirely prudent—to relax.

Crow closed the door and blurted out, "He's gone."

"Gone?" I did not need to ask who he meant.

"I went up to the attic after you and Oksana Timofeyevna left. The trapdoor to the roof was open. He wrote 'thank you' on the wall, so that I feel fairly certain he doesn't intend to come back."

"After the edifying spectacle of us fighting over him like two dogs over a bone? I can't think why not."

"He and I talked that night after you . . . left. About whether his oath was enough of a defense to save him from hanging. I had to tell him I *think* so, but I don't know. Marriage oaths are. And it was a serious oath that Small made Anuvadaka swear, serious enough that I really do think he would be acquitted."

"Maybe he will turn himself in," I said. "Or maybe he will find a way back to India and we will never know what becomes of him."

"He wants to go home," Crow said and sighed. "I *do* see your point, Doyle. I just wish we could have helped him."

"We kept Jones from arresting him," I said dryly. "And that's quite enough."

Crow opened his mouth to argue, then visibly changed his mind. "Oh, never mind! What happened to *you*?"

I told the story as simply as I could, given that Crow interrupted every other sentence to demand more details. When I mentioned the vampire, he became very still, staring at me with intensity worthy of the Angel of Waterloo, and when I mentioned the vampire's name, his wings snapped wide and he shouted, "Moriarty!" adding in a lower voice as he went to pick up the end table he had knocked over, "I hope you did not trust a word he said."

"You know him?"

"Oh, yes," said Crow. "My business has taken me among the vampiric hunts several times. They are unfortunately excellent places to look for missing persons. I know most of the East End hunts, and the Moriarty Hunt is the worst."

"Then you really won't like this part," I said and folded back my cuff.

Crow's wings snapped wide again, this time making a clean sweep of the breakfast table. Luckily, Mrs. Climpson had learned after the first disaster not to put out the good china. This was all secondhand mismatches—if not precisely *intended* to be broken, then certainly *expected* thus—although the clatter and crash they made hitting the floor was every bit as cataclysmic as the good china, and brought Jennie up immediately.

"I am so sorry," Crow said. He was already crouched down, carefully picking up half a cup here, a jagged seventh of a plate there, making a pathetically tidy pile of the wreckage.

Jennie said, "Let me, Mr. Crow," and gently nudged him away from the broken china.

"I think some of it is mendable," Crow said hopefully.

"I'll take it all to Cook," Jennie promised. "She's good at mending things." And she left with her apronful of broken china.

"Oh dear," said Crow, standing up and pulling his wings in tightly against his back. He stood a moment, wringing his hands like the fussiest old maid imaginable, then abruptly turned to me and said, "Show me."

I was half inclined to tell him to go to the Devil, but I held out my hand and let him run his cold fingers over the mark. He said, more quietly, "How did this happen?" and I explained my choice between vampire and hemophage.

His eyes became very wide as he listened. "I certainly wouldn't have wanted you to choose differently," he said. "Do you think it's true that Small feeds on vampires?"

"He looked like it was true," I said and yawned jaw-crackingly.

"Oh dear," said Crow. "I don't want to keep you from sleep any longer, but . . . all right, tell me the rest *quickly*."

I laughed and yawned again. I described the fight between Moriarty and Small, and then it was easy enough: "Moriarty followed the noise of the trains to Waterloo Station, and then the Angel of Waterloo showed us the way out."

"You saw Waterloo?" Crow said. "He spends almost all his time up in the rafters."

"I think he sensed us," I said. "We were down where the public don't go, and I suppose a vampire and a hell-hound together isn't something one comes across every day."

"Even Waterloo becomes curious," Crow said. "He and Victoria—the Angel of Victoria's Station, I mean, not the Angel of the Needle, nor the Queen, for that matter—are both a little peculiar. I don't think we're really meant to watch over that many people all at once."

"Is that what you think angels are designed to do?"

"Well, of course," he said. "Shepherds watch over their flocks. And angels watch over shepherds."

"But then why bind them to habitations?"—a question that had perplexed me greatly as a child.

"So that we don't have to choose *which* people to watch," he said. "It's why I take clients, as a way of limiting how many people I feel responsible for at any one time. We are very bad at making choices. It is a kindness of our Maker to remove that choice from our remit."

"You view it as a blessing?" I said, surprised.

"A mixed one," he said, one shoulder and one wing shrugging together. "I would give a great deal to have a habitation again—just not any of the things I should have to give up for that to happen. But you need to sleep, and I've been distracting you. Come along, Doyle."

I let him chivvy me to my bedroom, but there he stopped and said, quite seriously, "We were going to rescue you. Oksana Timofeyevna has had her brother trying to find out more about the hemophages' warehouse. And she herself—we had heard rumors that they had captured a vampire, and she was going to . . . oh *crumbs*. I have to send her a telegram that she doesn't need to go to any of the vampiric hunts! You go to sleep."

I was only too happy to comply.

❖

My SLEEP WAS patchy; I kept dreaming I was turning into a hell-hound and jerking awake to be sure it wasn't true. Somewhat to my own surprise, I was still human when I got up again at four o'clock, even if not noticeably better rested.

I came out of my bedroom, feeling as if someone had been striking matches on my eyeballs, and found Crow scribbling furious notes to himself on a piece of foolscap.

"You look perturbed," I said, sitting down.

"'Perturbed' is perhaps a little strong," said Crow, "but I'm definitely vexed. The Nameless cannot find Anuvadaka, and prior to this I would have said there was no one in all of London whom they could not find."

"He grew up hiding from tigers and ghouls," I said.

"True," said Crow. "But I cannot help him if I cannot find him."

"I think it's safe to assume he doesn't want your help," I said, as gently as I could.

"Yes," Crow said gloomily, "I think so, too. But I think I ought to help him all the same."

"Is this legal help or illegal help?" I said. "He *is* a murderer."

"Yes, I know that, too. But I don't think he will be well served by the British system of justice." He fixed me with one of his penetrating stares. "If I found him, would you turn him in?"

"No," I said, "but I am able to lie to the police about it."

"Touché," said Crow. "You think I should just drop the matter?"

"I suspect," I said, "that Anuvadaka can take care of himself, especially now that he's free of Jonathan Small. I might feel differently if he did not speak English."

"If he did not speak English, he would already be dead—although I keep expecting to see a notice in *The Times* or the *Standard* that they've pulled a 'savage child' out of the Thames. London's not really less dangerous than the jungle, just dangerous in different ways."

I opened my mouth to argue, thought of the rookeries of the East End, and subsided.

Crow sighed. "But you're right. If he doesn't want to be helped, then my help is useless to him. I just . . . it seems such a terrible position to be trapped in."

"Being Jonathan Small's traveling companion was worse," I said with certainty.

"I suppose that's . . ." His head jerked up. "There's someone at the door. Someone . . . Good *Lord*."

"Crow?" I said, as he shoved violently to his feet.

"It's . . . I can't believe . . ."

There was a tap at the door and Jennie came in with a card on a salver. "There's a lady to see you, Mr. Crow."

Crow took the card and held it so that I could see it. In an elaborately engraved script, it read: KATHERINE MORIARTY.

"Moriarty's Master," I said, a little numb with the surprise.

"Oh the infamy I am bringing to Mrs. Climpson's respectable house!" said Crow, half laughing, half dismayed. "I invite her in, Jennie. You can show her up."

"As long as Mrs. Climpson can't smell vampires," I said; any vampire going out in daylight was sure to have masked its true nature.

Crow said, "The aetheric disturbance—" and then Jennie opened the door to admit our visitor.

Fashionably hatted and heavily veiled, Master Moriarty had golden-blond hair and a tall, statuesque figure. Her nails were hidden by kidskin gloves (no doubt padded at the fingertips), and the inhuman whiteness of her skin, like the baleful yellow of her eyes, was camouflaged by the combination of hat brim and veil. She closed the door carefully behind her and said, "Thank you for seeing me." Her voice held a hint of Ireland, worn almost smooth by centuries in England.

Crow, unable to lie, said, "Curiosity trumps most things."

She raised her veil and said, "That is perhaps the only thing vampires and angels have in common."

She was quite lovely, if one ignored the eyes that did not belong in a human face, and she knew the art of cosmetics: she could almost have powdered herself that stark paper-white. Almost.

"How else is an existence measured in centuries to be tolerated?" Crow said, quite seriously.

"A telling point," said the vampire. "My name is Kate Moriarty—as you know, but I do like proper introductions."

"My name is Crow, and this is Dr. Doyle."

"Forgive me for not standing," I said. "I am still most abominably fatigued."

"James was afraid you had worsened the injury to your leg," said Master Moriarty.

"No," I said. "It aches, but nothing untoward. I admit I would have preferred *not* to know what lies beneath Lambeth, but I have taken neither permanent nor serious hurt. I trust you were able to get the manacles off?"

She gave me a curious look—no doubt she smelled what her husband had smelled—but said, "Oh, yes. One of my friends is a locksmith," with the most delicate possible stress on "friend" to indicate that she meant an addict. "Poor James is very bruised, but thankfully nothing worse." She gave me another, harder look. "James said he marked you. Is that true?"

I folded back my cuff and let her see the mark. She inspected it nearly as carefully as Crow had. "He should not have done it, but at least he did a nice clean job."

"Shouldn't have done it?" Crow said indignantly. "What, pray tell, should he have done instead?"

"We only mark those we have asked to join our hunt," said Master Moriarty. "James has no intention of asking Dr. Doyle, and I am sure Dr. Doyle would not consent if he did."

"No, I would not," I said, with more force than tact.

"Therefore he shouldn't have done it," she said. "But now that he has, there's no use fretting over it. Dr. Doyle, you are welcome to our hunt."

It was the last thing I had expected her to say, especially since we'd just agreed I had no intention of becoming a vampire. I managed to say, "Thank you very much."

"Show that mark to any vampire of the Moriarty Hunt, and they will help you to the best of their ability. In return, we would ask you the same consideration."

"I can't imagine how I could be of assistance to a vampire, but I certainly owe your hunt a debt. Yes, as long as it's legal, I will offer help to the best of my ability."

"We would not ask you to do anything illegal," Master Moriarty said, so gravely that I suspected her of secret amusement. "But that is only one of the reasons I have come."

"And what is the other?" said Crow.

She looked at us, her golden eyes burning in her white face, and said, "We want the treasure."

◇

IT WAS NOT a surprise. I had not missed James Moriarty's keen interest when the treasure was mentioned. He had been polite about the matter, not demanding details, but I had not imagined he would forget it. Vampires, unlike angels, do not forget, any more than they forgive. It would have been surprising if the vampires had *not* evinced interest in the Agra treasure.

That did not, however, mean that either Crow or I was prepared to deal with Master Moriarty's announcement. After a moment of rather scrambling silence, Crow said cautiously, "We do not know where the treasure is."

"No," said Master Moriarty. "Only Jonathan Small knows that."

"We don't know where Jonathan Small is, either," I said. "And Mor—James knows where the warehouse is as well as I do."

"Ah," said Master Moriarty, looking uncomfortable. "That's the problem. The hemophages have decamped from the warehouse."

"An unexpected display of intelligence," said Crow.

Master Moriarty gave him a brief, dimpled smile. "Thus, you see, we need to find Jonathan Small, and while we have our own ways of searching, it occurred to me that we might easily double or triple our chances of success if we pooled our resources, you and me and the Russian girl—necrophages know more about what goes on in a city's understory than anyone."

I said, "What about the police?"

"What about them?"

"Jonathan Small is a murderer and a burglar and is wanted for questioning in the death of Bartholomew Sholto, and while I don't know to whom the treasure properly belongs, if anyone, I think it is safe to say Her Majesty's government will want its share."

Master Moriarty said—sullenly, if that word can be used of the Master of a vampiric hunt—"I don't see that there's any reason the police need to know."

"Master Moriarty," Crow said sternly, "I hope you are not suggesting that we should dispose of Jonathan Small in some clandestine and illegal manner."

"Good gracious, nothing like that!" said Master Moriarty, either genuinely surprised or a very talented actress. "I just see no reason the police need to be involved until *after* we find Small."

"He will not hold his tongue if his treasure gets appropriated," I said.

"Possession is nine-tenths of the law," she countered. "And unless there's a manifest—"

"Please don't plot illegality in front of me," said Crow. "Recollect that I cannot lie to the police about it."

"So inconvenient that must be," murmured Master Moriarty.

"Ha," said Crow. "He will be looking to get out of London as quickly as possible; we had best proceed with some dispatch. We are looking for a hemophage with a wooden leg and a Benares-work iron box. If my 'forces' find him first, I will notify you, and I trust I may rely on you to do the same?"

"Yes," said Master Moriarty, lowering her veil. "My word is not as good as a werewolf's, but you may trust me that far." She held out her hand; after a dubious moment Crow shook hands with her.

"Good afternoon, Mr. Crow, Dr. Doyle." And the Master of the Moriarty Hunt took her leave.

Crow went to the bow window to watch her progress along Baker Street. "I *don't* trust her," he said, as if I had voiced a protest. "Vampires are liars—it's how they hunt. But at least this way, we have some information about what they're doing, instead of being wholly in the dark."

"We wouldn't have known about the hemophages deserting the warehouse if she hadn't brought us word," I said. "There is at least some reason to believe she wants what she says she wants."

"True," said Crow. "Maybe it is just greed. But regardless, I must get the Nameless searching for Jonathan Small and send another telegram to Oksana Timofeyevna. I'll only be a minute."

I leaned back in my armchair and thought about covetousness and jealousy and the swath of disaster the Agra treasure seemed to leave in its wake. Three men murdered, four men imprisoned for life (with one escape—but he only escaped the prison at Port Blair, not the treasure), Major Sholto's life consumed with the obsessive fear that someone would take the treasure away from him, Bartholomew and Thaddeus searching for six years and quarreling so bitterly that Thaddeus moved out. Bartholomew, I thought, would never have agreed to share; he had been infected by his father's greed. And now we had the hemophages of Lambeth, the Moriarty Hunt, the necrophages of Madame Silvanova's brother's circle, the Nameless angels of London, the Metropolitan Police . . .

When Crow returned, I asked him if he thought the treasure was cursed.

"It certainly could be," he said. "The original owner might have cursed it to keep his courier honest—if you steal it, it will destroy you—which rather makes one wonder what the *courier's* plans were, given that he was eaten by hemophages." He shuddered, his wings rising protectively and then settling again. "And then Small and Singh and Khan and Akbar stole it, and then Major Sholto stole it. And then Small stole it *again*. You're quite right, it does seem to be accompanied by, well, evil, if that's not too strong a word. I personally want nothing to do with it."

"Nor do I," I said. "Nor does Thaddeus Sholto—or, at least, so he claims—nor does Miss Morstan."

"Her indifference may very well have saved her life," said Crow. "Although I do note that she *kept* the pearls, rather than selling them as Mr. Sholto seems to have intended."

"It isn't as if he sent instructions," I said.

"No. And perhaps she kept them for the mystery of it—which, I admit, is what I would do if I were a governess and someone started sending me flawless pearls."

"It must have been rather a disappointment to find that the sender was Thaddeus Sholto," I said, suddenly seeing a certain black comedy in the matter. "Hardly the preux chevalier of a maiden's dreams. Much more like Carroll's Tweedledee."

"He *has* been a paragon of chivalry," Crow pointed out.

"Is he still imprisoned?"

"No. Most fortunately for him, it was proved that Bartholomew Sholto was still alive and yelling at the servants after Thaddeus left the house. And he has an unimpeachable alibi for the rest of the night. He went to a salon. There are at least twenty people prepared to swear in court that he did not leave until nearly five o'clock in the morning."

My eyebrows rose. "It must have been a most remarkable salon."

Crow smiled. "Even without Small, Thaddeus Sholto is safe. Mrs. Bernstone and Mr. Rao are in a slightly tighter spot. But Jones can't really make a case out against them."

"Have you informed Jones of the new plan?"

"I've told him he has to swear not to arrest or collect evidence against anyone but Small and his confederates. I don't know which way he'll jump. I *do* prefer working with Lestrade. Or even Gregson. Either of them would have sworn in a heartbeat."

"You are asking Jones to ignore a great deal."

"I personally have no proof that the necrophages of Grigori Timofeyevich's circle are committing any crimes—and I'm taking care to keep it that way. It is not a crime to be a necrophage."

"No," I said. "As long as you remember not to ask if any of them are registered."

"Exactly," said Crow.

We had no news of any kind that evening. Crow went back to his press cuttings and I went gratefully to bed at nine o'clock. I was too exhausted to remember my dreams, and if I turned into a hellhound in the night, it did not wake me.

The morning brought fresh headlines and a wire from Athelney Jones. Seven people had been savaged by hemophages in a dosshouse in Lambeth. Only one of them had survived, and she would almost certainly die before the day was out. All of the witnesses agreed that the leader of the hemophages had had a wooden leg.

Jones's wire read, IF CATCH SMALL BLIND TO ALL ELSE.

❦

THE NAMELESS WERE in and out of our flat all day. At two o'clock, Madame Silvanova arrived, beautifully dressed and coiffed, with small but obviously genuine emeralds glinting at her ears and throat.

She saw my glance and smiled a little wryly. "When you are fleeing your country one step ahead of the police, do be sure to pack all your jewelry. Easy to carry, easy to hide, easy to sell. And if you do not sell it, you can always wear it and look like a lady of quality."

"You would look like a lady of quality regardless," I said without thinking and then blushed hot scarlet to the roots of my hair.

Madame Silvanova said, "You are gallant, Dr. Doyle. But I am glad to see you unharmed?" There was just enough lift in her voice to make it a question.

"Aside from the loss of my second-best walking stick, yes. Quite unharmed." I tried not to think about James Moriarty's mark on my wrist.

I told her a short and somewhat expurgated version of my imprisonment and escape. She listened with great attention, saying when I had finished, "Always the hemophages causing trouble. And

Jonathan Small is surely the worst."

Crow came back in from one of his frequent forays to accost a Nameless on the street and demand a report. Because of the Consensus, he said, they all had equal access to information gathered by any one of them. This time, he had one of them trailing after him. It looked faintly alarmed, for which it could not be blamed. Crow seemed frenetic. He remembered to greet Madame Silvanova, but immediately turned back to the Nameless and said, "Tell them."

"Sir," said the Nameless. "There is a steam launch called the *Aurora,* which many people say is the fastest on the river. She is owned and captained by a man named Mordecai Smith. One of our sisters heard him complaining about a client who hired the boat, canceled the hire at the last minute, hired the boat again, and this time wants to bring three other men with him. He made derogatory references to a wooden leg and said with great emphasis that he was going to demand payment before allowing this client on board. Our sister thinks that Smith is afraid of this client."

"And can you lead us to this launch?" Crow said.

"I can lead you to her dock. She isn't supposed to cast off until sundown."

"Perfect," said Crow. "I have to go summon the others."

"Others?" said Madame Silvanova as Crow flung himself out of the room again, the Nameless at his heels.

I explained about the augmentation of the hunting party and reassured her that Inspector Jones knew better than to ask awkward questions.

"Do you trust him?"

"Crow does."

"Crow trusts everyone," she said.

"Jones wants the hemophages, not anyone else. I don't think he'll ask."

"Then I suppose we must stay. I had come only to report that my brother's friends had provided reams of rumors, but nothing that could be acted upon. Pray excuse me. I must go pay off the cab and bring Grigori up to join us." She departed, but was back in mere moments, shepherding a man nearly twice her size. She introduced him as Grigori Timofeyevich Silvanov, and after peering anxiously at my hand, he engulfed it for a handshake. He was mountainous, much darker than his sister, and clearly nervous of people in much the same way an elephant is nervous of a mouse. He muttered something that was almost lost in a strong Russian accent, but which I thought might have been, "Pleased to make your acquaintance," and sat obediently in the wing chair his sister pointed him to. She resumed her seat by me and said, "I am impressed that Master Moriarty came to you rather than compelling you to visit her."

"Compelling?"

"Threats, bribes, blackmail, her bullyboys. The Master of the Moriarty Hunt is subtle only when it pleases her."

"I think she was curious," I said, "and Crow has had some sort of dealings with the Moriarty Hunt in the past, though I don't think directly with the Master. It doesn't seem to have gone terribly well."

She gave an unladylike snort of laughter. "I do not think vampires are the strict opposite of angels—that would be the Bodiless Ones, the demons—but they are close. Most angels would ban vampires from their dominions if they could." She gave me a curious sidelong look. "But Mr. Crow allows the Master of a hunt into his home?"

"He said curiosity trumps everything else."

Her laugh this time was a restrained chuckle. "He does remind me of my cat, who must know what is on the other side of every closed door."

"A cat is not the worst comparison," I said.

Silvanov said something in Russian to his sister, who replied in the same tongue. "Grigori says there are two angels approaching," she said to me, "one white as snow, the other black as night."

"Your brother is a poet?"

"A folklorist."

Crow bounded back into the room as energetically as he had bounded out. A Nameless followed him. It might have been the same one—a man with dun-colored hair and a gray suit. I saw what had caught Silvanov's eye. They were the same height, almost the same coloring, and their suits were the same soft fog gray. Swan's wings and crow's wings stood out dramatically, as if Crow had planned the spectacle, although I knew such a thing would never occur to him.

And it *was* the same Nameless; it had the same wide-eyed expression.

Madame Silvanova introduced Crow to her brother. Silvanov shook hands even more tentatively and seemed grateful to be able to retreat to the wing chair.

"Now we have to *wait*," Crow said with considerable horror. "You said the *Aurora* is due to cast off at sunset?"

"That is our sister's information."

"And it's already three o'clock. Well, the good part is that we can't wait long. Anyone who can't be here by four will have to be left behind."

But the hunters were all eager. Jones arrived at quarter past, bringing with him Sergeant Forbes and a good deal of suspicion. "Another of your secret informants, Mr. Crow?" he asked in a tone that might have been anywhere from jocular to menacing.

"Not at all," said Crow. "I've told you before where I get my information, Inspector. There's no mystery, and you know perfectly well I can't be lying about it."

"I know you *say* you can't, but the angels I've talked to aren't so sure."

Crow made an exasperated noise that defies transcription and said, "I am not Fallen. It isn't the sort of thing one can hide."

"But you don't have a habitation."

"I have London."

"I was nearly killed by one of the Fallen in Afghanistan," I said. "If Crow were Fallen, I would not be anywhere near him."

I don't think Jones truly believed Crow was Fallen; I don't even think he was truly concerned. He said grudgingly, "All right. Where are we going?"

"Wherever the Nameless lead us," Crow said solemnly but with mischief glinting in his eyes. He waited until Jones was on the very verge of expostulation, then said, "Which will be a steam launch called the *Aurora*. That's where we will find Jonathan Small." He drew Jones and Forbes into a discussion of the evidence and their theories until ten minutes to four, when Master Moriarty arrived.

She and Inspector Jones eyed each other with wary hostility, while Silvanov seemed to shrink even farther back into the wing chair—which, as he had already made himself as small as possible when Jones came in, was an impressive feat. Jones had barely glanced at him, all his attention on Crow; Master Moriarty gave Silvanov a long, thoughtful look, but said nothing. Madame Silvanova, who had joined her brother when Jones came in, glared back at Master Moriarty as if daring her to attack.

Crow interrupted before either of them said anything. "We'd best be going. And I believe we're going to need more than one cab."

He was correct about that. We in fact had a bit of a fox-goose-corn conundrum, since neither Master Moriarty nor the Silvanovs wished to share a cab with Inspector Jones, and the Nameless, evincing the first sign of personality I had ever seen in any of them, refused to be parted from Crow. It was not ideal for Moriarty and the Silvanovs to share a cab, either, but Crow gave me an imploring look, and I made the fourth in their cab, while Jones and Forbes squashed in with the angels.

The Silvanovs sat on one bench, Madame Silvanova almost invisible beside her brother's bulk, and Master Moriarty and I on the other. I was very aware of the taffeta of her skirt brushing my leg, and although a vampire's normal temperature is only a few degrees below that of a human being, I felt as if I were sitting beside an ice sculpture, for she seemed both that cold and that inhuman.

It was only a few minutes before she spoke, sounding amused. "You needn't worry. I'm not going to denounce you or eat you or whatever it is you're imagining."

"I do not know what you mean," Madame Silvanova said stiffly.

"Of course not." Master Moriarty still sounded amused. "But your brother does." She said directly to Silvanov, "Truly, you need not fear me. I have no love for the Metropolitan Police and no grudge against necrophages, and I do not attack people wantonly in the street. If I bite you, it will be because you asked me to." I did not imagine she lacked for willing victims.

Madame Silvanova was looking at her with loathing. "Vampires are liars."

Master Moriarty laughed, the cold chiming of the Devil's clock. "True," she said, "but whatever you may choose to believe, I have no interest in you." She turned her head to look at the street, dismissing Madame Silvanova from existence.

"In Moscow," Madame Silvanova said to me, "the political prisoners are given to the vampires." Which I supposed explained as much as I needed to know.

The dock where the *Aurora* was moored was dreary and uninviting, but it was clear she was preparing for a journey. A number of half-grown boys were running back and forth with sacks of coal, under the direction of a man who had to be Mordecai Smith. He was no very prepossessing figure, and drunk into the bargain, but the *Aurora* herself looked trim and well-maintained. There was no sign of Jonathan Small. He must have been expecting pursuit, but he did not seem to have banked on the pursuit getting to the dock before the *Aurora* was ready to go.

"Finally," Crow said, "we might be one step ahead of him instead of lagging three steps behind."

"We just have to be careful he doesn't get scared off," I said.

"Jones is an old hand at this part," Crow said. "As far as I can tell, most of police work is waiting for the suspect to show up. I'm sorry you got dragged into that earlier. It drives Jones insane that I can get information from the Nameless and he can't."

"He can't?" I said. "Why not?"

"They talk to me because I'm like them."

"You mean, because you're an angel?"

"No. I'm so terribly close to Nameless, Doyle, I don't think you can understand. All that stands between me and them is a chunk of marble and a name given to me mostly by accident. I won't Fall, but it would be so easy to fade back into the Consensus."

"But you won't," I said, more than a little alarmed.

"Oh no," said he, cheerful again. "There's too much I haven't learned yet."

Jones arranged his forces with considerable expertise, putting Crow and the Nameless together in a recessed doorway where they would look like two Nameless, gathered together as Nameless always were, waiting for another job; put the rest of us in a knot of conversation, like sightseers who had gotten themselves lost; and himself went down on the dock to have a word with Mordecai Smith.

"Isn't that taking an awful risk?" I asked Forbes.

"Your odds are about fifty-fifty," Forbes said. "Either you spook him by talking to him or you spook him by *not* talking to him. Because even if old Mordecai hasn't spotted us, you can be sure his kids have." And a glance showed me one of the younger boys staring at us.

We had not been there long when I heard the uneven sound of a wooden-legged man's footsteps. I resisted the impulse to turn and look. Presently, between the passersby, I could see a pair of bulky shoulders making their lurching way out to the *Aurora*. Jones was still out there, having what looked like a fairly vehement argument with Smith. I saw the moment when Small realized something wasn't right. Another two steps, and he stopped completely, halfway between the quayside and the *Aurora*.

"Right, then," said Forbes and signaled to Crow.

We converged on the dock: two angels, a necrophage, an augur, a vampire, a detective sergeant, and a half-lame doctor. Small looked around wildly, then with another burst of his surprising speed and dexterity, dodged past Jones and onto the *Aurora*.

"You can't run her yourself, Small!" Jones shouted. "Come out peaceable-like and it'll go the better with you."

There was no answer from the launch. Mordecai Smith started to bluster, but Jones stared him down. "I told you, Scotland Yard. That man's an escaped murderer. Best get your boys to safety."

Smith stopped blustering.

At this point, another cab pulled up and three men got out of it; I recognized them as Overton and his friends. They came rushing angrily down onto the dock, shouting for Small, and only belatedly seemed to realize what they were walking into. By then, Forbes was already there, with Silvanov looming silently behind him. I couldn't hear the exchange, with Jones shouting at the *Aurora*, but after only a few moments, Forbes blew his police whistle to summon any nearby constables, and Overton lowered his head into his hands in resigned and disgusted defeat.

Jones said to Crow, "We're going to have to go on the boat after him."

"He can't go anywhere," Crow said, "and he's hardly going to jump in the Thames. Why not just wait him out?"

"He might do away with himself, jumping in the Thames or otherwise. Alternatively, he might start laying booby traps. It's best not to give him time to think."

But then Small appeared on deck, carrying an ornate iron box. His eyes were burning red, and his fangs were very close to dropping. "If I can't have it," he shrieked, "no one can!" and he heaved the box into the river.

All of the assembled made noises of dismay and outrage, and Jones rushed onto the *Aurora* to arrest Small before he could follow his box into the Thames.

"You'll never find it," Small was exulting as Jones herded him back to the quayside.

"We can send divers down after the box, you fool," said Jones.

"Of course you can," said Small, who was giggling now in a truly disturbing manner. "But the box is empty. I threw the treasure over the other side, piece by piece. No bigger than pebbles, those diamonds. Who's to say how far the current will take them?"

Someone—I think it was Master Moriarty—let out an anguished moan. The box had gone over the leeside of the *Aurora* and could well have gone straight down. But anything caught by the Thames's current might make it all the way to the sea.

Then the hemophages started yelling again, louder than ever, and the first constables appeared in answer to Forbes's whistle, and the scene devolved into utterly predictable chaos.

19

THE CHRISTIAN NAMES OF DR. DOYLE

MUCH LATER THAT evening, I made a reluctant pilgrimage to the house of Mrs. Cecil Forrester. Miss Morstan deserved to know what had happened to the treasure, a share of which had hypothetically been hers, and more than that, she deserved that I should tell her the truth about myself, so that she would not be left wondering whether she had been imagining things or, worse, whether, since she was not an heiress, I considered her literally not worth my time. I dreaded the conversation, but the idea of her thinking I had merely been making a cynical gamble was excruciating.

The first part went well enough. Miss Morstan and Mrs. Cecil Forrester were both agog at the adventure yarn (in which I had carefully changed all the names, just as I have done here), and when I had done, Miss Morstan said, "I can't very well repine for a fortune I never had and don't want. I'm just glad neither you nor Mr. Crow came to harm." Her eyes widened. "But I owe you your fee, and Mr. Crow never even said what it is."

"You don't owe *me* anything," I said, "and Crow will not charge you anything exorbitant. He doesn't really do this for the money."

"He almost forgot to bill me at all," Mrs. Cecil Forrester chimed in.

"But you've been to all this trouble," Miss Morstan said. "And I'm perfectly capable of paying."

"No one said you weren't," I said. "But I help Crow as a friend, and what he charges you is a matter of his business, not of mine."

"You are a remarkable friend, Dr. Doyle," said Miss Morstan, and I saw in her eyes the exact light I had hoped not to see.

Mrs. Cecil Forrester made some transparent excuse and swept out of the room.

The silence was paralyzing. I could think of no way to say any of the things I needed to, nor of any conversational gambit that might get her to talk while I tried again to find some way of explaining the matter without actually having to explain.

Miss Morstan began to look uneasy. "Dr. Doyle? I thought you must want to speak to me. . . ."

"I do," I said. "That is, I feel that I owe you an explanation."

"An explanation?" Her expression changed from uneasy to angry. "No, there is no need for an explanation. I can give it for you: 'I regret if any actions of mine, Miss Morstan, led you to believe I had any interest in you greater than pure and Christian friendship, for such was never my intent.' Am I right?"

Really, I should have said yes. Let her think of me what she would and disappear from her life as *good riddance to bad rubbish*. But at least half her anger was directed at herself, and I could not bear to let her go on thinking she had made a fool of herself.

"No," I said. "That's not it."

"It isn't?"

"No, you weren't wrong. I did—do—feel more for you than friendship. But I cannot ask you to marry me."

"*Cannot?* Why on Earth not?"

And, God help me, I blurted out the truth: "I'm not a man."

"Not a man . . . Were you wounded?" Her gaze dropped involuntarily to my crotch. "I knew you had been badly hurt, but—"

"No!" I said. "No, that's not it. Mary, I am . . . I am my father's only daughter. My Christian names are Joanna Henrietta."

"You're joking." She stared searchingly, almost pleadingly, into my face. "You *must* be. . . . You're not joking."

"I'm sorry," I said, knowing full well it was inadequate.

She turned sharply away from me; after a pause in which I could hear my own painful heartbeat, she said, in a voice that she could not quite hold steady, "I think you had best leave."

"Yes," I said. "I thought I might."

I was grateful not to encounter Mrs. Cecil Forrester on my way out.

<>

It was nearly midnight when I returned to Baker Street.

"You're back," Crow said, surprised.

"Of course I am," I said. "Where else would I go?"

"You and Miss Morstan aren't celebrating?"

"Celebrating what?"

"Your engagement."

We stared at each other.

"I am not engaged to Miss Morstan," I said finally. "There was never any possibility of my being engaged to Miss Morstan."

"But you liked each other," Crow said, his head tilting in bewilderment.

"Good God, I need a drink." I limped across to the sideboard, splashed whiskey into a glass, came back, and did not quite collapse into my chair.

Crow had set aside his scrapbook and scissors. "Did you not want to marry Miss Morstan? I thought you did."

"That doesn't enter into it," I said and took a hard swallow of whiskey. I deplore drunkenness, but tonight it seemed like an awfully good idea. "I can't marry her."

"I don't understand. If you want to marry her, why can't you?"

"Because it would be incredibly cruel." He tilted his head, obviously confused. "You know I'm a woman, Crow." If he knew I was a hell-hound, he had to know that.

"Yes," he said, "but what does that have to do with it?"

"Well, for one thing, it isn't legal for two women to marry. For another thing, I feel quite sure that Miss Morstan doesn't want to marry a woman."

"I don't understand," Crow said again, plaintively. "I can see that she likes you, just as I can see that you like her. Why does it matter that you are both the same sex?"

There were so many answers to that and so many of them led to discussions I didn't want to have. I settled on, "Most people, when they get married, want to have children. Miss Morstan and I wouldn't be able to because I don't have male sexual organs and therefore cannot reproduce with her."

"Oh," he said and was silent for a long time, his brows knitted in the frown he showed when he was thinking hard. I sat and watched the fire in the grate and from time to time knocked back another slug of whiskey. The silence went on long enough that I thought maybe the conversation was over, but then he said, "Is that why you didn't want to have sexual congress with me? Because you don't have the correct organs?"

I said, "No. I didn't want to have sexual congress with you because I don't like rape."

I was already drunker than I usually allowed myself. The word was vulgar, blunt, ugly; Crow flinched from it, his wings rustling. "But it isn't—"

"Isn't it? You don't feel sexual desire. Or is that not true?"

"No, it's true," Crow said reluctantly, staring now at his hands. "God gave to Adam and Eve that which he gave not to the Angels of the Garden."

"Saint Augustine," I said, recognizing the quote. "If you don't feel sexual desire and someone coerces you into having sexual relations with them, I don't see how it's anything *other* than rape."

He did not answer. I took another swallow of whiskey. "You know," I said, "the worst thing about pretending to be a man is that my name has to be a secret."

He did not look up, but his wings lifted, just slightly.

"I told Miss Morstan," I said, "because I didn't know how else to make her understand, but it feels wrong that she should know and you should not. You were close, you know."

"I was?"

"When you guessed that the *H* stood for a variant of Henry. It's for Henrietta."

He was looking at me shyly, sidelong. "What does the *J* stand for?"

"Joanna," I said, and I felt something vague, foolish, but undeniably heavy roll off my shoulders. "My name is Joanna."

"Thank you," he said softly, and I knew that he, of all people, understood.

PART FIVE

THE DISAPPEARANCE

OF

EUPHEMIA RUCASTLE HEBRON

20

A Most Unusual Case

I woke the next morning with a headache and a skin-crawling sense of embarrassment at my own behavior. There were reasons I did not get drunk, and keeping secrets was only one of them. But when I went out, Crow said, "Good morning, Doyle," as cheerfully as ever, so that at least I knew he had forgiven me, as angels do and the Fallen do not.

He read me bits of the newspaper stories about the arrests of Jonathan Small, Elias Overton, John Simpson, and Georg Richter, noting almost gleefully the way Jones seemed to absorb all the credit for the arrest, while the rest of us disappeared, except for phrases like "using his influence with the vampiric hunts."

"Of which Jones has exactly none," Crow added.

"Master Moriarty said she had no love for the police."

"Vampires prefer to have no dealings with the police at all. Although they are very careful about obeying the law, it's not because they're law-abiding by nature. It *is* true that if a vampire actually gives their word, they will keep it. It's why they go to such lengths to avoid it."

The *Star* had gotten Jonathan Small's exclusive interview, which was a tissue of self-justifications and lies. We were both indignant at the way he turned Anuvadaka into a bestial savage, claiming "Tonga" had murdered Bartholomew Sholto before he, Small, was even in the room. There was no mention of Small's hemophagic condition.

"Can Jones even prove he's lying?" I asked.

"He can prove he's an unregistered hemophage, and there's that attack in Lambeth that will get him convicted of murder again. But the only person who can disprove his story is Anuvadaka himself, and then it would be down to which one of them the jury believes. Small *does* admit he made 'Tonga' swear an oath of loyalty, so that if Anuvadaka *does* reappear, at least he'll have that much protection."

I hoped Anuvadaka had the sense to stay hidden. It wasn't as if Small was going to escape the gallows.

We were interrupted by the doorbell, and Jennie ushered in a man and, surprisingly, a little girl.

The man, over six feet tall and densely muscled, had an African complexion. He wore a dark suit, of good quality but plainly not bespoke by the way his shoulders strained at the fabric. He wore a brightly colored waistcoat, as the airmen did.

He nodded politely to me and to Crow. "Good morning, gentlemen," he said in a decidedly American voice. "My name is John Hebron, and this is my daughter, Lucy. We are hoping very much that you can help us."

The little girl was no more than eight, not as dark as her father; she was dressed soberly, and with her hair in two thick, beribboned plaits that nearly reached her waist. Her expression was solemn but hopeful.

"I will certainly endeavor to do so," said Crow. "My name is Crow, and I am the Angel of London. This is my friend, Dr. Doyle, whom you may trust as you trust me. Pray take a seat and tell us of your troubles."

John Hebron sat down, and his daughter climbed into his lap, where she gripped his waistcoat with both hands, as if fearing he should be taken from her.

"Thank you, sir," he said to Crow. "The matter concerns my wife, Euphemia. We fear very much that something terrible has happened to her." Carefully, he removed a carte de visite from his waistcoat pocket and showed it to us. A young Caucasian woman, fashionably dressed with her hair braided around her head. The engraved name was Mrs. John Hebron.

Crow, standing now in the middle of the room where his wings had at least a little space to move, nodded and said, "She is missing?"

"No, I know where she is. But I cannot get in to speak to her."

Crow cocked his head. "Perhaps you had best begin at the beginning."

"You must understand that Effie is a faithful wife and a devoted mother. She would never willingly desert us." The little girl hid her face in her father's chest. "I am an engineer on the airship *Friesland,* and am away from home for long stretches. Our household consists of me, Effie, Lucy, Miss Macfarlane—who was Effie's maid before we married and is now our housekeeper and Lucy's nurse—and a 'tween maid named Susan. I returned two days ago from the Cairo run and learned that Effie had gone missing only a few days after I had left. Miss Macfarlane told me that she—Effie—had received a letter in the morning post that had distressed her a great deal, and that afternoon, she had gone out without saying where she was going. She never returned. Miss Macfarlane was able to tell me that the letter was addressed to Miss Euphemia Rucastle—Effie's maiden name—and it seemed obvious that it had to be from her father."

"He disapproved of your marriage?"

"I've never laid eyes on him," said Hebron. "All Effie ever said was that she did not care if he disowned her. I do know that he lives in Balham, in a house called the Copper Beeches. I did the logical thing and went to ask him if he knew where Effie was."

"And?"

"The servants would not let me in the house and threatened to set the dog on me."

"Gracious," said Crow.

"I went back the next day, and the next. Finally a man answered the door actually holding the collar of a giant mastiff, and I do believe he would have let it savage me. After that I did not set foot on the property, but I have gone there daily in the hopes of at least *seeing* Effie. And then yesterday, something very strange happened. From the road, one has a particularly good view of the drawing room, and yesterday my attention was immediately attracted by a chair that had been placed before the center window, for it had not been there the day before. There was a woman sitting in it, in Effie's favorite electric blue dress and with hair of Effie's color—which is an unusually vivid chestnut. All of these things matched Effie's appearance exactly, but I swear to you, Mr. Crow, it was not Effie."

"You are sure."

"I have been married to her for thirteen years, and I love her as much today as I did the day I married her," John Hebron said with great dignity. "I am sure."

"I think we may trust your observations," Crow said.

"After only a few minutes, the woman turned and gestured to me to go away. I was not close enough to see her face, but it was not Effie. All the details were right, but she was the wrong woman. I can't explain it."

"I might be able to," Crow said darkly. "Mr. Hebron, can you tell us anything else?"

Hebron shook his head. "I wish I could."

"How about you, miss?"

"Lucy?" Hebron said encouragingly.

The child lifted her chin as if defying some inward fear and said, "Mama didn't want the letter, for she waited until we were done and Susan was clearing the plates to open it. Usually she opens her letters right away."

"That's a splendid piece of reasoning," said Crow, and the little girl hid her face again, embarrassed by praise.

Hebron said, "Macfarlane says Effie went white as a sheet, and she was distracted all morning. And then, of course, she went out and did not come back."

"I assume you do not have the letter, but do you by chance have the envelope?"

"No," Hebron said, but his daughter tugged on his waistcoat. "Lucy?"

She whispered earnestly to him.

"Well," he said, looking both proud and embarrassed, "Lucy says she has the envelope, but she doesn't want to give it to you."

"Why not, Lucy?" Crow asked gently.

Her face was still hidden against her father's waistcoat, but she said, audible though muffled, "It has Mama's name on it. She has to come back to it."

"Lucy, where did you learn such superstitious nonsense?" said her much discomfited father.

"Gran'mama said," the child explained. "She makes me sign all my letters to her with my full name so that she knows I'll come back to her."

"Lucy . . ." said Hebron.

But Crow said, very seriously, "Did she tell you not to give your full name to anyone you don't trust?"

"Yes, sir," said Lucy, turning her head enough to regard him with one wary eye.

"Good," said Crow. "Your grandmother is right. Your real name has power. I promise I will give the envelope back to you if you let me look at it."

Lucy considered and Crow waited patiently. "You promise?" she said finally, only the slightest waver in her voice.

"I promise," Crow said.

Lucy nodded, making up her mind, and wriggled to pull a grubby and battered envelope out of her skirt pocket.

"Thank you," said Crow and took the envelope over by the window to examine it, both Hebrons watching him anxiously. "As you say, addressed very legibly to MISS EUPHEMIA RUCASTLE. Is the address correct?"

"Yes," said Hebron.

"So that's deliberate. It's a man's handwriting with a very distinctive flourish to the tails. Postmark—legible, huzzah!—Balham. Which confirms you were in the right place." He returned the envelope to Lucy, who immediately put it back in her pocket.

"They never said Effie wasn't there."

"And yesterday's charade suggests that they want you to think she *is* there, but unwilling to speak to you."

"And that makes no sense, either," said Hebron. "If Effie wanted to leave me, she would tell me to my face, and she would *never* go back to her father. He didn't even send Lucy a christening present."

"I wouldn't have wanted it," the little girl said firmly, and made her father laugh.

"We shall be happy to take your most unusual case, Mr. Hebron," said Crow. "I shall be in touch as soon as I find anything, and I pray you do the same, especially, of course, if Mrs. Hebron returns home." He saw the two Hebrons out and came back upstairs, frowning.

"I do not like this, Doyle," said he. "The leaving is one thing, but why would she not return to her little girl? Why would she not write, or at least send a telegram? And that strange pantomime yesterday . . . No, Euphemia Hebron is either being held against her will or she's dead."

"She seems the sort of woman who would, if she were leaving her family, at least have written them a note," I said.

"Exactly. When she left, she expected to return home again in a matter of hours, not long enough to worry her household. Certainly not *days*." He paced thoughtfully up and down the room a couple of times. "The person I want to talk to is Miss Macfarlane. Depending on how long she's been with Mrs. Hebron, she may know a great deal. Will you come?"

"Yes," I said, "I think I will."

THE HEBRONS LIVED in a new two-story villa in St. George's in the East, the part that wasn't holding up the ruthless iron spires of Victoria's Needle. The neighborhood was mostly airship men, whom I supposed to be less likely to take offense at the spectacle of a white woman happily married to a black man. I myself had come to feel Christ's words about the first stone far too keenly to judge.

I followed Crow to the tradesmen's entrance, where the woman who answered the door was clearly Miss Macfarlane; she looked on the verge of tears.

"Good afternoon," Crow said, tipping his hat with the utmost politeness. "My name is Crow, and I am the Angel of London. This is my colleague, Dr. Doyle. Mr. Hebron has hired us to look into Mrs. Hebron's disappearance. May we speak to you for a few moments?"

"Yes," said Miss Macfarlane. "Any help I can be."

She had been Euphemia Hebron's maid for three years before her marriage, but even then Mrs. Hebron had been estranged from her family. "Miss Effie had some money of her own, from her mother, and there was bad blood over that. Her father wouldn't give her any peace about it, wanting her to sign some paper that would let him control it, so that first she moved out and then when he didn't let up, she went to America. I believe she thought it would be safe to come back. It had been nearly fifteen years, and her father didn't want anything to do with Mr. Hebron and Miss Lucy. I believe she thought he would leave her alone."

"You think her father is definitely behind her absence."

"*Yes*," said Miss Macfarlane. "That look on her face when she saw the letter—I never have seen a lady feel so guilty as Miss Effie for doing nothing wrong."

I felt a pang of kinship for Euphemia Hebron.

"Thank you very much, Miss Macfarlane. You've been a great help."

"Will you find her?" said Miss Macfarlane.

"We'll do our best," said Crow, and we took our leave.

"That answered one important question," he said when we'd crammed ourselves back into the hansom. "If her father summoned her, Mrs. Hebron would go."

"But wouldn't expect or want to stay," I said, catching his point.

"Exactly the conditions under which she vanished. Now, I think, our destination is Balham."

◆

WE TOOK THE Underground out to Balham. Crow's wings did look amazingly like an overcoat if you weren't paying attention, and most people weren't. The few people who *did* notice obviously decided he was Nameless. "People see what they want to see," Crow said, startling me out of my train of thought.

"How did you . . ."

He laughed, delighted with his success. "It wasn't hard. You wear most of your thoughts on your face, you know."

"What an uncomfortable notion," I grumbled.

He laughed again, and then, as if in apology, began telling me the life histories of the other people in the car. Even the Nameless, for he could tell me where they'd been that day and what they'd been doing. One of them was a postal angel—and Crow made some deductions about its route that he said cheerfully were most likely wrong—and the other was a lawyer's courier, taking important documents to someone in the suburbs.

I was reminded of something I'd been meaning to ask him. "The Nameless who brought the information about the *Aurora*—he said it was from his sister. But I don't think I've ever seen a female Nameless."

"Ah," Crow said and actually looked uncomfortable. "The truth is, you've never seen a male Nameless. Or a male angel, for that matter. We're all female." My expression was no doubt thunderstruck, for he added, "I did tell you bees were the best analogy."

"You're all female," I said after a moment.

"Insofar as it makes sense to apply gender to asexual beings, yes."

"But . . ." I gestured incoherently at his suit, at the suits of the two Nameless at the other end of the car.

"Human beings give us habitations and names," said Crow, "and also gender. We become what they expect us to be." He eyed me uncertainly for a long moment before he said, "I was female before."

I looked at him hard, then at the two Nameless, thinking about the dun-haired Nameless, soft-voiced and soft-featured. "But if you are all female, why do the Nameless not wear female clothing?"

He raised an eyebrow at me pointedly.

"Yes, sorry," I said, for I'd realized how stupid the question was as soon as I'd asked it. "But I don't see in that case how any of you become 'female' at all."

"Have you ever seen an angel in the process of acquiring a name?"

"No, I don't believe so."

"It is terrifying," Crow said. "We go to the very verge of dissolution—we may spend weeks so incorporeal that we cannot support so much as a pillowslip. But when we cohere again, bound to our habitation, the building owner names us, and our name makes us what we are. In my particular case, I don't actually know how long it was before I was corporeal enough to pick up a pebble." And I knew he meant the chunk of marble that was at the moment in his inside waistcoat pocket. "No one I encountered ever doubted for a second that I was male."

"Good Lord," I said. "I still can't see you as female."

He grinned. "My face and voice changed a good deal, and I'm quite a bit taller. When they named me Crow, I became what they expected." Then he said anxiously, "Don't say that's too peculiar for you, Doyle, please. I know it's a little . . ." He made a helpless double-handed gesture.

I said, "No, it's not too peculiar. Just unexpected."

"Fair enough," said Crow.

❖

BALHAM WAS INCREDIBLY bourgeois, but Crow entertained me, as we sought the home of Jephro Rucastle, with the convoluted story of the Bravo murder, which had also taken place in Balham: "The upshot of it all being that Charles Turner Bravo died of antimony poisoning. No doubt there. It's such a horrible way to die that suicide seems a ludicrous hypothesis—despite both the widow, Florence Bravo, and the hired companion, Jane Cannon Cox, asserting that it had to be. And no matter how many times they questioned him, Bravo himself repeated that he took nothing save for some laudanum he rubbed on his gums. Two people had reason to want him dead. And they were the two people best positioned to murder him. But nothing could be proved against either of them. Jane Cannon Cox did too good a job of destroying the evidence."

"You think she was the murderess?"

"No," Crow said. "I think she was too canny to murder a man with a great walloping dose of antimony like that. She'd have been like Dr. Pritchard and stretched it out over months—made it a mysterious wasting illness instead of this sudden, inexplicable death that made people ask all sorts of inconvenient questions. Now *Florence,* on the other hand. Florence was just the sort of person to dump an unconsidered dose of antimony in her husband's bedroom water pitcher and then go completely to pieces . . . as Florence Bravo definitely did. I think Florence committed the murder, and Jane Cannon Cox committed the cover-up. And although neither of them got the slightest joy from it, they did escape the gallows."

"But how could they possibly have been tried and not—"

"Ah, but they weren't tried. The Coroner's jury brought in willful murder, but that 'there is not sufficient evidence to fix the guilt upon any person or persons.'"

"Hardly the usual formula," I said.

"No, but it was good enough to close off the scandal, which was all the families wanted. Florence Bravo died a lonely alcoholic's death, and for good and faithful service Jane Cannon Cox was sent to Jamaica, whence she had come."

"So much for being an accessory after the fact."

"If she'd hoped it would give her blackmail material, she miscalculated badly. It gave her power over Florence, but Florence was persona non grata with her own family as well as with the Bravos, and Jane Cannon Cox could only take Florence down in a sort of Pyrrhic victory, which—again—she was far too canny to accept."

"Evidence against one was evidence against the other."

"Yes, and any defense counsel worth his fee would ask if the lady who covered up so competently might not be the mastermind behind the murder, with poor Mrs. Bravo as a mere innocent catspaw. Juries have believed more unlikely things than that."

"Here we are, guv," called the hansom driver. "The Copper Beeches."

The house was a handsome one, large enough to make the Hebrons' trim villa look dowdy, and with a quite respectable expanse of grounds. It was immediately obvious how the house had gotten its name, for the stand of copper beeches by the driveway was exceptionally fine.

The door was opened to us by a colorless and frightened-looking maid, who disgraced whoever had trained her by shrieking at the sight of Crow and fleeing into the recesses of the house.

"Well, *that*'s a first," Crow said, sounding hurt. "Usually they at least *ask* if I'm Fallen."

"If you were, of course, they would have had no chance to ask."

"This cold, machine-like logic will make you no friends, Dr. Doyle," he said mock-loftily. "But hark! Someone is coming to find out what's frightened Eliza into fits."

The new arrival was a tall, dour-faced woman, who raised her eyebrows at Crow's wings but stood her ground.

Crow tipped his hat politely. "Good afternoon. We're looking for Mrs. Hebron. Is she in?"

"Who's asking?" she said suspiciously.

"My name is Crow, and I am the Angel of London. This is my

colleague, Dr. Doyle. We only need a minute of her time."

By then, the woman had realized her error. "There's no one here by that name," she said. "This is the Rucastle residence."

But Crow, not at all discomfited, offered his card and said, "Then may I speak to Mr. Jephro Rucastle? It may take longer than a minute."

She hesitated, but she clearly hadn't been told to deny that Mr. Rucastle was at home, and by then Crow was in the house, having used the average human tendency to step back from angels to shameless advantage.

"I'll go see," she said and retreated. I joined Crow in the front hall.

"Someone forgot to rehearse the staff in their lines," I said.

"Slipshod," Crow agreed, and then a woman appeared at the top of the stairs and hastened down them.

"Oh, come quickly!" she said. "Please, come quickly!"

Her hair was vivid chestnut, and she was wearing an electric blue dress. But her round, freckled face was nothing like the portrait of Euphemia Hebron we had been shown.

"You must be the young lady from the window," Crow said.

"What? Oh, yes, but please, it doesn't matter. Just come *quickly*, before he gets here."

Infected by her anxiety, we followed her down a long hallway, through a baize door and then through a door which the woman unlocked. "I'm not supposed to have this key," she said over her shoulder. "I'm forbidden from going anywhere near this wing. But I must help her."

"Her?" said Crow as we started up a narrow staircase carpeted in drugget.

"I don't know her name, but her hair is the same color as mine and I'm wearing her dress. Oh God, I sound like a madwoman."

"Not at all," said Crow, "for you are quite correct. The lady's name is Euphemia Rucastle Hebron. We are here at the behest of her husband, whom I believe you saw yesterday." Being an angel, he was of course not out of breath, though both the false Euphemia and I were panting with the pace we were taking up the stairs.

"Oh!" she said on a gasp. "The . . . the African gentleman!" I wondered what phrase she had thought better of.

"Yes," said Crow. "He and their little girl are most distressed by Mrs. Hebron's disappearance."

"I swear I knew nothing of this," the false Euphemia said. "Mr. Rucastle hired me as a governess, but he had such strange stipulations. . . . I should have been quite nervous about accepting, but Balham seemed safe enough, and the salary is ridiculous."

"I would guess he did not hire you sight-unseen," Crow said, and then we were finally at the top of the stairs, where the false Euphemia led us across the hallway to *another* staircase, this one precipitous and so narrow I could brace myself with a forearm against each wall. At the top of these stairs, we found a half-floor under the gable of the roof, with unfinished plank flooring and low windows.

"She's up here somewhere," the false Euphemia said. "I heard him yelling at her."

Crow shouted, "Euphemia!"

I had never heard him raise his voice indoors before; I was not prepared any more than the false Euphemia was for the way his voice rang, nor for how disproportionately loud it was. It was a little like being caught under a ringing bell.

After a moment's startled silence, someone started banging on the third door down the row, and a woman yelled, "I'm here! I'm here! Please, God!"

The door was locked, but the false Euphemia said, "Let me try." She pulled another key out of her pocket and said with a grimace, "I thought if I was going to be a thief, I might as well do it properly."

"Quickly!" said Crow.

She tried the key and the door unlocked, disgorging a red-haired woman, wild-eyed and exhausted-looking and an uncanny double of the false Euphemia, save for the shapes of their faces.

Mrs. Hebron stared from her double to Crow to me. "What on Earth . . . ?"

"Mrs. Hebron?" said Crow. "My name is Crow, and I am the Angel of London. Are you hurt?"

"No," she said, frowning. "Who is this woman wearing my clothes?"

Crow raised his eyebrows at the false Euphemia, who blushed blotchily. "My name is Violet Hunter, and I seem to have been hired under false pretenses."

That was when a fat man, dreadfully red in the face, appeared at the top of the stairs. *"Euphemia!"* he bellowed, although his voice seemed thin and hoarse compared to Crow's.

Mrs. Hebron said, "Yes, Father? What are you going to do now? Lock us all up?"

He glared, eyes bulging apoplectically. For a moment, he had no answer, and then he shrieked, "The dog! I shall set the dog on these trespassers and this spying vixen!" He turned and rushed down the stairs.

"The dog?" Crow said.

"Carlo the mastiff," Violet Hunter said. "He is quite savage. Usually Mr. Rucastle doesn't go near him without Toller."

"Stay close to me," Crow said. "He's highly unlikely to have had anti-angelic training."

"Oh, he isn't trained at all," said Miss Hunter. "Just half-starved and ill-treated."

"Lovely," said Crow. "Mrs. Hebron, are you all right?"

"Yes, yes. Anything to get out of here!" Mrs. Hebron said fervently.

We had descended the first staircase and were starting down the second when the screaming started.

"Carlo," Miss Hunter said, barely a whisper.

"Oh my God," said Mrs. Hebron.

Crow said nothing, for he was already running pell-mell down the stairs.

I would only fall and break my neck if I tried to keep up with him. I stayed with the women and descended the stairs as quickly as I could.

When we were on the first-floor landing, Carlo began barking frenziedly, and I knew Crow had managed to back him away from Mr. Rucastle. The sound mingled horribly with Mr. Rucastle's screams.

We were just reaching the ground floor when the screaming stopped, though the barking continued.

"Oh God," said Miss Hunter.

"Which way?" I said urgently. "I'm a doctor. I may be able to help him."

Miss Hunter pulled herself together admirably. "I'll show you."

We went, at the fastest pace I could manage, back through the baize door and then along a different hallway and out a side door into an otherwise pleasant garden, where Crow, his wings spread to their fullest extent, had Carlo, still barking furiously, backed against a sort of shed-cum-doghouse, and Mr. Rucastle lay on the ground, motionless and bleeding horribly from the throat.

"All right," I said and got to work trying to save his life.

—◇—

I FAILED. THE damage from Carlo's teeth was too extensive and the blood loss too severe to save Jephro Rucastle. He died there in the garden, killed by his own dog, and although it was callous and un-Christian of me, I could not keep myself from thinking he deserved it.

I met Crow back at Baker Street. Once Toller arrived and took control of Carlo, Crow had escorted Mrs. Hebron to her home, and had not returned to the Copper Beeches, there being nothing further he could do. I answered his questioning glance with a headshake.

"I wasn't fast enough," he said.

"*I* wasn't fast enough, more to the point," I said. "But I think it was too late as soon as Carlo got his teeth set. A mastiff's jaws are a terrible weapon."

Crow nodded and seemed to accept my reassurance, such as it was, but he spent the next day staring out the window instead of immersed in his newspapers. By teatime I was unnerved enough to say something.

"I did warn you I get like this sometimes," he said.

"If this is about Jephro Rucastle . . ."

"It's not that simple," he said irritably, being unable to lie and tell me it wasn't about Rucastle at all. "I just . . . I just don't like getting people killed."

"You didn't get him killed," I said, a little nonplussed. "He did."

"If I hadn't been there—"

"He would still be holding his daughter captive, which I do not think is a better outcome. Did you find out what he wanted from her?"

"His second wife gave birth to a son six years ago. He was trying to consolidate his property. Apparently, he still believed that Mrs. Hebron's inheritance properly belonged to him." But he was not distracted. "Doyle, there must have been something I could have done. We knew there was a dog."

"We didn't know it was so savage it would attack the nearest human being," I said, "nor do I think it is reasonable of you to expect of us that we would. Nor could you have predicted that Rucastle would be fool enough to let the thing out without whatever measures were usually used to control it. Crow." I waited until he was looking at me, not minding for once the intensity of his stare. "There was no point before the screams started at which you could have predicted what was going to happen, and as I said yesterday, at that point, it was too late. On a man with less fat protecting him, Carlo would simply have torn his throat out. And then I suppose gone rampaging the neighborhood, and you *did* prevent that." Crow had kept the beast contained until Miss Hunter found Toller, a drunken old man who nevertheless had a remarkable way with the dog, for he got it back in its shed in a matter of minutes. Carlo would probably have to be destroyed, now that he had killed his master, but that was a matter for the widow, not for us, and I did not mention it to Crow.

"I suppose," he said unhappily. "But I just . . ."

"You feel responsible," I said. "I understand."

"I suppose you must," he said, with more interest, "being a surgeon. How do you stand it?"

"I did the best I could," I said, "and I know that my best is equal to or better than anyone else's best. In war, that *has* to be enough, or the sheer number of dying men you don't save will kill you— sometimes quite literally, for you leave yourself open to hauntings. Guilt calls to ghosts, often more strongly than grief, and any ghost that can move an object can kill a man. Before you ask, yes, I did once see it happen."

His eyes were wide. "Do you think . . ."

I coughed instead of laughing. "I think Jephro Rucastle's ghost, should there be one, would be so tightly focused on either the moment of his death or on his preoccupation with his daughter's money that nothing else would register on it. But I am not a necromanticist, so that's really only a guess."

His look was suddenly suspicious. "You aren't making a game of me, are you?"

"No," I said. "I'm not. I truly did witness the ghost of a soldier kill a surgeon, one of the young ones who wasn't calloused yet. It was . . . not pretty." I hunched one shoulder against the memory and poured myself another cup of tea.

Crow did go back to his newspapers after that, although only *The Times,* and in a subdued mood. The next day he was better, more like himself, and I thought he was making an honorable effort not to brood. I deliberately asked him questions, encouraged him to elaborate on his theory of the Whitechapel murders, which at this point was largely exasperation at the obtuseness of the police. "You can't trust witnesses," he said. "And especially you can't trust witnesses who think they know something. This woman who saw a man talking to a woman she swears was Annie Chapman . . . well, for one thing, you'll never shake her that the woman she saw was Annie Chapman—but you know that's not even a given. For another, she never saw the man's face and yet somehow perceived that he looked 'foreign.'"

"In fairness, one can often pick out a foreigner by the cut of his coat or the shape of his hat."

"Yes, but she doesn't say that." He flipped through his press cuttings. "She says she didn't see his face. But he was a dark-complexioned man over forty, wearing a deerstalker—which is *not* a particularly foreign hat—and he looked to her like a foreigner. All this from a passing glance at the back of his head. That witness isn't worth a halfpenny, and she's the best witness they have."

He was just as scathing about the saga of John Pizer, otherwise known as "Leather Apron," whom the police had been pursuing as a suspect based on the not unreasonable evidence that the prostitutes of Whitechapel were terrified of him. "But he has no reason to start disemboweling them," Crow said. "He has his tidy little racket all worked out—and I don't suppose he ever had to do much more than give a woman a black eye. A man like that is not the sort of man we need to find."

"What do you mean?"

"A criminal. John Pizer is a criminal, and I would bet you a guinea the Whitechapel murderer is not."

"Your Jekyll and Hyde theory."

"Yes. Of course, the problem with my theory is that, unless somebody really does see something, it doesn't provide anything to go on. At least you can *look* for a man called Leather Apron who extorts money from East End unfortunates. But my hypothetical virtuous citizen—well, there *isn't* anything to point to him. If there were, the police would be following it. They know how to proceed with an ordinary murder investigation. But this is something quite different. He's not killing them for any traceable reason. He's almost certainly not known to them, nor they to him."

"Why—"

"Again, if he were known to the prostitutes in the East End, the police would have found him by now. That's the sort of person they're looking for. I suspect he does live in Whitechapel or Spitalfields. He knows the ground too well to be a stranger. But he doesn't *talk* to prostitutes, whether to extort money from them or otherwise. And I doubt he patronizes them. He kills them and somehow leaves no trace of himself behind."

"You *would* think there would at least be a bloody footprint or two."

"Maybe there were at the scene of Polly Nichols's death. There wasn't enough light to tell—not until the car-men and the constables and the bystanders had been trampling all over the place. And a boy had started washing away the blood. But no, he's very careful and very sly, like a fox is sly. And maybe he has a charm like the ones Oksana Timofeyevna makes, so that people don't notice him as he slips away."

"That makes it even worse, for that way no one will *ever* see him."

"Not unless he makes a mistake," said Crow.

PART SIX

LONDON'S NIGHT FACE

21

DEAR BOSS

On the afternoon of the twenty-ninth of September, a wire came for Crow. He read it with a puzzled frown and said, "Well, I wasn't expecting *that*."

"Expecting what?"

"This is from Lestrade. He says they've got a letter from the Whitechapel murderer."

I truly believed I had misheard him. "They've got a what?"

"A letter. Lestrade wants to know if I want to look at it."

"I assume the answer is yes."

That got me a flicker of his smile. "Oh, of course. Do you want to come?"

"I am agog with curiosity," I said. "Let me get my coat."

I changed from my dressing gown to a suitable coat, picked the stoutest of my three remaining sticks (for the one I had lost at the hemophages' warehouse had never been recovered), and joined Crow on the pavement outside the glossy black door of 221 Baker Street.

He hailed a hansom. I was getting very good at squeezing myself into a two-person carriage with the equivalent of three people. The touch of Crow's wings was still unpleasant, but practice was making me better at enduring it, and the drive to Scotland Yard was not long.

Lestrade met us at the door. The Angel of Scotland Yard, who was standing in the broad lobby, beautiful swan's wings half-spread, looked pointedly away from Crow. I noted that he (she?) was haggard and almost translucent, and then remembered the new building going up and felt like an idiot. New Scotland Yard would have a new angel. Whatever plans there were for the old building, the Angel of Scotland Yard would no longer be the Angel of Scotland Yard and might well be forced back into the ranks of the Nameless. No one was supposed to coerce angels into renouncing their habitation—and I had come to feel very strongly about that, knowing that it was essentially the same as death—but of course it happened all the time. Angels were civic-minded creatures.

Lestrade took us to an empty office, where there was a piece of paper lying on the desk. "There it is," he said. "You, too, Dr. Doyle. The more eyes on this, the better."

Crow read the letter and handed it to me. It was written in red ink, in a well-formed and literate hand. It read:

25 Sept: 1888.

Dear Boss

    I keep on hearing the police have caught me, but they wont fix me just yet. I have laughed when they look so clever and talk about being on the <u>right</u> track. That joke about Leather Apron gave me real fits. I am down on whores and I shant quit ripping them till I do get buckled. Grand work the last job was. I gave the lady no time to squeal. How can they catch me now. I love my work and want to start again. You will soon hear of me with my funny little games. I saved some of the proper <u>red</u> stuff in a ginger beer bottle over the last job to write with but it went thick like glue and I cant use it. Red ink is fit enough I hope <u>ha. ha</u>. The next job I do I shall clip the lady's ears off and send to the police officers just for jolly wouldnt you. Keep this

letter back till I do a bit more work then give it out straight.
My knife's so nice and sharp I want to get to work right away if
I get a chance. Good luck.

Yours truly,
Jack the Ripper

Don't mind me giving the trade name.

And there was a postscript, written sideways:

wasnt good enough to post this before I got all the red ink off
my hands curse it
No luck yet. They say I'm a doctor now ha ha

I put the letter back on the desk and said inadequately, "What an unpleasant person."

"That's not the murderer," said Crow.

"What?" said Lestrade.

"The man who wrote that thinks he's funny. 'My funny little games.' He has quite a turn of phrase—Jack the Ripper, indeed—and he's ridiculously verbose. I don't think the real murderer is playing games. I don't think he could talk about what he does that way. And I don't think he'd take the incredibly stupid risk of writing to the police. I don't think he needs to."

"That's a very elaborate explanation," said Lestrade. "Ain't—aren't you the one always going on about the gentleman with the razor?"

"Occam," Crow said reflexively. "And, no, I don't think that's simpler. Aren't you already getting letters from people about the murder?"

"Well, yes, but—"

"You've never gotten a letter like this," Crow said. "That's because it's a fraud."

"We've never had murders like these, either," said Lestrade. "A man vicious enough to do one is vicious enough to do the other."

"You can't equate them like that! Vicious as they are, these are just words. Words, not murder."

Lestrade shook his head. "But why should anyone *but* the murderer write such a letter?"

Crow shrugged. "To make a stir. Which they most certainly have done. I wouldn't be surprised if it turns out they sent letters to the newspapers, too."

"Well, actually," Lestrade said, looking embarrassed.

"What? This *was* sent to a newspaper?"

"The editor at the Central News Agency sent it to us," said Lestrade. "He actually got it on the twenty-seventh, but at first he thought it was a hoax."

"Did he indeed?" Crow said, one eyebrow rising pointedly.

Lestrade stared at him. "You're not suggesting . . ."

"I think you should be alive to the possibility. To me this looks like how someone thinks the Whitechapel murderer *ought* to talk."

"I think you are making this complicated because you love complicated things," said Lestrade—which was an accurate character assessment, if nothing else.

"You aren't listening to me," said Crow. "It isn't complicated. It's a hoax. That's a much simpler explanation than trying to explain why the man who murdered Martha Tabram, Polly Nichols, and Annie Chapman should write *that* letter."

But I could see in Lestrade's face that his mind was made up. Crow saw it, too; his wings flared and settled, and he said, "Clearly I cannot persuade you."

"It's always good to hear your opinion, Mr. Crow," said Lestrade.

Crow snorted, his wings resettling again. "There's no point to this conversation. Do let me know, Lestrade, the next time you want to waste my time by not listening to me."

He stalked out. I shrugged at Lestrade and followed.

—◈—

CROW GRUMBLED ALL the way home and spent the rest of the day muttering at intervals, "It *must* be a hoax. *Must* be."

Finally, I said, "If I tell you I think you're probably right, will it help?"

"*Do* you think I'm right?" he asked, eagerly enough that I had my answer.

"I think something is off in that letter," I said truthfully. "I find it unlikely in the extreme that the murderer wrote it. But I don't think any of us really knows what such a man would be likely to do."

"I suppose not," Crow said grudgingly. "But still—!"

"No, no! Pax! I believe you! If the police proceed on the assumption that the letter writer is the murderer, I believe wholeheartedly that they will make fools of themselves."

"Thank you," said Crow. We were silent for a long time before he added, "Lestrade was right about one thing."

"Was he?"

"It is a vicious letter," said Crow, and I agreed.

We heard nothing from Scotland Yard all the next day, but I was awoken at one-thirty on the morning of the first of October by men's voices in our sitting room. After a moment's tense listening, I heard Crow—his voice recognizable by its timbre—though I could not make out any words. I lay down again, debating whether or not I would be able to get back to sleep, and was just deciding probably not when there was a knock at my door.

"Who's there?" I called, alert all over again.

"It's I," said Crow. "There's been another murder. Do you want to come?"

Part of me wanted merely to go back to sleep (although that was seeming increasingly unlikely), but more of me was at once consumed by curiosity. "Give me a minute to dress," I said, and shoved back the bedclothes.

When I came out, I found Crow talking to a young constable; he broke off to smile at me. "There you are, Doyle! Shall we?"

The night was cold and wet, and when we reached the scene of the crime, a dreary corner of the East End called Dutfield's Yard, the dead woman was lying in the mud like a discarded doll.

Two doctors were already present, a Dr. Blackwell and his assistant, but they were not at all territorial (who would be, with such a corpse?) and were happy to let me examine the body. She was a smallish woman, dressed in layers of shabby clothing that were most likely everything she owned. There was a red rose pinned to her jacket, and for some reason that and the packet of lozenges clutched in her left hand stayed with me more vividly than anything else.

She was a long-faced woman with pale eyes. Between the dark and the rain—and the mud—it was impossible to tell the color of her hair. Her clothing was undisturbed, except that her dress was unfastened at the neck, and Dr. Blackwell's assistant had done that. She was still warm.

The wound that killed her was a terrible gash that had severed her windpipe and all the vessels on the left side of her neck. The blood had pooled on the ground and run up the alley toward the door in the wall.

"Well?" said Crow.

"She certainly died from having her throat cut," I said as he braced me to my feet. "But there's no sign that her murderer tried to get at her abdomen."

"When she was found," Crow said, nodding toward a very pale-faced young man talking to Lestrade and another detective, "blood was still flowing from her neck. I don't think her killer was done with her. He was scared away from her corpse like a scavenging dog."

"Any chance somebody saw him?" I asked, looking at the crowd of gawkers being interviewed by the constables.

"No," Crow said with a sigh. "I'm sure he was gone before Mr. Diemschutz even realized what he had found."

"Does anyone know her?"

"No one yet."

The divisional surgeon, Dr. Phillips, arrived, and I was drawn into colloquy with my fellow doctors. I am not sure how long it was before Crow appeared and began literally dragging me by the hand toward Berner Street.

"Crow! Wait! What—"

"There's been another one," he said, not stopping. "There's been another murder."

<>

IT WASN'T FAR from Berner Street to Mitre Square, where there was another pair of doctors, very white-faced in the lantern light, and another corpse, this one so dreadfully mutilated that I said, "He was angry at being interrupted."

"He might have been," said Crow. "It would explain why he would take the foolish risk of killing a second woman an hour and a mile away."

"And dear God," I said as I got a closer look. He had literally eviscerated this woman; I knelt awkwardly beside the body and saw that he had mutilated her face, drawing designs with the point of his knife. Somehow the delicacy of the cuts—barely more than scratches—was worse than the savage, careless disembowelment. Not that the disembowelment was not bad enough. He had removed her intestines from her abdominal cavity—as he had done to Annie Chapman. Just as I was remembering other details from the Chapman inquest, the knowledge hit me like a sandbag. "Oh God," I said. "Crow!"

He was there immediately and helped me stand.

"He took part of her," I said in the softest voice I possibly could. "I have to follow."

"Well, of course you do," he said. "He's *carrying* it, whatever it is. Lead on."

No one noticed us go.

I was not familiar with the City of London, and even if I had been, I doubt I could have made sense of it in the dark. Crow, however, seemed to know exactly where we were the whole time, and it probably wasn't more than ten minutes before he said, "Doyle, stop! STOP!"

I stopped, and he said, "You're heading straight for the Thames. Whatever he had, he threw it in the river. And while you *can* follow it further, I beg of you not to."

"God," I said. For a moment I thought I wasn't going to be able to stop myself, that I *was* going to plunge into the Thames after whatever part of her body it was that her killer had stolen. But then rationality reasserted itself, reclaiming its precarious throne, and I took a staggering step backward.

"Doyle?" Crow said anxiously.

"I'm all right," I said, a few moments before I was sure it was true.

"Good," said Crow. "For if you jumped in, I don't believe I could pull you out again."

"Nor do I. I'm not going to jump."

"Good," said Crow again, and I realized he was almost as rattled as I was.

We made our way back to Mitre Square, which Crow found with perfect assurance, as if it were not the dead of night in an unfamiliar part of town—but then I wondered if any part of the metropolis was truly unfamiliar to him. He took his self-appointed duties as the Angel of London very seriously, and he had had some unknown number of years—and no need to sleep—to learn its streets, its courts, its mews and rookeries and cul-de-sacs.

No one in Mitre Square had noticed our absence. I went back over by the body, where at least they had gotten a little more light and were playing a macabre sort of Easter egg hunt, looking for her belongings. Even though I knew it was foolish of me to kneel down again, I joined them. Crow swept off in the other direction, but came back only a few minutes later and said, "The constables swear there weren't more than fifteen minutes between the time the square was empty and the time they found the body. Do you think that's possible?"

"Hmmph," I said. "I suppose so, if this fellow has their beats memorized—we already know he's a fast worker. He'd have to have it timed exactly right. But given how dark this square is, I think it's more likely that somebody just missed the body—and probably the murderer."

"I think I won't share that theory," Crow said.

"It would not make you popular with the City Police," I agreed. "And just because I don't think it's *likely* he could do all this in fifteen minutes, that doesn't mean he didn't."

"No one heard anything, either," Crow said.

"Of course they didn't," I said. "I would be disappointed if they had."

The police surgeon, Dr. Brown, had made a sketch of the body's position, and they were now ready to move it to the City mortuary. Crow was helping me to my feet when someone said, "Look alive, it's himself!"

"Oh dear," said Crow.

"What?" I said.

"Major Smith, the Acting Commissioner of the City Police. He and I have had encounters before, which he will not remember any more fondly than I do. Let's just . . ." He pulled me back into the shadows with him, where we disappeared rather as I thought the murderer had probably done.

Major Smith bustled into the square, snapping questions without waiting for answers and bringing with him a sense of anxiety that he probably thought of as urgency, if he noticed it at all. I recognized his type immediately, having encountered it among both doctors and military officers. He would never get the best out of his men, and he would never know why.

Crow waited until the Major was fully involved in the kicked beehive he had made of Mitre Square, then murmured in my ear, "We should go back to Berner Street. See if they've found any witnesses."

We began edging toward the exit from the square farthest from the body. I know for a fact at least one constable saw us, for he winked at me. But we were only in front of Kearley and Tonge's warehouse when another constable came running in from Mitre Street and said something to Major Smith that I could not hear, but that made Crow go stiff.

"Oh God, not another one?" I said and was appalled at the pleading note in my voice.

"No, not that," Crow said. "The Metropolitan Police have found a piece of her apron in Goulston Street and some kind of graffiti."

"Goulston Street it is, then," I said, and we were lucky that Major Smith was much too busy to hear Crow's giggle.

❖

THE NIGHT HAD been full of nervous constables, and here was another one, standing in a perfectly ordinary-looking doorway, where there was a piece of bloodstained apron and, as Crow had said, some very odd graffiti.

I got out my notebook and copied it down carefully, It read:

> *The Juwes are*
> *The men That*
> 　　*Will not*
> *be Blamed*
> 　　*for nothing*

"What does that even *mean*?" I said to Crow.

"Somebody doesn't like Jews," he said. "Will you wait for me?"

"Of course," I said.

He went to talk to the constable, and I puzzled over the graffiti. It was very fresh, so that it was possible it was only two hours or so old, but it was hardly the only message chalked on the walls of that entryway, nor even the only anti-Semitic one. The fact that the murderer had dropped that piece of apron beneath it might merely be a coincidence.

But this was a murderer who didn't drop things. Not after Martha Tabram, not after Polly Nichols, not after Annie Chapman, not after the poor woman in Dutfield's Yard. Why did he drop this piece of apron now?

The obvious answer was: to write the graffiti. But there had been a lot of obvious answers in the Whitechapel murders that had turned out to be wrong. Much like that awful jeering letter, I found myself baffled by the question: if the murderer was going to chalk incoherent anti-Semitic messages on walls near his crimes, why was he only starting *now*? Or—a horrible thought—had the police just missed his previous efforts and he'd dropped the piece of apron to be sure they didn't miss this one?

But if he was anti-Semitic, I countered myself, why was he murdering Gentile prostitutes? And what was this incoherent graffiti supposed to mean? That a Jew was the murderer and was escaping blame? The only reason for the murderer to write that was if he himself was *not* Jewish, in which case it defeated its own purpose—and that didn't seem much like the Whitechapel murderer either.

And yet he *had* dropped the piece of apron. Perhaps he agreed with the graffiti? Perhaps it was simply an accident? There was, after all, rather a lot of graffiti in the East End, and if a fellow was going to stop in a doorway to clean off his knife, he might find it hard to *avoid* anti-Semitic sentiments.

Crow came back and said, "It's much the same as with the body. One minute it wasn't there, the next minute it was."

"Now you see it, now you don't," I said, frowning.

"Quite."

"Do you think the murderer wrote the graffiti?" I said and gave him a summary of my conjectures.

"The fundamental question," said Crow, "is: why should he? To which, of course, there is no answer."

It was at this point that constables and detectives started arriving, both Metropolitan and City, and with them an argument. The Metropolitan Police wanted to erase the graffiti, on the grounds that it was inflammatory; the City Police wanted to preserve the graffiti long enough to photograph it, on the grounds that it was evidence. The argument became more and more heated as daybreak came closer and closer, and reached its apogee with the appearance on the scene of Sir Charles Warren, the Commissioner of the Metropolitan Police, who—over the agonized objections of a City detective—obliterated the graffiti.

Crow said, "He won't make himself popular with that move."

"He was unpopular enough already," I said and, out of curiosity, asked, "Do you think he's right?"

"I think he has good reason for concern," said Crow, which was a neat evasion of either no or yes. "Let us go before Major Smith arrives."

❖

LESTRADE, UNLIKE GREGSON, shared new discoveries with Crow willingly, almost reflexively, so that we had a reliable conduit of information beyond Crow's infinite newspapers. The first thing we learned of was a postcard, received by the first post on Monday morning. Lestrade let us come and see it. It was indubitably the same hand as the letter, and it read:

> *I wasnt codding dear old Boss when I gave you the tip. youll*
> *hear about saucy Jackys work tomorrow double event this time*
> *number one squealed a bit couldnt finish straight off. had not*
> *time to get ears for police thanks for keeping last letter back*
> *until I got to work again.*
>
> *Jack the Ripper*

Crow was just as dismissive of the postcard as he was of the letter. "A man who follows the case as closely as this one does could easily have found out about the murders on Sunday, and besides, he's guessing. The murderer wasn't interrupted because the woman screamed. He was interrupted because Louis Diemschutz came home."

"He said he'd cut their ears off," Lestrade countered, "and part of the second woman's ear *was* cut off."

"But that's not what he took with him," Crow said, because by then we knew that the second woman was missing her uterus and left kidney. "Besides, I saw that cut, and it was accidental. He wasn't *trying* to cut off her ear. I think it's safe to say that if he'd tried, he would have succeeded."

But Lestrade, and the Metropolitan Police behind him, were convinced enough by the letter and postcard that they had facsimiles made of both and placarded them outside their stations. They sent them to the newspapers as well, and the only result was the inevitable one: overnight the Whitechapel murderer became known as Jack the Ripper.

For reasons that I did not fully understand, this development infuriated Crow, never more so than when he caught *himself* using the killer's new soubriquet. It made him sulky and inclined to say "I told you so" when Lestrade bemoaned the deluge of "Jack the Ripper" letters that had begun flooding Scotland Yard.

He was more sympathetic about the muddle of testimony surrounding the woman found dead in Dutfield's Yard, beginning with her identity. On Monday, she was identified by Mrs. Mary Malcolm as that lady's sister, Mrs. Elizabeth Watts. Mrs. Malcolm's identification was quite certain and accompanied by a visitation, for Mrs. Malcolm said that at 1:20 on Sunday morning she had very distinctly felt three kisses on her cheek. Since she had been giving her sister weekly assistance for the past five years, it was indeed plausible that the woman's spirit would have been compelled to express gratitude. However, Mrs. Malcolm's timing was off, for the woman in Dutfield's Yard had been dead well before 1:20, and for all her certainty on Monday, she had been unable to identify the corpse on Sunday.

Moreover, the police had secured a second identification: the woman was Elizabeth or Elisabeth Stride, known among the lodging houses of Flower and Dean Street as "Long Liz," on account of the shortness of her stature. This identification, with multiple witnesses to attest to it, made Mrs. Malcolm's story look even less credible, although the police couldn't discount it entirely, especially when it turned out that Elisabeth Stride had had a vivid imagination of her own. She had accounted for an old injury to her mouth by claiming to be a survivor of the wreck of the *Princess Alice* in 1878, in which (she said) her husband and two children had drowned. Elisabeth herself had been kicked in the face. The trouble was that there was no record of anyone named Stride among either the victims or the survivors of the *Princess Alice,* and while Elisabeth was missing her two top incisors, her claims that the roof of her mouth had been damaged were demonstrably untrue.

The last night of Elisabeth Stride's life was just as confusing as everything else about her. Where with the previous murders there had been no witnesses, in Dutfield's Yard there were too many.

And the most baffling of them was Israel Schwartz.

Schwartz presented his information to the police on the thirtieth, before there was anything in the papers, and he told a very strange story about two men and a woman, who he thought was Stride, that he had seen on Berner Street fifteen minutes before Elisabeth Stride's body was found. Since Mr. Schwartz was Hungarian and spoke not a word of English, he could not be questioned directly, a fact which frustrated Lestrade no end, but the story he told through his interpreters, both to the police and to an enterprising reporter who tracked him down on the first of October, stayed extremely consistent, and there seemed little doubt that he was telling the truth.

What to *make* of that truth was an entirely different matter.

Schwartz had seen a man attacking a woman, and that man had yelled, either at Schwartz or at a third man who might or might not have been with the first man, "Lipski!" Schwartz had fled, and he thought the third man had chased him, but admitted he wasn't sure.

"'Lipski' seems a strange thing to yell," I said.

"Israel Lipski," said Crow, who had brought me the story from Scotland Yard. "Did you not see the reports of the Angel poisoning case last— No, you would've been busy not dying in Afghanistan. Never mind that. Israel Lipski murdered a woman named Miriam Angel by forcing her to drink nitric acid."

"Good God," I said.

"He confessed and was hanged, but his name has become a slur used against Jews in the East End. So that the man who shouted 'Lipski!' might have been shouting *at* Schwartz, who apparently has a strongly 'Jewish' appearance. Or he might have been shouting *to* the third man. But either way, he himself was clearly *not* Jewish, which is a point the Home Office seems to be having a good deal of trouble with, both there and with the graffiti in Goulston Street. I have a theory about *that,* but Lestrade has forbidden me to pursue it."

"What's your theory?" I said, obliging his clear desire to be asked.

"Well, I was thinking about the way the graffiti just seemed to appear along with that piece of apron—now you see it, now you don't—and you said something about it being difficult to accept as a coincidence, and I thought that, really, there's one other person who could willfully make the graffiti and the apron appear together, and that's the person who found them."

"The *constable*?" I said. "I quite see Lestrade's point."

"PC Alfred Long 254A," Crow said. "He's been loaned to Whitechapel from Westminster, so that he has reason to be bitter about this endless investigation, and he's far from the only person to believe a Jew is to blame. And how easy would it be for him to find the piece of apron and simply chalk his opinion on the wall before he blew his whistle?"

"I'm surprised Lestrade didn't kick you out of Scotland Yard."

"Oh, Gregson tried that once," Crow said, grinning. "He just ended up having to apologize and ask me to come back."

He looked so reprehensibly pleased with himself that I laughed even though I didn't mean to. "Is this a serious theory or just a way to wind up Lestrade?"

"Oh, I'm quite serious," he said. "If the constable is the author of the graffiti, we're left with only the one mystery: why did Jack drop—I mean, why did the murderer drop that piece of apron, and that may truly be an accident."

"Two mysteries," I said.

"Two?"

"Why was he going *back* into Whitechapel? He must have known what he'd find there."

"He likes taking risks," Crow said. "We do know that about him. I would guess, in fact, that the risks he takes are part of why he does it. Or, of course, heeding the gentleman with the razor, we might deduce that he resides in Whitechapel."

"Which we'd already deduced," I said. "And even so."

"It suggests Whitechapel is where he's most comfortable," said Crow. "He was confident of evading the police there—and rightly so, as it turned out—less confident anywhere else."

"I suppose," I said, "he might even have dropped that piece of apron to *show* that he'd gone back the way he'd come."

"It's more likely than that ludicrous postcard," Crow said. "This man is not a letter writer, and I shall keep saying that to Lestrade until he believes me."

"I understand his attachment to the theory."

"Oh, so do I! They've a chance of *catching* the letter writer—although not, I think, a very good one. But unless he makes a mistake, I don't think they've any chance of catching Jack at all." And then he went back and corrected himself: "The Whitechapel murderer." But it was a losing battle and he knew it.

22

ERRANDS

THREE DAYS AFTER the inquest on Elisabeth Stride adjourned, Crow reverted to the topic of names again.

He had asked me to go on some errands with him—being unusually close-mouthed about their nature—and I had willingly agreed. We took the Underground first to the nearest thing to a habitation the Nameless had: St. Paul's. They thronged its steps like pigeons, a great restless ever-shifting flock of men with dull gray suits and glorious wings. I tried to think of them as women and could not, even though I knew myself for a hypocrite.

The Angel of St. Paul's was not pleased to see Crow, but at least he acknowledged him. They spoke together in low voices for several minutes; I deliberately admired the architecture rather than trying to listen. Crow came away thoughtful, and on the next leg of our journey, he said, apropos of nothing, "I don't think human beings understand how dangerous names are."

"Probably not," I said.

"They shouldn't have given the Whitechapel murderer a name. Not like that."

"You mean the newspapers?" For the newspapers had pounced so gleefully on the name "Jack the Ripper" that it was now difficult to imagine him being called anything else.

"And the police. By giving credence to that letter, they gave credence to the name, and having a name makes him more powerful, especially because he isn't bound to a habitation."

"Like you," I said, and wished I hadn't.

"Well, yes, if I were a murderer," Crow said, unoffended. "But this is more like one of the Fallen being given a name."

"Could that happen?" I said, alarmed by the mere thought.

"No. They're *not* like me. They can't take a name without taking a habitation, and since the nature of the Fallen is to destroy, no habitation could survive them. You can't un-Fall."

I shivered. "What do you mean by 'more powerful'? He's not a magician."

"No, but—oh, for example, 'Jack the Ripper always evades the police.' Having a name makes it even less likely that the police will catch him. 'No one ever sees Jack the Ripper.' Well, not now they won't. Having a name makes him *more* what he already was. And that was already bad enough."

"Yes," I said, thinking of the mutilated corpse of Kate Eddowes. She had been identified by her common-law husband, based on a tattoo on her arm. Her story was much the same as those of her four sisters in murder: lodging houses, casual prostitution, too much liquor, the Ripper's brutal knife. In a piece of painful irony, she had assured her husband the last time he saw her that she would not let herself be caught by the murderer.

"Here's our stop," Crow said, and we emerged from the Underground at Aldgate, where Crow made directly for the Great Synagogue. I followed him up the steps (and through another throng of Nameless who watched us out of the corners of their eyes), and the Angel of the Great Synagogue met us at the top. "Crow, my friend!" he said with evident pleasure. "What brings you here?"

"Many things," said Crow. "Doyle, this is the Angel of the Great Synagogue of London." I shook hands with the angel, barely even noticing the static discomfort of his touch. He was shorter and stockier than Crow, with dark hair and an olive complexion.

I noted that Crow had not introduced me to the Angel of St. Paul's.

"It is a pleasure to meet you, Dr. Doyle," said the angel, who knew what I was as surely as Crow did, but did not recoil. "You may call me Mal'akh."

Because we had just been talking about names, I noticed that he did not say his *name* was Mal'akh, only that he could be called that. Later, Crow told me that *mal'akh* was the Hebrew word for "messenger," or "angel."

"Likewise," I said.

Crow said, "I wanted to talk to you about the Whitechapel murders."

"Of course you did," Mal'akh said, resigned, as I supposed all of Crow's friends, whoever they were, must be, to the inevitable topics of conversation.

"I don't think he's Jewish," Crow said, possibly as reassurance. "But I'm puzzled by the way the Stride and Eddowes murders seem to be"—he paused, visibly fishing for a word—"haunted, in a metaphorical sense, by anti-Semitism." He explained Israel Schwartz's story and the Goulston Street graffiti (leaving out his theory about the real author), and finished by saying, "Elisabeth Stride was killed next to a predominantly Jewish social club, and Catherine Eddowes was killed in Mitre Square, which is what? A literal stone's throw from here?"

"About," said Mal'akh.

"These things don't fit with the first three murders, but I can't decide if there's something really there or not."

"Leave out the graffiti," said Mal'akh. "It's most likely a coincidence that has mistakenly been assigned meaning. That kind of graffiti is too common to bear any weight. We wash similar sentiments off our walls all the time."

"That's fair," said Crow.

"Have you considered that Elisabeth Stride might not have been killed by the Whitechapel murderer at all? I've been reading the papers, and her murder seems different from the others."

"Well, we have to assume it's unfinished," Crow said. "He killed her but didn't have time for more before Mr. Diemschutz and his pony showed up."

"But he only needed fifteen minutes for what he did to Kate Eddowes," I said.

"He wasn't surprised," Crow said. "He knew exactly when the constables would come through Mitre Square on their beats. He planned for them. He didn't plan for Mr. Diemschutz."

"But the testimony of Mr. Schwartz is also different," said Mal'akh.

"If that was the murderer, if it was Elisabeth Stride, and if he was even in Berner Street at all," said Crow.

"You're arguing with my theory before I've finished presenting it," Mal'akh said mildly.

"Sorry," Crow said, and his wings hunched.

Mal'akh said, "These murders are creating a great deal of anti-Semitic sentiment, but in and of themselves . . . murdering a prostitute is neither Jewish nor non-Jewish, and while there may indeed be ritual in what he does to the bodies, it's *his* ritual. It's certainly not Jewish or connected to the Kabbalah or any of the other poisonous nonsense being whispered around the city." He sighed. "And I do think poor Elisabeth Stride may have been killed by someone else. These murders make a perfect blind."

"London is a city of great opportunity," I said dryly, and both angels looked at me as if they had forgotten I was there.

Crow said, "Thank you, Mal'akh. I just wanted a better opinion than my own—and to warn you that the Home Office seems to be warming to the theory that all these murders are the work of a mad Polish Jew."

"Oh dear," said Mal'akh.

"The police don't agree, but you know how it is with pressure from that high up."

"I shall warn the Rabbi," said Mal'akh. "Thank you, my friend."

As we walked back toward the Underground, Crow said, "He was one of the few angels who spoke for me at—I can't call it a trial because that implies a lot of things that weren't there. He spoke for me when I was judged by a jury of my peers and found unfit to join in the Consensus. It took considerable courage on his part—angels like harmony, not discord, and none of us likes to dissent—and without him and those one or two others, I might have been driven out of London to perish in the wilderness."

"The rest of England is hardly a wilderness," I said.

"Oh, but it is," he said, and he was quite serious. "No other Consensus would have taken me in if London threw me out."

"There's a difference between finding you unfit to join in the Consensus and throwing you out?"

"One is . . . I'm not allowed to join in the Consensus, but I'm still part of it. It's like I've been sent to bed without any supper. The other is being thrown out of the house. They didn't *disown* me, and they could have."

"It seems like some of them must have wanted to," I said, thinking of the angels who stared past Crow as if he weren't there.

"It's . . . complicated," Crow said.

I said, "Most things involving families are."

⊷

THIS TIME WHEN we emerged from the Underground, Crow led me through a warren of side streets to a quite unremarkable green door. We went inside and up two sets of stairs, and at the second-floor landing was an angel with jackdaw wings. He said, "Good afternoon, Crow. I'm glad to see you remembered our appointment."

Crow winced a little and said, "Doyle, this is the Angel of Whitehall. Whitehall, this is my friend, Dr. Doyle."

"What a remarkable friend," said Whitehall, and I went hot from my collarbones to my hairline.

Crow said, "Whitehall is my . . . I guess I have to say my guardian."

"I keep him out of trouble when I can," Whitehall agreed, "and I appreciate your efforts in that same direction, Dr. Doyle."

I had no idea what to say. He was politely soft-spoken, unremarkable in appearance, and utterly terrifying. The sharp feeling most angels gave off was in the Angel of Whitehall at least doubled, maybe tripled. He was, I knew, a very old angel, and perhaps that accounted for it. He had also been the confidant of kings and princes for centuries.

Fortunately, Crow was impatient. He said, "Can't we just get this over with?"

Whitehall said reprovingly, "You are graceless," but then to me, "If you will excuse us, Dr. Doyle." He opened one of the doors off the landing and ushered Crow through it, shutting it firmly behind them.

I was uneasy, although I did not know exactly why. Perhaps it was how silent it was; this part of Whitehall seemed to be absolutely deserted. Perhaps it was the Angel of Whitehall's crackling aura still unsettling me. But when there *was* a noise, I jumped like a startled cat, and then wasn't even sure what the noise was. It had been a cry of some kind, but I couldn't tell in my memory of it whether it was animal, human . . . or angelic. I wasn't sure if it had been a cry of startlement, of anger, of pain. I couldn't tell where it had come from, and above all else, I didn't know what to do.

It is a sign of how unnerved I was that I actually considered leaving, just going back to Baker Street and letting Crow find his own way home—which he was eminently capable of doing. But that was rank cowardice, and I was appalled at myself for considering it, even if only for a couple of seconds.

My second option seemed to be going in search of the noise, but there I was paralyzed by choice: there were three doors, plus stairs leading both up and down, and the noise had echoed so strangely that it might have come from anywhere.

Or I could stay where I was and do nothing—which was the result all my dithering achieved. I was still standing in exactly the same place when Whitehall reappeared, carefully closing the door behind him.

He was alone.

"Where is Crow?" I said and cursed the perfectly audible suspicion in my voice.

"He'll just be a moment," said Whitehall. "He asked me to ask you to wait for him."

"Of course," I said.

"You really are a most remarkable friend," Whitehall said. He sounded bemused.

I could feel the disturbance he made in the aether from where I was standing. Nevertheless, I asked, "What happened? I heard something."

"Yes," said Whitehall. "I thought you might." He folded his hands carefully in front of him and said, "It is the consensus of London that only the Nameless shall fly."

The silence returned, even more oppressive than before, while I stared at Whitehall, trying unsuccessfully to understand what he was trying, even if obliquely, to tell me.

"The Nameless fly," I said slowly, repeating a fact I'd known since earliest childhood.

"Yes," said Whitehall.

"But you . . . the angels of the London Consensus, if I have that right, do not fly."

"Correct. So far as I know, the only Consensus whose angels fly is the Consensus of Madrid."

"Crow isn't Nameless," I said, feeling like the world's slowest student trying to solve an equation for x. "And he isn't allowed to join in the Consensus, but . . . is he an angel of the Consensus or not?"

"He is a disgraced angel of the Consensus. He agreed to accept our judgment on him in return for being allowed to stay in London."

"Your judgment . . . did you do something to him?"

"He consented," Whitehall said, still as mild as milk. "It is a binding, much like clipping a bird's wings. And like that, it must be repeated periodically."

"It sounded like it hurt."

"It is . . . not pleasant," Whitehall admitted.

"Then why don't—can't you just accept his word that he won't fly?"

Whitehall made a pained face. "There are certain members of the Consensus, the Angel of the Tower and the Angel of Buckingham among them, who do not entirely believe Crow is not Fallen."

"But how could he be?"

"They think that instead of finding a way not to Fall, he has found a new kind of Fallenness." He added dryly, "It is not a particularly rational belief."

"How could Crow agree to something like that? How often do you have to do it?"

"Once every three months. Tinker with it though I will, I cannot make it last longer than that."

I was somewhat heartened by that sign that Whitehall did not like this situation, either.

I said, "It seems cruel. And why on Earth do the angels of the Consensus not fly?"

"We separate ourselves from the Nameless in every way we can," said Whitehall. "If they fly, then we do not."

That sounded insane, but before I could say that, or anything else disastrous, Crow came out. He looked shaken, his feathers rumpled, and he flicked a glance at me without meeting my eyes.

"Shall we go?" he said, trying for lightness and failing.

"Certainly," I said. If he wanted to pretend nothing was wrong, I would happily follow suit.

Whitehall looked amused, but said, "It was a pleasure to meet you, Dr. Doyle. Crow, you should bring your friends to visit more often."

Crow's wings hunched around him, but his voice was much steadier when he said, "I'll take that under advisement. Good-bye, Whitehall."

"Good-bye," I echoed, although I could not manage a platitude.

"Au 'voir," said Whitehall, smiling.

I waited until we were in the Underground carriage, our words protected by the noise of the train, to ask, "Are you all right?"

Crow hesitated long enough that I knew he was trying to find a way around saying *no*. Finally, he said, "You don't need to worry. I'll be fine."

"Interestingly," I said, "neither of those statements answered the question I asked, which, of course, is an answer in itself."

Crow's wings hunched even tighter, and I thought I would do better to change the subject. "Why are the angels of Madrid the only angels who fly?"

"The Consensus of Madrid is the only one that might accept me if London were to throw me out. They are considered renegades."

"Because they fly?"

"Among other reasons. I only know about them what I have read in books, which say they circle their habitations like doves of peace, singing with unearthly beauty."

"That sounds lovely," I said dubiously.

"So I'm told," said Crow. "But I don't want to find out."

PART SEVEN

THE SECRET

OF

THE MIRE

23

A Third Appeal
for Help

The stick was a good one, of the type called a Penang lawyer. The plate on it read: *To James Mortimer M.R.C.S. from his friends of the C.C.H., 1884.* The iron ferrule was much worn down, and the stick itself was quite banged about, with what looked like teeth marks below the plate.

"As a carte de visite, this leaves a great deal to be desired," I said to Crow.

Crow said from his fortress of scrapbooks, "Assuming that it has not been stolen—or, I suppose, inherited—we at least know the fellow's name."

"And profession," I agreed. "And he has a dog which he allows to carry his stick."

"Between that and the remarkable amount of wear he's put on it in four years, I think we can safely call him a country practitioner."

"CCH—Charing Cross Hospital or Coursers of something-something?"

"Charing Cross, almost certainly. On the occasion of his leaving for his country practice with the great esteem of his colleagues."

"Not an iota of ambition, then."

"Or some other circumstance in his life that required him to leave London." Crow sounded vaguely horrified at the thought.

"Such as?"

"An invalid wife. A nervous breakdown. Mostly, people move to the country for their health, don't they?"

"Some people," I said dryly, "do not like the city."

He gave me the look that meant he thought I was making a joke that he did not understand. "Do you not . . . like London?"

"It is a cesspit," I said.

He stared at me. "Well, yes, I suppose it is. . . . But why do you stay if you do not like it?"

"The I.A.F. doctors are here," I said, "and I have nowhere else to go. My family has disowned me, no hospital in the Empire would take me on, and I have not the faintest hope of being able to maintain a private practice, even if I could afford to buy one, which I cannot. London was invented for people like me: half-pay officers, loungers, idlers, wastrels."

"You are harsh," said Crow. He had put aside his scrapbook and was watching me intently.

"I am truthful," I said. I turned away from his gaze and crossed to the bow window.

"You haven't been to an aetheric practitioner yet, have you?"

"Well, you see," I said wearily, "there's a snag. Any aetheric practitioner I go to is going to recognize instantly that I'm a hell-hound and probably that I have a vampiric binding. Any *respectable* practitioner will refuse to treat me until I am registered, and any *non*-respectable practitioner will probably at once stoop to blackmail. And besides, I don't want the aetheric equivalent of a backstreet abortionist."

"Have you spoken to Oksana Timofeyevna?" asked Crow. "There must be aetheric practitioners who are sympathetic to the plight of the unregistered."

I said nothing.

"Doyle? We aren't fighting again, are we?"

He sounded so alarmed that I blurted out the truth: "I'm afraid that the practitioner will agree with the doctors that there's nothing more to be done. *Assuming* they don't turn me in to the police."

"I'm quite sure that there's something the practitioner can do," Crow said. "We will talk to Oksana Timofeyevna and see whom she recommends."

It was childish, but what made the difference was the word "we."

"You will come with me?" I said, knowing full well how pathetic I sounded.

"Of course," said Crow.

The whole time I had been staring blindly out at Baker Street, and now my attention was caught by one of the pedestrians. "I say, Crow, I think I see the man who belongs to that stick."

"What makes you say that?" Crow said, getting up to come see.

"The length of his stride. You see, there, how he keeps having to pull himself up short to keep from bumping into the people ahead of him?"

"The tallish skinny fellow?"

"Without a walking stick, yes."

"I see nothing to contradict your theory. And, yes, look! He's ringing our bell. Well done, Doyle!"

The approbation in his voice was perfectly sincere, and my face heated.

"It's nothing compared to—"

Jennie tapped on the door. "Please, Mr. Crow, it's that gentleman who was here last night."

"Show him up, Jennie," Crow said, and I limped back to my chair to be out of the way.

The gentleman who belonged to the stick suited it, being also clearly once high-quality, but now shabby and covered in dog hair. He was tall, rather lanky, and possessed of a pair of mild, myopic, rather dream-fogged eyes. I was not surprised that he had left his walking stick behind.

"My stick!" were the first words out of his mouth. "Oh, thank goodness. I've been racking my brains to think where I left it.

You would be horrified at how often that happens." He blinked mildly at Crow. "You must be the Angel of London."

"I am," said Crow, delighted. "And you must be James Mortimer."

"How did you—oh, yes, of course. My stick."

"Pray have a seat," said Crow, "and let me know how Dr. Doyle and I can help you."

The mild eyes blinked at me. "Are you a medical doctor?"

"I served with the I.A.F.M.C. in Afghanistan," I said.

"Good gracious," said Dr. Mortimer. "Perhaps you *can* be of help to me. It would certainly benefit from someone whose physical courage is greater than my own."

"What would benefit?" said Crow.

"It's about the Hound."

I prayed I had not jumped visibly. Crow said, "The Hound?"

"Of the Baskervilles," said Dr. Mortimer.

"Perhaps you had best start at the beginning," said Crow.

"I shall endeavor to do so," said Dr. Mortimer, "although it is difficult to know where the beginning is." He pondered for a moment and finally said, "I suppose it begins with Sir Hugo. The Baskervilles have preserved a transcript of the testimony at the inquest into the death of Sir Hugo Baskerville in 1656. The original manuscript is lost, but there is a clean copy that was made in 1742, and there is no reason to doubt its accuracy. I shall summarize it as best I can." He cleared his throat. "Sir Hugo was a bad man, violent and profane and cruel as a cat is cruel, so much so that he was actually examined for possession in 1653 and pronounced clear of demons. He was simply one of those men who enjoy other people's pain and fear. In 1656, he became enamored of a village girl, and the more she refused him, the more determined he grew to have her. Eventually, the inevitable happened, and one day when her father and brothers were gone, Sir Hugo carried the poor girl off to Baskerville Hall. He locked her in a first-floor bedroom, and then he and his friends proceeded to get vilely drunk, and the girl—who could hear them, of course—finally, in utmost desperation, climbed down the ivy and ran.

"She was lucky in that no one saw her go, unlucky in that shortly thereafter Sir Hugo took it into his head to bring her some food—and God only knows what else he meant to do—and found that she had escaped."

Dr. Mortimer took off his glasses and fiddled with them nervously. "He was infuriated beyond anything any of his friends had ever seen. He leapt onto the table and shook his fist at the rafters and howled that he would give himself entire to the forces of darkness if he could but catch the girl that night."

"That seems a singularly reckless oath," Crow said disapprovingly.

"I believe it may fairly be said that Sir Hugo was a reckless sort of person. Also, the local people all believe he had sold his soul to the Devil long before that. In any event, none of his friends seem to have been bothered, and one of them had the bright idea of putting the hounds on her scent. The Coursers of Baskerville were known then and are known now for their bravery and tenacity on a scent, and the poor girl had left behind a handkerchief in her flight. The hounds set off baying, with Sir Hugo right behind them, and his drunken friends following as best they could.

"They quickly lost sight of Sir Hugo, but kept following the noise of the hounds. It was unfortunately a full moon and a clear night, so that no one was tempted to give up. They followed the baying of the hounds for some length of time that none of them could later agree upon, until quite suddenly the baying stopped. Moments later they heard a terrible scream, which cut off even more terribly. They drew close together, but kept going, there being both courage and foolishness in numbers. Very shortly, Sir Hugo's black mare bolted past them, broken reins trailing, and then they came upon the hounds, who were clustered whimpering at the head of a deep dip in the moor. The local word is 'goyal,' and they can still show you Hugo's Goyal with perfect certainty.

"In the goyal were two dead bodies, and here I want to be as exact as I can. Sir Hugo was lying flat on his back with his throat torn out. Nearby was the girl with her throat cut and Sir Hugo's hunting knife in her hand. She was naked."

"Naked?" Crow and I said in near unison.

"Stark naked," said Dr. Mortimer. "But her clothes, lying nearby, were not torn as a man would tear them off, but—still perfectly layered—torn as if from the *inside*. And all around Sir Hugo's body were the footprints of a hound far larger than any in the Baskerville coursing pack."

"The girl was a hell-hound?" said Crow.

"That was the conclusion of the inquest," said Dr. Mortimer. "No human being could have made the wound in Sir Hugo's throat, and with all of Sir Hugo's friends accounted for, where else could the beast have come from?"

"And it explains her suicide," I said, cold despite the fire in the grate.

"Her family swore she was not a hell-hound, but I think it's rather an open question whether they'd been hiding her affliction—which was a capital crime during the Protectorate—or whether Sir Hugo's oath had perhaps crossed some desperate prayer on the girl's part. For he did indeed catch her."

"Indeed," said Crow. "This is a most interesting piece of local history. But why has it brought you to my sitting room?"

"Well," said Dr. Mortimer with a deep breath, "when the next baronet, Sir Rodger, was dying, the servants reported seeing 'giant glowing eyes' outside the windows at night. And on the morning after his death, the footprints of a gigantic hound were discovered in the flower beds beneath his bedroom windows. There was then, and continues to be to this day, considerable argument over whether it was the ghost of the unfortunate girl—Constance Burry was her name—or an actual fetch. But it has faithfully appeared for the death of every baronet since. Which brings me to Sir Charles, who is the most recently deceased baronet, if you will forgive the infelicitous phrasing. Sir Charles was my patient, and I must tell you that he was a man with a serious heart condition. He was also a timid man, a hypochondriac, and a man with a morbid fear of dogs. When he assumed the baronetcy, it was the first time that anyone could remember someone *other* than a Baskerville being Master of Hounds for the Baskerville Course. They are quite hoping the new baronet will be a man of different mettle."

"They don't know the new baronet?"

"Sir Charles was unmarried and childless. The new baronet is a Colonial. His father, Sir Charles's younger brother John, having quarreled with their father over his choice of a Colonial wife, followed his wife back to her home—in Virginia, I believe—and never returned to England, dying when Sir Henry—for that is the new baronet's name—was still a small boy. Sir Henry, the estate solicitors found farming in Canada. But I have become sidetracked. My point was simply that Sir Charles dreaded dogs, even lapdogs. He believed wholeheartedly that the Hound is a fetch, and he dreaded meeting it. When he began to think he was catching glimpses of a spectral black dog on his evening walks—on the grounds of the Hall only, for he would never venture on the moor at night—I admit I did think it might be his imagination. True fetches are so rare, and the legend of the Hound is so dramatic, that it would be very easy for an overimaginative man like Sir Charles to talk himself into his own death. But when he did die, in the yew walk at Baskerville Hall, the footprints of a giant hound were found around his body; therefore, I decided that the Baskervilles did indeed have a fetch and it had been warning Sir Charles as best it could."

"But now you are not so sure," said Crow.

"Now I am beginning to wonder if there is not some other explanation. Sir Henry is only just reaching England today, but yesterday one of the gardeners came to me, white as a sheet, and said he'd found a dog's footprints, too large to be natural, in the flower beds along the south wall of the house. Those rooms aren't in use any longer, but one of them is the window Constance Burry climbed out of in making her escape. Another is the bedroom window of that Restoration Sir Rodger. And I do not know what to think."

"It can hardly be a death visitation for someone who isn't there," said Crow. "Are there any other Baskervilles—cousins or the like—at

Baskerville Hall?"

"No. Sir Charles's father, another Hugo, was an only child, and of his three sons, Charles had no children, John had only the one and himself died in Virginia, and Rodger, the black sheep of the family in the good old-fashioned sense, made England too hot to hold him and went to South America, where he died of yellow fever in 1876. Sir Henry is the last of the Baskervilles."

"Then perhaps it is the ghost of Constance Burry," I said.

"But the footprints have never before shown up *except* when one of the baronets was dying. Certainly never when the baronet wasn't even *there*."

"You think it is an actual living hell-hound," said Crow.

"I don't know *what* to think," said Dr. Mortimer. "But I am concerned for Sir Henry's safety. For if there is a mortal hell-hound, the possibility exists that Sir Charles was deliberately frightened to death."

"Murder," said Crow.

"It is what I fear," said Dr. Mortimer.

Sir Henry Baskerville was arriving at Waterloo Station that morning, and the crux of Dr. Mortimer's visit was what he ought to do with the new baronet.

Crow was perplexed. "Why should he not go to the home of his fathers? Any evil which can befall him there can just as easily befall him in London—more easily, perhaps. After all, a fetch *predicts* death. It does not cause it."

"And if the footprints belong to a living being?"

"Then Sir Henry can be defended with locked doors and a load of buckshot," said Crow.

"You are flippant, Mr. Crow."

"Not at all. A shotgun is an excellent defense against almost all mortal creatures, and I would suggest you purchase one, for peace of mind if for no other reason."

"But Sir Henry!" said Dr. Mortimer. "I am to meet his train in less than an hour!"

"And you should certainly do so," said Crow. "Give me twenty-four hours to consider your problem. At ten o'clock tomorrow morning, come back—bring Sir Henry with you—and I shall give you my best opinion on the matter."

"Thank you," said Dr. Mortimer, scribbling a note of the appointment on his shirt cuff. "I shall do that." And he hurried out—at the last moment remembering to take his stick with him.

24

SIR HENRY
BASKERVILLE

THE NEXT MORNING the doorbell rang at ten o'clock, so promptly that I was immediately sure it was not Dr. Mortimer's doing. And indeed, when Jennie led our guests upstairs, it was Sir Henry Baskerville who came in first.

He was a small, alert, dark-eyed man about thirty years of age, with thick black eyebrows and a square jaw. He wore a tweed suit of Colonial cut and had the deep crow's-feet of one who has spent the great majority of his time out of doors, but he most definitely had the bearing of a gentleman.

"This is Sir Henry Baskerville," said Dr. Mortimer unnecessarily.

The baronet's sharp eyes were taking in everything: the double-stacked and overflowing bookcases, the chemical apparatus, the bulging scrapbooks, Crow's ink-black wings, my cane, finishing with a quick assessment of our faces. He said, "The odd thing, Mr. Crow, is that if Dr. Mortimer had not told me of his appointment, I might have suggested coming 'round myself. I understand that you think out little puzzles, and I've had one this morning which wants more thinking out than I can give it."

He had a decided Colonial accent. I wondered how many Englishmen would hear the voice, not notice the watchful eyes, and take the new baronet for a rube. Anyone who did would be in for an ugly surprise.

"Pray take a seat, Sir Henry," said Crow. "Do I understand that you have had some adventure since you arrived in London?"

"Nothing of much importance. Only a joke, as likely as not. It was this letter, if you can call it a letter, which reached me this morning."

He laid an envelope on the table, and we all bent over it. It was of common quality, grayish in color. The address "SIR HENRY BASKERVILLE, NORTHUMBERLAND HOTEL" was printed in rough characters, the postmark Charing Cross, and the date of posting the preceding evening.

"Who knew that you were going to the Northumberland Hotel?" asked Crow.

"No one could have known. We only decided after I met Dr. Mortimer."

"But, of course, Dr. Mortimer was already stopping there?"

"No, I had been staying with a friend," said Dr. Mortimer. "There was no possible indication we meant to go to *any* hotel, never mind which one."

Crow cocked his head and regarded Sir Henry. "Someone seems to be very deeply interested in your movements." Out of the envelope, he took a half sheet of foolscap paper folded into fourths. This he opened and spread flat upon the table. Across the middle of it a single sentence had been formed by the expedient of pasting printed words upon it. It ran, "AS YOU VALUE YOUR LIFE OR YOUR REASON KEEP AWAY FROM THE MOOR." The word "moor" only was printed in ink.

"Now," said Sir Henry, "perhaps you can explain, Mr. Crow, what is the meaning of that? And who can possibly have taken such an interest in my affairs?"

Crow raised his eyebrows at Dr. Mortimer. "There is certainly nothing supernatural about this."

"No, but that in itself means nothing. Anyone knowing of this business might send such a warning."

"What business?" asked Sir Henry sharply. "You gentlemen seem to know a great deal more than I do about my own affairs."

"We shall share our knowledge," Crow said. "Perhaps you will have a different perspective on it. Do you know of your family legend?"

"What, you mean the Hound?" He laughed. "My father scared me half to death with stories of the Hound when I was a little boy. I remember when he was dying, I didn't sleep for two nights, trying to listen for the Hound to make it go away and leave my daddy alone. But I was too little to understand what a fetch was. What does that have to say to this?" And he flicked the paper with his fingernail.

"That's the part that isn't clear," said Dr. Mortimer. He explained to Sir Henry what he had told us the day before, finishing with the footprints of a giant hound in the south flower beds two days earlier.

Sir Henry listened intently, eyebrows drawn together. "You think someone in the house is a hell-hound and they scared my poor Uncle Charles to death?"

"Someone with access to the house," Dr. Mortimer said. "And I don't know that I *think* that, precisely. But I am concerned."

"It seems very unlikely," said Sir Henry. "Perhaps the ghost of Constance Burry got riled up with not having a baronet around all these months. It's a ghost, not a clockwork toy. It doesn't have to do the same thing every time. Besides which, why should anyone want to scare Uncle Charles to death? Aside from me—and I hope you're not suggesting I had anything to do with it."

"Oh, good Lord, not at all!" Dr. Mortimer said, horrified.

"Who is the next heir?" Crow asked.

"We did go into that," said Dr. Mortimer. "After Sir Henry, we have to go back to Sir Rodger, Sir Hugo's father—they all have the same names, the Baskervilles. Sir Charles had an elder brother Hugo, but he died before Sir Hugo did. But Sir Rodger had a younger brother, and we traced his line to an elderly, childless, and utterly unambitious vicar in Westmorland."

"After him?" said Crow.

"After him, we should have to hire an augur or similar professional, and I don't think that putative heir can have any more idea than we do that they are third in line to the baronetcy."

"Did my uncle have any enemies?" said Sir Henry.

"He was a most uncontentious soul. Even the Baskerville Course was only *disappointed* when he shut the kennels, not angry."

"He shut the kennels? But even in America, they recognize the name Baskerville in foxhound lineages."

"Sir Charles was terrified of dogs," said Dr. Mortimer. "He couldn't bear to have them on the estate."

"Good Lord," said Sir Henry, clearly taken aback. "Well, I guess I know what I'm doing first off."

"McAllister will weep with joy," said Dr. Mortimer. "He was Sir Hugo's kennel master and he's never gotten along with Mr. Tenby quite the same."

"Well, there's someone who wanted Uncle Charles dead," Sir Henry said, perhaps a shade flippantly.

"It can't be McAllister," Dr. Mortimer said. "He has forty dogs which would betray him instantly if he were a hell-hound."

"I didn't mean it," Sir Henry said. "And anyway, you said *disappointed,* not *swearing vengeance.*"

"No, Sir Charles insisted that McAllister's employment went with the pack—even if Mr. Tenby had wanted to get rid of him, and as far as I know he didn't. There was no enmity there. And even those who might have disliked Sir Charles personally would never want to do anything drastic, not when having a Baskerville at the Hall affects so many people's livelihoods. You, ah. You will be very popular when you arrive."

"Will I?" Sir Henry looked even more taken aback than at the news his uncle had closed the Baskerville kennels.

"Your uncle was a very good landlord, and a charitable one, which is not the same thing."

"No indeed," said Sir Henry. "But that makes it all the more unlikely that someone deliberately set out to kill him."

"Except for this letter," said Dr. Mortimer, "which certainly has been sent by someone who wants to keep Baskerville Hall empty."

"You yourself said they might be referring to the ghost, or the fetch, whichever it is," said Crow.

"Yes," said Dr. Mortimer, but he looked dissatisfied.

"For myself," Crow continued, "the more I think about it, the less I believe this letter writer to have any benevolent intentions. If he did, why not come to Sir Henry in person? Or at least sign his epistle? Or at least use his own handwriting, which he seems to have been at great pains not to do—you notice that 'MOOR' is written in the same capitals as the address. None of this suggests a person with any legitimate concern for Sir Henry's welfare."

"No, it does not," Sir Henry agreed.

"Or, if perhaps this warning is genuine, it has been written by someone who, for some other reason, most passionately desires to remain anonymous. It does seem to have been composed in a state of great agitation—which seems unlikely for someone plotting your doom. But either way, it makes it unlikely that the footprints in the flower beds belong to the ghost. And even makes it unlikely that what Sir Charles was seeing was the genuine Hound. Do you know of anyone in the neighborhood who is a hell-hound, Dr. Mortimer?"

"I don't," said Dr. Mortimer. "And since all of the local landowners course, like McAllister they would be betrayed at once."

"And the servants at the Hall?"

"Sir Charles made do with just a butler and a housekeeper—he'd shut up most of the house. They're a married couple, the Barrymores. And I suppose I don't positively *know* that neither one of them is a hell-hound, but I cannot think it very likely."

"That seems like a good first line of inquiry," said Crow. "We have hell-hound footprints in a flower bed—I don't suppose anyone thought to take a cast of them? No, of course not. We need to find a hell-hound to match them."

Dr. Mortimer scribbled a note on his cuff.

"But we cannot do that from here," said Crow. "From here, we can only decide whether Sir Henry ought to go to Baskerville Hall or not."

"Why shouldn't I go?" said Sir Henry.

"This is either a threat or a warning," said Crow. "Either way . . ." And he shrugged.

"That's only if all this *isn't* the fetch or the ghost. If it's the fetch, it doesn't matter where I go. I'm not afraid of the ghost of Constance Burry, nor am I afraid of dogs. And if it *is* someone who wishes me ill, I'd much rather face them *there,* where I can see them, than to try to do it in London. I can't even keep track of my own boots here."

"You've lost your boots?" said Crow.

"Just the one," said Sir Henry with a self-deprecating smile. "And I only bought them last night. Good brown boots. It's enough to make a cat cry."

"I'm sure it's only mislaid," said Dr. Mortimer. "We shall look thoroughly, and I've no doubt it will turn up."

"I hope so. Six dollars I paid for 'em, and I haven't even got them on my feet yet."

"The question remains, Sir Henry," said Crow, "what are you going to do?"

"Well, how the . . . how the Sam Hill should I know? This is an awfully heavy load of information to dump on a man all at once. Look. It's eleven-thirty now, and I'd like a quiet hour or so to myself to think things through. If Dr. Mortimer and I go back to the Northumberland now, and you and Dr. Doyle come around at two and lunch with . . . oh." His face fell. "You don't eat, do you?"

"No, but I don't mind watching," said Crow. "And Dr. Doyle eats, so that it's not as though your invitation is wasted."

"Would that be satisfactory to you, Dr. Doyle?" asked Sir Henry.

"Perfectly," I said. "I am long used to Mr. Crow watching me eat."

"Excellent. Then we will see you at two o'clock. I want a walk, Dr. Mortimer, do you care to join me?"

"Gladly," said Dr. Mortimer.

No sooner had the front door closed behind them than Crow was all but hauling me out of my chair. "Quick, Doyle, your boots, your boots, oh my sainted hat, how are you still in your dressing gown?"

He chivvied me into my outdoor clothes as relentlessly as any nanny.

I said, "If you wanted to walk with them, I'm sure you had only to say so."

"Yes, but I most particularly do *not* want to walk with them. Come on!"

Bewildered but game, I followed him down the stairs and out onto Baker Street, where Dr. Mortimer and Sir Henry were still visible about two hundred yards ahead of us in the direction of Oxford Street.

"Are you sure?" I said. "You could easily catch them up."

"I am perfectly satisfied with your company, if you will tolerate mine," said Crow. "It is certainly a beautiful morning for a walk."

That much was true. It was rare to have a truly blue sky over London, but this was as close as it came; the air was crisp with the promise of winter without actually being uncomfortably cold.

Crow might not have wanted to walk with Dr. Mortimer and Sir Henry, but he certainly wanted to keep them in view. He edged us closer, bit by bit, into Oxford Street and down Regent Street, until we were only about one hundred yards behind them, and I could see that Sir Henry was talking animatedly and Dr. Mortimer was nodding periodically. When, once, they stopped and stared into a shop window, Crow grabbed my elbow and we did the same. "Looking for another pair of boots?" I said.

Crow said, "I hope you aren't suggesting he should give up on the one lost at the Northumberland. It hasn't even been twenty-four hours yet." Then he gave a cry of satisfaction, and following the direction of his glance, I saw that a hansom cab with a passenger, which had halted on the other side of the street, was now proceeding slowly onward again.

"Come on!" said Crow. "We'll get a look at him, if nothing else."

At that moment, I was aware of a bushy black beard and a pair of piercing eyes turned upon us through the side window of the cab. Instantly the trapdoor at the top flew up, something was screamed to the driver—I could not for the life of me make out the words—

and the cab clattered madly off down Regent Street. I was just in time to keep Crow from dashing into the street in pursuit.

"It's too late," I said urgently, remembering not to grip as hard as I wanted to, for I did not know if angels were breakable and did not want to find out. "He's driving like a man demented—you'll never catch him."

"No," said Crow, "no, I suppose not. Blast it all!" I thought for a moment he was going to fling down his hat and stomp on it.

"Who was that man?"

"I have not the least idea."

"A spy?"

"It would seem so."

"But for *whom*? And *why*?"

"Both excellent questions, to which at the moment I have no answers, except the surmise that it is someone who knows Dr. Mortimer by sight, for otherwise how should he recognize his quarry?"

"Not just someone who knows Dr. Mortimer," I said, "but someone who knows—and is passionately interested in—his errand. For I can think of no other reason why anyone should be following him."

Crow laughed. "You need to exercise your imagination more, Doyle. I can think of several. But I agree with your principle that Sir Henry is the object of our spy's attention rather than the good doctor . . . and these things together suggest that the spy is interested in something happening *before* Sir Henry reaches Baskerville Hall. For if not, why bother coming to London? Why not just wait for Sir Henry to come to you?"

We had resumed walking, still toward the Northumberland, although the doctor and the baronet were out of sight. "Well," I said, "why *not* just wait for Sir Henry to go to Baskerville Hall? You're right—it would make him infinitely easier to find."

"But, on the other hand, it is much harder to hide oneself. There's no convenient crowd in which to become lost. Did you, by chance, get a good look at him?"

"I could swear only to the beard."

"And so could I—from which I gather that in all probability it was a false one. But I got the cab number, 2704. The cabman should at least have an interesting tale to tell. Hold up a moment, Doyle."

The Nameless collect in front of houses of worship and also in front of bakeries. Bakers believe they are good luck and, at least in London, any bakery without a few Nameless clustered in front of it tends to be regarded with suspicion. The bakery we were passing was no exception to the rule, and I waited obediently while Crow plunged into discussion with the handful of Nameless standing in front of it. I watched as one turned, took three strong steps, and jumped into flight, passersby ducking his wings as a matter of course. After a few more minutes of animated discussion, two others hurried away in the direction of Charing Cross.

"There," said Crow with considerable satisfaction. "Two lines of inquiry started."

"Which are? Or do you not intend to tell me?"

"Of course I— Oh, you're teasing. Well, I sent one off to find out the driver of hansom 2704, and the other two are going to canvass the hotels around Charing Cross and see if they can find a copy of yesterday's *Times* with some very particular words missing."

"Do you really think they'll find it?"

"No. It's most likely been burned. But if they are successful, it could prove exceedingly instructive."

"He won't have registered under his real name."

"No, that would be too much to hope for. But if someone has remarked the beard, we'll know it's the same man as the one in the hansom—which, I confess, I'm inclined to assume it is. And someone might have seen him *without* the beard. Or someone might remember his voice. There are a thousand details I can tease out that he wouldn't have thought of disguising. In any event, it is certainly worth the effort. And it gives two of my Nameless kindred something to do. One of the things I remember very vividly about being Nameless is how *boring* it is." He paused a moment, considering the matter, and said, "Although, of course, having a habitation is not necessarily better in that regard."

"That's a radical opinion," said I.

He shrugged wings and shoulders together. "They've already blackballed me."

"But I thought angels were kept very busy with the . . . with the household work, for want of a better term."

"And that isn't boring in and of itself?" said Crow. "Yes, as the Angel of the Sherlock Arms, I supervised the maids and the porters and the cooks, but they were all people who knew their jobs. I spent most of my time in the lobby waiting for guests to greet. It was *horrifically* boring."

He made me laugh, as he had intended, and shifted the topic of conversation. "I have been thinking about the matter of finding an aetheric practitioner. Have you any objection to going 'round to see Oksana Timofeyevna now? We should have just about the right amount of time."

"No, no objection. You'll be tactful, though?"

"My dear Doyle!" said Crow. "How you wound me!" He was grinning as he flagged down an empty hansom.

CROW HAD BECOME closer friends with Madame Silvanova than I had realized. This time when we reached Southwark, he led me around to the mews behind Madame Silvanova's shop and there without hesitation rang the doorbell beside a bright red door—which was answered, very swiftly, by the lady herself.

"Mr. Crow!" Her face lit up, making it less composed of angles and more composed of facial features. "And Dr. Doyle! Do pray come in."

We followed her up a narrow staircase—I noted the door that had to lead to the back room of the shop—and into a warren-like apartment of tiny rooms that opened into a common hallway or into each other or both without any discernable system. Madame Silvanova led us into a sitting room so tiny that a person on the settee was nearly knee to knee with anyone in the armchair, and the second chair was wedged back in the corner as if it feared the settee would do it a mischief. The window was tall and deep, and the cream-colored tabby on the windowsill was sleeping soundly in the sun.

"I regret that the accommodations are not better," said Madame Silvanova, "but please have a seat." She chose the chair in the corner, I took the armchair, and Crow managed to arrange himself on the settee.

Madame Silvanova smiled at us both. "I do not think this is a social visit. How may I help you?"

"We have need," said Crow, "of an aetheric practitioner who is morally opposed to the Registration Act."

It was in fact a very tactful way of phrasing the matter.

Madame Silvanova clearly understood what he meant. She said, "There are very few who are trustworthy. Oxborrow when he's sober, but that is only about a fourth of the time. Blundell wouldn't turn anyone in, but she's a ham-handed wretch—Grigori's friends call her Charlotte Blunder. No, Martha Damon is your best choice. Excuse me one moment." She left the room by the door we had not entered through.

Crow said, "So many things are a matter of knowing whom to ask."

I said nothing, for in truth I found it difficult to believe it could be so easy, and Madame Silvanova returned before either of us spoke again.

She said, "I've given you three addresses, just in case. Martha Damon, Cyrus Oliphant, and Thomas Oxborrow. Oxborrow's the best of them, in truth, but his wife's death . . . he is killing himself with laudanum as fast as he can. All of them are honest, and all of them hate the Registration Act." She handed a folded piece of paper to Crow, who squirreled it away in his waistcoat.

"Thank you," he said as he stood up. "We have another engagement, so that we cannot stay, but I will come back on a better afternoon."

"Please do," said Madame Silvanova with more than mere politeness in her voice, and I heaved myself up out of the armchair, wondering despite my best efforts where the catch was.

—◇—

THE NORTHUMBERLAND HOTEL was smallish and decidedly genteel: just the place to bring a baronet fresh from the wilds of the Colonies. The clerk was expecting us and was puzzled but politely agreeable when Crow asked to see the register.

"There, you see?" said Crow to me as if continuing a conversation which we had decidedly not been having. "Theophilus Jones." And he demanded of the clerk, "The airship captain, is it not? Tall, stout man with blond side-whiskers?"

"No, sir, this Mr. Jones is a coal-owner and a very active man."

"A coal-owner?" Crow said as if deeply disappointed. "Surely you are mistaken in his trade?"

"No, sir," the clerk said apologetically. "He has stayed with us for many years on his visits to town. All the staff know him well."

"And this lady, Mrs. Oldacre—do forgive my curiosity, but I know a Mrs. Oldacre. Is she a youngish lady, quite sprightly and much concerned with good works?"

"No," the clerk said, even more apologetically. "This Mrs. Oldacre is a widow, an invalid lady. Her husband was the Mayor of Gloucester. She lives here in between her trips to Bath and various spas on the Continent."

"Certainly not a lady I know," said Crow, and he did a good job of sounding as if the admission pained him rather than being flat truth. "Ah well."

"Who is the Mrs. Oldacre you know?" I murmured as we crossed the lobby.

"Former client," said Crow. "And she *is* a sprightly lady much addicted to charitable work."

I thought I would do well to remember just how close Crow could come to falsehood. That clerk would certainly swear an oath that Crow had told him there was a tall, stout airship captain named Theophilus Jones. It further and most uncomfortably occurred to me, as the swallow-winged Angel of the Northumberland turned pointedly away from Crow, that Crow might do well to be rather more careful. The clerk, after all, would *offer testimony*—and sincerely believe its truth—if called on to do so, and thus he would prove that Crow was a liar. And if Crow was a liar, he was Fallen. And if he was Fallen . . .

But there was no time for that train of thought, for just as we started up the stairs, we met Sir Henry Baskerville coming down. He was furious, nearly knocking Crow flat as he turned to snap over his shoulder at a flustered waiter, "Then *find* it."

I caught Crow's elbow to keep him upright. He said to Sir Henry, "Still looking for your boot?"

"Oh! I beg your pardon, Mr. Crow. And, yes."

"But"—Crow frowned at the dusty black boot in the baronet's hand—"surely you said that it was a new brown boot."

"So it was. And now it's an old black one."

"What! You don't mean to say—"

"That's just what I *do* mean to say. Look. I had three pairs of boots in the world: the old black ones, the new brown ones, and the patent leathers, which are on my feet right now and I'll sleep with them under my pillow if that's what it takes to keep them safe. Last night it was one of the brown ones, and this morning they've made off with one of the black ones."

"I see you've sent out a search party," said Crow.

"Well, it's ridiculous!" said Baskerville. "One boot is one thing, but I'm now out two of my three pairs of boots, and Mortimer's already reminded me that I can buy another pair, but that's not the point! But—" He coughed, clearly embarrassed at his own passion. "I apologize for creating such trouble about a trifle."

"I think it's well worth troubling about," said Crow. "For example, how do you explain it?"

"Well, I don't," said Baskerville. "The clerk assures me the Northumberland has never been troubled by poltergeists."

"I am sure they have not," said Crow.

"What do *you* make of it? You're the puzzle-solver."

Crow laughed. "Puzzle-solver, not miracle-worker. I do not profess to understand it yet, but I do not despair of doing so. But come, I see Dr. Mortimer approaching."

We lunched very pleasantly—three of us eating and Crow asking questions about the food, as cheerfully curious as always about something he could never experience himself—and afterward retired to a private sitting room. Sir Henry, as he relaxed into our company, proved to be an excellent raconteur. He had served as a light-boy on the airship *Antioch* in his teens, and had come away from it with a fund of stories ranging from hilarious to hair-raising.

"Why did you not return to Virginia?" Crow asked. "I admit my grasp of Colonial geography is imperfect, but isn't Canada a dreadfully long way from where you were a child?"

"Some of it is farther than that," said Baskerville. "Which is an advantage when you've quarreled with everyone you're related to in three counties. My mother was quite the black sheep of the family for bringing home an Englishman, and there were some things said at her funeral that I have not yet forgiven."

"Gracious," said Crow. "I had no idea anti-English sentiment still ran so high."

"Oh, mostly it doesn't," said Baskerville. "The Buller side of the family is just the sort of people who can never let an argument die. You know . . . 'And another thing!' two days later."

"I had an uncle like that," I said. "The bane of every family gathering."

"Yes," said Baskerville. "Now multiply him by ten and you have my Buller cousins. No, I don't miss Virginia. And Canada was beautiful, but very lonely. I'm hoping England will be less so."

"You will not have many close neighbors," said Dr. Mortimer, "but most of us are sociable. And naturally you'll join the Baskerville Course."

"How could I not? I shall have to buy a couple of hunters and hope they don't go the way of my boots."

Crow said, "Then you've definitely decided to go down to Baskerville Hall?"

"Yes, at the end of the week."

"On the whole," said Crow, "I think that decision is a wise one. Did you know that you were followed this morning from Baker Street?"

Dr. Mortimer startled violently, and Sir Henry said, "*Followed?* By whom?"

"That is an excellent question. Dr. Mortimer, do you number among your neighbors and acquaintances in Dartmoor a man with a very full black beard?"

"I thought you said the beard was probably false," I said.

"Oh, I still think so," Crow said. "But it would be stupid to act as if we'd proved that when we haven't."

Dr. Mortimer was pondering. "There's no one I can— No, wait! Barrymore. Sir Charles's butler is a man with a full black beard. He's rather vain of it."

"Splendid," said Crow. "And where is Barrymore?"

"At Baskerville Hall."

"Hmmm," said Crow. "It wouldn't hurt to find out if he is really there. Or if by chance he has deserted his post for a jaunt to London."

"But how can you possibly determine that?" asked Baskerville.

"Easily enough," said Crow. "A telegraph form will do the trick. 'Is all ready for Sir Henry?' Address to 'Barrymore, Baskerville Hall.' Which is the nearest telegraph office?"

"Grimpen," said Dr. Mortimer.

"Thank you. Then we'll send a second wire to the postmaster, Grimpen: 'Deliver telegram into Barrymore's own hand. If absent, please return wire to James Mortimer, Northumberland Hotel.' That should let us know by evening whether Barrymore is there or not."

"Clever," said Baskerville. "By the way, Dr. Mortimer, who *is* this Barrymore fellow?"

"He was Sir Charles's butler. The Barrymores have been at Baskerville Hall for four generations. This Barrymore's father was the groundskeeper, and Sir Charles never did enough in the way of entertaining to want much of a staff. Mrs. Barrymore is the housekeeper." He added anxiously, "They are an extremely respectable couple."

"Who are sitting very pretty with no one at the Hall," said Baskerville. "Did my uncle leave them anything in his will?"

"Five hundred pounds each," said Dr. Mortimer.

"Did they know that?" said Crow.

"Yes. Sir Charles was fond of discussing the provisions of his will."

"That," said Crow, "is very interesting."

Dr. Mortimer said, "I hope you are not suspicious of everyone who received a legacy from Sir Charles, for I, too, inherited a thousand pounds."

"Indeed," said Crow. "Anyone else?"

"Insignificant amounts," said Dr. Mortimer, "and a number of charitable bequests. The residue all goes to Sir Henry."

"And how much is that?"

"Seven hundred and forty thousand pounds."

"Good Lord," I said.

Crow's eyebrows had gone up. "I did not realize there was so much at stake."

"On those grounds," said Baskerville, "I believe I'm my own best suspect."

"We did not know how wealthy Sir Charles was until we came to examine his securities," said Dr. Mortimer. "It was a dreadful task. I felt like a vulture."

Crow's wings rustled, and I wondered how close he'd come to having Vulture as his name. He said, "I remember that you told me the next heir after Sir Henry is a clergyman."

"Yes. His name is James Desmond. He came to visit Sir Charles once, not very long after Sir Charles had come back from South Africa and reopened Baskerville Hall, and he refused to accept a settlement of any kind, although Sir Charles pushed him hard."

"And if Sir Henry dies, he inherits . . . ?"

"Everything," said Baskerville. "The title and the estate are entailed, and I have no intention of leaving the money to anyone else—it seems directly counter to my uncle's wish to restore Baskerville Hall to its former glory."

"Indeed," Crow said, frowning deeply. "Well, Sir Henry, I agree that you must go to Baskerville Hall, if only because someone seems so insistent that you must not, but we must make provisions for your safety."

"For my *safety*?" Baskerville burst out laughing. "You can't protect me from a fetch, Mr. Crow!"

"No," Crow agreed, "but if it is not a fetch, then some measure of defense may prove necessary. And if it *is* a fetch, it does no harm. I suggest you hire a cerberus—there is a company I can recommend— and above all else, you must not go alone."

"Well, no," said Baskerville. "Dr. Mortimer accompanies me."

"Dr. Mortimer has his practice and his family, to whom he is no doubt eager to return, and his house is miles from Baskerville Hall. With the best will in the world, he may simply not be there when you need him. I meant that you need a companion, someone who can remain by your side."

"Is it possible that you could come yourself, Mr. Crow?" the baronet asked hopefully.

"Regrettably, I cannot."

I said, "I can go."

"Would you?" said Baskerville, and I realized that he was more nervous than he was trying to appear.

Crow said, "Are you sure, Doyle? It may not be . . . restful."

"I believe I can manage," I said, knowing that he was referring as much to my hell-hound manifestation as to my health. "A change of scenery will probably do me good."

"Only, the thing is," said Sir Henry Baskerville, "I don't know a soul in London beyond Dr. Mortimer and the two of you, and I should be truly grateful to have someone to watch my back."

"You cannot ask for anyone better than Dr. Doyle," said Crow, acquiescing to my plan with sudden enthusiasm. "And it will be a simple matter to keep me apprised of developments."

"I shall write you faithfully," I promised.

"It is *very* kind of you," said Baskerville. "We are planning to leave on Saturday. Does that suit you?"

"Perfectly," said I.

"Then on Saturday," said Dr. Mortimer, "unless you hear otherwise—or there are further incidents, I suppose—we shall meet at the ten-thirty train from Paddington."

We had risen to depart when Sir Henry gave a yelp of triumph and, diving into one of the corners of the room, he dragged a brown boot from under a cabinet.

"My boot!" he cried.

"But how very odd," said Dr. Mortimer. "I searched this room quite carefully before lunch."

"So did I," said Baskerville. "Every dratted inch of it."

"There was certainly no boot there then," pursued Dr. Mortimer. "Do you think the waiter would have put it there?"

"It seems prodigiously unlikely," said Crow. "But we are honor-bound to inquire."

But none of the waiters, none of the maids, none of the clerks could shed any light on the matter of the brown boot. In desperation, Sir Henry even asked the Angel of the Northumberland, but she never went into the private rooms and said she had noticed nothing.

"*You* would have noticed," I said to Crow as we walked home.

"My situation is rather different," he said. "I *listen* to what I hear, because I have no protection from attack except myself, and I have no dominion any more than I have a proper habitation. Most angels *hear* a great deal more than they *listen* to. She genuinely does not *listen* to the private rooms—they are not part of her dominion."

"Then a dominion is different from a habitation?"

"Sometimes. Her habitation is the entire building. Her dominion is the part of the building under her aegis. My dominion at the Sherlock Arms didn't include the cellars. I never went down there—they could have been doing anything at all for all that I knew, because I wasn't listening to them." He considered a moment and added, "Think of it as a strategy to keep from going insane."

"A strategy you have abandoned."

"Any angel you ask will tell you I'm already insane. But that's neither here nor there. The relevant part is that the journeys of that boot remain a mystery from start to finish."

"We have quite a collection of mysteries over the past two days," I said. "The anonymous letter, the black-bearded spy in the hansom, the loss of the new brown boot, the loss of the old black boot, and now the return of the new brown boot."

"Plus," said Crow, "the mystery of the hound's footprints in the flower beds of Baskerville Hall."

"Yes. Those, too, although they *might* be the ghost of Constance Burry."

"I think they almost certainly are not," said Crow. "*If* they'd appeared the night after Sir Henry's arrival, perhaps. But a night when there was no baronet whatsoever at the Hall? No, Constance Burry is not the explanation of those footprints. I wish I knew what was."

We continued to puzzle over this cluster of mysteries, receiving no illumination either from a telegram which Jennie brought up just before supper (*have heard Barrymore is at the Hall—Baskerville*) or from the report of the Nameless who had investigated the hotels around Charing Cross. They had visited twenty-three hotels and had had no luck at any of them.

"It was a long shot," Crow said philosophically. "I have more hope of the hansom driver."

But that Nameless, too, reported failure. He had found the cabdriver, sure enough, but the cabbie, like Crow and myself, remembered only the bushy black beard, and while the man had given a name, it was so common as to be patently false. "He could only have been more insulting if he'd called himself John Smith," said Crow. "'John Watson,' indeed."

"He knew we would ask."

"Yes. He was entirely prepared to be flushed out of hiding, false name, false beard, and he had the cab drop him at Victoria's Needle."

"Whence he could go absolutely anywhere."

"With perfect ease," Crow agreed bitterly. "Check and mate."

25

AN AETHERIC
INTERLUDE

SIR HENRY BASKERVILLE's plans left me Thursday and Friday for preparations—and for Crow's grim determination to drag me to an aetheric practitioner before I left London.

"It's waited this long," I protested. "There's no reason it can't wait a few weeks more."

"And no reason it should," said Crow. Which of course was unanswerable.

We went first to Martha Damon, as Madame Silvanova had suggested. She lived and worked on a street of prosperous artisans, one of the East End's dwindling pockets of respectability . . . and she was not seeing new patients. No argument Crow made could move her doorkeeper, and we were forced to try the next name on the list, Cyrus Oliphant.

Oliphant lived above a public house in Shoreditch. It was not precisely a bad part of town, but it was seedy and down-at-heel, and Oliphant himself was much the same. I disliked him on sight, and five minutes later was leaving the premises, in preference to punching him in the nose, although the latter would have been a good deal more satisfying.

"No," I said to Crow when he caught up with me. "I don't care. *No.*"

"All right," he said, "but you realize that leaves us with the opium-eater."

"Better that than a jackass," I said.

"Well, it's probably a good time of day to visit Mr. Oxborrow," said Crow. "Even if he has already started measuring out his drops of laudanum, he can't have measured very many."

Oxborrow lived in a tenement, one shaky step up from a doss-house, and he was even shabbier than Oliphant. But his room was clean, and the pale green eyes in his ashen, mournful face were intelligent. He didn't bother hiding the bottle of Battley's and the cracked cup on his one unsteady table, whether it was from defiance, honesty, or just indifference.

He looked at us without interest when we came in, and barely batted an eyelash at Crow; then he looked at me a second time and said, possibly involuntarily, "Good God."

"Do you think you can fix it?" said Crow, who never noticed when he skipped over the social niceties. Perhaps he had decided, long ago, that they were not part of his dominion.

"I don't know," said Thomas Oxborrow. He got up and came closer, but hesitantly, as if he wasn't sure he wanted to get too close. "You have encountered one of the Fallen."

"In Afghanistan."

"And it touched you."

"Barely."

"Well, yes, or you wouldn't be standing here talking about it."

"Is there anything that can be done?"

He raised an eyebrow in appreciation of the distinction between Crow's question and mine. "There's certainly something that can be done, although I don't know how much. But why have you come to me? Anyone who gave you my name would have told you I'm an opium addict."

"I'm . . ." This part was harder to say than all the rest of it put together, and not only because I was admitting to a felony. "I'm unregistered. The . . . the friend who recommended you *did* say you were an addict, but she also said you wouldn't turn me in."

"Well, that's true enough," he said, almost reluctantly. "But I'm hardly the only one."

"We tried two others," said Crow. "And our friend said you were the best of them anyway."

He blinked. "That encomium makes me doubt your friend's judgment. But, well, you are here, and I'm not far gone enough yet to be incompetent. Let us have a talk about your spectral wound." He gestured me to the only chair, while he sat on the bed. "Tell me what happened."

I did the best I could, although he unnerved me by asking detailed questions about the position of the sun and the prevailing wind, and we ended up using his cup, my watch, all the farthings and halfpennies in Crow's pockets (and the Battley's to represent the Fallen) to make a diagram of the attack. I could at least tell him the date, and he consulted a battered almanac to find the phase of the moon.

He read my palm, although he did not say what he found there, and being given the date and hour of my birth, worked out my horoscopical information with the help of an even more battered set of astrologer's tables that he dragged out from beneath the bed. Then he said, "I need to examine your aetheric aura in more detail."

"All right," I said. "What does that entail?"

He looked uncomfortable. "First, I need to assure you that nothing I discover will leave this room. I do not gossip and I do not trade in my clients' secrets."

"That is good to hear," said I. "I have trusted you this far. It would be foolish to cavil now."

"Thank you," he said, and he did seem relieved. "Then if you will give me your hands and be patient—it generally takes between five and ten minutes."

I extended my hands and said, "I will curb my natural impatience."

His smile was hesitant and fleeting, as if he wasn't sure whether I was making a joke or not. His grip on my hands was firm, surprisingly warm, not unpleasant. He bowed his head, and we were silent for a length of time sectioned off by the ticking of my watch. Behind me, Crow was as perfectly silent as a stone angel in a cemetery.

After what felt like a very long time, Oxborrow spoke without raising his head: "It is a very ugly wound, and its effects are all through your aura. I cannot heal the wound itself, but I can free your aura of the darkness—of at least some of the darkness that is preventing the wound from healing."

"All right," I said. "Can you do it now?"

"No. It requires a fair amount of preparation, and you need to come to it fasting. If you will return tomorrow morning at six o'clock, having eaten nothing and drunk nothing but water since six o'clock this evening, I will do what I can. I must warn you that it will be painful."

"Thank you," I said dryly. "And can I trust you with the preparations?"

"Touché," he said, and lifted his head to look at me, the pale eyes clear and determined. "You have given me a problem to wrestle with, and since I take opium in order to escape my thoughts, you have relieved me of much of the temptation. I know only a fool trusts the word of an addict, but I give you my word anyway: you can trust me to stay sober today."

I felt the barely there spark of his oath—he was right that the word of an addict was not to be trusted. "Then I will return at six o'clock tomorrow morning," I said, and Oxborrow released my hands.

⇥

I FASTED OBEDIENTLY that night, and in the morning, Oxborrow's tiny room was covered in chalk symbols, red on the walls, white on the floor, and he himself was waiting for us, clear-eyed and apparently eager to work.

"You're not Nameless," he said to Crow, as if it had taken him this long to notice what he was seeing.

"No," Crow said. "My name is Crow, and I am the Angel of London."

Oxborrow looked intensely puzzled—he was apparently one of those rare people who actually understood the nature of an angelic habitation well enough to know that London could not be one—but he made an actual gesture of pushing something to one side, and said, "Dr. Doyle, if you would remove your boots and stockings, I will show you where to stand."

The floor was cold against my bare feet, but at least it was clean. I positioned myself as Oxborrow showed me—quite alone in the middle of the room now that the table and chair were upside down on the bed—and nodded to show my understanding when he said, "It is very important not to smudge the *diagrammata*." He put Crow in the bare half circle in front of the door and himself stood with his bare feet positioned one to either side of a smoothly curving line.

My Latin was disgracefully rusty, so that I could not follow most of what he said, but I felt it, almost immediately, first in my femur, but swiftly in all the bones of my leg and hip, something like buzzing, something like heat, something like the sharp pain of breaking and the dull pain of healing. I inhaled hard, but kept my feet, and then set myself to endure.

Oxborrow did not work as swiftly as a surgeon, but of course he did not have to worry about his patient bleeding to death before he finished. He did work steadily and without hesitation, which I thought was a better sign than speed, no matter how much I wished he'd hurry up.

And then I felt . . . if shadows had weight, I would say I felt a shadow fall off me. I felt it so distinctly, I would almost have sworn I heard it hit the floor, like an Indian viper shot out of the thatch roof of a hut.

I shuddered, and this time my knees did give out. I landed hard, but without any of the sick pain I expected.

"Are you all right, Dr. Doyle?" said Oxborrow. "No, don't try to get up, I'm almost done."

"I'm all right," I said, and coughed, inwardly cursing my voice for skying like a boy's.

He was truthful about being almost done, for it was less than five minutes before he said, "There, that's it," and began using a dishcloth to erase his chalk symbols and equations.

Crow came to help me up and said, "In layman's terms, what did you do?"

Oxborrow said, "In layman's terms, I balanced Dr. Doyle's aura so that it will rotate smoothly like the sublunary sphere that it is."

"Ah," said Crow. "Doyle's aura is much brighter now."

"Do you see auras?" I asked, although I didn't know why I was surprised.

"That's most of what I do see," he said, more than a trifle apologetically. "I have to concentrate to make out the details of a human being's physical appearance."

"Is that why they say it's impossible to hide from an angel?"

"Well, first of all, it's perfectly possible to hide from an angel, and that is an idiotic saying," he said crossly. "But it's much harder to hide from an angel who knows *you* are the person whom they seek. You could never hide from me, Doyle."

"I hope I never have occasion to try," I said. "Mr. Oxborrow, what is your fee?"

"I generally charge a guinea for a balancing like this," said Oxborrow.

"A guinea?" I said. "Are you quite sure that's enough?"

He smiled in what looked like genuine amusement. "You're a woefully bad hand at haggling, Dr. Doyle. Yes, I'm sure. Anything more will only be spent on opium anyway."

"All right," I said, though dubiously, for I'd come expecting to pay at least twice that, and even then I suspected I would be underpaying. I felt, not only close to free from pain, but also immeasurably lighter and—no matter how much I told myself it was my imagination— cleaner, as if the aetheric darkness staining my wound had been truly physical.

I paid him, and we gratefully left the tenement, which was clean only in Oxborrow's room.

The effect of his work was not miraculous, although it seemed very close. My leg still ached, and I would not be discarding my collection of sticks, but the feeling of brittleness was gone, a feeling that I now recognized as being aetheric rather than a sign that my leg was not healing properly. There was an article for *The Lancet* in that, if there had been any chance they would accept a contribution from me.

"It seems as if it helped," said Crow.

"I think so, yes." I sighed, but I knew I had to say it: "You were right."

He laughed. "You needn't sound so disillusioned, Doyle. My job is drawing correct conclusions from data sets of varying completeness. Yours was quite tolerably complete. I just hope you don't suffer any regression. From what I've read, people sometimes do."

"What a horrid thought," I said.

"I don't know that it happens very often," he said, with what I recognized as his own particular style of reassurance.

"Then I will have to hope it misses me," I said. "Come, I have a number of errands to accomplish if I am to leave for Dartmoor on Saturday. Will you accompany me?"

"Of course," said Crow.

26

BASKERVILLE HALL

I MET SIR Henry Baskerville and Dr. Mortimer on the platform of the 10:30 train from Paddington. (The cerberus was being shipped separately and would arrive, the leasing company promised, on Monday.) They were both glad to see me—Sir Henry wrung my hand so effusively that I felt it for an hour afterward; they had had no further adventures or mysteries, but had both become a little jumpy, fight it though they obviously had.

Crow came with me to the station, as full of advice as an anxious parent. He was particularly emphatic on the subject of my letters to him—or "reports" as he insisted on calling them. I was not to try to theorize, but only to report the facts as fully as I could.

"What sort of facts?" I said irritably.

"I'm quite interested in Sir Henry's neighbors," said Crow, "and what they think about the Hound. Any fresh details you can dredge up about Sir Charles's death, and I should rather like to know what his neighbors thought of *him*. Obviously, you should be on the watch for men without bushy black beards."

He caught me with that one, and I burst into laughter, causing a passing matron to give me a most withering stare.

"Also, of course, the servants at the Hall," said Crow, "starting with the Barrymores—who may be entirely blameless—and then I believe there is also a groom. He, too, may have feelings about the Baskerville Course."

"Even the greatest fanatic would agree that's hardly a reason for murder."

Crow shook his head. "If brooded over long enough, *anything* can be a reason for murder. I had a case once where a murder was committed over a birdcage. Merely keep an open mind and report all."

The whistle blew and I parted from him with one injunction of my own: "If you need me, send a wire. I'll come at once."

"Stay close to Sir Henry!" he said in return, and I closed the compartment door.

I looked back at the platform, when we had left it far behind, and saw Crow, his wings half spread as if for flight, standing motionless and looking after us.

"You are good friends," said Baskerville.

"Yes," I said.

He hesitated, possibly on the brink of asking another question, but if so, he must have seen I would not answer it, for he said, "In Virginia, they say that a man who has an angel's friendship has the Devil's luck."

"Let us hope so," I said lightly, "for I cannot help but feel we are going to need all the luck we can come by."

The journey was a swift and pleasant one. I spent it in becoming better acquainted with my two companions for, as Baskerville quite rightly said, it might all be nothing or we might be traipsing into considerable danger.

Dr. Mortimer was able to provide particulars about all of Baskerville's new neighbors, although he did not always notice things with the acuity that one might wish. He knew, for instance, that both Misses Tenby were prone to bronchial complaints, but could not remember whether Caroline or Marianne was the elder. He had had a great many interesting conversations with Mr. Stapleton, a naturalist living with his sister at Merripit House, but had no idea where the man was from. Himself being a keen courseman, he knew all the members of the Baskerville Course, although even there he was more likely to recognize the horse than the rider. "My wife would do better," he said apologetically.

"Does Mrs. Mortimer course?" asked Baskerville.

"Yes, but more to the point, she's a local girl, one of that old reprobate Frankland's daughters, and herself a keen amateur historian. We must have you over soon so that she can fill you in on a hundred years of gossip."

"We should be delighted," said Baskerville. "Now tell us about that 'old reprobate Frankland.' *He* sounds like a lively sort of neighbor to have."

Dr. Mortimer snorted. "Frankland could be a brilliant legal historian, except that he *will* keep putting his knowledge to practical use."

"Litigious?" I said.

"Does not even begin to describe it," said Dr. Mortimer, and told us stories of Frankland from there to our stop.

There was no station at Grimpen or Coombe Tracey or any of the other hamlets surrounding the Hall. We disembarked at a small wayside station where it was immediately obvious everyone knew who Sir Henry was and had been waiting for him. He handled the situation quite gracefully—more gracefully than I would have expected of him, and I commended his Colonial mother for teaching him manners—but it was some time before he was able to climb into the waiting wagonette and say to the driver, "Take us home," and then to me, "That feels better to say even than I had imagined."

As we started away from the station, Dr. Mortimer leaned forward and said, "Jernigan, why are there so many soldiers about?"

"Escaped convict, sir," said the driver. "Selden, the Notting Hill murderer."

"Dear God," said Dr. Mortimer. "Has anyone . . ."

"Not so much as laid eyes on him," said Jernigan.

"None of the ladies . . ."

"Safe as houses," said Jernigan.

"How long has he been free?" I asked.

"It's been a week," said Jernigan grimly. "Princetown keeps sending more guards and all they do is stand around and not find him. Begging your pardon, sir, if I spoke too free."

"Not at all," said Baskerville. "Who is this Selden, then? He must not have made the Colonial newspapers."

"He is a beast," Dr. Mortimer said bluntly.

Crow had followed the case with considerable interest. I said, "He murdered his common-law wife, mutilated and outraged the corpse, dismembered her, and was caught trying to throw her left arm in the Thames. He nearly killed a constable and it took four men to get handcuffs on him. His sentence was commuted because the examining doctors agreed that he was not at all sane. He's only been in prison a matter of months."

"Quick work on losing him," said Baskerville.

"He clubbed a guard with his manacles," said Jernigan. "They say the poor man went down like a tree, and he may yet die of the skull fracture."

"And now that monster is out there on the moor," said Dr. Mortimer.

"Between ourselves, sir," said Jernigan, "they don't know how to search for him. There's too many places to hide, and too many places where he could see anybody coming from miles off."

"The perfect place for an escaped beast," I said.

"Except for food," said Baskerville. "The brute must be starving by now."

"They think someone's helping him," said Jernigan. "Maybe not of their own free will, as it were."

"Well, you *wouldn't*," said Baskerville, and we fell uneasily into silence.

⬥

BASKERVILLE HALL PROVED to be exactly the sort of massive Elizabethan pile I had expected, with additions from several later monarchs.

Baskerville whistled. "'Home' may have been a little presumptuous."

"You'll grow used to it very quickly," said Dr. Mortimer, in what I thought was meant to be a bracing tone.

"I don't blame my uncle for being fearful," said Baskerville. "What this place needs is real electric lights."

"Your second act as the eighth baronet," I said. "After restoring the coursing pack to their rightful home."

"You only think you're joking," said Baskerville, and gave me a sidelong grin.

We were greeted by the infamous Barrymore, who was standing at the front door with a lantern. He was a tall man, quite handsome, and his beard, although black, was impeccably trimmed. "Welcome to Baskerville Hall!" he said. "Welcome, Sir Henry!"

"Swann and Edison," muttered Baskerville, still thinking about electric lights, and I kicked him. "What? Oh! Thank you, it's good to be here. And you must be Barrymore." He and I descended gratefully from the wagonette while Jernigan and Barrymore unloaded our luggage. Dr. Mortimer did not get out.

"Won't you stay for supper?" said Baskerville.

"I can't," said Dr. Mortimer. "I must get home to my wife. I cannot imagine the terror she must have undergone this past week, alone in the house with George Selden on the loose."

"But I thought you lived in Grimpen," said Baskerville. "He won't dare go near towns."

"Women are delicate creatures," said Dr. Mortimer. "I only hope the strain has not made her ill. But I shall walk over tomorrow. Good night!" And he and Jernigan rattled away into the dark, leaving Baskerville and me to face Baskerville Hall.

"I thought better of Mortimer," Baskerville said, only half joking.

"He loves his wife," I said. "I cannot fault a man for love."

"No, I suppose not," Baskerville said, and sighed heavily. "Let's go in."

The main hall was very Elizabethan, with the enormous rafters, the stained glass, the coats of arms on the walls. We huddled by the fireplace, which was built on the same scale as the rest of the room, and tried to restore feeling to our cold hands.

Barrymore had returned from taking our luggage to our rooms. He stood now at the edge of our circle of light and said, "Would you wish dinner to be served at once, sir?"

"I would," Baskerville said frankly. "Is it ready?"

"In a very few minutes. You will find hot water in your rooms." He hesitated. "My wife and I . . ." He hesitated again, and I got the impression that whatever he was going to say was painful to him. "My wife and I will be happy to stay with you until you have made your fresh arrangements, but you will understand that under the new conditions, the house will require a considerable staff."

"What new conditions?" said Baskerville.

Barrymore looked acutely uncomfortable. "Only that Sir Charles led a very retired life, and we were able to look after his needs. You will naturally wish to do more entertaining, and thus you will need changes in your household."

"But that doesn't mean . . . Barrymore, are you saying you wish to leave?"

There was a considerable pause before Barrymore said, "Only when it is quite convenient to you, sir," which I noted was not an answer to the question asked. Besides, it was quite obvious that Barrymore did *not* wish to leave.

"But your family has been with us for several generations, haven't they? I should hate to begin my tenure here by breaking such an old family connection. What is the problem? It can't be me—I haven't been here five minutes."

Barrymore now looked acutely unhappy. "I feel that also, sir, and so does my wife. But, to tell the truth, sir, we were both very much attached to Sir Charles, and his death has made being at Baskerville

Hall very painful to us."

"But what on Earth will you do?"

"I have no doubt, sir, that we shall succeed in establishing ourselves in some business. Sir Charles's generosity has given us the means to do so, and now, sir, perhaps I had best show you to your rooms."

We followed Barrymore up a magnificent staircase, around a balustraded gallery, and down a long hallway to the very end. Barrymore said, "These are considered the best rooms of the house. Sir Henry, you are in the east room, and I have put Dr. Doyle to the west."

"I've gotten completely turned around," I said, not entirely untruthfully. "Are we on the north end of the house or the south end?"

"This is the north wing, sir," said Barrymore. "Most of the rooms in the south wing are closed up these days."

I decided this was not the time to ask about footprints in the flower beds. Instead, I went into the west room and found it to be unexpectedly modern and cheerful, complete with electric lights and a delicately patterned wallpaper. It was like being in a different house, and I was thankful for it. I made use of the hot water, and then went across the hall and tapped on Baskerville's door.

"Come in," he called.

I found him still staring about in considerable bemusement. "This still all seems like a dream," said he. "I keep expecting to wake up and be back in Alberta, having fallen asleep while darning a sock or something, and this house! We jumped three centuries in as many steps!"

"Sir Charles seems to have put his money to excellent, if rather eccentric, use," I agreed.

"I must find out if anyone knows more of his plans than Dr. Mortimer," said Baskerville. "For if he had some grand design, I should like to feel that I was honoring it."

"Barrymore might be the best person to ask," I said. "He would at least know who visited most frequently."

"It's a place to start," said Baskerville. "I would rather find a friend than a lawyer. And it's a better topic of conversation than the family fetch."

And indeed, when asked over supper, Barrymore proved very willing to help—suggesting that his reasons for leaving had nothing to do with distaste for the new baronet. He said, as had Dr. Mortimer, that Sir Charles lived a retired life, seeing very few people socially. "He said it tired him," said Barrymore. "Indeed, I believe Dr. Mortimer was his only truly close friend, although he was certainly not on *unfriendly* terms with anyone, and I know he enjoyed his conversations with Mr. Stapleton."

"Stapleton?" said Baskerville.

"The naturalist," I said, remembering Dr. Mortimer's rather disorganized remarks. "Living at Merripit House."

"With his sister, yes, sir," said Barrymore. "Sir Charles said he had a lively and well-informed mind. They worked together a great deal on Sir Charles's charitable efforts."

"Oh Jehoshaphat," said Baskerville. "I didn't even think . . . What kind of charitable work did Sir Charles do?"

Barrymore pondered for a moment. "He liked to help individuals in need, and he liked to do so anonymously."

"Thank goodness," said Baskerville with great sincerity. "How did he find these individuals?"

"Mostly through the churches. The curate of St. Michael on the Rock and the Methodist minister in Grimpen and the Presbyterian minister in Coombe Tracey all knew to come to him, and then there was Mr. Frankland's daughter, but that was a bit different."

"Mr. Frankland's daughter. You mean Dr. Mortimer's wife?"

"No, sir. Mr. Frankland's *other* daughter. Dr. Mortimer married Miss Lydia. It was Miss Laura who made a bad marriage and found herself in trouble."

"And she couldn't go to her father?"

"Her father never spent a cent he didn't have to on those girls," said Barrymore with sudden venom. "And besides which, he'd disowned her when she married that Lyons fellow. There were a number of gentlemen, not just Sir Charles, who combined to help her start a typewriting business in Coombe Tracey."

We were silent for some time as Barrymore cleared the plates and brought out the port. "I don't know," Baskerville said. "All these ancestors disapproving of me. Barrymore, the Hall isn't haunted, is it?"

The question clearly took Barrymore by surprise. "No, Sir Henry. Unless you mean . . . you *do* know about the Hound?"

"Yes. I didn't mean him," Baskerville said. "I meant all these Baskervilles. Which one is the wicked Hugo?"

"That would be this Sir Hugo," said Barrymore, indicating a cavalier with a thin, rather stern face and fanatical eyes.

Sir Henry said, "He certainly doesn't look like a man you'd want to cross. I'm glad he got what was coming to him."

I asked Barrymore, "Does anyone but the Baskervilles ever see the Hound?"

"That's hard to say, sir. There are *stories* about people seeing the Baskerville fetch, but never anything reliable. But that's all they are. Just stories." He bowed sharply and stalked out of our little circle of light.

"Note," Baskerville said after a moment. "Barrymore does not like talking about the Hound."

⬦

I WENT TO bed that night feeling both weary and alert, which is a dreadful combination. I tossed and turned, dozed and woke. Finally, at one o'clock, I got up, pulled on my dressing gown, and went down the long north hall to the lav, which had been wedged into an oddly shaped space between the main building and the north wing. I was just grateful Sir Charles had included a W.C.

I washed my face and hands, and had my hand on the doorknob to start the trek back to my room, when I heard a noise. I would not have heard it at all if it had not been for the odd acoustical properties created by Sir Charles's renovations, and as it was, I had to listen carefully for quite some time before I could be confident in my identification: a woman, crying softly but heartbrokenly, somewhere in the Hall.

The question was whether she was living or dead.

I opened the door and immediately ran into Baskerville. We both started back as if the other were the Hound. "What are you doing?" he whispered.

There was no one in the north wing to disturb, but I whispered, too, "Lav. You?"

"Can't sleep," he said, and held up a book. "Went to raid the library."

"Did you hear her?"

And I knew the answer before he said, "Yes."

I went back to bed, but it was a long time before I was able to sleep.

27

LETTERS

FROM DR. J. H. Doyle to Mr. Crow

Baskerville Hall, October 11th

My dear Crow,

Pursuant to your fiat, I have been doing my best to meet all of Sir Henry's neighbors. Mr. Stapleton made it easy; he came over the first morning and introduced himself, begged us to consider him a guide as needed, and took us out to the spot where the wicked Sir Hugo met his end.

It is a dreadfully grim little coombe—or goyal, which is the local word—with two great stones in it, sharpened at the upper end, where you can make out the marks of the tools that sharpened them, and then worn by time until they look like the fangs of some monstrous creature just beneath the earth. Sir Henry was most interested and asked Mr. Stapleton a number of questions, both about the goyal and about the story, and they got into an almost heated discussion about whether Constance Burry had been a hell-hound before Sir Hugo got his hands on her or if Sir Hugo, having sold his soul to the Devil, did in fact carry enough *metaphysicum morbi* to contaminate the girl. Mr. Stapleton held that Constance Burry's extremely watchful and protective family must have been guarding her secret as much as her honor while Sir Henry seems convinced, having seen Sir Hugo's portrait, that he did indeed make a deal with the powers of darkness, and Constance Burry was merely his day of reckoning made manifest.

When we returned from that expedition, two carters from Coombe Tracey were in the stable yard unloading the straw-stuffed crate in which the cerberus had traveled to Baskerville Hall. It is not the same model as McMurdo, being designed specifically for bodyguard work and thus having a somewhat lighter chassis. The three heads are designed to look like an Alsatian's rather than a mastiff's. Its name is Wiggins. It ate Sir Henry's American penny and has followed him faithfully ever since. (It is easily able to keep up with a horse.) Sir Henry worries about what the locals will make of it, but I know he is safe in that regard; the announcement that the Baskerville coursing pack is returning to Baskerville Hall is rapidly making Sir Henry the most popular man in Devonshire.

And no one is happier than Mr. Ralph Tenby, a stick-thin and jauntily active man in his sixties who says the hounds were eating him out of hearth and home—"but you couldn't ask Sir Charles to take them back. I've never seen a man so sincerely terrified of anything as that poor man was of dogs."

"Did he ever give a reason?" I asked curiously.

Tenby said, "No. And it was *all* dogs, not just hounds, although I know the fetch preyed on his mind a good deal."

"Do we *know* the fetch is a hound?" said Baskerville. "Has anyone but a Baskerville ever *seen* it to know?"

"Only the family can see a fetch," Mr. Tenby said, scandalized.

"Yes, but I've heard there's another theory," said Baskerville.

"That it's the ghost of that poor girl? Hardly likely, is it? Hell-hounds don't haunt. They don't have souls."

It is a common opinion, and I did not make the foolish mistake of arguing. Sir Henry said, "Do you know of any local traditions about Constance Burry?"

"Oh, they all say it was Sir Hugo, that he was some sort of walking miasma of evil."

Sir Henry changed the subject and got Mr. Tenby's opinion on a number of other things, for he is the sort of person who has an opinion on everything, whether he knows anything about it or not. But he has kept the coursing pack in excellent condition, so that I try not to think too harshly of him.

Our other near neighbor, Mr. Frankland, he of the two daughters and the litigious ways, also came to inspect the new baronet. He is elderly, energetic, red-faced with choler, and completely devoid of any true human feeling. He cares only for points of law, and I no longer wonder at his treatment of his daughters. They can only barely have impinged on his consciousness to begin with.

We have also met one of the daughters, Dr. Mortimer's wife Lydia, for he had us over to dinner as he had promised. She is a tall lady, startlingly beautiful in a Burne-Jones fashion, with eyes that are not at all dreamy, but are always looking at something in the far distance that only she can see. Sir Henry found her unnerving; I rather like her.

She knows more about the Burry family than anyone I have yet encountered. They lived in the tiny village of Firley, where Constance's father was the blacksmith, with the help of his four sons. Constance's mother had died when her only daughter was still an infant. Mrs. Mortimer thinks Constance's spinster aunt must have moved in to help raise Constance and her four older brothers.

I asked her how Constance could have become a hell-hound. She said, "That's an interesting question, Dr. Doyle. The most logical answer is that Sir Hugo was a demoniac—he certainly gave every evidence of being either possessed or insane—and he infected her, but it's also possible that someone in Constance's family was a demoniac— her mother, for instance, who died young—and she was infected that way. *Or* it's possible that *Constance* wasn't the hell-hound at all."

"You think Sir Hugo was the hell-hound?"

"Stories metamorphose," said Mrs. Mortimer. "A dead hell-hound and a dead girl become a dead hell-hound and a dead baronet. Perhaps it seemed more plausible than that Constance could have actually killed a hell-hound before it finished dismembering her."

"Is that likely?"

"No more or less likely than Constance Burry being a hell-hound. It is an incredible story, and frankly I would not believe it at all except for the curious location of Constance Burry's grave."

"Where is Constance buried?" I said.

"You've probably stepped on her" was the disconcerting reply. "She's buried in the mouth of Sir Hugo's goyal, which James tells me Mr. Stapleton took you to see."

"So where is Sir Hugo buried?"

"With all due pomp and circumstance in St. Michael of the Rock with the rest of the Baskervilles. There was no mark of the Devil on him."

"Therefore *not* a demoniac."

"Not according to the story," said Mrs. Mortimer.

For all her eccentricity—and indeed, she is well matched to Dr. Mortimer, for neither of them will ever mind, or possibly even notice, if the other isn't paying attention—Mrs. Mortimer proved a good hostess. Sir Henry managed to steer the conversation toward coursing, and she became quite animated, as any true courseman does, in talking about courses she'd followed and horses and hounds, and from hounds to the Baskerville fetch and the supernatural in general. "The moor is full of ghosts," she said. "Especially around Grimpen Mire."

"Grimpen Mire?" echoed Sir Henry.

"The Great Grimpen Mire," said Dr. Mortimer. "You should get Stapleton to show it to you. I doubt anyone knows it better, even men who have lived here their entire lives."

"That's because they have more sense than to go near it," said Mrs. Mortimer. "Stapleton says he actually goes *in* it after his butterflies and whatnot."

"Stapleton is very intrepid," said Dr. Mortimer, perhaps a shade wistfully.

"Stapleton is reckless," said Mrs. Mortimer. I got the impression that she does not care for Mr. Stapleton.

Of Mr. Frankland, I find that I hardly know what to say, except that if he had any enmity toward Sir Charles, he would have sued him, and I suspect he understands the entail better than Sir Henry does. Even though I think him ruthless enough for anything, I do not believe he is our man.

I may, of course, be utterly wrong.

Sir Henry spends much of his time in the study, trapped with Sir Charles's man of business, Arthur Holland. I spend my days walking, learning the grim and austere countryside.

Until I have something further to report, I remain,

Most obediently yours,

J. H. Doyle

❖

From Dr. J. H. Doyle to Mr. Crow

Baskerville Hall, October 13th

My dear Crow,

I did not expect to have more to report quite so soon, but a couple of very peculiar incidents have occurred in the past two days.

First was my second encounter with Mr. Stapleton. I was out walking, Sir Henry being once again immured with Mr. Holland, when I heard someone calling my name, and turned to find Mr. Stapleton, complete with butterfly net and tin specimen box, bounding toward me.

"Good morning, Dr. Doyle!" he cried upon reaching me, not in the slightest out of breath. "I see you are out taking in the beauties of the moor."

He was not, as far as I could tell, being at all sarcastic.

"Good morning, Mr. Stapleton," I said. "It is a happy chance that I should meet you, for Dr. Mortimer said that I should ask you to show me the Grimpen Mire."

"Of course!" said Stapleton enthusiastically. "It is a most remarkable part of the moor. It looks as innocent as a dove," and he gestured with his free hand out over a great low-lying plain to our north, "but it is perilously easy to put a foot wrong, and even that small a mistake can kill you. In dry seasons it is merely dangerous to cross, but after the autumn rains, it is an awful place. And yet I can find my way to the very heart of it and return alive."

I ignored his boasting. "But why should you wish to?"

"Well, you see the hills beyond? They are really islands, cut off on all sides by the impassable Mire, which has crawled round them in the course of centuries. That is where the rare plants and butterflies are, if you have the wit to reach them."

Really, a most unconscionable braggart, even though I quite believed he was telling the truth. I remembered Mrs. Mortimer saying he was reckless, and definitely agreed with her. Before I could say that—or any other tactless remark—there came a sound I barely know how to describe, whether to call it a moan or a howl or a roar. It came from nowhere and everywhere, rising from a murmur to a sound as air-filling as the tolling of a bell when you stand directly beneath the belfry, and then sinking back to a murmur and slowly dying away.

I stared at Stapleton, who had the oddest expression on his face: anxiety, curiosity, almost pain—I have been wrestling ever since with the question of what it was I saw on Stapleton's face.

"Queer place, the moor," said he.

"What in the name of God *was* that?" I said.

He smirked. "The locals claim it's the Hound of the Baskervilles calling for Sir Hugo's soul."

"Fetches don't do that," I said, which was an idiotic thing to say, but the noise had unnerved me.

"I don't think the Hound *is* a fetch," said Stapleton. "I've had too many people tell me they've seen it or that their grandfather saw it. But I don't think this is the Hound."

"No?"

"Bogs make queer noises," said Stapleton with a shrug. "It's the mud settling or the water rising, or something."

"No," I said. "That was a *voice.*"

Perhaps I was imagining it, but I thought he looked a little taken aback. "Have you ever heard a bittern booming?"

"No, I don't believe I have."

"It's a very rare bird—practically extinct—in England now, but all things are possible upon the moor. Yes," he said, warming to his own theme, "I should not be surprised to learn that what we have heard is the cry of the last of the bitterns, somewhere out in the Great Grimpen Mire."

"It is by far the strangest noise I have ever heard," I said.

"That would be the moor," said Stapleton. "Look at the hillside over there. What do you make of those?"

The whole steep slope was covered with gray circles of stone, a score of them at least.

"What are they? Sheep pens?"

"No, they are the homes of our ancestors—or at least the homes of the ancestors of those of us native to Devon. Prehistoric man lived densely on the moor and no one in particular has lived there since. The ghosts are as thick out there as gnats in summer, for prehistoric man was no less bloodthirsty than his modern descendants. Probably they fought over the tin mines." He pointed to a great trench in the opposite hill, then said, "Oh, I beg your pardon, but it is surely *Cyclopides.*"

A small butterfly or moth had fluttered across our path, and in an instant Stapleton was darting in pursuit of it with extraordinary energy. The creature flew straight for the Mire, but Stapleton never paused for an instant, bounding from tuft to tuft behind it, his green net waving in the air. His gray clothes and jerky, zigzag, irregular progress made him not unlike some huge moth himself. I was standing, watching his pursuit with a mixture of admiration, however reluctant, for his extraordinary activity and fear lest he should lose his footing in the treacherous Mire, when I heard the sound of steps, and turning round, found a woman near me upon the path.

She had to be Miss Stapleton, since there were very few ladies to be found upon the moor, and I had already met the Misses Tenby and Mrs. Mortimer. Moreover, I remembered that I had heard someone describe her as being a beauty. That she most certainly was, and of a most uncommon type. There could not have been greater contrast between brother and sister, for Stapleton was neutral-tinted, with light hair and gray eyes, while she was darker than any brunette whom I had seen in England—slender, tall, and regal. She had a proud, finely cut face, so regular that it was almost like a statue's, save for the sensitivity of her mouth and her vividly dark eyes. With her perfect figure and fashionable dress, she was, indeed, a strange apparition upon a lonely moorland path, and I admit I thought for a second of the lamia and the Lorelei. But she was clearly human from the heaving of her chest and the sound of pebbles shifting beneath her feet as she walked.

Her eyes were on her brother as I turned, and then she quickened her pace toward me. I had raised my hat and was trying to think of some explanatory remark that did not include the question: *Is your brother a madman?* But she did not wait; she said at once, "Go back! Go straight back to London immediately!"

She caught me wrong-footed, and I stared at her in sheeplike blankness.

Her eyes were blazing with urgency. "You must leave," she said, and I noticed that she had a very faint lisp.

"But why?" I finally managed.

"I cannot explain," she said, "but you *must* leave."

"I won't abandon Sir Henry," I said.

It was her turn to stare at me stupidly. "But aren't you . . . Oh God, here comes my brother. Not a word of what I have said. Would you mind getting that orchid for me among the mare's-tails yonder? You wouldn't think orchids would grow in such a desolate place, would you?"

Stapleton had abandoned the chase and come back to us, breathing hard and flushed with exertion.

"Hello, Beryl," said he, and it did not seem to me that his greeting was entirely cordial. "I see you have met Dr. Doyle."

"Yes," she said with a brilliant, flashing smile that looked as fake as a papier-mâché mask. "I was just telling Dr. Doyle that it is rather late in the season for the true beauties of the moor. Did you catch your prey?"

"No," Stapleton said, "he eluded me. It is a great pity, for it cannot have been *Cyclopides,* but I could not get close enough for a proper identification."

"My brother is a great hunter," Miss Stapleton said, lightly but with a glance full of meaning. "You should come see his collection and lunch with us."

"I would be delighted," I said, mostly truthfully.

A short walk brought us to Merripit House, which was as bleak as the moorland surrounding it.

"Pray ignore the ghost," Miss Stapleton said as we walked through the stunted orchard toward the house. "She is some eighteenth-century farmwife who died in childbirth. Why she haunts the orchard, I do not know."

The indifference in her voice was unexpected and repellant, especially given the blood-soaked, sobbing apparition that stood beside the path, her bloody hands outstretched beseechingly.

"As ever, my sister's command of the facts is rather treacherous," said Stapleton with some asperity. "She wasn't a farmwife, she was a hired girl, unmarried. There used to be a barn here, and she gave birth out here alone and bled to death because she was trying to conceal her pregnancy from the farmwife. Also, she's not eighteenth-century. She died in 1832."

"Poor girl," I said. "What happened to the baby?"

"Stillbirth," said Stapleton with a sigh. "But come in, please. Anthony, we have a guest for lunch!"

We were admitted to the house by a wizened old manservant, dressed in rusty black, who seemed much of a piece with the moor and the stunted orchard and the ghost. But inside Merripit House, there were large rooms, furnished with an elegance in which I thought I detected Miss Stapleton's hand. I looked out at the moor and could not help wondering how a highly educated man and a lady with taste, assurance, and beauty had ended up *here*.

"Queer spot to choose, is it not?" said Stapleton, with quite your trick of answering one's thoughts.

"Have you been here long?" I said.

"Only two years. The residents still consider us newcomers. We came shortly after Sir Charles settled. And we contrive to make ourselves fairly happy, do we not, Beryl?"

"Quite happy," she said with another of her fake, flashing smiles and no conviction at all.

"I had a school," said Stapleton. "It was in the North country. The work to a man of my temperament was mechanical and uninteresting, but the privilege of living with youth, of helping to mold those young minds and of impressing them with one's own character and ideals was very dear to me. However, the fates were against us. A serious epidemic broke out in the school, and three of the boys died. My school never recovered from the blow and much of my capital was irretrievably swallowed up. And yet if it were not for the loss of the charming companionship of the boys, I could rejoice over my own misfortune, for with my strong tastes for botany and zoology, I find an unlimited field of work here, and my sister is as devoted to Nature as I am." He coughed. "I beg your pardon. I did not mean to say all that, just to answer the expression on your face when you looked out at the moor."

"I'm afraid the moor has not won me over yet," I said.

"You've hardly been here long enough," said Stapleton with a peculiar sort of gaiety. "Come look at my treasures, Dr. Doyle. Lunch will be ready soon."

I am not a squeamish person, but Stapleton's "treasures" nearly made me one, case after case of creatures—moths, butterflies, beetles, other things I wasn't sure how to classify—each neatly pinned and labeled. Here and there two specimens of the same species were pinned side by side to show both sides of the wings. Other pairs showed male and female. In places, there were neatly labeled gaps where he had yet to acquire his sacrificial victim.

Stapleton darted among the cases much as he had darted after the butterfly that might or might not have been *Cyclopides,* pointing out particularly rare finds, telling little scraps of stories about tripping full length in ponds or almost falling off cliffs; balancing on fence posts; being chased by angry dogs; finding—very nearly disastrously—a wasp nest the size of his head. He seemed especially proud of the specimens he had collected from that adventure and looking at their sleek and deadly shapes, I supposed he had every right to be.

I was staring in horror at a case of enormous South American beetles when Miss Stapleton appeared in the doorway and said, "Anthony is serving lunch."

The food was better than I had expected—Anthony's unprepossessing exterior concealed quite a talent—and the company was . . . I decided as I walked home that the right word for Stapleton was "overbearing." He certainly ruled his sister; I had been conscious of her glances at him throughout the meal, watching for disapprobation with no small degree of anxiety. As a schoolmaster, he had probably been a petty tyrant; men who talk about "molding" youth usually are. All those butterflies on pins!

I was just out of sight of Merripit House when I rounded an outcropping and found Miss Stapleton sitting on a rock beside the path. She was flushed and panting and had one hand pressed to her side.

"I did not think to see you again so soon, Miss Stapleton," I said.

"I have run all this way in order to cut you off, Dr. Doyle," said she. "I had not even time to put on my hat, and I must not stop or my brother may miss me. I wanted to apologize for my foolish mistake in thinking you were Sir Henry. Please forget what I said, for it has no application to you."

"But I cannot forget, Miss Stapleton," said I. "I am Sir Henry's friend, and his welfare concerns me deeply. Tell me why you were so anxious for Sir Henry to return to London. Please."

"A woman's whim, Dr. Doyle," said she. "When you know me—"

"No," I said. "I don't believe that for an instant. You were entirely serious. Please be frank with me—ever since I have been here, life has become like the Great Grimpen Mire, with treacherous ground everywhere and no guide to point the track. Tell me what it was you meant, and I promise I shall convey your warning to Sir Henry."

For an instant, an expression of indecision passed over her face, but then her eyes hardened again. "You make too much of it, Dr. Doyle. Sir Charles had a morbid fancy that the fetch of the Baskervilles was actually a curse tied to the house and perhaps I have become infected by the idea. That is all."

"But that is a very serious matter," I said. "Did Sir Charles ever have a practitioner in for an assessment?"

She looked surprised by the idea, which made no sense. Surely it is the obvious step if you believe yourself or your family or your residence to be cursed? She said hesitantly after some considerable pause, "I believe Sir Charles was more afraid of being proved right than of living with the uncertainty."

"But if it preyed on his mind—"

"I don't know!" she said, almost angrily. "But if you are truly Sir Henry's friend, tell him to leave Dartmoor at once. I must go." I got the distinct impression, perhaps unfair, that she was fleeing from my questions.

I watched her go—very fleet of foot is Miss Stapleton for a woman who dresses with such elegance—and then I walked thoughtfully back to Baskerville Hall, where I found Sir Henry in the mood for escape. His meetings with Holland, aside from being long, must be unutterably tedious, for they leave him restless and frequently looking like he wants to give it all up and go back to Canada.

I suggested a ride; he was out the door almost before I finished speaking, Wiggins all but bounding at his heels. Later, as we ate, I told him about my encounter with the Stapletons and Miss Stapleton's strange warning.

"She certainly seems to know *something*," said Sir Henry. "I just wish we had some guess as to *what*."

"She seems to feel you will be safe away from the moor," I said, "but experience suggests that that is probably not true."

"He can steal my boots," Sir Henry agreed. "Stands to reason he could do worse."

"Which I suppose begs the question of why he didn't."

"The fetch," Sir Henry said promptly—which I think indicates he had asked himself that question more than once already. "It's the perfect blind for murder, when you think about it. Once I see a giant dog, I'll be *expecting* to die, and from there a fellow this clever will have no trouble in orchestrating the actual event."

"I shouldn't have let you go out alone," I said.

Sir Henry snorted. "One, you most certainly should. Two, you couldn't have stopped me. Three, I had Wiggins with me, and what's the point of hiring a cerberus if you're going to insist on doing his job?"

I shoved aside my most dreadful imaginings and said, "All right. But for God's sake keep Wiggins with you."

And this brings me finally to my second peculiar incident.

I had been aware that all was not still and peaceful in Baskerville Hall of a night. I do not often sleep soundly, as I suppose you are aware, and even in my "human phase," if I have that term correctly, my hearing seems more sensitive than it was before. Thus I was aware of someone pacing in the servants' quarters, aware of a woman sobbing—and the only woman who lives here, as opposed to coming in by the day, is the stolid and stone-faced Mrs. Barrymore, whom I would judge about as sensitive as a turnip. In the middle of the night I tend to convince myself the weeper is Constance Burry; during the day I consider that I am doing Mrs. Barrymore an injustice. Thus far I have not wanted to confront her. Relations with the Barrymores are awkward, with both sides aware that the Barrymores are leaving *and* that they do not want to. And Sir Henry is up to his ears in estate matters, trying to learn how to manage his inheritance responsibly. He has no time for staffing concerns—and I think is inclined to drag his feet a little, in hopes that the Barrymores change their minds. I have said nothing. But about this, I really shall have to speak.

For the past several nights, I have heard footsteps. The first time, I thought nothing of it. The second time, I was puzzled, but at that point too sleepy to be concerned. Last night, well past midnight, I heard footsteps come up the servants' stair beside my room. Barrymore's tread, but neither of us had rung for him, and his footsteps turned away from our rooms. I listened as they paced softly and steadily down our hall to the balustraded gallery, and then I opened my door and slunk out after them.

Barrymore was quite right, by the way, not to use the main staircase, which is magnificent but noisy as sin, and I thought I remembered a conversation, overheard and only half listened to, about the servants' stair in the south wing being unsafe. But it made for a dreadfully long walk through the dark and deserted corridors.

I was fortunate, being no paragon of stealth, that Barrymore is rather deaf, so that I did not need to worry that he would hear me. I followed him down the length of the south wing, becoming more and more perplexed. Finally, at the very end of the hall, he opened the door on the west side and entered the analogue of my room at the other end of the house. I think it almost certain that this was the room from which Constance Burry had escaped.

I crept closer, as close as I dared.

Barrymore was standing at the western window with his unshielded lantern, staring out across the moors. His profile was toward me, and I could read tense expectation in his face and what looked to me like deeply bitter resolve. For some minutes he stood, watching intently. Then he gave a groan (of impatience? of relief?) and shielded the lantern again. I did not wait, but slunk back to my own room, and a few moments later I heard Barrymore's stealthy footsteps going back down the stairs.

I lay awake for some time puzzling over Barrymore's behavior, and this morning Sir Henry and I made a plan of action. We both feel strongly that we want answers to *some* part of the mysteries surrounding us, and I believe my next letter to you will make for interesting reading.

Yours sincerely,

J. H. Doyle

❖

FROM DR. J. H. Doyle to Mr. Crow

Baskerville Hall, October 15th

My dear Crow,

As I promised, I believe this letter does at last contain some answers.

To begin with, before breakfast on the 14th, I walked down the corridor to the end of the south wing and examined the room that Barrymore had chosen in the night. There was nothing remarkable about it save for the fact that the window through which he had stared so intently commands the best and nearest outlook onto the moor. There is an opening between two trees which enables one to look right down upon it, while from all the other windows, only a distant glimpse can be obtained, if that. Ergo, since he went to considerable trouble to reach this window, meaning no other window would serve his purpose, he must have been looking for something or someone on the moor. Given how dark the night was, he must have been looking for a light. I wondered if he might have had an assignation—he is certainly good-looking enough to attract that sort of attention, and if he is not behindhand in reciprocating, it would explain, perhaps, the weeping I had heard and why Mrs. Barrymore, for such a stolid woman, seems sometimes so ill at ease. It cannot be easy knowing that your husband carries on intrigues behind your back.

But whatever the meaning, it was not something I felt I could keep to myself. After breakfast, I retired with Sir Henry to his study and told him all I knew.

His eyebrows climbed higher and higher as I spoke, and when I had finished, he said, "I don't like the sound of that at all."

"It's difficult to imagine an innocent explanation," I said.

"Difficult?" said Sir Henry. "Try impossible. If there were an innocent explanation, Barrymore wouldn't be creeping around in the middle of the night." I waited while he considered the matter. "I should like to confront him right away, but if he denied it, we would be at an impasse. We shall stay up tonight together and catch him red-handed. That is, if you are game?"

"Of course," I said.

"It will be something to look forward to," he said with a sigh. "I expect Mr. Holland at any moment."

Out of curiosity, I walked out on the moor this morning, along the line of sight from that same window, trying to figure out what Barrymore had been looking for. I saw nothing but the bleak landscape of Dartmoor, the tors rising like strange castles from the rough and rocky ground. There was certainly no house visible, nor anything that seemed to explain Barrymore's strange pilgrimage.

I ate lunch alone; Barrymore was grimly silent. I felt as if I had fallen into *Wuthering Heights*. After lunch, I explored the library. I fear that none of the Baskervilles have been great readers, although I found an interesting book about the supernatural denizens of the moors, written by a past curate of St. Michael of the Rock. He says there are redcaps in most of the tors and jenny greenteeth in the Grimpen Mire, making the moor an even less pleasant place than I had previously considered it. I definitely should not have let Sir Henry go out alone. I shall have to tell him to take Jernigan. I do not think my leg will let me ride, even improved as it is, and in any event it would take a London cab horse to let me near enough to try. But Jernigan seems steady enough to be a good riding companion.

I have spent the remainder of the afternoon in writing this letter. I shall not close, as I anticipate having a good deal more to say after tonight.

October 16th

Well, at least I was not incorrect about that. I do indeed have a good deal more to say.

I entertained Sir Henry over dinner with an account of some of the things I had read in the Reverend Hubbard's book, and it only seemed natural after the covers were cleared to take the brandy decanter up to Sir Henry's room to continue the conversation, which by then was ranging far afield. Sir Henry told me about the buffalo spirits of the American plains, and I talked about the ghosts in Afghanistan. I then told him a carefully censored version of my childhood encounter with a jenny greenteeth. "They like irrigation ditches, and their arms are always longer than you think. I was saved purely because I was holding my pony's reins, and she was stronger than it was. I don't think it got a very good grip, to be honest, but I still must put it down to the grace of God that the reins didn't break. I never told anyone, for I should only have been punished for being so stupid."

Around midnight, we extinguished the lights and settled down to wait in silence. After about half an hour, Sir Henry whispered, "What if he doesn't come tonight?"

"Then we try again tomorrow," I whispered back. "But I don't think he saw what he was looking for last night. I believe he'll return."

Sir Henry had a good fire; there was nothing unpleasant about sitting silently next to it. I reminded myself to let him hear Barrymore "first" unless there was no choice. I didn't want to rouse any suspicions about my unusually good hearing. Although I think Sir Henry might refuse to entertain such suspicions, I do not want to put him—or myself—in the position of having to find out.

As it turned out, I didn't need to worry. At two o'clock, we both heard Barrymore on the stairs. Sir Henry gripped my wrist, and we waited, holding our breaths, as Barrymore crept down the hall. When he had reached the gallery, we got up and crept after him.

Barrymore led us to the same room, and as we watched, he unshielded his lantern and raised it to the window.

All at once, it was too much for Sir Henry. He strode into the room, saying sharply, "What in blazes is going on?"

Barrymore whipped around, blank horror on his face. "Sir Henry!"

"What are you doing here, Barrymore?"

"Nothing, sir." His agitation was so great that he could hardly speak, and the lantern threw great shuddering shadows on the walls. "It was the window, sir. I go round at night to see that they are fastened."

"On the second floor?" Sir Henry said, almost derisively.

"Yes, sir, all the windows."

"You choose an odd time to do it."

"I . . ." Barrymore is clearly not one of Nature's liars. He had no idea how to answer that, and after a moment Sir Henry took pity on him and said, "Suppose you just tell us the truth."

"I was doing no harm, sir. I was holding a lantern to the window."

"And *why* were you holding a lantern to the window?" said Sir Henry, very much in the manner of my father.

Barrymore drew himself up and said, "I cannot tell you."

Sir Henry seemed dumbfounded, and Barrymore said in a rush, "I cannot tell you. It is not my secret. I would not—if it involved only myself, I would not try to keep it from you."

Sir Henry said, "But who else can it involve that has you creeping around my house in the middle of the night?"

I remembered my idea about an assignation, and stepped up to the window to peer out. Nothing but the black shapes of the trees against the blackness of the moor met my eyes.

"You'll see nothing out there, Dr. Doyle," said Barrymore.

"But then what are you *doing*?" Sir Henry demanded. "What confederates are you signaling to?"

Barrymore's face became defiant. "I will not tell you."

"Then you leave my service at once," said Sir Henry. "Whatever you are plotting against me, you shall not do it in the comfort of my home!"

"Not against you, sir! I swear no harm is meant to you or Dr. Doyle!"

It was only a minor vow, but I did feel the pricking of it for a moment. And it wasn't Barrymore's voice.

We all three turned in startlement. Mrs. Barrymore, paler and more horror-struck than her husband, was standing at the door.

"Eliza," said Barrymore, warning in his voice.

But she would not be silenced. "My God, have I brought you to this? It is my doing, Sir Henry, my doing and my secret. He has done nothing except for my sake, and because I asked him."

"All right," said Sir Henry. "Speak out then. What does it all mean?"

"My unfortunate brother," Mrs. Barrymore began, broke off as she choked back a sob, and began again: "My maiden name is Selden."

It took me five thunderous seconds. "As in George Selden?"

"Yes, sir. He is my younger brother—the youngest of us. We spoiled him when he was a little boy and gave him his own way in everything, and he grew up believing that the world was a toy for his pleasure and that he could do whatever he liked with no consequences. I suppose a boy like that was bound to fall into bad company, and George certainly did. It was almost like a demon had entered into him—although indeed his lawyers hired a practitioner and it was not possession—until he broke my mother's heart and dragged our name in the dirt. He grew worse and worse, seeming to seek always the worst thing that he could do, until finally it is only something—the grace of God? The luck of the Devil?—that has kept him from the scaffold. I know he has done atrocious things that no one, wolf or man, can forgive, but when I look at him, I still see Georgie, the curly-headed little boy who always ran to me when he was in trouble, and I just could not—" She broke off again, and this time seemed unable to go on.

Barrymore said grimly, "When he escaped, he came straight to us, as straight as a homing pigeon."

"He was cold and hungry and scared to death," said Mrs. Barrymore, "and I could not turn him away. I could not. I am the oldest, you see, and Georgie was like my own child, the child I cannot have."

"We took him in," said Barrymore, and I could see how that decision had eaten at him. "We hid him for a week, but then word came of your arrival, Sir Henry, and—"

"You hid him," I said. "In the south wing?"

"Yes, sir," said Barrymore.

"Then did *Selden* leave those footprints in the flower bed?" I didn't wait for an answer, because I already knew the truth. "The Notting Hill murderer is a *hell-hound*?"

"It was that filthy prison infected him!" cried Mrs. Barrymore.

"Where is he now?" Sir Henry asked pragmatically.

"I don't know!" Barrymore said. "He hasn't answered my signal for four days."

"He promised," said Mrs. Barrymore distraughtly. "He *promised* he wouldn't bother anyone, not the farmers and not the gentry, but would wait on the moor until we could arrange passage to South America."

"Which we have done," said Barrymore. "The ship sails in three days."

"And I know we should turn him in," said Mrs. Barrymore, "but I cannot do it. That is the whole truth, sir, as I am an honest Christian woman, and you will see that if there is blame in the matter it does not lie with my husband, but with me, for whose sake he has done all that he has."

"Is this true, Barrymore?" said Sir Henry.

"Yes, sir. It is the truth of the matter."

"Well, I cannot blame you for standing by your own wife. Forget what I have said. Let us all go to bed, and we can talk further in the morning."

When the Barrymores had gone, we looked out the window again. Sir Henry had flung it open, and the cold night wind beat in upon our faces. And as we stared out into the darkness, looking for God knows what, there rose suddenly out of the vast gloom of the moor that strange cry which I had already heard upon the borders of the Great Grimpen Mire. It came with the wind through the silence of the night, a long deep mutter, then a rising howl, and then the sad moan in which it died away. Again and again it sounded, the whole air throbbing with it, strident, wild, and menacing. Sir Henry caught my sleeve, and his face was white as bone in the lantern's light.

"What in the name of God is that?"

"I don't know," I said. "It's apparently a sound they have here on the moor. I heard it once before."

It died away, and an absolute silence closed in upon us. We stood straining our ears, but nothing came.

"Doyle," said Sir Henry, "that was the cry of a hound. It cannot be anything else."

"Stapleton says it is a bittern booming."

"Oh, nonsense," said Sir Henry. "What do locals call it?"

"Well, of course, they say it's the Hound of the Baskervilles."

"Of course," said Sir Henry with a hollow laugh.

"Let us follow the Barrymores and go to bed," I said, shutting the window. "We can do nothing useful right now."

"How like a doctor," Sir Henry said, but he was only half grumbling. "Very well. But in the morning . . ."

"In the morning, everything will look more manageable," I said firmly, and pushed him ahead of me out of the room.

With the help of another tot of brandy, I got Sir Henry in bed and asleep, but I myself am wide awake. I have occupied myself in finishing this letter. The sun is coming up, and I shall close here, so that it can go out in the first post.

At least the mystery of the Barrymores is solved.

Yours sincerely,
J. H. Doyle

❖

From Mr. Crow to Dr. J. H. Doyle

Baker Street, October 18th

My dear Doyle,

For a change, it is I who have information to impart to you, for I am too impatient to wait until I should see you again in person.

I had a most peculiar set of visitors today: three men, distinctly of the petit bourgeoisie, and frightened almost out of their wits. They had heard of me through some torturous connection of employers and aunts and brothers-in-law, and they had a matter on which they wished my advice.

They put the matter on the table. A small box, addressed to GEORGE LUSK (Mr. Lusk being one of my three visitors), and reeking vilely.

"I received it through the post," said Mr. Lusk. "There was a letter with it." And he put the letter on the table.

Dreadful handwriting and worse spelling.

From hell

   Mr Lusk
      Sor

I send you half the Kidne I took from one woman
praeserved it for you tother piece I fried and ate it was very
nise I may send you the bloody knif that took it out if you only
wate a whil longer
   signed   *Catch me when*

                                you can
                     Mishter Lusk

I looked again at the reeking box. "Is that . . ."

"It looks like half a kidney," said Mr. Aarons. "Human kidney, I don't know."

"You should probably take it to someone who can find that out," I said. "If it *is* the kidney of the Mitre Square victim, it's important evidence."

"But what about the letter?" implored Mr. Lusk. "Why is this madman sending things to *me*?"

"You were in the papers," I said, for I had recognized his name, "as the chairman of the Mile End Vigilance Committee. Perhaps he thought you were the most proper person with whom to communicate."

The third man, Mr. Harris, turned a laugh into a cough, not very well.

"It's also possible," I said, "that this is just a very ugly prank. Do you have any enemies, Mr. Lusk? Anyone who would want to frighten and offend you like this?"

"I . . . I don't think so," said Mr. Lusk, clearly bewildered by the mere question—which suggests, in fact, that he has no such enemies at all.

"There are a lot of very peculiar folks in London," offered Mr. Harris.

"That's true enough," said Mr. Aarons.

"I don't think there's anything the police can do with it, even if it *is* Mrs. Eddowes's kidney," I said. I could not, of course, tell them that it could not be Mrs. Eddowes's kidney because that kidney had been thrown in the Thames, but just because the fellow sending half a kidney through the post is not the Whitechapel murderer does not mean he is not a nasty piece of work. "But you should take it to them, nonetheless. I promise they will take it seriously."

"I don't know," said Mr. Lusk. "I don't want to cause any trouble, and surely it's not anything. . . ."

"Suppose it happens again," I said. "If he writes to you once, it's worth considering the possibility that he will write to you twice."

"Oh dear God," said Mr. Lusk.

"Who should we take it to, to find out if it's a human kidney?" said Mr. Harris ungrammatically but practically.

"Well, I can look at it first," I said, "although I'm only an amateur anatomist."

"Please," they said in a chorus. I had gathered, as they told the story, that I was a compromise position between ignoring the half a kidney entirely and going straight to the police, and I could appreciate that what they all most dearly wanted was to be rid of the vile thing.

Thus, I looked at the half a kidney.

It had been divided longitudinally, trimmed up, and preserved in spirits. "It's definitely human," I said. "And I should say it was the left kidney of an adult. Which would fit with it being Mrs. Eddowes's kidney, as it was the left one which was removed."

"Oh God," said Mr. Lusk.

"It doesn't look healthy," I said. "Pale, bloodless, rather congested at the base of the pyramids. Which also fits with it being Mrs. Eddowes's kidney, according to the inquest testimony. But that's hardly conclusive. Take it to Inspector Lestrade and tell him I advised you to do so. He will listen to you."

"Oh God," said Mr. Lusk again.

"Come on, Lusk," said Aarons. "You want to do the right thing."

"Yes, of course," said Mr. Lusk. I closed the box and found some fresh paper for them to wrap it in. "But. Do you think my family is in danger?"

It was not an unreasonable question.

"As far as we know, the Whitechapel murderer, if this is indeed his work, has only preyed upon the prostitutes of the East End. He hasn't gone after men or children, and no respectable woman seems to be in danger from him. I don't think at this point you need fear for your family or yourself. If he continues to write to you, I might change my mind."

Mr. Lusk did not look comforted.

"Send them to the country for a spell, if you're worried," I said. "There's nothing wrong with getting them out of this poisonous cloud of fear, whether this particular man is a danger to them or not."

"It is that," said Mr. Aarons. "Like breathing in a bad fog."

"Yes, though this is detrimental to the spirit rather than the lungs."

"All right," said Mr. Lusk, seeming to pull himself together. "Thank you for your time, Mr. Crow."

And they left with their grim little package.

I don't quite know what to make of it, Doyle. On the one hand, we know this *isn't* Mrs. Eddowes's kidney and the Whitechapel murderer has shown no inclination to write people letters (leaving out entirely those ludicrous fakes of which Lestrade is so enamored). On the other hand, this seems more *like* something the Whitechapel murderer would send, both the letter itself and the ghastly half a kidney. And yet, as Mr. Harris said, there are a lot of very peculiar folks in London. Lestrade has been showing me some of the *other* letters they've been receiving, now that they've been idiots and put the idea of writing "Jack the Ripper" letters into everybody's head, and there are a *great many* people in London I should not like to meet in the East End after midnight. Whitechapel murderer or not, this man is one of them. I feel sure, however, that Lestrade can be trusted with Mr. Lusk's safety, even if I fear he will go tearing off after this fresh red herring with his customary enthusiasm.

Please continue to send your excellent letters. It maddens me that I cannot be there myself, even though I know you are just as capable as I of guiding Sir Henry safely through this mystery.

Your friend,
Crow

FROM DR. J. H. Doyle to Mr. Crow

Baskerville Hall, October 17th

My dear Crow,

This afternoon, Sir Henry and I (and the ever-faithful Wiggins) went out walking on the moor. We were both far too curious *not* to try to find George Selden's camp and also to figure out what happened to him. If he had met his demise upon the moor, as seemed all too probable, it would be better that we find him than poor tormented Barrymore.

It was an excellent day for walking on the moor, crisp and bracing, and although I still need my stick, my leg is enough better that I could keep up with Sir Henry without difficulty. We kept ourselves on a line with the window Barrymore had been looking out the night before, the only window of the Hall visible once one had passed through that gap in the trees. We looked back frequently to check our reckoning, since neither of us was confident about our ability, in the barrenness of the moor, either to keep a straight line or to discern landmarks.

"Baskerville," I said, "have you found any record of Sir Charles having an aetheric practitioner out to cast for a curse?"

"No, and he kept good records," said Sir Henry.

"I wonder why he didn't?"

I had told him about my two solo encounters with Miss Stapleton, so that he had no difficulty in following my line of thought. "Either he found he truly did not want to know, or he knew it wasn't a curse."

"I can't think why he wouldn't want to know," I said. "Curses can be removed."

"Then it wasn't a curse."

"If it wasn't a curse, what killed him?"

"A bad heart and his own terror of our family fetch," said Sir Henry. "I'm more interested in this fellow Selden who leaves footprints in my flower beds."

When we reached any outcropping or cairn that was on our direct line with the window, we would stop and cast about for first, a candle that when lit would serve as a beacon for Barrymore, and second, any sign of Selden's camp. We had failure after failure, and were both getting discouraged when we found Selden's camp by almost literally falling into it. It was a natural declivity in the lee of a jagged spur of rock. It was easy to see someone had been camping there, and he had left a scrap of paper under a stone.

Dreadful handwriting, as you said of the unfortunate Mr. Lusk's correspondent, and worse spelling:

> *Dear Lizzie*
> *I hav fownd a better deel*

No signature, but I suppose there wasn't anything to write that wouldn't incriminate his sister. At least there is *something* he balks at.

"A *better deal*?" said Sir Henry. "What on Earth does he mean by that?"

"I can't imagine he *wants* to go to South America," I said.

"No, he'd rather stay in England and break his sister's heart," Sir Henry grumbled. "Where do you suppose he's gone?"

I shook my head. "I can't even hazard a guess."

There was no other detritus in that miserable little hollow and nothing to show what direction Selden had taken when he left it. We did find his signal point, with the stump of a candle still in a hollow in the rock, shielded from view in all directions except that straight line with the window, still just visible, of Baskerville Hall.

"Clever brute," said Sir Henry. "I suppose that's what makes him dangerous."

"That and a much too sentimental sister," I said. "Are you going to report the Barrymores to Princetown?"

"I can't," said Sir Henry. "It won't do any good, since Selden has obviously moved on, and Mrs. Barrymore is going to be hurt enough by her brother's defection. Dash it all, Doyle, the Barrymores have been at Baskerville Hall for four generations—I can't throw them to the wolves!"

"They were aiding and abetting an escaped felon," I said.

"And probably, if it were my brother, I'd do the same. Wouldn't you?"

"Yes," I said reluctantly, thinking of poor, doomed Henry, "but that's not the point."

"I think it's exactly the point. And, no, I am not going to report them."

Ethically, I think I should have kept arguing. But I don't have the heart to turn the Barrymores in, either, especially after the way Mrs. Barrymore *crumpled* when she read Selden's note. She has all the punishment she can bear, simply in being George Selden's sister. As for Barrymore, he would clearly do anything in his power to make his wife happy, and yet there is nothing he can do, either about her brother or about their childlessness, which must pain her a great deal. It isn't as if there's more information that can be extracted from them, and I confess I do not myself want the careful scrutiny of the law, especially so far from London and Lestrade's benevolent blindness.

Just as we started back to Baskerville Hall, we heard again that terrible howl that I have described to you. It froze both of us in our tracks as it rose, and only when the moor was silent again were we able to move on.

"That's not a bird," Sir Henry said flatly. "I don't care what Mr. Stapleton says."

I managed a laugh, although it was not easy. "We are hunting a convict and a hound from hell is hunting us, as likely as not. I only hope its luck is as bad as ours."

Sir Henry was struck by a thought. "You don't suppose that's Selden, do you?"

"I think Selden is long gone from the moor," I said.

We walked back to Baskerville Hall in silence.

Mrs. Barrymore, as I said above, was devastated by her brother's note, but with that great secret revealed, both Barrymores seem much easier, and I don't think they will revert to the idea of leaving Baskerville Hall.

We have had a visit from Mr. and Miss Stapleton, which seemed a transparent attempt to throw Miss Stapleton at Sir Henry. Sir Henry thought so, too, because he smiled beatifically and started talking about the wife he had left in Alberta. He claimed her name is Ermentrude. Miss Stapleton didn't seem to know quite what to do—I noticed her anxious glances at her brother just as I noticed them the other day—as if her instructions hadn't included that contingency. Stapleton himself merely conversed about the butterflies and moths of the moor and asked about the *Lepidoptera* of Canada. I had one of those moments of pseudo-telepathy one sometimes has with friends and kicked Sir Henry just before he could say, "You'd have to ask Ermentrude."

He coughed and said, "I'm afraid I'm not the person to ask."

"Pity," said Stapleton with what I feel sure was perfect sincerity.

Sir Henry sat in frowning silence for some time after they had gone, then said, "He reminds me of someone. Who on Earth does he remind me of?"

"I don't think it can be anyone you've met since you came to England," I said.

"No," said Sir Henry. "And I don't know that it's someone I've *met*. It may just have been someone I've *seen*. Argh! Nothing to drive a man crazy like that tip-of-the-tongue feeling."

I must end this letter here, but you will no doubt be hearing from me again soonest.

Yours sincerely,

J. H. Doyle

‹›

Telegram from Mr. Crow to Dr. J. H. Doyle

20OCT1888
S IS SCHOOLMASTER VANDELEUR STOP HE IS MARRIED
STOP—CROW

❖

Letter from Dr. J. H. Doyle to Mr. Crow

Baskerville Hall, October 20th

My dear Crow,

I promise you that your news has had all the impact you could have wished. We were both much taken aback when we had figured out your meaning, and I believe Sir Henry murmured *Thank God for Ermentrude.* He would indeed have been in an uncomfortable situation if he had attempted to woo an already married lady, even if both the lady and her husband seem inclined to encourage it. We cannot go out walking without falling over one or more of the Stapleton-Vandeleurs. He buttonholes me with discussions of butterflies or—more frequently since he has drawn the correct conclusion that I am not a budding lepidopterist—the oddities of the moor, while she walks apart with Sir Henry and tries (he says) to encourage him to bigamy. It would take a blind man not to find the lady attractive, but Sir Henry took a dislike to her even before we knew that she was not Stapleton's chaste and maiden sister, and I fear that her repeated attempts at enticement merely make her look foolish. I do not think she is a lady who relishes the fool's role; there are definite signs of rupture in the Stapleton-Vandeleur alliance. But she clearly fears him—which makes me think all the more ill of him—and will not defy him. Nor, Sir Henry says, can he persuade her to admit that she is only attempting her seduction because her brother (husband? this starts to look very incestuous) has ordered her to. But we are agreed that it is very hard to imagine that he has changed his name and made his wife into his sister for any innocent purpose.

I'm sure you will be pleased to know that the coursing pack, with Mr. McAllister in dour Scottish attendance, has returned to Baskerville Hall. Sir Henry is delighted with himself and with Mr. McAllister and with his forty-odd foxhounds. The dogs are noisy brutes; I have refused to go anywhere near them—and should have refused even if they were not all but guaranteed to betray my uncomfortable secret. I was never much for coursing to begin with, and although Sir Henry seems determined to persuade me otherwise, he will not change my mind. There is talk of perhaps putting a course together next month.

Sir Henry is full of other plans for Baskerville Hall, for modernizing it properly and restoring the formal garden and a host of other things as numerous and noisy as the foxhounds. He is particularly concerned to continue his uncle's charitable work, and that has led to another interesting encounter, as Mrs. Laura Lyons (née Frankland) came to the Hall to plead her case.

She is the perfect image of her sister Lydia, except for a rather harder expression about the eyes and mouth. She was very anxious that Sir Henry should see the good use to which she had put Sir Charles's gift, and indeed she seems to be scraping a living from the typewriting jobs to be found in Coombe Tracey and Grimpen. Dr. Mortimer helps by giving her his articles for publication, and Mr. Stapleton has promised to do the same when he has something worth writing up.

She seemed uncertain whether she was making what in vulgar parlance is called a dead set at Sir Henry, or if she was being a businesswoman, and Sir Henry seemed rather more interested than he had been in the manifest charms of Miss Stapleton, if I may so still call her. Ermentrude did not make an appearance in his conversation.

And it is no business of mine with whom Sir Henry chooses to entangle himself romantically, but I noticed Mrs. Lyons's uncertainty, and I noticed the way she reddened when she mentioned

Mr. Stapleton, and I caught her on her way to the stable—Sir Henry having been snagged again by the ubiquitous Holland.

"Dr. Doyle, is it?" said Mrs. Lyons.

"Yes," I said. "I was just wondering what he told you when he put you up to it?"

She went scarlet with mortification and then tried to cover. "I'm sure I don't know what you mean."

"I'm sure you do," I said. "Mr. Stapleton persuaded you, somehow, to try to engage Sir Henry's interest, but you are too honest to be comfortable with a subterfuge like that, just as you are too honest to be comfortable lying about it. I just want to know what reason he gave you?"

She gave falsehood up as a bad job. "He said . . . he said the baronet was bothering his sister. He said I didn't have to commit to anything, just to get him to come walking or riding with me someday soon. But you're right. I've never been a good liar."

"How did he persuade you, then?"

"He . . . we are to be married next year."

My eyebrows shot up. "*Are* you? I beg your pardon for intruding in personal business, Mrs. Lyons, but it would be criminal of me not to tell you that the lady you know as Miss Stapleton is actually Mr. Stapleton's wife."

The interesting thing is that she believed me—and not in the way a credulous child will believe anything it's told. I could see it in her eyes as she looked back over their relationship, and that single truth, like Occam's razor, swept away a hundred puzzles that had seemed too small to bother with at the time. "*God,*" she said with considerable vehemence. "Played for a fool *again*. I beg your pardon, Dr. Doyle—thank you—but I have to go."

It is not exaggerating to say the lady fled, and I felt I had done more than enough damage, so that I came back to the house to finish this letter to you before the post.

Sincerely yours,
J. H. Doyle

28

THE HOUND
OF THE
BASKERVILLES

AFTER I HAD put my letter to Crow in the mailbag, I wandered back into the library to prospect through the shelves, hoping (as one always *does* hope, no matter how often disappointed) to find treasure among the stuffy and stolid eighteenth- and early-nineteenth-century volumes. I found *A History of Dartmoor*, written by the Reverend August J. B. Chesham, and was flipping through the pages when I came across a really rather splendid woodcut of the hell-hound standing over Sir Hugo's dead body. The artist had not stinted in imagining the thing's bulk and its phosphor-dripping jowls and the way its head was lowered, more like a bull's than a dog's, and I was staring at it, thinking about Constance Burry and footprints and the howling on the moor, and the thing that made everything make sense was the simple realization that Laura Lyons wasn't the only one Stapleton had played for a fool. He'd told me that the locals said the howling was the Hound of the Baskervilles, and then had offered me a series of more-or-less plausible explanations for the noise, but it had never once occurred to me to check with anyone that the locals *did* call it the Hound of the Baskervilles—or that the locals had ever heard it before Sir Henry came to Baskerville Hall.

I still could not quite run, but I almost ran to the kitchen, where Mrs. Barrymore was washing dishes. "Mrs. Barrymore," I said, and made her jump a foot.

"Oh, I beg your pardon, Dr. Doyle, I didn't hear you."

I waved it off. "The howling noise on the moor—you know the one I mean, the one that sounds like it's going to rip your soul from your body—how long has that been going on?"

She stared at me as if I'd turned bright green and started reciting Wordsworth backward. But she said, "That dreadful noise just started maybe the day that Sir Henry came? The day after?"

"I *knew* it," I said, and flung myself out into the stable yard, across to the yew walk where Sir Charles had died, and through the gate onto the moor. My first thought was to beard Stapleton in his den, but I realized, as I cooled off a bit, that that was foolish. There was nothing I could do by myself, and at that point every reason for Stapleton to ensure that I disappeared. Instead of Merripit House, I started to walk to Grimpen and the telegraph office to send a telegram of my own, already beginning to regret the clipping pace at which I'd set out.

It was with a tired sense of déjà vu that I found Miss Stapleton in my path.

I raised my hat. "Good afternoon, Miss—"

"I am terribly sorry, Dr. Doyle," she said. "I have never been able to stand against him."

That was true enough, but I realized a second too late what she meant by it. Just as I was starting to turn, there was a blinding crack against the side of my head, and I suppose I must have gone down like a felled ox.

❖

WHEN I WOKE, I realized at once that several hours had passed, then that I did not have the least idea where I was. I was inside, for I was lying against a cold stone wall, but I was outside, because I could see the sky shifting in slow shades toward violet and dusk. It took me a long, painful period of cogitation to figure out that I was inside a stone building without a roof. And then I think I knew where I was before I made it to my feet to stagger to the doorway.

Nothing to be seen on any side except the low verdant death of the Great Grimpen Mire. Stapleton had marooned me.

My first concern was the whereabouts of the convict, but I was entirely alone on this island with its huddle of ruined buildings. There were signs that Selden had been there—a store of tins, a wodge of blankets. No fire, of course, and I shuddered at the thought of eating tinned peas cold.

My second concern was that it might very well come to that. Stapleton had said that to try to cross the mire without knowing the path was a lethal mistake—and of all the things he had said to me, that seemed the one most likely to be true. Thus, unless his purpose for me somehow, miraculously, involved coming out here and rescuing me, I was stuck.

And I thought I knew what his purpose was. Mrs. Lyons had said that Stapleton wanted her to get Baskerville to go walking or riding on the moor. Which meant he wanted Baskerville on the moor *at a time of Stapleton's choosing.* Thwarted by Mrs. Lyons and threatened by my knowledge of his secret—and it should have occurred to me that she would go straight to Stapleton to have it out with him—he must have been delighted to discover me out on the moor alone, for he could kill two birds with one stone. He could get rid of me and he could ensure that Sir Henry would be out on the moor tonight, looking for his lost and very stupid friend.

Stapleton brought my unconscious body out, fetched Selden, and then went back to find the perfect place to release the hell-hound on the baronet. I wondered if he'd wanted Mrs. Lyons to persuade Baskerville to leave Wiggins behind for their tryst on the moor, or if he felt a real hell-hound could make scrap metal out of a cerberus.

Possibly it could. I had no enthusiasm for the experiment.

At that point in my reasoning I had to stop to be sick. When I'd recovered, wishing mightily for clean water to rinse out my mouth, I realized that I'd done exactly the thing I'd spent days telling Baskerville not to do: I'd gone out on the moor alone and without bothering to tell a soul where I was going or what my plans were.

"Brilliant, Doyle," I said. "What do you intend to do about it?"

That was the true question. Even if Stapleton *was* planning to rescue me, which I doubted, I did not want to wait for him. I found a stick and went down the hill to test the ground. One step out . . . two steps out . . . three steps out and the solid ground turned into water. I scrambled back to safety and watched my stick sink inch by inch.

If I yelled, would anyone hear me? Would it do any good if they did? Stapleton was the only one who knew the way out here, and that wouldn't change no matter how many farmers knew there was a fool stranded in the middle of the mire.

An alternative occurred to me.

It was a bad idea. I knew it was a bad idea, and yet compared to starving to death while Baskerville was ripped to bits by Selden, it seemed like a genuine option. The sky was getting darker by the minute, and while I thought Stapleton would wait until full dark to release his Hound—just in the unlikely event Baskerville survived, or if there were witnesses—I didn't *know* that and I had no way of knowing where exactly Stapleton's trap was laid.

My idea would take care of that problem, too.

I forced myself to sit and think it through carefully, step by step, but really it came down to a perfectly simple choice: starve to death in the middle of the Great Grimpen Mire, or shift phase and deliberately become a hell-hound.

I felt like a burned child faced with a fire. The last thing I wanted was to become a hell-hound *on purpose,* but the hell-hound's superior sense of smell would enable me to backtrack Stapleton and Selden out of the maze of the Grimpen Mire, and while as a human being I was twigs and tissue paper as far as a hell-hound was concerned, as a hell-hound myself, I might be able to fend off Selden's attack if Wiggins couldn't. Oh, it was all so perfectly logical and reasonable and I hated it.

Hated it, and did it anyway.

I knew I would need somehow to bring my clothes with me. I tore one of Selden's awful blankets into strips and knotted two strips together, which made a strap long enough to tie my boots and clothing into a bundle, with enough left over for a loop that I would hopefully be able to pick up in my teeth. At that point, naked and starting to shiver, I realized I'd more or less committed myself to this venture, since it was either untie my careful bundle, get dressed again, and pray for rescue like the heroine of a yellow-backed novel, or shift phase and try to save Sir Henry's life.

For several agonizing minutes, I didn't think I was going to be able to do it. It was like trying to flex a muscle I didn't actually have. But the hell-hound was so close—as the hell-hound was always close—that I kept trying and finally, by an accident of the "try everything" variety, I discovered that it was not that I needed to flex anything, it was that I needed to relax the (mostly metaphorical) muscles I was holding tensed against the change. I grappled with that in increasing frustration, but then I very abruptly caught the trick of it, and I was, without warning, a hell-hound.

The scents of my enemies, one the rancid sweetness of a rotten orange, the other like burning metal, made the island vivid, and as I had expected, their path through the mire was just as vivid. But before I followed it, there was another scent, a bad scent, that needed to be investigated.

In another of the buildings, I found the corpse of a gigantic dog—a true dog, not like me, but almost as big. His throat had been torn out, and I smelled hell-hound all over him. I nosed the corpse, whining under my breath, and smelled hunger and anger and the hot itch of an intact male. There was an old gnawed boot beside him that smelled of *friend*.

I left him there, stopped my own whining, and set out to track the sweetly rancid scent that was the most vivid to me. It was easy to follow, even though I had to keep my head raised to safeguard the bundle. The path through the mire twisted and turned, but my feet stayed on dry land. There was one place where I did not follow, where his scent diverged from the scent of the burning man, heading for an obvious shortcut. I didn't need to track his scent to see what had happened, for he got maybe seven steps before he started to sink and had to scramble back. I whined again, knowing the burning man had laughed, and then pressed on, more and more eager to get to solid land.

I came out at last on a little spur of rock. I dropped my bundle and lay panting for a moment, but the sickly-sweet scent was in my nose, and I needed to follow it.

I nudged my bundle into the lee of a jumble of rocks, where hopefully it would go unnoticed until I came back for it. It was almost full dark; although it made no difference to me, I remembered that it meant something, something bad, and I remembered that I was looking for *friend*, that *friend* was in danger from the burning man and the hell-hound whose scent was cloying in my nose and mouth, the hell-hound whose scent said *enemy.*

I lowered my nose and followed it.

He was making no effort to hide or confuse his trail, he and the burning man. Their trail was easy to follow, and I ran along it, pausing every so often to cast for *friend* and finding occasional traces, old and dim, nothing more.

As I ran, the fog began to rise, a nuisance at first and then a danger, as it obscured the ground in front of me. I slowed my pace, mindful that the ground was not to be trusted. But it made me anxious not to be able to see clearly, and it got harder and harder not to bay, to call my sisters to hunt with me.

No sisters in earshot, I reminded myself, only *enemy*. Even with the fog, his scent was growing thicker and thicker, and then I heard a sound I recognized, the clank clunk of the metal dog who went everywhere with *friend* to protect him. I couldn't tell where the sound was coming from, and I knew I couldn't let *friend* see me. And *enemy* was somewhere nearby, his smell was too fresh for him to be far away. I froze, and in that same moment, a man yelled, "NOW!"

I heard *friend* cry, "Who's there?" and then he screamed. It gave me a direction, and I ran full-out, barely noticing my bad leg. The fog eddied, and I saw my enemy smash the metal dog aside, already leaping for *friend*'s throat.

I finally gave tongue and hurled myself between *friend* and *enemy*. I collided with my enemy, and we went tumbling, slamming hard into the ground. We rolled. I ended up on top and would have ripped his throat out, except that he got his back legs between us and shoved me away. I snarled and rushed him again. This time he turned so that my teeth closed on his ear instead of on his jugular. It made him yelp, but it wasn't what I wanted.

He turned his head, pulling against my grip on his ear, and tried to get his teeth in my throat. I pushed away, his blood running down my jowls. Both men were shouting. My enemy got to his feet and was backing away. In another moment he would flee the fight entirely. I couldn't let him. There was too much sweet-reeking rottenness in his scent.

I had to keep him here, so that he could not use his great advantage, which was that he had four strong legs.

I started another rush, but pulled up short with a yelp, and then began hopping awkwardly away backward, favoring one front paw. It got his attention; his body quit looking like he was going to run, and instead he began stalking me, body low to the ground.

I hopped awkwardly and carefully away until an outcropping of rock blocked my path. The instant I looked trapped, my enemy charged at me. I rolled with him as he came and heaved him into the rock behind me. He dropped to the ground dazed, and I flung myself at him. My teeth closed in his throat, and that was the end of him.

Blood gouted. I backed away, shaking my head and snorting to get his blood out of my nostrils and sinuses, and then I realized that I was *visible*. Both *friend* and the burning man could *see* me.

I bolted.

I remembered where the bundle was, and I ran to it, splashing through every puddle and scrim of standing water I could find. It was not far—I had tracked my enemy in an arc, but could take the straight line path back. I outran the fog and only wanted to run faster.

I was damp and muddy but clean of blood when I reached the bundle. I stood, my chest heaving, and tried to think of why I should change. I knew that I had to, that it was important, but the reason made no sense, and the moor was full of scents to follow and prey to catch and a thousand thousand fabulous things that I would not be able to hear or see or smell if I changed.

Still, memory insisted that I had to do it, that I could not simply spend the hours until dawn in exploration. Memory insisted, but could not tell me *why,* and I was pacing along the edge of the mire, grumbling to myself, when I heard, far away but coming closer, the thud of running feet.

I knew it was the burning man, and the knowledge terrified me. He had trapped my enemy. He might trap me as well. The thought was a spur. I lowered my head and changed . . .

. . . into a person who was equally terrified of Stapleton's approach. Fortunately, years in the Medical Corps had taught me how to dress in a tearing hurry in conditions ranging from darkness to artillery fire. I flung my clothes on, praying that I had succeeded in getting all of the blood off myself. I raked my fingers through my hair, winced at the lump Stapleton had left, although at least it might explain blood on me if no one inquired too closely. I thought suddenly, *How do I explain* myself? Stapleton had left me in the middle of the Grimpen Mire and there was no reasonable explanation for how I could have found my way out.

I threw myself flat on the ground at Stapleton's approach. He had a small lantern, which lit his face into the mask of a monster, and he was raving to himself in an incandescent fury. I caught scattered syllables, enough to be sure that Baskerville was still alive and that Stapleton had not connected me with the unexpected second hellhound—though that would change when he reached his island and found me gone. If I'd had my revolver, I would have shot him, but I had left it, quite safely, in my locked valise.

From the darkness, Baskerville cried, "Stop!"

Stapleton spun around. I noticed that he had one foot on the rock that marked the start of his Daedalian path. "Sir Henry?" he said with what almost sounded like real cheerfulness. "What can I do for you?"

"Who in God's name are you, and what have you done with Doyle?"

Stapleton laughed—actually laughed—and said, "I suppose you can call me cousin."

Baskerville made the connection more swiftly than I did. "Uncle Rodger got married."

"Indeed. To a lovely German girl who died in giving birth to me. He did not marry again, remaining quite faithful to my mother's memory. He told me often of the great estate in England where my grandfather lived—this was after my father had 'died,' you understand. He was infected with necrophagy and could not bear the thought that his father and brothers might learn of it. It is very easy to fake your own death in Brazil."

"Did you kill Uncle Charles?"

"He was so scared of the family fetch that any large dog could serve to make him scare himself to death. An interesting paradox, is it not? And it gave me the idea, when you were too foolish to renounce your claim and stay away, *despite* being warned. Because no one would wonder if a Baskerville was killed by a hell-hound."

"Well, that's one question answered," said Baskerville grimly. He had come closer, though not quite to the edge of Stapleton's circle of light, and I saw as I looked that direction that the fog was beginning to curl close. "Now what did you do with Doyle?"

"Oh, the good doctor is safe," said Stapleton. "Quite, quite safe." He began to giggle, a thin note of hysteria riding the edge of his laughter. "I'll be sure to tell him you send your kind regards." And he whirled and started into the mire.

"Stop!" said Baskerville, and when Stapleton did not stop, Baskerville shot his lantern out of his hand—an excellent shot if that was what he had intended to do. I have never asked him.

"You can't really think that will stop me," called Stapleton. "I can walk this path blindfolded." And there was just enough moonlight that I could see him bounding through the mire, as I had seen him bound after the butterfly that might or might not have been *Cyclopides*. Baskerville ran forward, but there was not enough light for him to take a shot.

Now or never, I thought, and called, "Baskerville? Is that you?" My voice came out in a distressingly persuasive croak.

"Doyle!" He immediately dismissed Stapleton from his attention. "My God, man, are you all right? Say something so that I can find you."

"I think so," I said, and asked before he could: "What happened?"

"That villain Stapleton," said Baskerville, as he found me, a damp, muddy hand clutching my damp, muddy arm to help me up. "He set an actual hell-hound on me!"

"Good Lord," I said. It seemed a rather weak response, but it satisfied Baskerville, who went on to tell me the whole story, including the corpse of the hell-hound turning back into George Selden in the end.

"His 'better deal' must have been with Stapleton," I said.

"One devil making a deal with another," said Baskerville. "And I fear he's smashed poor Wiggins to pieces, although someone can come out tomorrow and collect the pieces, and maybe the company can mend him. But what happened to *you*? I've been searching the whole moor for you, and Barrymore is out searching still."

I told him the story up to my encounter with Miss Stapleton, and there had a stroke of luck, for he said, "Good God, Miss Stapleton, we must catch her before she realizes the game is up. Come on, before the fog swallows us whole!"

I followed him willingly—though I was starting to feel the aches and pains attendant on the punishment I had given my body as a hell-hound—grateful to have gained a respite before I actually had to lie to him. We found Merripit House ablaze with lights and apparently deserted, not unlike the *Mary Celeste*. No trace was ever found of the servant Anthony, and we searched room after room for Miss Stapleton without success, until we came to a locked door.

"This is Stapleton's dreadful museum," I said.

We had found a key in the door of Miss Stapleton's bedroom—on the outside, suggesting that that unhappy lady was not infrequently locked in—and when Baskerville tried that key in the museum door, we both heard the tumblers turn over.

The sight that met our eyes was truly one of the strangest I can recall. In the middle of the room was a beam, supporting the rafter, and to this beam, in the midst of Stapleton's nightmare creatures, was tied a human form, so swathed in bedsheets that it was almost unrecognizable. One towel passed around the throat and was secured at the back of the pillar. Another covered the lower part of the face and over it two dark eyes—eyes full of grief and shame and, as she recognized us, amazement—stared back at us.

"Good *God*," said Baskerville.

I jerked free the gag, and we rapidly unswathed the bedsheets. Miss Stapleton sank to her knees in front of us, her chest heaving as she took her first free breaths for what must have been hours. As her head dropped forward, I saw the clear red weal of a whip-lash across her neck.

Baskerville muttered something that I pretended not to hear.

"You are lucky he did not asphyxiate you," I said.

"I know," she said in a raspy voice. "I think he wanted me to die that way, but he couldn't bring himself to . . . to make it certain. But, Sir Henry, how is it that you are safe? What happened to . . . what happened to the Hound?"

"It is dead," said Baskerville, "and your husband has fled into the Grimpen Mire."

"Oh thank God," she said.

I said, "Are you hurt, Miss . . . see here, what is your name? Your real name?"

She hesitated, then nodded. "I am Beryl Garcia. I no longer accept any of his names as mine."

"Good for you," said Baskerville. He laughed suddenly, startling himself as much as us. "Sorry. It just occurred to me what an awful name 'Beryl Baskerville' would be."

"It is not mine," she said. "I will not touch it."

"Are you hurt, Miss Garcia?" I said.

"Only bruises," she said wearily. "What he has done to my soul is worse than anything he could do to my body. I have followed him for years, changing my name, colluding in his crimes, clinging always to my belief that, no matter what words he used or how he ill-treated me, that he *did* love me, that at least I had that—but I didn't. It was just another of his endless, endless lies." She broke down sobbing, and I found I could not fault her.

She regained her composure after barely a minute, and raising her head, saw through the window the fogbank that now surrounded the house. "Fog!" she said, like a child seeing snow at Christmas. "You said my husband went into the Grimpen Mire?"

"Yes," said Baskerville.

She laughed brilliantly. "Then he is doomed, the fool. He may find his way in, but he will never find his way out, not when he can't see the guiding wands."

"He said he could walk his path blindfolded," Baskerville said doubtfully.

"And I'm sure he thinks he can," she said, her lips curving with tigerish amusement. "But he's never tried it, has he?"

Baskerville and I both shuddered at the thought, suddenly vivid, of trying to navigate the Grimpen Mire in this white, evasive, endlessly obscuring fog.

Beryl Garcia saw and smiled. "He will never come out of the Great Grimpen Mire alive," she said, and in that she was correct.

◈

THE FOG LIFTED a little after midnight, and Baskerville and I were able to walk home, each of us tremendously glad for the other's company. We found Barrymore had returned just as the fog was getting bad and was in the middle of getting ready to go out again—which doubtless contributed to his pleasure in seeing me. He suggested a hot toddy before bed, "to throw off the fog," and Baskerville and I agreed it sounded like just the thing.

We talked rather aimlessly; I think we were both too conscious of avoiding the subject of the Grimpen Mire and Stapleton's probable, horrible fate for real conversation. I was just getting up to go to bed, every muscle now protesting overexertion and cold and damp, when Baskerville said, "Y'know, there's one thing I cannot for the *life* of me figure out?"

"Oh?"

"Who was the second hell-hound? It can't have been Barrymore, because I saw very clearly that it was a bitch, but it can't have been Beryl Garcia, because she was wrapped up like an Egyptian mummy."

"Hmm," I said, and swallowed panic. "Perhaps it was Constance Burry."

"Perhaps it was," he said. There was nothing conscious in his gaze, no sign that he was covertly telling me that he knew both of my secrets. He was genuinely baffled. "Well, goodnight, Doyle."

"Goodnight, Sir Henry," said I, and limped off to bed.

PART EIGHT

THE SURREY VAMPIRE

29

A New Errand

I RETURNED TO London on the twenty-third. Crow was on the platform to meet me, and we shook hands as effusively as if I'd been gone for years.

"I *missed* you," Crow said, almost indignantly.

I startled myself by saying, "I missed you, too," and it was worth it for his smile.

And it was good to be back in the Baker Street flat, where everything was in the right place and the cook knew how I liked my eggs. I slept well for the first time since I had left for Dartmoor.

Crow wasted no time in acquainting me with all that had happened in the search for Jack the Ripper in my absence. It was, as he described it, "a series of successive failures," with every new suspect, seeming so likely at first glance, turning to ashes in the investigators' hands.

"And Gregson and Lestrade keep looking at me as if they expect me to pull the murderer out of a hat like a street magician."

"They have seen you solve some remarkable cases."

"I can't solve everything," Crow said. He sounded tired, which was alarming. "I don't know who killed the Marrs and the Williamsons. I don't know who's dismembering women and dumping them in the Thames. And I don't know who Jack the Ripper is. There are limits to the power of deduction."

He was standing by the bow window, staring out at the street, but I thought for once he wasn't observing the passersby.

I said, "No one expects you to solve every case you come across."

"No, only me," he said with something that was almost bitterness. "How else can I justify my existence, Doyle? What other reason do I have for not embracing the Consensus?"

"Is that why you do it? Solve crimes?"

"Well, no," he said. "Yes? I mean, it's the thing that I *do,* that no one would do if I weren't here. I suppose . . . is it?"

"If you continue your existence, you may yet solve those murders," I said. "And I think it's safe to say no one will solve them if you don't. Scotland Yard is never going to find Jack the Ripper. They don't even know how to look for him."

"I don't, either," said Crow.

"No, but you might figure it out. Which is more than I can say for Gregson, or Abberline, or Swanson, or any of them."

Crow turned from the window and smiled suddenly. "You don't have to persuade me not to throw myself in the Thames, you know."

"No?"

"No. I'm frustrated, not despairing. At least, not despairing to that extent. This case is *maddening.*"

"Yes," I said, "but it's not your fault you can't catch him."

"How do you make that out?"

"Well, what can you deduce from the corpses, since that's the only evidence we've got?"

He gave me a baffled look, but said, "They're all prostitutes."

"Yes, and?"

"He most likely strangled them before he got his knife out. It's the only reason I can think of that none of them screamed."

"Unless Israel Schwartz really did see Elisabeth Stride and her killer."

"What he describes, though, is not a woman who realizes she's in an alleyway with Jack the Ripper. If she'd known who he was, she would have screamed the place down. And the Ripper's too canny a lad to let them see the knife."

"He strangles them before he cuts them—and he just had bad luck with Stride all the way around. First Israel Schwartz and then the fellow with the pony."

"Louis Diemschutz."

"Yes. And, of course, that's assuming Elisabeth Stride was killed by the Ripper in the first place."

"You think Catherine Eddowes was a *coincidence*?"

I shrugged, inwardly pleased that I'd gotten him to start arguing with me. "It would make sense of why he went back into Whitechapel. He didn't know Berner Street was full of policemen."

Crow thought about that and nodded almost reluctantly. "And Elisabeth Stride was killed by a copycat?"

"It would explain why the fellow made such a hash of it."

"I don't know, Doyle. It's an awfully big coincidence."

"Oh, I'm not saying it's true. Just that it's possible. We don't have enough evidence to tell us either way. Which is my point. You don't have enough data to be able to deduce more than the most general attributes of this man. Nobody's seen him, so that there's no one to ask questions of, and I think he's much too smart to let anyone know what he's doing. Nobody's sheltering him—although I know there are plenty of theories that say otherwise—and nobody's working with him. And he's not a lunatic. He's probably the sanest man in London."

"Certainly he has the coolest head. Your theory is that we can't catch him?"

"My theory is that none of the tactics that work on other murderers will work on him. He doesn't know his victims, he doesn't have a motive—or at least nothing *we* recognize as a motive—and unless he has a moment of phenomenally bad luck, he's not going to register as anything but another Londoner to the people who meet him on the street. *Nobody knows they know him.*"

"We need a new set of tactics," Crow said.

"Yes, and I haven't the least idea what they are."

Crow's wings mantled up protectively around him. He said, "All we have to work with are the victims he leaves behind. They all lived and died in the East End, but there's nothing in that, is there?"

"Only that the East End is his hunting ground, and the prostitutes who live there are his prey—and *that*'s most likely because they are so easy to hunt. They are already letting men pay to prey on them. The Ripper and his knife are just an exaggeration of these women's daily business."

Crow's wings mantled even further, so that he was almost invisible behind them. "And he steals organs," he said. "Why does he do that? What possible purpose can he have?"

"He steals them to steal them," I said. "I would guess he took the uterus twice because it's the most 'female' organ."

"And the kidney?"

"I don't know."

"I think he took it because it's so difficult to get at. To prove that he knows what he's doing."

"You think he reads the papers?"

"Everyone in London either reads the papers or hears them read. Or at the very least hears them talked about. He *has* to know that that's the big debate, and of course he wants to weigh in. He botched the uterus that second time, so that he had to do something really difficult—which, given how fast he was working and in what little light, that actually *was*."

"Do you get the feeling," I said—hesitantly, because this was one of those ideas that had a horrible sort of plausibility in the middle of the night but looked ridiculous during the day—"that he's looking for something?"

"Looking for what?"

"I don't know. I don't think *he* knows. But the way he rummages around inside their bodies . . . I don't know. It's just one of those ideas—once it occurred to me, I couldn't get rid of it."

"But rummaging around after *what*? You must have some idea, or it wouldn't bother you so much."

Which, of course, was true. "Well, he's clearly a man who hates women. You don't go after someone with a knife like that unless you either hate them personally or hate something about them so fundamental that it can't be changed. And since we know it wasn't a personal motive, or the police would have dug it out, it must be fundamental. And given how he poses them, and how he goes after their lower bodies and wombs, it's their womanhood he hates. But it fascinates him at the same time. He can't just leave it alone. He's trying to find the thing he hates and he can't."

Crow said, "That really *is* bothering you."

"It's such a horrible idea," I said, knowing it was an inadequate explanation.

"It's a *theory*," Crow said kindly. "You've probably given the matter more thought than he has."

"I know," I said.

⟨◇⟩

ON THE THIRD night after my return, I went to bed early, still fatigued from my adventures in Dartmoor. I woke, suddenly and completely, some time after midnight, when a voice said in the darkness, "Good morning, Dr. Doyle."

I did not have to ask who was there. I did say, stupidly, "How . . . ?"

There was a cold, chiming laugh. "Mr. Crow *did* invite me in," said the Master of the Moriarty Hunt.

At that moment, Crow began knocking frantically on the door. "Doyle? Doyle! Are you all right? Doyle!"

"Dr. Doyle is entirely unharmed," said Master Moriarty, "and will remain that way."

"That's good to hear," I said. "But if not to harm me, why are you here?"

Master Moriarty sighed and said, "I need your help."

"*My* help? Are you sure you don't need Crow's help?"

"No," she said with flat finality. "Mr. Crow cannot help with this."

"But I can?"

"The Master of the Gilbraith Hunt has stolen one of my Chosen. I cannot go in after him, but you can."

"You want me to go into a vampiric house after one of your addicts?"

"Gently, Dr. Doyle," said Master Moriarty. "I may need you, but I will not tolerate insult."

"I spoke no insult, Master Moriarty," I said. "Any Chosen of yours must be addicted to your blood. But I apologize for my harshness. Still. Is that what you want?"

"No vampire can touch you," she reminded me. "And the Gilbraith Hunt isn't strong enough to turn Isa's will. He is still *my* Chosen. They will not be able to stop you."

"Is this part of some vampiric skirmish?" I said. Vampiric hunts were always skirmishing with each other, jockeying for power and wealth, and in general human beings were well-advised to stand clear.

"She has gone too far," said Master Moriarty. "But that need be no concern of yours. I wish you only to bring Isa out of the vile Gilbraith den."

"I don't see that I can refuse," I said.

"Doyle!" said Crow from the other side of the door.

"I promised," I said. "And I don't believe Master Moriarty would ask for my help if she had not exhausted all other avenues. Give me a moment to get dressed, and we can go."

Master Moriarty unlocked my door without apparently touching the key and drifted out, much as she must have drifted in. I yanked yesterday's clothes on and followed her into the sitting room, where she and Crow were glaring at each other like rival cats.

"Oh, stop it," I said. "This isn't a pleasant errand, but it's not going to harm me."

"She could have waited until morning," said Crow. "You need your sleep."

I thought of the many nights when Crow kept me up, excitedly explaining his new theory about the Ripper or stewing over his current case, but did not say so. "Don't look to a vampire for consideration," I said and bowed slightly to Master Moriarty. "Shall we?"

"I have a hansom waiting," she said, and I followed her out into the cold, wet night.

◈

THE GILBRAITH HUNT also kept its seat in Lambeth, the telltale red windows glowing luridly over a tobacconist's shop. "I will wait here," said Master Moriarty when the hansom stopped, the first time either of us had spoken since she gave the address to the cabbie. "You are looking for Isa Whitney."

"Right," I said.

I climbed the stairs, narrow and reeking rather of tomcat, and pushed open the door at the top. The vampiric house was dimly lit, and it was a maze of passages and tiny rooms, each barely big enough for the fainting couch it contained. Of the sixteen such rooms I counted, only five had anyone in them, that paltry number suggesting why Master Gilbraith had done something as dramatic and foolish as trying to steal one of Master Moriarty's Chosen.

I asked each of the addicts I found, three men and two women, if he or she either was or knew Isa Whitney. They all said no.

Then I came to a red baize door, the first actual door I had found in the entire house. Beyond it, presumably, were the Gilbraith vampires, and where the addicts had merely been puzzled to see me, the vampires would be actively displeased. I wanted, badly, to go back to Master Moriarty and tell her Isa Whitney was not here, but I did not think she would believe me. I certainly did not think she would let me go home.

Then the decision became moot, for a stocky blond vampire opened the door and stared at me in bewilderment.

"I am looking for Isa Whitney," I said, before he could ask.

The blank look I got in return suggested that perhaps Master Gilbraith was not being discriminating enough in her Chosen.

"Excuse me," I said, and stepped past him. He did not stop me.

Behind the red baize door the house became more houselike, with a parlor and a sitting room and closed doors that were probably bedrooms. Before I quite nerved myself to start opening doors at random, I found another, smaller set of rooms with fainting couches. All six of these had an addict on the couch, and I recognized by their waxy complexions that these were Chosen who were near making the transition to vampire kits.

I asked a young man in a rumpled brown suit, "Are you Isa Whitney?"

It had been a guess, based on the fact that he looked like a good bourgeois and the others looked like they'd been pulled at random off the streets.

He opened his eyes (brown starting to sheen gold) and frowned dreamily at me. "Yes. Who are you?" His voice was slow and slurred, but at least he was cognizant enough to understand me.

"Master Moriarty sent me."

His eyes widened. "Master Moriarty?" He started floundering upright. "I didn't mean to worry her. I wasn't going to stay long."

I knew, as any child knows, the ability of vampires to beguile their prey. The vampires of London generally had no need to use that ability, as their prey came willingly to them, but it would certainly make it easy for a Master to lure in anyone she wanted to.

"What o'clock is it?" said Whitney.

"Nearly three in the morning."

"Of what day?"

"Friday," I said. "The twenty-seventh of October."

"Friday! It can't be Friday!" He had half risen, but now he sank back onto the couch. "It's only Wednesday. It has to be Wednesday. Don't frighten me like that."

"I am sorry," I said, "but it is Friday. Master Moriarty has become very concerned about you."

"Oh no," moaned Isa Whitney.

"She's waiting outside in a hansom," I said, offering a lure of my own, and Whitney made it upright.

"Give me your arm," he said. "I can't worry Kate."

I chose not to say any of the things I could have said and simply helped him maintain his balance.

We were just through the red baize door when Master Gilbraith caught up with us. She was stick thin, with a sharp, rather ratlike face and long red hair that she wore loose like a child or a Burne-Jones painting. "Isa!" she said. "Where are you going? And who is your companion?"

"Madame," I said, "I am an emissary from Master Moriarty."

Her lip drew back from her upper teeth, making her look even more strikingly ratlike. "Master Moriarty has no right to send her . . ." She broke off, staring at me in bafflement.

"Master Moriarty was concerned about Mr. Whitney," I said. "And Mr. Whitney has indicated that he wishes to leave, which you must acknowledge he has every right to do."

Master Gilbraith glowered, but her play had been based on the same principle: until Isa Whitney was actually turned from human to vampire—and he wasn't quite there yet, although he was close—he could come and go as he pleased, and no hunt had a legal claim on him.

And Whitney proved he was listening by saying, "I want to leave."

Master Gilbraith snarled at me over Whitney's head; she did not, however, attempt to come any closer. It was some comfort in a most discomforting situation, that apparently it was true that no vampire other than James Moriarty could harm me. I had truthfully hoped never to test that proposition at all.

"Good evening, madame," I said to Master Gilbraith, and Whitney and I continued our slow progress out of the Gilbraith house. No one tried to stop us, although there were suddenly vampires with all the addicts in the outer part of the house, and they all watched us as warily as cats watching a strange dog.

As we neared the front door, four vampires appeared seemingly out of nowhere to block it, three women and one man. The women all wore their hair down, as their Master did.

"Isa," said one, "why are you leaving us?"

"Do you not love us?" said another. "Did you not promise to stay?"

"Did I?" said Isa Whitney, sounding alarmingly uncertain.

"Remember that Master Moriarty is waiting for you," I said urgently.

"Master Gilbraith will forgive you, Isa," said the male vampire coaxingly. None of them was trying to come near us, but they weren't moving aside, and I was afraid that if we approached them, they would simply remove Whitney from my arm like taking custody of a lapdog. I wasn't at all sure, looking at his dazed face, that Whitney would protest.

A voice said from behind us, "Dr. Doyle?"

Startled, I turned, keeping my hold on Whitney's hand, and found James Moriarty, looking just as startled as I felt. "Moriarty!" I said. "What are you doing here?" I turned back far enough to keep an eye on the Gilbraith vampires, all of whom were looking sour.

"Visiting a friend," he said, with a wry twist of his mouth. "What on Earth are you doing in a vampire den?"

"Your Master," I said, "asked me to come fetch Mr. Whitney."

His eyebrows went up. He looked from me to Whitney to the four vampires between us and the door. "I see. That venture seems to be proceeding most prosperously."

"You might provide assistance."

"So I might," said Moriarty. "I have no objections." And he smiled at the Gilbraith vampires, letting his teeth show.

They shifted uneasily.

Moriarty came to stand on Whitney's other side. "Isa Whitney is Master Moriarty's Chosen. Master Gilbraith has no right to interfere. Which," he added, "would be why she's not stopping Mr. Whitney herself."

The four Gilbraith vampires glanced at each other.

"Possession is right enough," said one, but I could see that it was only bravado.

"Strength is also right," said Moriarty. "I suggest you stand aside."

And, somewhat to my surprise, they did.

"Come along, my dear," Moriarty said to Whitney, and the two of us led him out and down the stairs and out onto the street, where Master Moriarty leaned forward in the hansom and said, "James! What are *you* doing here?"

"Looking for help and finding none," he said pointedly. "I know why *you*'re here, but you shouldn't have sent Dr. Doyle in alone. The Gilbraith Hunt are a stupid lot, and they almost tried something." He handed Whitney up into the hansom.

"Pay mind to your own business, James," said Master Moriarty, and then, just as it was crossing my night-fogged mind that hansoms had room for only two passengers, James Moriarty turned back to me and said, "Dr. Doyle, I, too, need your help."

The hansom drove off without so much as a "good-bye" from Master Moriarty.

I took a deep breath, exhaled slowly, and said, "I don't seem to have very much choice. What sort of help do you need?"

He had the grace to look guilty. "I don't mean to entrap you. If you hear me out and want nothing to do with it, I will not bother you further, I promise."

"Must we do this *here*?" I said. "Or can we return to Baker Street, where at least I can sit down?"

"Of course," he said. "I do not disdain Mr. Crow's advice, either. I left a hansom over here." And he led me to a side street where a black horse and a hansom cab were almost invisible in the shadows.

"We ready, sir?" the cabbie said cheerfully. I wondered if he specialized in vampire fares.

I climbed into the hansom and Moriarty followed me after giving the cabbie the address.

The cab started off. Moriarty said, "I had no idea Master Gilbraith had been foolish enough to interfere with Mr. Whitney. Our paths have crossed by chance."

"What was your business with the Gilbraith Hunt, then?"

"Let me tell the story coherently and in one piece. I notice that your leg seems a good deal better, and the *metaphysicum morbi* has subsided."

"Yes. I did take your advice."

"Even vampires can have good ideas."

"But are rarely so altruistic as to share them."

I caught the motion of him shrugging in the darkness. "I like you. I would have let those hemophages eat you if I didn't."

If he meant to silence me, he succeeded. He either didn't notice or demonstrated the consideration vampires most often disdain, for—rather than waiting for me to find a reply—he began telling me, in distinctly slanderous terms, about the Gilbraith Hunt, a topic which took us easily from Lambeth to Marylebone.

In Baker Street, I used my latchkey and Crow had the flat door open before I'd closed the front door behind us. He showed heroic self-restraint and said nothing until all three of us were in the flat and the door closed again. Then he demanded, "What *happened*?" Unspoken, but still very nearly audible, was the rider, "And why is *he* here?"

I had invited Moriarty in, wondering at my own stupidity as I did so; therefore I answered the unspoken question first: "Mr. Moriarty has a case for us."

As I expected, this distracted Crow completely. He immediately turned his uncomfortable gaze from me to Moriarty and said, "You do?" sounding both hopeful and dubious, like a child promised a treat by a stern great-aunt.

"I suppose so," Moriarty said, shifting uneasily. "Certainly, I have a problem."

"Please," Crow said. "Tell us your problem."

"Well," said Moriarty, gathering himself, "I imagine you know that not all vampiric Masters start from an advantageous position?" He looked from me to Crow, brows raised.

"You're talking about vagabond hunts," said Crow after a moment's perplexity.

Moriarty made a face. "I dislike the term, but yes. The acquisition of property is every Master's first goal, but not all established Masters will give their daughters a seed house. The Master who made me—the Master of the Hunt Flannagan in Dublin—wants no competition. If one of her sisters turns Master, she buys her a ticket to Liverpool and there's the end of it."

"Liverpool is a dreadful place for vampires," said Crow.

"It's overrun," Moriarty agreed. "Which is why no new Master can stay there. Vagabondage is a terrible thing for a vampire—we are meant to have a house and a hunt. One of the reasons 'vagabond hunts' have such a bad name is that they *aren't* hunts. A vagabond hunt is a Master who can't start a hunt because she doesn't have a house. They resort to all kinds of crimes because they are desperate."

"You have a friend," I said.

"She is my sister, as vampires reckon such things, for we were both made by Master Flannagan. Her name is Judith Shirley."

"Not an Irish name," Crow observed.

"Her parents were English," said Moriarty. "I forget how they came to Dublin, but Judith was born there and loves the city as passionately as anyone ever has. When her parents wanted her to marry a Londoner, she ran away and turned vampire. She was utterly content as a sister of the Hunt Flannagan . . . and then she turned Master."

"I thought vampiric Masters were made as vampires are made," said Crow.

"Which is what the Masters prefer for everyone to believe, but—and I shall doubtless be in trouble with Master Moriarty if she learns I have told you this—the truth is that we do not know what makes a sister become a Master. It isn't desire, for Judith desired nothing less. She either had to challenge Master Flannagan—and quite certainly be killed—or be exiled from Dublin."

"The city she'd become a vampire to stay in," I said, understanding the cruel double-bind her biology had put Judith Shirley in. "Obviously, she chose to leave."

"There's always a chance that someday she will be able to return," said Moriarty. "But she needs a house and a hunt and property, and at the moment she has none." After a moment, he continued bitterly, "At the moment, she is in a Surrey jail on suspicion of murder."

"Murder?" said Crow. "But vampires don't commit murder. Haven't for centuries."

"Even a vagabond like Judith has no need to," said Moriarty. "That's only one of the peculiar things about the story."

"How did you come to hear of it?" said Crow. "There's been nothing in the papers."

"A letter," Moriarty said. "She managed to smuggle it out of Stoke Moran with the help of a family of Roma."

"Suppose," said Crow, "you start from the beginning. I know, of course, that your people have been kind to the . . . Roma, did you say?"

"It is what they call themselves," said Moriarty, "and is thus surely to be preferred to 'gypsies.'"

"To the Roma," Crow continued, "thus that part of the story needs no explaining. But why should anyone think a vampire was a murderer? Wait. Who was the victim?"

"A woman named Julia Stoner. She—Judith, I mean—had been foolish enough to let herself be seen talking to Miss Stoner, and apparently the fact that Miss Stoner's death was mysterious created an assumption that Judith must have killed her."

"That is remarkably shoddy logic," Crow said, "even for people unaccustomed to the practice."

"I really don't know any more than that. But Judith is my sister and she has no hunt to stand for her. I must help her if it is possible to do so."

"And of course you need a doctor," I said. "Unless an autopsy has already been done?"

"Judith's letter says the family is agitating against autopsy—strange, considering that Miss Stoner's stepfather is a doctor."

"Very strange," said Crow.

"Will you come, Dr. Doyle?" said Moriarty—beseechingly, if the word can be applied to a vampire.

"I think you should go, Doyle," said Crow. "*I* would."

"You'll go anywhere for a puzzle," I said, "but I suppose I'm no better. Yes, I'll come."

"Thank you," said Moriarty with unmistakable relief. "Master Moriarty agreed that I could go, but she called it a fool's errand and said she would waste none of her sisters on it, and my friend in the Gilbraith Hunt . . ." He shook his head. "There's a seven-fifteen train from Paddington this morning."

"Good," I said. "Then I'm going back to bed."

30

INTO THE COUNTRYSIDE

WHILE I SLEPT, Moriarty and Crow stayed in the sitting room and talked about murder. When I came out again, they were arguing about whether John Thurtell was or was not guilty of the murder of William Weare.

I said, "I'm going to ring the bell for tea. You decide if we're going to terrify Jennie out of her wits."

Moriarty smiled a small and alarming smile. "She won't see me," he said. He settled in the wing chair by the bow window and picked up one of the stack of the *East End Observer* on the side table.

I hesitated, but Moriarty said, "No, I promise. She'll have no idea I'm here."

"All right," I said, and rang the bell.

Moriarty was perfectly correct; Jennie never even glanced his direction. She brought me tea and toast and *The Times* as if everything was normal and there was no vampire in our sitting room.

After I'd poured my tea and the door was firmly closed behind Jennie, I said, "How did you do that?"

Moriarty laughed. "Watching the pair of you trying not to look at me was more entertainment than I've had in weeks. But to answer your question—and this is another thing I'll probably get in trouble for telling you—it's much the same as a beguilement, except instead of *drawing* attention, you repel it. It's much harder to do, and it's really only effective on one person at a time. It's not much more than a parlor trick."

"Useful in this instance," said Crow.

Moriarty shrugged.

I thought Moriarty might have exaggerated the difficulty of his reverse beguilement, for I noticed as we made our way through Paddington Station that no one ever seemed to look directly at him, even the ticket clerk. We had no trouble securing a first-class compartment and settled in across from each other. Moriarty leaned back with a sigh as if exhausted.

"Were you beguiling them?" I said, with a wave of my hand to indicate the whole of Paddington.

"Not in the same way as I beguiled your maid," he said. "This is just a minor deflection. We practice it all the time."

"It must save a good deal of trouble."

"That is one word for it, yes."

To spare myself from trying to make conversation with a vampire, I had bought a raft of newspapers, and unlike some traveling companions I have had—my mother springs instantly and horribly to mind—Moriarty proved amenable to spending our journey in silent reading.

We alighted at Leatherhead per the instructions in Judith Shirley's letter. Moriarty succeeded in hiring a dog cart, while I found the station master and got directions for Stoke Moran.

My scent made our hired horse, a dark bay gelding with two white socks, uneasy, but we found that he calmed considerably if I sat in the back of the dog cart and left Moriarty to do the driving alone.

The hamlet of Stoke Moran was big enough to have an inn. I took a room there, Moriarty having vanished to find Judith Shirley, and then took my medical bag and set out to find the body of Julia Stoner.

I found the police station easily enough; as in the villages near where I had grown up, the station doubled as the constable's home. He was there, a sharp-featured young man with tow-blond hair. I said, "I'm here about the autopsy," and his face brightened perceptibly.

"Oh thank goodness," he said. "No disrespect to the dead lady, but she needs to be buried."

"I'm happy to start right now," I said, and he brightened further.

"Let me take you over to St. Anne's," he said. "We've been keeping her in the crypt. It seems like the most respectful thing to do."

Aside from being respectful, the crypt would most likely have been warded to retard decay—a church crypt was the smartest place to put a body if you couldn't put it directly in the ground.

"I was rousted out in rather a hurry," I said truthfully. "What can you tell me?"

"The deceased's name is Julia Stoner, age thirty-five. Lived with her stepfather, Dr. Grimsby Roylott, and her twin sister Helen. A kind lady, a good churchgoer, much afflicted in her stepfather, who is a man with odd ideas and a terrible temper. Deceased was heard to scream in the middle of the night. She unlocked her bedroom door, said—her sister swears—'the speckled band,' and collapsed. She died four hours later without regaining consciousness."

That didn't sound at all like someone dying of exsanguination, which was the only way I could see a vampire killing someone—aside from the normal and non-mysterious methods like strangulation or a knife to the belly. Their teeth weren't as vicious as those of a hemophage, but they could certainly tear open an artery if they wanted to.

I followed the constable in the side door of St. Anne's and down the tight corkscrew of stairs into the crypt, which was as cold and airless as I had expected.

"I'm going to need more light," I said.

The constable said, "Yessir," lit a match, and began going around the room lighting candles, of which there was a frankly insane number.

He caught the look on my face and grinned. "The Vicar believes in thinking ahead."

By candlelight, I took my first look at Julia Stoner.

Someone had had the sense to leave the body as it was, in a nightgown and with a thick, dark, white-streaked plait of hair that hung over the edge of the flat-topped crypt on which she had been laid. I hoped the vicar was offering prayers for that crypt's rightful inhabitant. Even the long dead could be touchy about that sort of thing.

I'd become as callous as any successful medical student to the presence of a cadaver—and certainly had not been softened by the experience of war. But there was something about this dead woman, in her nightgown with the sad little frill at the collar, her face sallow and rather gaunt, with frown lines in her forehead that even death couldn't smooth out, that made me feel like a callow youth profaning something sacred.

"I'm trying to help," I muttered as I stripped her. "I want to find out what happened to you."

There was no obvious and immediate sign of what had killed her, but after I had assured the constable that I did not need help and he had left, I made a careful, thorough inspection of the body. Along with the usual blemishes and imperfections—and the first signs in finger-and toenails that the crypt's wards were losing the battle—I found two neat dark puncture marks, all but invisible, in the crook of her left elbow.

"This may not be a fool's errand after all," I said.

I detected no particular scent when I made the Y-cut, no bitter almonds to warn of cyanide, no scent of camphor or chloroform. Her esophagus and stomach were unharmed—although if she'd lived longer, it looked like she would have had a bleeding ulcer to contend with. I found petechial hemorrhages in her eyes and lungs, but nothing to show her airway had been closed, either manually or by ligature. I brought a candle over and looked carefully at her face, and, yes, the cyanosis was faint, but it was there. She had died of respiratory distress, the inability to breathe. But what had caused it?

The liver looked all right, but the kidneys were a mess, delicate structures sloughing into a necrotic sludge. That was the hallmark of a toxin, but it wasn't a toxin she had ingested, and it wasn't a toxin she had inhaled.

I stared again at those neat, almost demure punctures on her arm. They looked like a snakebite, but I'd seen a number of snakebite cases in Afghanistan, and they had all been distinguished by coagulopathy, which Julia Stoner did not display at all.

Mentally digging around, racking my brains for anything I knew about snakes and snakebites, I remembered one of my colleagues, an old warhorse of a doctor who'd served in India for thirty years before being assigned to our regiment, talking about cobra bites. He'd never discussed the pathology, but I remembered him saying—I thought I remembered him saying—that cobra bites didn't bleed.

But how could Julia Stoner have been bitten by a cobra in the middle of Surrey?

I was standing beside the crypt, staring at those puncture marks and trying to make sense of them, when a horrified voice said, "What in the name of God are you doing?"

I looked up, and for an awful disorienting moment thought it was Julia Stoner who had asked. The next second I realized this was a living lady, and therefore Julia's twin sister, Helen.

"Trying to find out what killed your sister," I said.

"But you mustn't—!"

She sounded so genuinely distressed that instead of pointing out that it was too late for warnings, I said, "Why not?"

That seemed to flummox her. I began sewing up my Y-cut and finally she said, "Dr. Roylott said it was too dangerous. We don't know what killed her."

"That's why one performs an autopsy," I said, and I tried to be respectful of her grief and say it kindly, though I don't know how well I succeeded.

"He said Julia must have some terrible disease for her to have died so quickly, and we were lucky not to have caught it."

"I don't think so. Come here, Miss Stoner." She came, though wincingly. "Have you ever noticed this mark on your sister's arm before?"

She looked, frowning, at Julia Stoner's arm, then I saw her head jerk down for a closer look. "No, never," she said with flat certainty. "What is it?"

"I think it's what killed her, but I can't see how it happened. Unless you know how your sister could have been bitten by a cobra?"

Her sallow face went chalk white, and I had to catch her as her knees buckled. "Oh my God, the Doctor," she said in a whispered rush. "He spent his professional life in India and when we returned to England—though why I say that when Julia and I were born in India—in any event, he had his friends ship him Indian animals, living ones. Macaques and langurs, a hyena, even a Bengal tiger. I don't know that he ever received a cobra, but he is a strange and secretive man, and it would not surprise me."

"Well, your sister died of something that stopped her breathing and did a lot of damage to her kidneys—which is generally the sign of a toxin. She didn't swallow it, and she didn't breathe it, and the only other damage I can find on her body is this mark on her arm, which looks to me like the bite of a snake. Not," I added pointedly, "a vampire."

She reddened. "My stepfather is a very persuasive man. The village is terrified of him, and I admit I am, too."

"Your stepfather is the one who accused the vampire?"

"I believe he meant only to divert attention from the gypsies who were camped in the lower field as he always lets them do. But the Mayor and the Chief Constable seemed to think it had to be the correct solution."

"But why didn't he just say, 'I have a cobra. It must have gotten loose.'"

She turned wide, dark eyes on me, and I saw that she was scared almost out of her mind. "Because my sister's door was locked. We *always* keep our doors locked, because my stepfather lets his creatures roam the house. If there was a cobra in Julia's bedroom, it could only be because he put it there."

"Why would he do that?"

"The money. My mother left her money—which is all that stands between him and penury, for he has no money of his own—such that when Julia or I get married, we get a third."

"And Julia was going to get married?"

"She was, although I didn't think he knew." She shivered. "It is impossible to keep secrets in that house, and he is Machiavellian in his plotting. I have always thought he had something to do with the death of my fiancé, even though I do not know how that could be true."

"How did your fiancé die?"

"He was lost at Bhurtee—he had volunteered to attempt to reach the relieving column and was never heard of again. The rebels killed him. I tell myself that Dr. Roylott could have had nothing to do with Harry's death, but he and my mother did not approve of Harry, and Dr. Roylott was always thick as thieves with Sergeant Barclay—it was no secret how much the sergeant hated Harry. He came courting me, when we knew Harry was dead, but I could not bear even to be in the same room with him. And my stepfather could not have prevented my mother from giving me part of her estate as a wedding gift, although I know he argued with her about it."

I had finished closing up Julia Stoner's body while her sister spoke and now redressed her in her nightgown.

"Thank you, Miss Stoner," I said. "You must have been very young."

"It was thirty years ago," she said, as if it were something she told herself often, and sighed a little. "I was seventeen."

"And you have lived with Dr. Roylott ever since?" It sounded like a sure recipe for madness.

"We see each other very little," she said. "Since my mother's death, he has shut himself up in his wing of the house to conduct his experiments and write treatises on the fauna of the Indian subcontinent, and I never venture there."

"Forgive my asking, but do you think you are safe?"

"Oh yes," she said with a twisted smile. "I will never marry, and he knows it. I do not wear mourning only for my sister. But thank you, Dr. . . . I don't believe I know your name."

"Doyle," I said. "J. H. Doyle, at your service."

"And I am Helen Stoner, but you already know that."

From somewhere above us and not very far away, a man's angry voice shouted, "Helen! Where are you?"

"Oh God, it's him," she said, and she gathered up her skirts to take the stairs almost at a run.

"Were you terrified of him, too?" I said to Julia Stoner as I covered her again with the crisp white sheet. "I imagine you probably were, and it seems you had good reason." Helen Stoner was safe for now—two mysterious deaths in a row would probably be too much even for the Chief Constable—but sooner or later, her stepfather was going to be plagued beyond bearing by how much money he was wasting on feeding and clothing her, and she would be killed.

I wondered about Mrs. Roylott's death, too.

31

A MAN WITH
A MONGOOSE

I MADE MY cautious way back to the inn—the last thing I wanted was my own encounter with Dr. Grimsby Roylott—and found Moriarty waiting in my room.

"Don't you need permission?" I said irritably.

"Not in a public space," said he. "Anywhere there's an angel, vampires can come and go freely. The Angel of the Rose and Tankard is in the tap room."

"And she won't come to find out what you're doing?"

"There's nothing for her to find," he said. "I'd hardly be so stupid as to commit rape where she could hear me. And anything else we may choose to do"—he gave me a comic-opera leer—"is no business of hers. But come! Tell me what you found out, and then I will share my story."

I described the bite and the evidence of a toxin. He said indignantly, "Vampires are not poisonous!"

"Venomous, actually," I said on reflex.

"How could they think—?"

"I think Dr. Roylott has a vested interest in keeping the authorities away from the truth, since he set a trap for Julia Stoner with a cobra he had shipped to him from India."

"A *cobra*?"

"Or some other venomous snake. He apparently has a number of Indian animals roaming his property."

"How odd," said Moriarty. "For that dovetails very neatly with my news. I have found an ally, and he is a man with a mongoose."

"A mongoose."

"Yes. He'll be up a little later, once he's finished entertaining the men in the taproom."

"All right. But you found Miss Shirley?"

"Yes. The jail is not terribly secure, but of course the iron bars are cage enough. She is unharmed—though angry—and says she has learned nothing save that everyone is terrified of Dr. Roylott."

"His surviving stepdaughter says the same."

Moriarty's eyebrows rose. "You encountered Miss Helen Stoner."

"She discovered me in the midst of conducting the postmortem on her sister."

"How very awkward," Moriarty said appreciatively, and I grinned back.

Crow, I thought, with some fondness, would not have seen the difficulty.

"I acquit the lady of any malice," I said. "She is terrified out of her mind by her stepfather. The stepfather is the one who first suggested Julia Stoner was murdered by a vampire."

"A cunning murderer, and as you say, one with a vested interest in pointing attention elsewhere. Perhaps a visit to Dr. Roylott is in order."

"A very cautious visit, if he has a cobra to send after unwanted visitors."

"Bah," said Moriarty. "He'll be hiding his snake for all he's worth—if he hasn't already killed and buried it, which would be the intelligent thing to do."

"He collects Indian animals. I doubt he could bring himself to dispose of the jewel of his collection. Besides, he might want to use it again."

"You think the remaining Miss Stoner is in danger?"

"Not *immediate* danger. But he killed Julia Stoner out of greed, to keep from having to give a portion of her mother's estate to her upon the occasion of her upcoming wedding. I cannot persuade myself that Helen Stoner is safe, even though she says she will never marry."

"Disappointed in love?"

"Her fiancé died in India. She believes Dr. Roylott had something to do with it."

There was a knock at the door.

"Ha!" said Moriarty. "My ally comes well upon his cue." And he called, "Come in!"

The door opened and a most remarkable human being entered the room. His face was handsome, though rather haggard, but his body was hunched and twisted in such a way that it was clearly impossible for him to stand upright. He carried a box slung on his back and from inside it, something rustled. He looked a little startled to see someone other than Moriarty in the room, and Moriarty said with great good humor, "Dr. Doyle, may I present Helen Stoner's dead fiancé—this is Henry Wood."

The crooked man looked even more startled, and I said, "Perhaps you had best elaborate."

"It is not my story," said Moriarty. "Corporal?"

"That I was," said the crooked man with a sigh. "Corporal Harry Wood, and although you may find it impossible to believe, I was once the smartest man in the 117th Foot. I was betrayed by my sergeant into the hands of the rebels, and they left me as you see me."

Moriarty said, "We were just speculating that perhaps Dr. Roylott had something to do with your unfortunate fate."

"It wouldn't surprise me," said Harry Wood, and clearly he was not surprised. "I've always known Barclay didn't act by himself." His lip curled. "He wasn't smart enough. He had the information, but somebody else had the idea. I would guess it was that somebody else who actually talked to the rebels—and that means it almost *had* to be Dr. Roylott, because there were only so many men in Bhurtee who could speak Hindi. And besides, it was his kind of plan, if you follow me. But I have no proof. I don't even have proof it was Barclay, except that he and I were the only two people who should have known where I was going and when."

The box on his back rustled again, and he said apologetically, "Do you mind? Teddy won't bite, and he can't stand a room he hasn't investigated."

"Not at all," said Moriarty, and I shook my head.

Wood shrugged the box carefully off his back and set it on the floor. "All right, Teddy," he said, and slid open the wire door.

Teddy proved to be a long, grayish-brown creature, short-legged, with a pointed nose and bright, horizontally pupilled red-orange eyes. He investigated the room rapidly, but thoroughly, as if he had some sort of checklist, and he showed no fear of either Moriarty or me. He came back in the end to Wood, who stroked his long back, saying, "Teddy is the most faithful friend I've ever had. I don't count the Maharanee, for she would kill me if she could."

"The Maharanee?" said Moriarty, as one who knows he will be sorry he asked.

Wood grinned, a remarkably sunny expression on his haggard face, and drew out of one of his overcoat pockets a long, dry, rustling thing that at first I could not even make sense of until suddenly the head came into view, and I realized it was a snake.

I might have yelped.

Wood let the snake slide through his fingers back into his pocket. "That's the Maharanee. She's a defanged cobra. Teddy catches her every night to amuse the punters."

"You are a man full of surprises," Moriarty said, and Wood laughed.

"No less than the pair of you. What's your story? Why are you in Stoke Moran?"

Moriarty and I explained in tandem, first about Judith Shirley and then about the findings of the autopsy. Wood listened intently, and at the end said, "What do you plan to do? I'll help you in any way I can."

Moriarty said, "We have to find the snake to prove the murder."

"It'll be somewhere in the manor house," I said. "This could be tricky."

"How certain are you that he killed Julia?" said Wood.

"Certain," I said. "She died of a poison that she didn't inhale, because there's no sign of it in her lungs or her trachea or her mouth, and she didn't ingest it, because there's no sign of it in her stomach or her esophagus. And she shows none of the signs of heavy metal poisoning. The only mark on her body is two little punctures on her left arm, and I do know what a snakebite looks like. If it was a snake, and it didn't get into her room by itself, which it didn't because Miss Stoner told me that she and her sister always kept their doors locked, there's only two people who could have put it there, and my money is not on Helen Stoner."

"Well, if there's snakes involved, I have the sovereign remedy," said Wood. He snapped his fingers, and Teddy came galumphing across the room—I can find no better verb than Mr. Dodson's—from where he had been investigating under the bed.

"Let us pay a visit to Dr. Roylott," I said. "And I am uneasy. Let us do it tonight."

"You said you didn't think Miss Stoner was in immediate danger," said Moriarty—not as an objection, for he was already standing up.

"I know," I said, as Wood half coaxed, half shoved Teddy into his box and slung the box on his back again. "But something . . .". I could not explain it. It was not even an instinct, just a vague, inchoate feeling that something was not right.

"He'll be awake," said Moriarty. "He's well known for insomnia in the village."

"I'm in," said Wood. "Let's go."

❖

WOOD AND I sat together in the back of the dog cart. He was cheerfully, blessedly incurious, talking of the places he and Teddy (and the Maharanee) had been, which seemed to be everywhere from India to Portugal.

"What brought you back to England?" I said, for clearly he had never meant to return, a position with which I could sympathize.

"Well," he said, "it was a funny thing. There was a tarot reader working a canteen in Gibraltar, and instead of getting mad when I came along, she offered to give me a reading. I'd watched her do a couple, and she knew what she was doing, so I said sure. And it was a good reading—pain and betrayal in the past, aimless wandering in the present, and every card that talked about the future said, GO HOME. And, well, if the aether tells you something that loudly, you do it. Teddy and the Maharanee and I stowed away on the *Nancy Devoy,* and we've been wandering 'round England ever since. The trouble is, I'm not sure where 'home' is supposed to be. My dad moved us around a lot when I was a kid, following the jobs, so nowhere ever really got to feel like home. My parents both died before I entered the service—thank God, for I'd hate for them to see me like this—so that's not the answer. I finally thought of Helen—no, that's not right, I think of Helen all the time—I finally thought that Helen might be 'home,' so I came to Stoke Moran as a test. And I think this time I was right."

"Yes," I said. "I think we may be very glad of you and Teddy before the evening is out."

The manor house was a Romanesque mansion made of dark gray stone. I have seldom seen a building I disliked more intensely on first sight. Moriarty drew up at the front door, and a surprised and sleepy-looking groom came out of the stable to hold the horse's head.

The butler looked just as surprised, if not as sleepy.

"Is Miss Stoner in?" I said. "It is a matter of some urgency."

"I . . ." He glanced over his shoulder, then pulled himself together. "May I ask who is calling?"

"Dr. Doyle. We met this afternoon."

He retreated, looking sorely bewildered; when he returned, Miss Stoner was with him.

"Dr. Doyle!" she said. "We must be very careful that my stepf—
HARRY?"

Beside me, Wood winced, but said staunchly, "Hello, Helen."

It is greatly to Miss Stoner's credit that she did not faint dead away,
but said, "C—come into the drawing room."

Moriarty said, "I think I'll stay with the horse." I glanced at him,
and he shook his head slightly. Miss Stoner had not noticed that he
was a vampire, and she did not need another shock—whether that
was Moriarty's reasoning, I could not say.

I followed Miss Stoner into the drawing room, and Wood followed
me. The instant the door had closed, I said, "I fear you may be in danger."

"Danger? But he has no reason to kill me."

"No, but listen," I said, "because I think I have it. He does not
know an autopsy has been performed—does he?"

"I have not told him."

"Then if he kills you tonight, in the same 'mysterious' manner as
Julia, it proves Miss Shirley's innocence, and if he is friends with
the gypsies, he cannot afford to get a vampire falsely convicted of
murder."

"No," she agreed, "and he always likes to talk to the vagabond
hunts if one is in the neighborhood."

"I think he accused Miss Shirley because he was thinking of the
bite mark, before he realized that he could actually keep there from
being an autopsy at all. Who is the coroner?"

"Mayor Winthrop's brother-in-law."

"Then, yes, you die in the same mysterious manner as your sister,
exonerating Miss Shirley, and I give you odds of ten to one that
Dr. Roylott will announce that you and Julia have succumbed to
the effects of some sort of poisonous miasma. The coroner directs
the jury, Dr. Roylott closes that wing of the house, and he's got
everything he wants."

"Dear God," she said, her eyes wide. "He has been asking me if I've
smelled anything strange in my bedroom. He even suggested I open
a window tonight."

"Yes," I said, although I will admit I was a little taken aback to have my theory so abundantly confirmed. "Would he have any difficulty in obtaining a key to your room?"

She shook her head. "The locks in this house are so old that one key works in all of them—except his. That one he had replaced with a Yale lock."

"Of course he did," I said. "Then I apologize for the necessity, but we must search your bedroom, for there is every reason to believe there is a venomous snake hidden somewhere in it."

"Name of God," she said. "It does make sense, but is he truly going to kill me just to save a vampire?"

"He may have some view in mind that would require spending some of your mother's capital; he may feel that you will leave the house in the wake of your sister's death and go beyond his reach; he may simply have decided that he wants to. Or I may be wrong, although I don't think I am."

"No," she said. "It makes too much sense of what has seemed senseless. Please, let us go search. But later—Harry, you and I have much to say to each other."

"I know," said Wood. "I won't turn craven."

Miss Stoner's bedroom was in a wing of the house even gloomier and more dismal than the main rooms—also chilly and rather damp. I said, "This is just the sort of place to have a poisonous miasma."

"I know," said Miss Stoner. "Julia and I—that is, I spend all winter coughing."

"Why *haven't* you left?" said Wood, appalled.

"I have nowhere to go," said Miss Stoner. "This is my bedroom."

It was a plain room, simply furnished. Wood slung Teddy's box off his back, careful again not to tip it too far or too hard, and said, "I suggest you leave this part to me."

"Gladly," said I.

"I'm no expert," Wood said, "but I do know a little bit about where snakes like to hide."

We watched as he searched, slowly and carefully, looking into all the dark corners and under every piece of furniture, using his stick to keep from having to get too close. Finally, he approached the bed.

"This may be the most likely spot," he said, "but I don't want to be doing anything in the middle of the room until I know there isn't a snake in the corner."

"You've hunted snakes before," I said, as he looked cautiously under Miss Stoner's narrow bed.

"You have to have more than one string to your bow when you live as precariously as Teddy and I do," Wood said, straightening as much as he could. He looked carefully up and down the bed, then his eyes widened and he said, "God help me, I think I know where it is."

He backed up as far as he could and began using his stick, very gingerly, to prod at the pillows.

"Oh dear God," said Miss Stoner. When I glanced at her, her face was bone white and she had her teeth set in her lower lip.

We all heard the pillows hiss.

"That's it, right enough," said Wood. "Dr. Doyle, will you let Teddy out?"

The door to Teddy's box was simple enough. I raised it, and Teddy shot out, straight for Wood.

"What is that?" said Miss Stoner in a strangled whisper.

"Teddy's a mongoose," said Wood, who seemed very calm now that he knew where the snake was. "Some people call them ichneumon, but most of the people I've met call them snake-catcher. That's what Teddy does."

He picked the mongoose up and set it gently on the bed, near the foot. Then he prodded the pillows again, making them hiss, and then—with the mongoose's unwavering attention now fixed on the head of the bed—he used his stick to flip one pillow completely off the bed.

I think Miss Stoner and I were both too paralyzed to make a sound.

There was definitely a snake, and as it reared up, hood flaring, we could see it was definitely a cobra. Wood took a healthy step back.

"The speckled band," Miss Stoner said, although her voice was barely audible, even to me. "If she didn't see the head . . ."

The body of the snake was indeed irregularly colored, enough so that "speckled" was not inaccurate. And no one could say what Julia Stoner had actually seen, in the light of a single wavering match.

Teddy darted up the bed with blinding speed, then bounded aside just as fast. The snake struck and missed. Teddy bounced from foot to foot, darted in again, darted back. The snake struck and missed. It began to come forward, trying to reach the mongoose that danced and darted and made odd little noises that sounded like laughter. The snake struck and struck again, and Teddy somehow wasn't there for either bite. He lured it farther and farther down the bed, until he could actually bound all the way around it. The snake hissed and struck and missed and Teddy darted in from behind and bit it just behind the head, shaking it like any rat-catching terrier.

"It's dead," said Wood. "Teddy doesn't miss his grip."

"Oh thank God," said Miss Stoner on a tremulous exhale.

"Come sit down," I said, knowing that her stays were probably keeping her from getting as much breath as she needed. There was one chair in the bedroom and I handed her into it. She might well choose never to sleep in that bed again, and I could not say that I would blame her.

"Teddy will carry off the body and stash it somewhere if we let him," Wood said, "and I gather we'll want it for—"

"Helen!" The same angry male voice I'd heard that afternoon. "What's this nonsense about visitors? Who the Devil is coming to pay a call at this time of night?"

Dr. Grimsby Roylott, when I finally laid eyes on him, was well over six feet in height, broad-shouldered, and with a dark brooding stare that promised ill for anyone who dared cross him. He loomed in the doorway of Miss Stoner's room, taking everything in: Miss Stoner not slumped in the chair only because her stays would not allow it; me beside her; Wood (Roylott's frown deepening) beside the bed; Teddy standing triumphantly over his enemy; and finally the long, limp body of the cobra, and his expression changed from anger to horror.

"My *Naja naja*! What have you done to her?"

"Kept her from killing Miss Stoner," said Wood. "Do you remember me, Dr. Roylott? My name is Henry Wood."

It took a moment for the import of that name to reach Dr. Roylott through his grief for the cobra, but then his face changed color, and if I hadn't been certain of his guilt before, that would have convinced me.

He stood for a moment, his mouth working although no sounds emerged; then his nerve broke and he turned and fled in long strides.

"Where is he going?" Wood said.

"I don't know," said Miss Stoner. "He must know he has no reason to fear. The Chief Constable will see to it that he is not arrested."

"There are ways around that," I said, thinking of Lestrade, "but nothing that we can do tonight."

Wood caught Teddy off the bed, making him drop the cobra's corpse, and put him firmly back in his box, despite Teddy's protests and wiggling.

"He's really a very handsome little animal," said Miss Stoner. "What did you say his name is?"

"Teddy," Wood said and added, almost shyly, "He has been my best friend for many years."

"How lonely your life must be," said Miss Stoner, then, inexorably, "Harry, we must talk."

"I know," Wood said, and I was just about to excuse myself, for I had no wish to be an audience for this reunion of Romeo and Juliet, when there came a bloodcurdling scream.

"What in the name of God?" said Wood, but I already knew.

"Moriarty," I said, and started back for the main wing of the house.

Moriarty was not with the horse in the yard, and the groom was unable to tell me where he had gone. But a moment later, the question was moot, for Moriarty appeared, yellow eyes gleaming in the dark, and said, "Someone had better go check on Dr. Roylott. I'm afraid that he may have just accidentally killed himself."

"And you happened to be a witness?"

"A cause," he said apologetically. "I was walking on the lawn behind the house when someone flung a window open. Naturally I went to see what was going on, and I found a gentleman whom I presume to be Dr. Roylott, in the middle of moving a snake from a glass tank to a bag of the sort snake charmers use. I said, 'Good evening,' and I'm afraid he lost his grip on the snake, which immediately turned and struck. He screamed and fell to his knees and then full length on the floor."

"In other words, you startled him to death."

"You could put it that way," Moriarty said. "Another reason for concern is that I don't know what happened to the snake."

"Oh dear," I said.

From behind me, Wood said, "What happened? What was that terrible scream?"

He looked unfinished without Teddy's box on his back.

I said, "Something unfortunate seems to have happened to Dr. Roylott." I glanced at Moriarty, who repeated his story.

"I'd best get Teddy," said Wood.

❖

IT WAS A grim sight that met our eyes when the butler and the groom between them finally managed to break down Dr. Roylott's door. The room had been ransacked, as Dr. Roylott in his hurry had simply pulled drawers out and dumped their contents on the bed or on the floor. Mercifully, of the cages and tanks that ringed the room, only one was empty. Two macaques chattered at us, scolding and excited. The doctor himself lay full length on the floor, as Moriarty had said, motionless and with the fixed stare of a corpse.

Wood said, "Well, Teddy, you've got your work cut out for you," and let the mongoose out to hunt.

I said to Miss Stoner, who had insisted on coming, "Is it true that there's a tiger?"

She managed a noise that could almost pass for a laugh. "There *was*. It was an old beast, and ill, and it died last winter. He grieved more for that tiger than he did for my mother."

"Any other creatures we need to worry about?"

"Not that I know of, but then, I didn't know about the cobra. The hyaena is in the stable block, I do know that much."

"Is there a will?"

"Somewhere in this room. I know he made one, because he told me about it. He left everything to Julia and me—it was the sort of joke that would amuse him." She paused, thinking, then said almost to herself, "He must have been planning our murders for a very long time."

I wondered again about Mrs. Roylott, and again held my tongue.

Teddy came streaking out from beneath the bureau, then turned and bounced and darted back again.

"He's found the snake," said Wood. "Let's see if he can lure it out."

Teddy advanced and retreated, darting in, bouncing back, and he was clearly *maddening*, for the snake, in its efforts to reach him, gradually emerged from beneath the bureau.

"That's a krait," I said, for I'd seen them in Afghanistan and seen what their bite could do. "Your stepfather had some odd tastes. I suppose we should count ourselves lucky he didn't get his hands on a hamadryad."

Miss Stoner shuddered. "When we were little girls, in India, he would sometimes take us along when he went to talk to the snake charmers. They knew all kinds of tricks and secrets. Julia and I were more afraid of them than of their snakes. Once I even saw the guardian of the temple, although my stepfather tried to avoid it."

Teddy danced in a circle. The krait struck after him and missed again and again, Teddy always—sometimes miraculously—just out of reach.

"How long can he keep doing this?" I asked Wood.

Wood grinned his unexpected sunny grin. "Longer than the snake."

As with the cobra, the end was abrupt: Teddy found the angle he wanted, darted in, and just like that, the snake was dead. This time he dragged it under the bureau before Wood could get to him.

"Oh blast," said Wood. "He's going to make a mess."

"Let him," said Miss Stoner. "There's no one left who cares."

❖

THERE WAS A great deal of officialdom about the death of Dr. Grimsby Roylott; I ended up getting paid to do the autopsy on him, as there was no one in Stoke Moran who was qualified. My findings were not quite what I had expected. I found the snakebite—the creature had twisted around and bitten him just above the wrist, at the base of his thumb. But I found no trace of the poison's work on his organs and concluded, with some bemusement, that Dr. Roylott had died of a heart attack, brought on by being bitten by the krait. "Death by misadventure" was the coroner's ruling.

We then turned around and held the inquest on Julia Stoner, with the body of the cobra as Exhibit A. I confirmed that she had died as a result of being bitten by the cobra; Miss Stoner testified that she and her sister had not even known that their stepfather possessed an Indian cobra. The coroner, a walrus-mustached old man, made harrumphing noises of sympathy and ruled the death an accident—and nothing to do with the vampire Judith Shirley, who was therefore released.

Judith Shirley was a small woman, thick chestnut-brown hair in braids around her head, with the vampire's eyes like golden coins in her face. She was brisk and forthright in her thanks, and it was clear that she and Moriarty were genuinely fond of each other; she called him "brother" just as he called her "sister," and I have known actual siblings who valued each other less.

"What will you do now?" I asked her.

She sighed. "Continue vagabonding until I either find a weaker Master I can displace or an abandoned house I can claim by squatter's rights and start working my way upward from there. There really is no good answer to being a Master without a hunt. I have not the money to do any of the more sensible things, like rent a room, and it is very hard for a vampire to find paying work except . . . as a vampire. No firm would hire me as a secretary, no mill would take me on even as a floor sweeper. I am not yet so desperate as to sink to prostitution, though some vagabond Masters do."

"You don't think keeping a vampiric house is prostitution?" I asked before I could catch myself.

Her eyebrows went up, but she laughed. "I see why James likes you. And, no, in keeping a vampiric house, we allow people to pay us for what we need. Prostitution is if anything the opposite. A woman engaged in prostitution must give away her body and hope the man pays her for it—rather than, for instance, carving her to bits. Do you see?"

"I'm not convinced it isn't casuistry," I said, "but I am no expert in such matters, and I accept that you are. I wish you luck, Miss Shirley."

"Thank you," she said. "I will need it."

—◇—

I RETURNED TO London that afternoon. Moriarty and I parted ways in Paddington, and I used a portion of my fee to hire a hansom—an extravagance I didn't usually allow myself when I was alone.

Indulging myself once was allowable, I decided. I had gotten less than four hours' sleep between the matters that needed to be tidied away in what was now Miss Stoner's house and the news that the coroner wanted an autopsy of Dr. Roylott, and I had that leaden, aching feeling that comes with too much action and too little sleep.

The hansom drew up in front of 221 Baker Street; I paid the cabbie and pulled myself together to climb the stairs. Crow was waiting on the landing by the time I opened the front door.

"You're home!" he said. "Will you tell me everything?"

"I will," said I.

PART NINE

THE
LORD MAYOR'S
DAY

32

No. 13,
MILLER'S COURT

THE NINTH OF November was the Lord Mayor's Day, James Whitehead's investiture as the Lord Mayor of London. Crow insisted that we attend. He had strong feelings about public ceremonies. I managed to persuade him that we did not have to go to Aldwych to see the swearing of the oath (although he was sorely disappointed in me), so that it was merely a matter of finding a suitable vantage point.

We were still arguing about that in an amiable fashion while I finished lacing my boots, when someone started pounding on the front door.

I finished my boots in a hurry and stood up just as Jennie said, "Mr. Crow, it's a police officer. Should I let him come up?"

"By all means," said Crow.

The police officer was young, long-faced, sweating profusely. "Inspector Lestrade says can you come right away? There's been another one."

Neither of us had to ask, *Another what?*

❖

DORSET STREET IN Whitechapel was another street of doss-houses and pubs, the two places where London's desperate poor would spend their money. Our guide said, "Here. Miller's Court," and we turned down a narrow, reeking alley into a cramped courtyard in which police officers and citizens seemed equally represented.

Lestrade strode up and shook Crow's hand, then mine, and said, "Good of you to come," as if he had somehow been worried we wouldn't.

"Of course," said Crow, frowning around the court. "What have you done with the body?"

"She's in there," said Lestrade, pointing to a room that jutted out at the head of the court. "We haven't gone in because Abberline's waiting for the werewolf."

"Did Sir Charles talk them into it, then?" said Crow. "Last I saw, the packs were still debating."

It was highly unorthodox for a human police officer to ask for help from the werewolf equivalents, who were called pack guardians. But Sir Charles was understandably desperate, and the packs of London had no desire for a monster like Jack the Ripper to be running around loose, either. One version said that the packs had actually approached Sir Charles, rather than the other way around—but if that had been the case, I was fairly sure Sir Charles would have said yes without hesitation.

"One of their younger guardians volunteered," said Lestrade. "His name is Clifton Barnaby, and Abberline sent a runner for him at the same time I sent for you, so he should be here soon. Then we'll see if he can find anything."

"You sound unconvinced," I said.

"Eh," said Lestrade. "Tracking in the city is hard, and werewolves aren't *magic*. It might work and it might not."

"It's certainly worth trying," said Crow.

"*Anything's* worth trying," said Lestrade. "This fellow's not going to stop until we catch him."

"Or worse," I said, "he *does* stop and you *never* catch him."

"Bite your tongue, Dr. Doyle," said Lestrade. "We don't catch him and we'll be the laughingstock of England."

"If you aren't already," Crow said with blinding tactlessness.

Lestrade was fortunately too used to him to take offense. He said only, "The newspapers are a cruel lot."

"Tell me about the victim," Crow said. "Do you know who she is yet?"

"The deceased is believed to be the occupant of the room, one Mary Jane Kelly. We aren't sure because, well, one, we haven't gone in yet and, two, the poor thing's been butchered so badly her own mother wouldn't know her. He really took advantage of having some privacy." Lestrade shuddered and shoved his hands in his overcoat pockets.

There was a little stir at the entrance of the court. "That must be Mr. Barnaby," said Crow. "Or, at least, it's definitely a werewolf."

The werewolf was a square-built young man, with a thick cap of reddish-blond hair and flourishing muttonchop whiskers. He went straight to the portly Inspector Abberline and shook hands vigorously. Abberline said something to him in a low voice, and then they walked over to the door of that single jutting-out room.

"Number 13," Lestrade said with gloomy satisfaction. "Couldn't be anything else, could it?"

Abberline reached through a broken pane of the window beside the door and freed the lock.

"Deceased had lost her key," said Lestrade. "We've got any number of witnesses to testify that she'd been getting in and out like that for weeks."

"That rather obviates the point of locking the door," I said.

Lestrade made a what-can-you-do face. "Deceased didn't have anything worth stealing, from the looks of it."

Abberline, having had another quick discussion with the werewolf, opened the door and he and the werewolf stepped inside.

"Come on," said Crow. "I want to watch what I'm eavesdropping on."

"Mr. Crow!" Lestrade expostulated, but Crow was already in the doorway of No. 13. I followed him.

The smell of blood hit me full in the face, the thick copper reek of it invading my sinuses, my mouth, blurring my eyes. I knew what was going to happen the instant before it did, but there was utterly nothing I could do. My knees were buckling, my stomach twisted into a sick knot, and I changed.

The smell of blood only became stronger. I struggled out of the torn and constricting clothes, snarling at the men surrounding me. The angel said, "Oh, Doyle, *no*," and I whined and edged sideways away when he tried to come too close. He stopped.

A man behind me said, "God almighty, what is *that*?" and another man said, "A hell-hound, Dew. Don't tell me you've never seen one before."

I lowered my head, scenting, then followed the scent to the bed, where lay bones and flesh and blood, all horribly disorganized and incomplete. I put my front paws up on the bed and inspected what was there, but I already knew it was missing.

He had taken her heart.

"What is it doing?" someone whispered. "It's not going to eat the body, is it?"

"It's scenting for something," said the wolf. "You gentlemen may not need me after all."

The angel said, "Doyle, this is very awkward."

I grumbled deep in my throat and turned to the door. Several men scrambled out of my way. The scent of *her* was thick, the trail unmistakable. I followed it out of the room, through the crowd (which shrieked) and up the alley back onto the street. People scattered; there were more screams. I lowered my head and started tracking.

I had to find the rest of *her*. I'd failed before, and I could not bear to think of failing again. I could pay attention to nothing but the scent of *her*. I loped along the track, moving as fast as I could, streets and streets and finally stairs. Stairs going down into an areaway, and then a locked door.

I whined, thwarted, and paced in a circle. There were voices from street level: "I think it's found something." "Who does the house belong to?" "Oh for God's sake, Dew, how should I know?"

I bumped the door, testing, then backed up and hurled myself at it. The door broke in a hail of splinters and I found the trail again.

The basement was dank, mold everywhere, but *her* scent was like a crimson ribbon, and I followed it easily through a twisting warren of hallways, then down a long, tight corkscrew of stairs, along a broader, danker, darker corridor, dirt and mold and cobwebs and *her*.

I ran faster, urgency coming from somewhere, the memory of the Thames in the middle of the night, up another set of stairs, through a hole into a tunnel. I was splashing as I ran, and the smell was rank and raw and like fists pounding on my nose and eyes, but *her* scent was still stronger, still clear, and I ignored everything else and followed it. Up a set of narrow, mossy, brick stairs and a door I hit without breaking stride.

It shattered and I leapt on the man in the room, a little man with a blotchy face and a broad overhanging mustache. He shrieked as we crashed together to the floor. *Her* scent was all over him; he had held her dying heart in his hands. I growled, glowing saliva dripping from my jowls, and started to lower my head. There were noises behind me, but they didn't matter.

"JOANNA, STOP!"

The voice was like a bell; it clanged through my head unforgivingly. I whimpered and dropped to the floor, pinning the little man beneath me.

The angel strode past me in a terrifying, painful blaze of light and said to the man, "Don't make me sorry that I saved your life just now. Especially when this thing on the table is clearly a human heart."

The little man said, "Oh my God, get it off me!"

The angel said, "No, I don't think so. *Is* this a human heart?"

"How should I know?"

"No, that strategy won't work. You have her blood all over you."

"I'm a slaughterman."

"Maybe. But that doesn't explain what you're doing here with what I am quite sure is a human heart. Any time you wanted to give me a proper answer so that I could stop employing this circular logic, I would very much appreciate it."

"I don't know what you want!"

"Well," said the angel. "You *are* Jack the Ripper, aren't you?"

"I don't know what you're talking about."

I growled and edged a little up his body. I smelled deception.

"That's a foolish sort of lie," said the angel. "There isn't a soul in London who doesn't know who Jack the Ripper is—or, rather, who doesn't know what Jack the Ripper has done. What's your name?"

"Beg pardon?"

"Your name. You must have one."

"Never give your name to strangers."

"Oh, quite right. My name is Crow. I am the Angel of London. This is my friend and colleague, Dr. Doyle."

"You're friends with a hell-hound?"

"No one is to blame for being afflicted by the *metaphysicum morbi*," the angel said. "Dr. Doyle encountered one of the Fallen in Afghanistan and is truly to be commended for not dying on the spot. Now. We only have a couple of minutes before the others catch up to us—they have a werewolf tracker, and your trail is not hard to follow. What is your name?"

"Why d'you want to know?"

"I can't protect you without your real name," said the angel, and the little man went off in what seemed to be genuine laughter.

"*Protect* me?" he said. "You'll do nothing of the sort."

The angel cocked his head. "Whyever not?"

"Well," said the little man. "I *am* Jack the Ripper."

A voice from below us shouted, "I see a light!"

"Quickly!" said the angel.

"Ta, guv, but I'll take my chances. I'm not giving my name to a bloody angel."

And then a voice said, "For God's sake, Mr. Crow, furl your

wings," and the police were there—the bulldog detective, a long-faced constable, a stout man in a homburg, and the werewolf.

"Good Lord," said the homburg. "Is this him?"

"That's certainly a human heart on the table," said the angel.

"Get this thing off me and I'll go peaceably," said the little man.

"Well, that'll be a bit of a trick, I reckon," said the bulldog. "Mr. Crow?"

"I can try," said the angel. "Doyle, we can't all wait here until dawn tomorrow. You need to let the police have him. Come here."

I whined.

"No, really," said the angel. "They'll telegraph to the Registry for a handler, and none of us wants that. Come *here*."

I went, though I kept my gaze on the little man covered in *her* scent.

"I'd say it was a pleasure to meet you," said the bulldog, "but it would be a lie. Up you come." He and the long-faced constable hauled the little man to his feet. "What's your name?"

"Jack Ketch."

"A comedian," said the bulldog. "Well, Mr. Ketch, you are under arrest for the murder of Mary Jane Kelly."

"Oh," said the little man. "Was *that* her name?"

<><

WE EMERGED FROM the tunnels under the city into the teeth of a mob. There were police officers guarding the areaway, but when we came up the stairs, the crowd drew back a little, then surged forward when they saw the little man.

"Jack the Ripper!" someone shouted. "They caught Jack the Ripper!" The crowd surged forward again, nearly breaking through the line of police officers. I began barking in warning. But nothing would deter the mob, which was growing larger by the second. They rushed the line of officers, clawing, straining, shouting obscenities, and someone yelled from the rear, "Let's get the bastard!" A second surge followed hard on the first, and the sheer weight of bodies shoved through the police officers' line.

The angel's hand descended onto the scruff of my neck, where it burned like a live coal. "Stay with me, Doyle," the angel said under the roar of the mob, so softly that I couldn't tell if it was an order or a plea.

My barking deepened, phosphorescent saliva flying in all directions, and I pushed against the angel's legs. We were quickly cut off from the bulldog and the others; they would have to look out for themselves. I herded the angel along the building, snarling and snapping at anyone who came too close. The crowd kept growing; we couldn't seem to get free of them, and I knew angels were fragile. I could not make enough space for the angel's wings to spread, not without actually savaging someone. The angel's hand stayed, burning, on my neck.

"Doyle," said the angel. "Doyle, I, ah, don't want to sound unnecessarily alarmist, but I think they're about to lynch our sanguinary friend."

My jaws nearly closed on the leg of a man in a sailor's uniform, who yelped and swore, but pushed ahead toward the center of the disturbance instead of trying to stand fast. Somewhere, I heard glass breaking.

"No, really," said the angel. "Someone's come up with a rope, and I can't see Lestrade or Abberline anywhere, but there's that carrot-orange hair. He may have wanted to take his chances, but he doesn't *have* a chance—they'll tear him apart like the Bacchae, and that's even if he manages to get free of them at all, which he's not going to. I should—"

The angel's hand left my neck. I swung my head around and growled a warning.

"Doyle! What do you think—but I have to do—"

I boxed the angel in along the wall, pushing always away from where the crowd was thickest and loudest and most dangerous.

"But I can't let him just be hanged in the street!"

I shoved the angel as hard as I dared, trying to get us both to open, safe ground.

"Doyle, stop! You have to let me—Doyle! *Doyle!* Let— Oh God, it's too late."

The crowd around us made a terrible noise. I got the hem of the angel's suit coat in my teeth and began pulling. The angel followed, face stricken.

"Oh God, I should have done something. . . . I should have *tried*. . . . I should have . . ." A dry sob, face now in hands.

I wished for a hansom or an Underground station or *anything* that would get us home faster. Behind us, the crowd was cheering hysterically. Someone shouted, "Bloody Jack the Ripper's bloody dead!" and I heard more glass breaking.

"I can't blame them," the angel said in a harsh whisper. "Well, that is, of course I *can*, but I understand. But what if he *wasn't* Jack the Ripper? What if there was some explanation, although I admit I can't think of one? But God help us, what if there *was*? What if they just hanged an innocent man and the Ripper is holed up somewhere laughing . . . He should have had a trial, whether he was innocent or not."

We had finally come to the end of the mob, around a corner where they couldn't even see us. I let go of the angel's coat and sat down, panting. The air tasted of fear and rage and something even darker, uglier, something like the smell of *her* blood on the little man's hands.

"They would have torn him apart," the angel said. "If there hadn't been a rope handy. And God, God, he was covered in her blood like he'd been bathing in it. And we don't know so much as his name. God."

Already, the noise of the crowd was getting louder, the news spreading. I got up and shook hard, as if I could get the reek of blood and death out of my fur, then tugged at the angel's coat.

"What— Doyle, that's a dreadful habit."

I tugged again.

"All right," the angel said. "I don't want to stay here, either. Let's go home. The rest of the story can find us there."

THE REST
OF
THE STORY

33

The Angel
and
the Solicitor

I SPENT THE rest of that day hiding in my bedroom. I could not find the way to change back as I had on the moor, even here where it was safe to. The angel came in and out, talking nonstop, bringing a bowl of water, which I drank gratefully, and a soup bone, which I disdained until sometime past midnight, when I gave in and crunched it satisfyingly to smithereens.

At dawn, I changed back, and found myself in too much pain to crawl into bed, as if for all the time I had been a hell-hound, my human body had been crammed into the animal's shape.

Crow was almost immediately in the room, saying, "Oh thank goodness, Doyle, are you all right?"

"I don't know," I said. "No, don't try to help me up, you'll just end up on the floor with me. The height of my ambition at the moment is to make it into bed."

I managed, awkwardly and painfully, to uncramp my limbs far enough to crawl from the floor into my bed, Crow dashing over to turn the sheets down as if it was the only thing he could think of to do that might help.

The mattress was a miracle of softness. I cautiously stretched limb after limb, reminding myself that this one was an arm, this one a leg, and finally the cramped pain receded enough that I could lie, if not comfortably, at least without actual agony. I looked over at Crow, who was watching with wide, anxious eyes.

"I'm not dying," I said, and surprised myself with a laugh.

"Oh. Oh! That's good!"

"Is it? I seem to remember that all Scotland Yard now knows I'm a hell-hound."

"Um," said Crow. "Yes. Well. That is true. But you also caught Jack the Ripper."

"And promptly let him get lynched by a street mob."

"*That*," Crow said firmly, "was not your fault."

"You might have saved him if I hadn't stopped you."

Crow shrugged. "I doubt it. It might have been an interesting experiment, to see if a lynch mob would balk at harming me, but if they were willing to overrun a line of police officers, I don't think I would have deterred them for long. And I don't actually want to explore the question of how much damage I can take before I am trapped and drawn down into dissolution. Thank you, because I was going to get myself in a great deal of trouble, and you stopped me."

"What happened to Lestrade? I heard his voice earlier."

"Inspector Abberline was hit in the head. Lestrade said he did his best to protect both of them—the inspector and the murderer—but he couldn't rally the constables fast enough to save Jack, as I suppose we must call him until he is identified—"

"*If* he is identified. No one is going to want to admit knowing him, and it isn't as though they'll pay the reward to someone who identifies a dead man."

"You are a cynic," Crow said.

"Yes. I'm also right. Where was that constable in all this? What was his name?"

"Dew," said Crow, "and he was under Inspector Abberline—they fell down the areaway stairs together."

"Oh dear."

"No bones broken, but no one can say he was shirking his duty."

"No, I suppose not," I said and yawned jaw-crackingly.

"Go to sleep," Crow suggested and closed the door behind him as he left.

I slept for a couple of hours, there being nothing more useful I could do, and when I woke, I was in a good deal less pain. I was able to get up and wash and dress and go out to the sitting room.

I did not know if Mrs. Climpson or Jennie had seen me the day before—although the fact that I hadn't been tossed out on my ear suggested they had not—and it took some considerable willpower to ring the bell as if nothing had happened. But if there was a charade, Jennie was part of it and an actress of more talent than I thought possible, for she brought tea and toast and the usual array of suggestions from the cook without any hint of alarm. Also *The Times*, which I eyed with dismay.

The rest of the story—or I suppose you might call it the other shoe—found us as I was halfway through my third cup of tea and a wincing perusal of *The Times*'s pronouncement on the capture and death of Jack the Ripper. The only mercy in the entire thing was that apparently no one except Crow and Lestrade actually knew who I was, and thus no one could give my name to inquisitive reporters: *The Times* merely called me the "Unknown Hell-Hound," which was an oppressive soubriquet, though better than the truth.

"Crow," I said, "have you seen—"

I was interrupted by someone pounding on the front door as if he wanted to break it down with his fist.

"It's Gregson," Crow said, listening intently. "And he has a warrant. Quick! You'll have to go out the trap in the roof."

"But—"

"Don't be ridiculous, Doyle. Go to Kate Moriarty. She'll have a solicitor who can keep you out of prison. Go!"

I barely managed to grab my cane before Crow physically shoved me into the attic stairwell.

I climbed as quickly as I could. As I was opening the door at the top, I heard Crow say, "Good morning, Inspector Gregson," and my heartbeat began thumping in my ears.

Part of my mind, cognizant of the fact that I was in Crow's sanctum, where I had never been before, was trying to look everywhere at once—at the cyclone of newspapers and the teetering stacks of scrapbooks—but I was mostly looking for the half door to the rest of the attic. I had to shove my way through the newspapers to reach it, and I mentally apologized to my friend, as I had no doubt that there was method to his madness and order in this paper chaos. Then through the half door, bad leg dragging, and I was in something that looked like an Egyptian tomb, if the pharaohs had been addicted to tea chests. The path between the looming rows was so narrow that I was surprised Crow could fit.

I passed the dividing wall where Anuvadaka had scratched the words THANK YOU, and then I was standing beneath the locked trapdoor to the roof.

Unlocking it was simple, and I threw it open. The question was whether I was going to be able to haul myself and my cane up through it.

I put my cane on the roof beside the door and then, desperate and out of options—for it couldn't take Gregson more than a few minutes to think of searching the attic—I gripped the opening and jumped, using my good leg, and just barely managed to get my floating ribs across the lip. I groaned and kicked and somehow got my legs to follow where my torso had gone.

I crawled up the roof far enough to close the trapdoor and then I sat for a second, steadying my breathing and looking around at the weird panorama of Marylebone roofs, trying to orient myself and figure out what to do. Crow had said to go to Kate Moriarty, but I found myself deeply reluctant to do so. James Moriarty had saved my life; I had saved Judith Shirley's life. We were even across the board, and I wanted to keep it that way. Besides, I thought as I picked myself up and started toward the next roof over, I wasn't sure that even a clever vampire lawyer—and vampires were the cleverest of lawyers—could help me. I had known I was a hell-hound for months, and I had not registered. I had broken the law, and I am sure some would argue it was mere wickedness that made me so unwilling to accept the consequences of my wrong-doing. But those consequences might well include being locked up in Colney Hatch for the rest of my life.

No, a solicitor couldn't help me. But I thought I knew someone who could.

—◇—

"I NEED TO speak to the Angel of Whitehall," I said to the polite young man.

"Do you have an appointment?"

"No, but this is a matter of great urgency. Tell him Crow sent me." True in spirit, if not in letter.

The young man looked dubious, but he said, "Just a moment, please, and I will inquire."

He was just starting to get up when the door behind him opened, and the Angel of Whitehall said, "No inquiry will be necessary, Fenton. Dr. Doyle, how pleasant to see you again. Please come in."

Whitehall's office was austerely furnished and painted clean, blank white. Whitehall sat on a backless bench and motioned me to the chair. "Please be seated. How is your leg?"

"Much better, thank you."

"*Did* Crow send you? It's unlike him not to come in person."

He knew I had lied, and in his own sideways fashion, he was inviting me to explain myself.

I took a deep breath and did the best I could.

Whitehall was an attentive listener, and he let me pour the whole story out before he said anything. "Certainly, it seems most unfair that you should be betrayed in the course of catching a murderer, and I admit I am not enamored of the Registration Act, which seems to create the very behavior it is meant to prevent. But I don't quite see what it is you think I can do."

"I don't know!" I said. "But if you want me to stay with Crow, you have to do something. Or he'll be visiting me monthly at Colney Hatch." Where all the occult prisoners were sent.

"And that if you can hold your temper and not get your privileges revoked," murmured Whitehall in a way that suggested he thought I couldn't. But something in what I had said had caught his attention. "Crow is better since your advent. More . . . I hesitate to use the word 'human,' but less like a machine devoted to murder." He looked at me, his gaze steady and his eyes very blue. "Less like someone who might Fall."

"Crow would never Fall," I said with considerable certainty.

"Maybe not," said Whitehall. "But he no longer has a habitation, and he refuses to embrace the Consensus. You must admit his options are few and his position extremely precarious. But you make it less so."

"He brought me to meet you," I said, suddenly understanding what that odd, awkward afternoon had been about. "You and the Angel of the Great Synagogue. His family."

"Are we?" said Whitehall, looking almost taken aback by the idea. "Gracious." He looked at me silently for long enough that I wanted to squirm; then the faint frown cleared, and he said, "I know who we need."

Going to the door, he said, "Really, I shouldn't do this." He opened the door and said, "Fenton, I need Sir Edwin. As quickly as possible." He returned to his bench and told me, "Fenton will find him."

As we waited, Whitehall said, "Forgive me, but my curiosity about this has been unendurable since we met. Your, ah, secret . . ." And he paused, eyebrows raised, until I nodded. "It must have been discovered when you were wounded. How is it that you receive an Imperial pension and continue to dress as a man?"

I smiled grimly and said, "I blackmailed the Imperial Armed Forces."

"Go on," said Whitehall.

"Almost nobody knew, you see. The doctor who first found out was a friend—a good friend—and he made sure that only he and the orderly who saved my life tended to me. Murray would have died before he betrayed me. I don't think he even cared, although things were very strained with Kilpatrick." I laughed suddenly, surprising myself, remembering some of those dreadful conversations. "But then my wound became infected, and I had to be sent to Dr. Sylvester. And Kilpatrick had a crisis of conscience and reported me to General Dr. Brook."

"Oh dear," said Whitehall.

"When I was well enough, I had a series of very nasty conversations with him and the nearest general to hand, in which I said that they would discharge me *with* a pension and *with* my medical rights and *without* discussing anything else, or I would go to the first war correspondent I saw and. Tell. Him. Everything."

"And was there a great deal of everything to tell?"

"Well, first there was the scandal that one of the I.A.F.'s best surgeons—I have medals to prove it, though I don't suppose I'll ever wear them—is actually a woman. Max Chesney could have run with that for *days*. But then . . ." I hesitated, and Whitehall said, "You're not going to shock my unsullied virgin ears, you know."

"All right," I said. "There's a great deal of corruption in the I.A.F. Corruption and incompetence and the most vile kind of nepotism, and I saw far more of it than I wanted to, for I'm afraid Brook may be the most corrupt of the lot. You know how the newspapers are about the war, and I'm sure you can guess the damage I could do."

"Quite," said Whitehall.

"They implored me to think of my Queen and my country, and I assured them that that and my foolish loyalty to the I.A.F. were the only reasons I hadn't gone to a war correspondent long ago."

"Clearly, they did not call your bluff."

"I wasn't bluffing. I would have told Max everything I knew, names and dates and places, and given him my diaries, and then, I don't know, I probably would have blown my brains out."

"My dear doctor!" Whitehall said, aghast.

"I'm not a man," I said, "but I'm not a woman, either. I've masqueraded as a man far longer than I wore long skirts and corsets, and I don't think I could go back. I certainly couldn't go back to the gossip and embroidery that are a woman's lot."

"Many women do other things," said Whitehall.

"I know. I . . . oh, it doesn't matter. But to be alone and friendless as a man is still far better than to be alone and friendless as a woman." I shook my head. "I wasn't bluffing."

"Well," said Whitehall, "I certainly feel—"

There was a tap at the door.

"Come in," said Whitehall, and a stout, cheerful, bald man with a tremendous red walrus mustache stuck his head in the door.

"Fenton said you had need of me?"

"Yes," said Whitehall. "Pray come in, and shut the door behind you. Sir Edwin, this is Dr. J. H. Doyle, who is in a quandary. Dr. Doyle, this is Sir Edwin Ottershaw, a solicitor who may be able to help you. You can certainly trust his discretion."

Whitehall got up, and he and Sir Edwin had a momentary, silent disagreement over who should sit on the bench, which Whitehall won. Whitehall went to stand by the window. Sir Edwin therefore sat down across from me and said, "I am bewildered, yet game. Tell me your story, Dr. Doyle."

Thus I went through the whole matter a second time, explaining things as I went in a most disorganized fashion. Sir Edwin proved himself as game as a pebble, for he listened raptly and asked incisive and uncomfortable questions, which I did my best to answer. His small, bright, wren-like eyes widened a little when he realized I was the Unknown Hell-Hound who had caught Jack the Ripper, but he rendered no judgment, good or bad, on the rest of my tale, and said when I had finished, "Yes, I see why Whitehall called me," as if he were entirely delighted to have my thorny and awkward problem dumped in his lap. "My sister is a hell-hound, you see, and I have very strong feelings about the Registration Act."

"Very strong," Whitehall said dryly from the window.

"And yours is a very interesting case from my perspective, because it shows that occult persons may act in the service of the law. But I quite see that, from your perspective, you don't want to go to prison."

"I don't," I agreed.

"And Whitehall has asked me in because angels can't lie, but lawyers can." From the way he twinkled at Whitehall, this was an old joke between them. "You will have to register, I'm afraid. There's nothing to be done about that."

"I know," I said and shivered involuntarily.

He saw my expression and said, "There's an anti-Registration movement, you know. The ladies marching for the right to vote march for occult rights, too."

"Wonderful," I said. The thought gave me a great dismal feeling in the pit of my stomach.

"Sir Edwin," said Whitehall, "you stray from the point."

"So I do," said Sir Edwin, cheerfully unbothered. "In any event, it isn't really the registering per se that bothers you—well, it *is*, but that's not the part with which I can help. What we're trying to avoid is the prison sentence handed down for not registering in the first place."

He thought for a time, so fast and hard I could almost hear the cogs turning. "Well!" he said at last. "I do see a way, although I will have to use up a favor with Sir Guy to achieve it. But I would not see anyone put in prison over the Registration Act if I could possibly help it, and you *are* the man who caught Jack the Ripper. The Queen was saying just this morning that you ought to be commended, and it doesn't reflect well on Her Majesty's government to be arresting you the same day. And this is a good story, very plausible. We inform Scotland Yard that you are an agent of the Home Office, and that it was crucial to your cover story that you *not* register. Perhaps we were sending you to spy among the unregistered. They certainly prey upon the Home Secretary's mind a good deal."

"Perhaps," I said, thinking uncomfortably of Madame Silvanova and her brother.

"In any event, those details are naturally top secret, and Scotland Yard need not know them. I will bring you a letter tomorrow—of the *to whom it may concern* variety. I can bring the Registry paperwork at the same time, make sure it gets done and all that." He shot me a bright, not unsympathetic look over the walrus mustache. "There is, however, a quid pro quo."

I had known there would be. "What is it?"

"I wish you to call upon a lady named Mary Josephine Dickerson—I will give you my card, so that you may assure her of your bona fides—and tell her your story. The true story."

I felt that great dismal hollowness in the pit of my stomach again. "I will do it, but may I ask why?"

"Miss Dickerson works for occult rights. She will find much to interest her in your tale."

"But I don't—" I stopped myself. I might not enjoy the thought of being made part of a cause, but what I did not *want* was to be sent to Colney Hatch. Whatever Sir Edwin's benevolent blackmail demanded was a small price to pay.

"She's a very pleasant young lady and hardly ever dines upon her callers," said Sir Edwin. "And you will be doing your brethren a great boon."

I bit my tongue and did not deny that the occult were my brethren.

◇

I SPENT THE night in the same hotel where I had lived when I first came to London, and was horrified anew at how oppressive and dismal it was. I realized what a great debt I owed Stamford and thought that I should find him and tell him so, although the thought made me feel nearly as hollow as the thought of talking to Sir Edwin's pleasant young lady.

I slept badly.

In the morning, I dared to return to Baker Street, where Crow gave me a vivid and gleeful account of Gregson's visit. "He wanted to arrest me for obstruction of justice—I could see it in his eyes—but there was nothing to show that I helped you escape, and how could I be obstructing anything when I answered all of his questions truthfully?"

"Yes, I've seen you do that," I said dryly, and he laughed.

"He'll be back, you know," he warned me.

"That's all right," I said, "and I must tell Mrs. Climpson we're having a guest for lunch."

Mrs. Climpson gave me a sour look—which I fully deserved for springing a lunch guest on her at the last minute—but whatever crises I caused in the kitchen, by the time Sir Edwin arrived, there was no sign of them.

We had spent a lazy morning, mostly discussing the discussion of Jack the Ripper in the newspapers. "Have you seen *The Times*?" I had asked Crow as he came back into the room from his stairs.

"Very much as one might expect," he said. "The *Star* is yelling about conspiracies and suggesting that the man who died on Monday wasn't really Jack the Ripper at all."

"Evidence *is* rather sketchy—which *The Times* is trying hard not to discuss."

"Evidence consists of Mary Jane Kelly's heart on his table," Crow said. "And Constable Dew and Inspector Abberline can testify to that. It isn't just my word for it."

"You can't lie. No one can ask for a better witness."

"No one will put me on the stand," he said. "No matter which side I would be a witness for, the other side would bring up the question of whether I *can* lie—being Fallen rather than merely . . ." He made an oddly precise gesture indicating inadequate vocabulary. "Whatever I am. Ergo, I'm no use as a witness. But that's not the point. The point is that Inspector Abberline saw that heart—human and extremely fresh—and—"

"We have no proof that it came from Mary Jane Kelly's chest."

"Yes, we do." He stared at me, his gaze as unnerving as ever. "You tracked it. And I don't think you *would* have lied about it, even if we could have explained to you how."

"But I can't testify, either," I said. "Not as a hell-hound."

"No, but Constable Dew and Inspector Abberline can testify to what you did, just as they would if you'd been a tracking dog. Or if Clifton Barnaby had ended up shifting. Or, rather, they would have been able to testify, if there had been a trial."

"Quite," I said.

"You don't think . . . I mean, do you think he *wasn't* Jack the Ripper?"

"No, I'm sure he was. I smelled *her* blood—Mary Jane Kelly's—on his hands. But that's what a trial is for, so that all the evidence can be laid out and everyone can see that it's true. This way, it's just going to be down to what people believe."

"And the *Star* yelling conspiracy," Crow said gloomily.

"Yes, exactly."

Sir Edwin was delighted to be introduced to Crow, and he achieved what I had never managed, to get Crow to talk about one of his old cases. Crow would talk endlessly about the history of crime in London, but was reticent to the point of muteness about his own part in the solutions side of it. Sir Edwin—or possibly Sir Edwin's mustache—induced him to tell us about his tangle with the League of Red-Headed Men and the talented and unscrupulous John Clay. I might have considered the escapades in the bank vault implausible, except that I knew—of course—that Crow did not lie.

We were just finishing the fish when someone started pounding on the door.

"Oh, not again," said Crow. "It's Gregson."

"Perhaps my memorandum did not reach him?" said Sir Edwin. "I assure you, I sent it to Scotland Yard yesterday."

"I believe you," I said, and Gregson flung our door open with a bang.

"You're paying for the plasterwork, Inspector," Crow said, but Gregson didn't even hear him.

"Aha!" he cried. "You see, Dr. Doyle, you are not sharp enough to fool old Gregson after all!" His enmity against me was shining in his eyes.

I took a sip of wine and said nothing.

"Good gracious," said Sir Edwin.

Crow said, "Gregson, you're about to make a fool of yourself."

"You can't evade arrest forever, Doctor," said Gregson.

"Inspector—" I tried.

"You may have pulled the wool over Lestrade's eyes, but you don't fool me! I knew there was something queer about you from the start. Dr. J. H. Doyle, you are under arrest for fraudulently posing as—"

"*Inspector!*" shouted Sir Edwin, and Gregson jerked to a halt halfway across the sitting room.

"Who are you, sir?" Gregson demanded. "Another of Dr. Doyle's pawns?"

"I am the very Napoleon of crime," I said sotto voce to Crow.

"My name," Sir Edwin said dryly, "is Edwin Ottershaw, and I am no one's pawn."

"Indeed," said Gregson, and much as I disliked him, I wished I could advise him not to sneer at Sir Edwin. "But you can have no idea—"

"On the contrary, I have a very good idea," said Sir Edwin. "I suppose I shall have to show you my credentials in the matter." He produced from the inner pocket of his coat the copy of the memorandum regarding my status that he had brought to show me.

Gregson took it suspiciously and scanned it with a deepening frown. "Is this some sort of joke?"

"Oh, Gregson," Crow lamented. "Always so predictable."

"No," said Sir Edwin. "It is neither a joke nor a ruse. Dr. Doyle has done significant and meritorious work in the service of Her Majesty, and does not deserve to be persecuted by the police."

Gregson looked like a man who had stepped on solid floor only to fall through into a pantomime. Or a man whose speeding locomotive had just encountered a solid wall.

He opened and closed his mouth several times without producing any words, until Crow took pity on him and said, "Come 'round the next time you have something interesting, Inspector. Dr. Doyle and I will be glad to see you."

Gregson at least had the wit to recognize a lifeline when he was thrown one. "Indeed," he said. "Good afternoon to you gentlemen then." He tipped his hat, mostly to Sir Edwin, and retreated heavily down the stairs.

"I'm quite glad I was here," said Sir Edwin.

"Gregson would have listened to reason eventually," Crow said. I was glad he believed it; for myself I had doubts.

"Well," said Sir Edwin, who might also have had doubts, "in any event, we'd best get the Registry paperwork done before this excellent lunch prompts me to forget it." He gave me a wry look. "I'd only have to come back."

The paperwork was prying and ill-natured, but the only difficulty came when it demanded the name of a "responsible person" who would vouch for my good behavior.

"I have no family," I said. "Or, none who would agree to such a thing."

"Don't be ridiculous, Doyle," said Crow. "I'm standing right here."

"And who better than an angel," said Sir Edwin, "to stand surety for a hell-hound's behavior."

"I think you've got that backward," Crow muttered.

"Is this a decision *I* make?" I said cautiously.

"It isn't valid without your signature," said Sir Edwin at the same time Crow said, "If you don't want it . . ."

"Are you sure *you* want it? It does rather tie us together, and we've only been rooming together for four months."

"Which is three months and two weeks longer than any other human being has ever put up with me," said Crow. "I'm quite sure."

"All right," I said. "But I want to read over everything before I sign it."

"Sound practice," Sir Edwin said, and produced a sheaf of paper from his briefcase.

While I read, Sir Edwin gossiped with Crow about the Ripper case and the odd mash of politics and reasoning ability that put both Tories and Whigs on each side of the fence about whether or not the alleged Jack the Ripper was the real thing. He also brought the welcome news that the person both sides wanted to get rid of was Sir Charles Warren, so that he was being blamed for an incident at which he had not been present. (And about which he could have done nothing, even if he had been.) Lestrade and Abberline were both free of the hook. "Inspector Abberline is already the Man Who Caught Jack the Ripper, which will do wonders for his career."

"But it was Doyle," Crow said indignantly. "The rest of us were just following as best we could."

"Let Abberline have the credit," I said. "Here. Hand me a pen, Crow, so that I can sign this."

I signed, Crow signed, Sir Edwin bowed to us both and tucked the document away. "Well," I said when our visitor was gone, "I guess you're stuck with me."

"I think you've got that backward, too," Crow said, and smiled like sunrise after the nightmare-dark.

Acknowledgments

Firstly, my most profound thanks to my editor and everyone at Tor Books. You people are amazing.

Secondly, thanks to my readers, Elizabeth Bear, Allen Monette, C. L. Polk, and Fran Wilde, for much-needed help and reassurance.

Thirdly, I must acknowledge my great debt to W. S. Baring-Gould's *The Annotated Sherlock Holmes,* which has shaped my reading of Conan Doyle for almost forty years. Maddening though it sometimes is, it is an invaluable resource and truly a labor of love.

Fourthly, books about Jack the Ripper that have shaped my understanding of the crimes and their context: Neil R. A. Bell, *Capturing Jack the Ripper: In the Boots of a Bobby in Victorian London;* Alexander Chisholm, Christopher-Michael DiGrazia, and Dave Yost, *The News from Whitechapel: Jack the Ripper in* The Daily Telegraph; L. Perry Curtis, Jr., *Jack the Ripper and the London Press;* Maxim Jakubowski and Nathan Braund, eds. *The Mammoth Book of Jack the Ripper;* Robin Odell, *Ripperology: A Study of the World's First Serial Killer and a Literary Phenomenon;* Donald Rumbelow, *Jack the Ripper: The Complete Casebook;* Philip Sugden, *The Complete History of Jack the Ripper.*

Fifthly, for more on the Ratcliffe Highway murders, I point you to P. D. James and T. A. Critchley, *The Maul and the Pear Tree*.

Sixthly, there are two books about the Thames Torso murders: R. Michael Gordon, *The Thames Torso Murders of Victorian London*, and M. J. Trow, *The Thames Torso Murders*.

Seventhly, Crow's theory about the Bravo murder comes from James Ruddick's excellent *Death at the Priory*.

Eighthly and lastly (but so very not leastly), my thanks go to my Patreon patrons, who make more possible than they can ever imagine: Sarah Wishnevsky-Lynch, Hilary Kraus, Jennifer G. Tifft, Meredith Katz, Kate Diamond, Linda Cox, Liz Novaski, Seth Carlson, Gail Morse, Sylvia Sotomayor, Christina Fayz, Meredith B., Jennifer Parrack, Elizabeth Monette, E.S.H., Anna Hedlund, K. Monahan, Marissa Lingen, Lindsay Kleinman, Gordon Tisher, ScottKF, Liza Furr, Lesley Hall, S. L. Ingram, Kris Ashley, Sasha Lydon, Caryn Cameron, Margaret Johnston, Lorna Toolis, Yvonne Lam, Rhiannon B-G, Gretchen Schultz, Bill Ruppert, Laura E. Price, Mary Kay Kare, Anna Davidson, Jennifer Lundy, Laura Bailey, Elizabeth Woodley, Celia Yost, Ruthanna Emrys, Danielle Beliveau, Eleanor Skinner, Mariam Kvitsiani, D. Franklin, Edmund Schweppe, Arkady Martine, Sylvia Hobart, Sarah Ervine, Danielle Beauchesne, Maddie Beauchesne, Lidija Feldman, Kitty, Katy Kingston, Norman Ramsey, Meghan Parker, pCiaran, Emily Richards, Nathaniel Eneas, Irene Headley, Megan Prime, Jack K., Asia Wolf, Amy Miller, Simone Brick, and Jen Moore.

AUTHOR'S NOTE

FOR THOSE OF you who do not know, there is a thing called fanfiction, wherein fans of a particular book or TV show or movie write stories about the characters. Fanfiction, as an umbrella term, covers a vast variety of genres and subgenres. One of those subgenres is something called wingfic, wherein a character or characters have wings. *The Angel of the Crows* began as a *Sherlock* wingfic.

ABOUT THE AUTHOR

KATHERINE ADDISON is the author of the Locus Award–winning novel *The Goblin Emperor,* and her short fiction has been selected by *The Year's Best Fantasy and Horror* and *The Year's Best Science Fiction.* As Sarah Monette, she is the author of the Doctrine of Labyrinths series and coauthor, with Elizabeth Bear, of the Iskryne series. She lives near Madison, Wisconsin.

FIND US ONLINE!

www.rebellionpublishing.com

/rebellionpub   /rebellionpublishing /rebellionpublishing

SIGN UP TO OUR NEWSLETTER!

rebellionpublishing.com/newsletter

YOUR REVIEWS MATTER!

Enjoy this book? Got something to say?

Leave a review on Amazon, GoodReads or with your
favourite bookseller and let the world know!